Gloria Cook is the author of well-loved Cornish novels, including the Pengarron and Harvey family sagas. She is Cornish born and bred, and lives in Truro.

Also by Gloria Cook

Trevallion
Trevennor's Will
Listening to the Quiet

The Harvey Family Sagas

Touch the Silence
Moments of Time
From A Distance
Never Just a Memory
A Stranger Light
A Whisper of Life

The Pengarron Sagas

Pengarron Land
Pengarron Pride
Pengarron's Children
Pengarron Dynasty
Pengarron Rivalry

The Kilgarthen Sagas

Kilgarthen
Rosemerryn

The Roscarrock Sagas

Roscarrock
Porthellis

The Leaving Shades Sagas

Leaving Shades
Reflections

Gloria Cook

TREVALLION

CANELO

First published in the United Kingdom in 1994 by Headline Book Publishing PLC

This edition published in the United Kingdom in 2022 by

Canelo
Unit 9, 5th Floor
Cargo Works, 1–2 Hatfields
London, SE1 9PG
United Kingdom

A CIP catalogue record for this book is available from the British Library.

Print ISBN 978 1 80032 819 8
Ebook ISBN 978 1 78863 645 2

Look for more great books at www.canelo.co

Printed and bound in Great Britain by Clays Ltd, Elcograf S.p.A.

In celebration of the birth of my first grandchild

Kerenza Naomi Webb

And love and thanks to her mum, my daughter,

Cheryl and her husband, Andrew

Prologue

He knew as his men scrambled up the ladders and netting from the trenches that their faces were as white with fear as his own, their eyes glazed to attention, their lips like his muttering goodbyes to their loved ones and snatches of prayer, their throats gulping at the sheer enormity of what would probably be their last act on earth. Over the top he led them, each man towards the place where he might die. They were fighting for king and country, for the peace and security of the world, in the Third Battle of Ypres in the month of August, in the year 1917.

Sergeant Georgie Gilbert followed his lead and urged the men on to glory with a bloodcurdling threat against the Hun. Sixteen-year-old Jimmy Clark was on the sergeant's heels fighting back the tears, singing his favourite music-hall song with grim determination. Cyril Dawkins was playing a mouth organ clamped between chattering teeth.

While he and his men ran onwards, aeroplanes roared overhead waging battle in the sky, British and German flying machines, adding to the carnage that lay all around them. They didn't look up. They didn't see the aeroplanes. They didn't hear them. They had to concentrate. They were rushing through a quagmire of French soil in which some of their comrades had drowned.

There was mud everywhere, in their eyes, noses, mouths and ears. There was mud ground into their flesh, filling their pores. The relentless heavy rainfalls had churned up the fields, flooding the trenches with black water.

Everything was black. Black smoke hung heavily in the air and shut out the daylight. Huge black rats were running for cover while he led his men on, their guns blazing. The world was black. The future was black. He knew it and so did his men.

New and highly sophisticated artillery was spewing death and destruction on all sides and after only a few feet of forward movement the first of his men fell. Others followed quickly and those dragging ammunition stumbled over the bodies. Shells and mortar grenades exploded, bullets whistled past, and as they got closer to the heart of the battle, machine-guns cut them down in a swathe as if they were a field of ripe corn.

He ran on relentlessly, showing his men the way forward, his gun barrel red-hot from firing at the enemy, and those who were left followed him. While they ran they cried, screamed, moaned, cursed and prayed. The men fought for breath, many shuddering out their last.

They dodged whinnying horses and fallen men. The guns continued to boom. Mud cascaded up into the sky and spattered them, spraying over the dead and dying. Bodies were strewn everywhere, bloodied, torn apart, mangled, twisted, flattened; once living, once human, once caring, loving, giving men; lying now in craters, over mounds of earth, over barbed wire.

Bodies of men who had fallen only a moment before were in the way but he had to keep running, so he ran over them, and his men, becoming smaller and smaller in number, followed him. It was madness, all this death and destruction, just to gain a few hundred feet of land. And the screaming never stopped. It was burrowing its way deep into his brain and echoing in his ears, screaming, screaming, screaming.

He shouted to Sergeant Gilbert that they would take out the nearest machine-gun sheltered in an almost impregnable position a few yards up ahead.

'We can do it!' he shouted, encouraging and cajoling his men onwards. His unit had recently captured a fortified farmhouse from the enemy; they might be but a few now but they could surely take out a machine-gun.

He and Georgie Gilbert, with Jimmy Clark and Cyril Dawkins hard on their heels, dodged in and out of the line of fire, crawling on their bellies the last few feet.

Suddenly all went quiet. The battle had stopped. He looked back to smile in blessed relief at his men. But they weren't there. No one was there. Where were they? Where were his men? Where was the enemy? He got to his feet. It was a terrible risk to take; he could be shot. But there was no one to shoot him. He spun round and round. There was nothing. No one. No unit, no enemy. No horses, no aeroplanes. No mud, no trenches, no war. Nothing but a vacuum of impenetrable blackness.

He ran but there was nowhere to run to, his feet wouldn't move. There was just black nothingness and the sound of his own breathing and panic inside his head where once the noise of the battle had been.

Then he was falling, falling deeper and deeper into the emptiness. He cried out and screamed, fighting against the blackness, fighting against the nothingness.

Someone was shaking him, something vile and terrible from the nothingness was trying to devour him and keep him there for ever. He struggled and fought.

There was a light. A small flickering light. Then there was a voice. 'Wake up, Major! Wake up, sir!'

Alex Fiennes woke with a tremendous shudder. There was a man. One of the men from his unit? No, a servant. There was a woman with him, another of his servants.

'Are you all right, Major?' she asked in soothing tones.

He wiped at the stream of sweat burning on his brow. He couldn't speak. He could only nod. They left him alone, leaving the bedside light on so he wouldn't be in darkness.

Outside the bedroom door his butler turned to the housekeeper. 'That's the third nightmare he's had this month.'

'It's a good thing the missus is out. She can't cope with him when he's like this,' the housekeeper whispered, shaking her head in despair. 'You'd think he'd be over it by now, after all these years.'

'Perhaps the journey down to Cornwall and a few weeks of sea and country air will do him good.'

'Oh, I do hope so. If something doesn't happen soon to help him come to terms with his ordeal, I fear he'll go completely mad.'

Chapter 1

'So there is an heir to Trevallion after all!' Trease Allen exclaimed, tapping the letter he was reading. 'It says so right here.'

'Are you sure, Dad? Let me see that.' Rebecca Allen sprang up from the kitchen table where she had been poring over an accounts book and tried to take the letter out of her father's hand.

A few moments ago she had paused in her work and watched anxiously as Trease had taken the letter down from the mantelshelf where it had been sitting unopened for the past three days. Rebecca knew why he had been reluctant to open it. The letter was obviously from Mr Robert Drayton, one of the trustees of the estate of which her father was negligent caretaker. Rebecca thought it probably contained a demand for the accounts she'd been working on, which were one of Trease's lapsed responsibilities, or even a formal confirmation of his dismissal. But now, here he was, after three long anxious days, telling her it was probably the good news they had been waiting so long to hear.

Trease held the letter up high and danced excitedly about the kitchen of their small cottage while Rebecca watched him in exasperation. He ended up in front of her with a wide grin on his face but she looked back at him severely.

'Well, Becca?' he inquired eagerly, smacking his thin pale lips and looking up under her disapproving chin. 'Aren't you pleased?'

'Dad! You've had that letter sitting up there for three whole days and all the time it contained the news that we've been hoping to hear for ages! That Mr Drayton has found an heir to the estate and we might not be out of our home and jobs after all. How many times have

I begged you to open it? But no, you had to be your usual stubborn self!'

Rebecca picked up the accounts book and waved it under her father's nose. 'I thought Mr Drayton was asking you yet again for these, the winter accounts that you've been taking so long over. It's nearly time to make up the spring ones! Why didn't you open the letter before? I've been worrying that you might have been dismissed, or that Mr Drayton was writing to say the estate was going to be sold, that the big house was going to be turned into a hotel for the holiday trade or something.' Rebecca pursed her lips and folded her arms tightly. She found it hard to share her father's sudden joy and optimism. 'Well? What exactly does the letter say?'

Trease had become subdued under his daughter's reprimand. She had got up early this morning to try to make sense of the scribbles he had put at sketchy intervals in the accounts book. Rebecca was always having to cover for his laziness. She had shouldered so much for him over the years, worrying constantly over him, that she had lost something of her youth.

Trease scratched at his thinning, prematurely grey hair and attempted to remove the deliberately blank look in his hooded colourless eyes. Putting on a businesslike face, he returned to his chair by the fireplace. He rubbed at the sides of his thick brush-moustache, placed his spectacles on the end of his nose and, after straightening out the pages of the letter, scanned its contents again with his one good eye.

Rebecca knelt down beside him. Her long black hair fell over his arm and he pushed it away. He didn't like her near him; she hadn't been able to get close to him in years. It hurt her feelings every time he did something like this. She craned her neck to read the letter with him. It began with the expected plea, accompanied with a threat of sorts, for the accounts covering the months of January to March, then moved on to what her father had become so excited about. After a moment Rebecca became excited too and began to read bits of it out loud.

'... am therefore pleased to inform you that the property has passed into the hands of a Major Alexander Fiennes... a second cousin of the late Captain Miles Trevallion... an industrialist... resides in Berkshire... Major Fiennes has expressed the wish to view the property and will shortly be journeying to Cornwall... with him will be Mrs Fiennes and her son, Stephen... Despite the fact that I've pointed out Trevallion House is presently uninhabitable the Major desires to stay on the property rather than at an hotel... Therefore I trust you will prepare appropriate accommodation at the gatehouse; it has sufficient rooms for the family's needs... my apologies this is such short notice... will be arriving – What!'

Rebecca snatched the letter from Trease's hand and swung it round as he jumped up and tried to grab it back. 'But that's tomorrow morning! Why weren't we told? Oh, Dad, we can't possibly get things ready for them by tomorrow. It will take weeks rather than hours. Oh, how can people be so inconsiderate!'

'Because they're our masters,' Trease said calmly, not including himself in her last remark. He took the letter back and placing it on the floral-patterned oilcloth over the table he reverently smoothed out the creases Rebecca had made as if it was the most important thing in the world. At that moment, to Trease Allen, it was.

Rebecca watched his actions and suddenly felt the same way. 'At least we know we have an employer again,' she said.

'Aye, and as this major wants to come down here and look over the place it could be the end of our worries for the future, Becca. He's an industrialist, a rich man, he might build up the estate to what it was in Captain Miles's day. We can't waste any more time, we've got a lot to do to get things ready for him. You can give work on the farm a miss today. 'Tis in Frank Kellow's interests as much as ours to get things in order. Go and fetch Jossy, Joe and Loveday here, m'dear. Tell 'em whatever they've got to do today, this is more important. I've got a bottle of sherry somewhere in the cupboard... left over from Christmas. We'll have a little celebration and get up a campaign of action on what we'll have to do to get ready for the people coming here tomorrow.'

Trease was already off to get the bottle and glasses. Rebecca frowned, her dark eyes flashing with extreme annoyance. She knew the sherry had not been left over from Christmas, no drink in her father's possession ever lasted more than a few hours. But she needed no encouragement to go and fetch Joe Carlyon.

–

Rebecca and Trease lived in a small pink-painted cottage close to the water's edge of Kennick Creek, a little inlet nestled in a sheltered spot, one quiet part of the winding course of the River Fal. Rebecca had been born in the cottage, known simply as Allen Cottage by the other creek inhabitants, who in turn were known locally as the 'Kennickers'. The few other dwellings of Kennick Creek were all whitewashed cottages and like Allen Cottage backed onto and were sheltered by the woods of the estate. On the banks of the creek bushes grew, hazel, ash and sloe, tightly packed and overhanging the basin which was now empty, soon to be refilled by lazy green water as the tide came back in. Rebecca had her own small rowing boat, left high and dry alongside Trease's at the moment by the receding tide.

She strode along the river in her loose-limbed manner, and jumped down onto the shaley, seaweed-strewn shore of the creek. Because the weather had been hot and dry for several days the shore gave firm footing. Despite her worries there was a proud lift to Rebecca's shoulders. She had a statuesque build, her skin was fine and flawless, her features as smooth as marble and looked as if they'd been sculpted with great love and care. Her mouth, red and full, was never given to sulkiness. Her eyes, dark, immense and almond-shaped, looked straight at those she spoke to but were guarded, as if they possessed secrets she would never share – although nothing had happened in Rebecca's life to give her what she considered a secret.

She made her way first to the boathouse. It was only a few yards away from Allen Cottage but was hidden by the trees and bushes that bowed down to the water's edge. There were three boats still kept there and Rebecca knew she would find Jossy Jenkins, a sprightly septuagenarian whose family had always been Trevallion's boatmen, somewhere in its vicinity.

She rounded the mooring poles and ducked under the hawsers of the Jenkins' family oysterdredger and half a dozen other boats belonging to the Kennickers, passing by several sheds of neatly stowed equipment up on the bank. The tide and wind had eroded much of the lower bank, exposing gnarled roots of the trees and making the sheds look as if they might fall from their precarious perches at any moment. Holly intermingled with the trees and streamers of ivy swayed in the fresh breeze.

Rebecca jumped onto the trunk of a tree fallen in a long-ago winter gale and spying Jossy on a bench outside the boathouse she waved to him. Jossy was proud of the bench which he had made himself from old wooden crates and painted green in keeping with the river. He watched her with a keen eye, puffing away on a big brown pipe as she approached him and climbed the eight wide stone steps that led up from the shore.

'Hello, maid,' he hailed her brightly, waving his pipe in his thick knobbly hand. 'Off to work then?' As he spoke his bristly white beard moved about his weather-worn face.

'Not today, Jossy.' Rebecca smiled, gazing momentarily across the creek up at a field of quietly grazing sheep where she often worked. She had good news to share with Jossy today, but his round wrinkled face peeking below his lumpy ancient cap automatically brought a smile to everyone's face. 'Can you go to our cottage? Dad's had a letter. It's news about an heir to the estate.'

Jossy puffed away thoughtfully for a moment. 'So that Truro bloke's found someone then, have 'ee?'

'Looks like it. I'm on my way to fetch Joe and Loveday.'

'See you in a little while then.' When Rebecca had gone, Jossy asked the silent creek what it thought about this piece of news.

Jossy Jenkins had received the news in his usual quiet way but Rebecca knew Joe and Loveday would welcome it as eagerly as she and Trease had, and share in their hopes that the interest Major Alexander Fiennes and his family were showing would end in them keeping their homes and jobs.

Things had been uncertain for the estate since the outbreak of the Great War eleven years ago. Captain Miles Trevallion had gone to fight, taking with him all the young men on the estate not needed to keep up the farming and sheep rearing. Ever since, the estate had been kept in a kind of suspended animation. The women, children and old men left behind had done what they could to keep the big house and its grounds in good order. They had done their best, but there hadn't been enough of them and they didn't have the right skills.

The war had ended seven years ago, it was now the summer of 1925, Captain Miles Trevallion had been returned home so badly wounded he had been forced to live in a nursing home at Truro, until four months ago when he had, mercifully, died. In accordance with the Captain's instructions, if injury in the war rendered him incapable or killed, limited funds had been periodically released for the upkeep of the estate by Mr Drayton. The Captain had been greatly respected, and Trease and Joe Carlyon, who had returned home relatively unscathed, had been deeply affected by his terrible fate, more so than by their own battle trauma and Trease's lost eye. Neither had felt particularly thankful to be spared, not even Trease for Rebecca's sake. They were glad, however, that Mr Drayton, who had known how much Miles Trevallion had cared for his staff, took them back to work on the estate.

Due to the Captain's incapacitation, Trease had not been needed as chauffeur and mechanic but was employed as caretaker of the big house and gardener in place of Stanley Wright who had been killed. As well as returning to his job as groom, Joe was responsible for the two hundred and fifty-seven acres of woods and grounds. Mr Drayton had turned a blind eye to Loveday Wright continuing to stay in the cottage where she'd lived from the day of her wedding to Stanley, and where she'd given birth to the daughter Stanley had never seen. She paid the weekly rent of one shilling and ninepence by taking in sewing.

Trease and Joe had coped with peacetime in different ways. Joe worked hard and relentlessly. Some days he worked until he nearly dropped, doing his own work and what he could with Rebecca to make up for Trease's laziness. Rebecca wished her father behaved in the same way. From the very first day, Trease had failed to carry out his duties. The big house, its gardens and grounds now showed signs of

9

serious neglect. Trease had returned home bitter. Bitter that Stanley Wright was dead, drowned in the mud at Passchendaele, bitter that Miles Trevallion, an intelligent young man, had sustained injuries that had left him legless and irreparably brain-damaged, bitter that soon after he had left Cornwall to fight for his country his wife had run off with another man, leaving Rebecca to live with Loveday and her baby, Tamsyn. Joe had understood Trease's moods at first and had made allowances for them, but as the years passed there had been no improvement and Trease had turned to drink. Joe had become resentful, then angry and offended on Miles Trevallion's part. Joe and Trease clashed often and this upset Rebecca greatly.

At a place where the creek path broke, Rebecca climbed the short hill to Joe's cottage. She took this path most mornings to help Joe exercise the four horses kept in the stables before leaving to work on Verrian Farm, which was tenanted from the estate. Rebecca waved a hand in front of her face. She was not usually bothered by insects, but she had just dabbed on violet scent from the tiny bottle hidden in her riding breeches, and the irritating little creatures were out in force in the warm midsummer air. The riding breeches were old and rough but she had topped them with a feminine blouse.

She found Joe sawing logs for the winter round the back of his cottage. His muscles were straining against the cloth of his collarless shirt, which was soaked in sweat. His shirt sleeves were rolled up and his well-developed arms and shoulders spoke of the hours of rowing he put in. He was rugged and deeply tanned, a man like a great dark oak, with a full head of thick black hair inclined to curl; dark pinpricks stood out on his face where his beard grew. Rebecca was attracted to his strong masculinity. Her hand automatically reached upwards to tidy her long hair, which flowed in waves down her back.

'You'll never tame it,' Joe called out in his deep accent.

'What? I mean pardon,' Rebecca said, as she reached him.

'Your hair.' He motioned at her while his meaty hands paused in his work. 'You smooth at it every time I see you but it just stays the same, wild and raven-black and beautiful.'

Rebecca's cheeks didn't flame often so she turned so he couldn't see her red face. That would only have amused him. Joe Carlyon was not many years younger than her father, who had recently gone on a drinking binge to celebrate his forty-first birthday, and it seemed that all Joe saw in Rebecca was his one-time friend's little girl. Rebecca often wanted to tell Joe she was now a twenty-year-old woman who did most of her father's work and ran her own household, albeit small, and it was time he noticed it.

She sighed and said, 'Dad had a letter a few days ago.'

'I know, from Mr Drayton. Loveday told me. She's been on tenterhooks ever since you showed it to her, wanting to know what's in it, says she thinks it might be something really important this time.'

Rebecca held on to the end of the log Joe was sawing off then put it on the woodpile. She stayed quiet, but Joe caught her feeling of excitement and he put the saw down.

'Has there been some sort of news about the estate then?'

'Yes, there has. It seems we have a new master after all. Mr Drayton had some trouble finding him owing to the three people named in Captain Miles's will all having perished in the war. He's a Major Alexander Fiennes from upcountry, a place called Berkshire, and he's coming here with his family tomorrow.'

The whoop of joy about to leave Joe's throat changed into an exclamation. 'What! Tomorrow?'

Rebecca nodded soberly. 'Dad wants you down at our cottage. I'll go and fetch Loveday.'

Loveday was hanging out washing, the pegs being passed to her by her daughter Tamsyn. She dropped the next item of clothing back in the basket and frowned. 'What are you doing here at this time of day? You'll be late for work by the time you've gone riding with Joe.'

'Dad's opened the letter at last. There's news about who's inherited the estate. Can you come to our cottage now? Dad wants to speak to you, Jossy and Joe about it.'

Loveday smoothed at Tamsyn's flyaway hair and without stopping to take off her wrap-around apron took the skimpy little girl's hand and hurried with Rebecca to Allen Cottage.

Despite being plyed with urgent questions, Trease insisted they first all drink a glass of sherry to the future, whatever that might be. Loveday refused to drink the sherry. 'Certainly not at this time of day!'

Trease winked at her, screwing up the raw puffy flesh under his eyes that told of his drinking habits. Loveday's primness amused him. She always looked uncomfortable in the presence of men, as though she found something not quite nice about them. She had rather startled eyes and her tight pink lips pursed out over her chin, and the nose she could look down stood out from her pale complexion. It had surprised all the Kennickers when she'd married the cheerful Stanley Wright at the age of sixteen and come to live among them. They had only known her before as the very serious-minded friend of Jossy Jenkins' granddaughters. She took a sip from Tamsyn's glass of lemonade and gave a disapproving grunt when the two men lit cigarettes.

Rebecca didn't want any sherry but took a sip to placate her father; he was usually offended when someone refused to drink with him and she didn't want to upset him today, of all days. She sat down and Tamsyn sat on her lap. The little girl, sired on Stanley's last leave and now eight years old, glanced at her outraged mother then grinned down at the glass in her hand; she knew if Trease Allen had his way, she would be sipping sherry too. Her piercing green eyes possessed the same mischievous glint that Stanley's had held. Jossy sat quietly with his cap pushed back, glass half-empty on his knee, waiting patiently.

Trease read the letter out loud to the gathering. There were gasps of wonder, hope and anxiety by the time he'd finished. When he'd put his spectacles safely away in their case, he looked around at the others.

'Goodness knows we'll have our work cut out,' said Joe, the first to offer a comment. 'We'll have to do something somehow though, to present a fine looking house to this Major Fiennes tomorrow. Trevallion's so rundown he might take one look at it and decide to sell up, and that could mean disaster for us.'

Trease's face darkened and he looked at Joe in challenge. Since he'd come back to the creek he took every comment personally as a judgement or criticism.

Loveday spoke up quickly before the men clashed. 'If this major's made up his mind to sell then nothing we can do will stop him.' She was always of a pessimistic nature since Stanley's death.

'Joe's right though. We've got to do something,' Rebecca said, her chin resting lightly on Tamsyn's head. 'If we had several days we could have made quite a difference to the big house. Folk round here would have been glad to help out. But if we could at least tidy up the front of the house and do something to the gardens and if we explained to Major Fiennes that we didn't know he was coming so soon, he might at least be impressed with our efforts.'

'I agree with Becca,' Joe said, flexing his powerful hands and looking as if he couldn't wait to get started. 'I don't like the idea of the estate being inherited by some upcountry Englishman who'll probably think we're just a quaint bunch of country yokels down here. He may be set on selling Trevallion, he may be coming down here to make up his mind. P'raps he'll keep the place on to use for summer holidays. But if he were to decide to build up the estate and keep us on, it'll bring us peace of mind and more work for the locals. Whatever we do, we can't simply do nothing. What do you say, Trease? Have you got a campaign of action over this?' This was said with sarcasm. To Rebecca's shame it had become a standing joke among the Kennickers that since his army days Trease Allen always had a 'campaign of action' that he never put to use.

Trease didn't seem to notice the insult. His brain had been rapidly ticking over since Rebecca had gone to fetch the others and now he wanted to say what he had in mind. He looked at Jossy Jenkins. Jossy never pushed his views on others but was content to wait for his opinion to be sought, and it was usually acted upon.

'I think you'll agree with this, Jossy. I'd like you to round up your family and go round the creek and get as many folk as you can up at the big house as soon as possible. Tell 'em to bring dusters, rags, brooms, grass cutters, gardening tools, anything they can, depending on who you're speaking to. Loveday, you go to Verrian Farm and tell Frank Kellow that Becca's needed here today and ask him if he can send someone over to exercise Trevallion's horses so Joe can get on with work up at the house. Round up as many workers as you can from the other farms too.

'Me, Becca and Joe can go up to the big house now and make a start on cleaning windows and pulling up weeds and cutting grass. The better the appearance of the front of the house, the better the impression Major Fiennes and his wife will have from the start. I've got the keys to the house and have permission to let people in at my discretion. The women can clean the ground floor and the stairs and we men can tackle as much as possible outdoors. The gatehouse can be left to air out today and Becca and Loveday can prepare it before I leave to collect the Major from the railway station. Then the four of 'ee, and the little maid, can get all done up and stand on ceremony outside to receive 'em. Well,' he finished proudly, 'what do you say to that? Jossy?'

The old man took his time looking for the place where he had put down his pipe. Then he said quietly, 'Sounds fine to me, Trease.'

Trease beamed and fetched a box of matches for him.

For the first time in years, Loveday was looking at Trease in admiration. When he raised an inquiring eyebrow at her she said, 'I say Amen.'

Trease didn't ask for Joe's approval. He had Jossy's and Loveday's and that was enough. He rarely asked Rebecca if she approved of his ideas.

Joe stretched his arms. Rebecca followed the movements, noting the bulging muscles on his bare forearms covered with dark hairs. He grinned at her, like an indulgent big brother, and she smiled back, half-resignedly, then got up to let Tamsyn slide off her lap.

'Let's get to work then, shall we, ladies?' Joe said enthusiastically.

Trease took one last drink from the sherry bottle and told his band of willing workers, 'If Major Alexander Fiennes does decide to sell Trevallion, it won't be because of the way he and his family see it tomorrow.'

Chapter 2

Rebecca's arms were aching when she started on the last window inside the front of Trevallion House. She was in the hall, where the sash windows, installed a hundred years ago, were nearly as high as the ceiling. She climbed up a stepladder to wash the top panes while Mrs Kellow of Verrian Farm did the lower ones. Loveday had managed to round up all the women in the creek and she and Ira Jenkins came behind them polishing the panes to a sparkling gleam.

Jenny Jenkins, Jossy's wife and Ira's ageing mother-in-law, was in the butler's pantry cleaning the brass. Mary and Edith Jenkins, two more of Jenny's daughters-in-law, had scrubbed the kitchen floor and tiles and were polishing the racks of copper saucepans and every utensil until they shone. Lilian Grubb, Jenny's only daughter, was assigned to laying fresh kindling in the grates and beating the carpets.

They had been hard at work for nearly three hours but were in good spirits. Jacky Jenkins, Jossy's brother, although too frail to work, had brought along his fiddle and was sitting on the top step outside the front door playing for those labouring hard. Rebecca had left the door and all the windows open to air the building and the merry tunes were filtering in on the fresh summer breeze.

Many of the workers were singing along with what breath they had to spare, but Rebecca was deep in thought. Would there be servants living again in the attic rooms upstairs? Or, if Major Fiennes wasn't interested in the estate, would the house be sold as a hotel for the county's growing holiday trade? The locals dreaded the thought but Mr Neville Faull, another trustee and solicitor in the same practice as Mr Drayton, was rumoured to be urging this course of action. These were times when many of the smaller estates in Cornwall were being sold off because the families could no longer afford to keep them going. Perhaps Major Fiennes was only coming to Trevallion so he could see for himself the best possible price he could get for it. It was a hopeful sign, though, that the Major was bringing his family down with him. If he stayed as master, what sort would he be? She'd only been a girl when she'd last seen Captain Miles but she knew Major Fiennes had a lot to live up to. But even if he kept Trevallion, she still had the worry that Trease would be dismissed.

Rebecca frowned. She could have done a lot more on the upkeep of the house but it would have angered her father. She stopped work to tie back her troublesome hair; it kept working loose from the scarf she wore.

Mrs Kellow pulled a pair of nail scissors and a ball of string out of her apron pocket and cut off a long length. 'Come here, maid. I'll tie it back for 'ee. I've never seen hair so long and thick. 'Tis lovely, you should make the most of it, use it to catch yourself a husband instead of slaving away for that lazy father of yours. Ira's daughter Gwen soon snapped up my Leslie, and he had her expecting in no time. Gwen would have liked to have come today but 'tis a bit too near her time. I'll have to get on here, can't leave her without a woman around for too long.'

Before Rebecca could thank Mrs Kellow for her contribution to the cleaning and speak up in her father's defence, Loveday said crossly, 'Rebecca is fine as she is, there's more to life than chasing men!'

'Hark at she,' Mrs Kellow laughed and motioned to Ira Jenkins. 'Do she good to find herself another husband. What do you think, Tamsyn?' she asked the little girl, who was sitting quietly on the bottom step of the stairs.

Tamsyn grinned cheekily but didn't get the chance to say anything.

'Well, really! What a way to speak to a child,' Loveday snapped. 'One more word like that and I'll go help Lilian outside with the carpets.'

'I think they're only teasing us, Loveday,' Rebecca said hastily. The last thing she wanted was a quarrel among the women; she heard cross words between Trease and Joe from outside.

As the men and women who had turned out saw the improvements they were making to Trevallion House, its grounds and gardens, their hopes that life would return within its walls grew. The house had been built in the late eighteenth century on a fortune made from tin and copper mining and the East India trade. The Trevallions had owned many properties but they were not good businessmen. With each succeeding heir, their fortune had dwindled, until a hundred years later, in the time of Roland Trevallion, Miles's grandfather, the small estate was all that was left. The house had not been spoiled in the Victorian era by bright colours and over-furnishing but retained a quiet solid charm. It was plain on the outside, with no pillars or Roman arches, but was strongly built and imposing. It was not as grand as Trelissick House, a short distance further along the Fal, but boasted a huge hall, twelve bedrooms, a balcony on the second floor which overlooked the river, two bathrooms, a long elegant drawing room, dining room, a big kitchen, conservatory, office and study, and a smoking and games room with a huge billiard table. The games room housed Captain Miles's trophies for rowing, cricket, rugby and motor racing, and there were many photographs of him about his physical pursuits. Mr Drayton had locked the trophies away in tall cupboards.

In the hall stood a long oak table which had borne, among others, Roland and Miles Trevallion's coffins. High up on the wall was a heraldic banner, painted on silk, depicting the arms of a more important branch of the Trevallion family which had died out long ago; with the death of Miles, all the Trevallions were gone and now the estate was owned by a stranger. Although it was old and faded, Rebecca found the banner more engaging than the many paintings that had been crammed on the walls, which she had seen in her child-hood. Now there were blank spaces where Mr Drayton had removed the valuable ones, some of them Opie portraits, for safekeeping.

Rebecca hoped Major Fiennes wouldn't notice the flakes of paint and plaster dropping off the walls, ceilings and wainscot. At least Trease had managed to stop up the leaks, and Rebecca was pleased there were no tell-tale dark stains on the wooden and tiled floors or spoiling the moulded ceilings. There was plenty of dust to get rid of, however, and the women coughed in their long aprons or frock overalls, their hair protected under scarves, as one by one each downstairs room had its dust covers removed and was made fragrant with lavender and beeswax polish.

When the windows were finished, Rebecca helped Lilian Grubb clean the wooden steps and long curving banister of the stairway, then she joined Loveday in Captain Trevallion's favourite room, the study. They hoped Major Fiennes might find this room appealing, a room to sit and work in, with its typically masculine dark and solid furniture. They sang to Jacky Jenkins' fiddle as they worked around Tamsyn who, with nothing to distract her since she had not been allowed to bring her huge mongrel dog along, was sitting at the desk pretending to write a letter to the King and Queen.

Rebecca stood on a chair to dust the frame of a portrait of a beautiful young woman in a wide straw hat and cascading red ribbons. The picture was of Miss Harriet Bosanko of Melvill Road, Falmouth, the late fiancée of Miles Trevallion. It had broken his heart when in 1912 she had died of influenza. Rebecca looked across the room at a smaller picture, one of Miles. If Miss Bosanko hadn't died, she would have been married to the Captain before the war broke out and there might have been a child as heir to the estate and the workers wouldn't be going through all this worry now. And perhaps if there had been someone for Miles Trevallion to come home to, he might not have been as brave and foolhardy as was rumoured of him, and so horribly wounded.

Rebecca helped Loveday dust the Captain's collection of 'modern inventions', a gramophone, home recorder and typewriter, and his collection of cameras and binoculars and telescopes. Tomorrow, as with the other downstairs rooms, Rebecca planned to put flowers in the study to make Mrs Fiennes feel welcome. Was she the sort of woman who was interested in the running of a small country estate? Rebecca wished she knew more about the new owners of Trevallion House.

'Here, my bird,' Loveday said to Tamsyn. 'Take this duster and clean round the bottom of that old chest there.'

Tamsyn was delighted to be included in the important grown-up work. She set to work with vigour, kneeling down and putting her stubby nose almost on the claw feet of the curious-looking chest. It was made of dark golden oak and was battered and scratched but had been greatly prized by Miles Trevallion. Tamsyn longed to see inside it. To be as thorough as the women, she pushed the duster in the space underneath the chest but when she tried to pull it out it was stuck fast.

'Ohh...' She was disappointed and worried that she'd done something wrong.

'What is it, Tamsyn?' Rebecca said, lowering herself down beside the girl.

'I can't get the duster out,' Tamsyn huffed.

Rebecca laughed kindly. 'Let me try.' She put both hands on the duster and tugged on it gently. It began to move but it was obvious something had caught on it. Loveday came to watch. A little bit at a time, Rebecca pulled the duster out. Tangled up with it was a doubled-over sheaf of ageing brown papers. She unfolded the papers at the middle. There was faint copperplate writing on the top page and she read the initials at the bottom, S. B.

'They look very old. What are they?' Loveday asked, looking over Rebecca's shoulder.

'I don't know, I'd better just put them back. If Major Fiennes decides to move the chest, he can come across them himself Can't be anything important.' Rebecca didn't mention that in her brief perusal she'd read part of what was a very intimate love letter.

'Put them back exactly as you found them, Becca,' Tamsyn whispered fearfully, tapping Rebecca's arm. 'We don't want the old man coming after us.'

Rebecca and Loveday exchanged looks. 'I've told you before, Tamsyn, many times, there's no ghost in Trevallion House,' Loveday said rather crossly. ''Tis just silly old rumours.' But like all the other women apart from Rebecca, Loveday was too frightened to be left alone in the house. The ghost was rumoured to be that of Roland Trevallion, Captain Miles's grandfather, who hanged himself in the cellar sixty years ago. Strange moans and noises were said to emanate from the cellar, heavy steps were heard on the cellar stairs and the door would creak open. The ghost was rumoured to roam the house at will.

Outside, Joe and Trease and the other men cleared the courtyard of its weeds and the wide stone steps that led to the front door of years of mossy growth and dead leaves. They hacked back the overgrown shrubbery and clipped the hedges. They mowed the sweeping lawns of tall grass and thick long-stemmed daisies to a short brown stubble, getting the children to run and fetch cans of water to spray over them, hoping it would give some green colour by the next morning. The flowerbeds were dug over and every border made neat. The deep rectangular ornamental pond, which had once held many exotic species of fish, was cleared of debris and refilled with fresh water. Joe was pleased that at least he had tended to the many beautiful varieties of rhododendron growing along the drive, now out in full bloom. Huge oaks and cypress trees towered protectively over the top of the house at the back, giving the building a majestic frame.

People came and went as they could and some of the women used Loveday's kitchen to make sandwiches and keep up the supplies of fresh tea.

In the late afternoon, Trease eased his aching muscles, puny now after lack of hard work, and made for the garage to polish the four-cylinder Spyker, the pride and joy among Miles Trevallion's three motorcars. While neglecting the work he was paid to do, Trease had kept the cars in immaculate condition and he would use the Spyker to collect the Fiennes from the station tomorrow.

But coming along the long driveway now was another motorcar, a small Austin Seven, an economical, reliable and durable car, driven by a middle-aged man who shared his car's attributes. Mr Robert Drayton stepped out of the car in a dull suit and very shiny shoes. A wide smile broke out on his unremarkable face as he took in the busy scene. Rebecca, Joe and Loveday gathered around Trease and Jossy to see what the solicitor had come for.

Mr Drayton doffed his hat to the ladies, momentarily revealing his big ears, and after breathing in the clean fresh smell of newly cut grass, addressed Trease. 'I must say I am impressed at what you are doing here, Allen. I was on my way to call at your cottage to make sure that you had received my letter but thought I'd call here first and take a look at the big house. This is a most pleasant surprise and I'm sure Major Fiennes will appreciate your efforts. You have the time of the train's arrival?'

'Aye,' Trease said tartly. He made no bones about the fact that he did not like Mr Robert Drayton. 'The eleven thirty-two. I know which platform it'll arrive at too.'

'Splendid, splendid. Mr Faull and I would be there ourselves to meet Major Fiennes and his family but he prefers to settle in before discussing business matters.' He looked at Rebecca. 'You have the gatehouse made ready, Miss Allen? You will be able to manage?'

'Everything will be in order for tomorrow, and yes, we'll manage. Mrs Wright was in service with Lord Falmouth before she was married and is helping me,' Rebecca replied, mentally going over how much more work they still had to do.

'Splendid, well done. I have arranged for some provisions to be delivered at the gatehouse shortly for the Major's stay.'

'I'll see to them,' Loveday said.

'Thank you, Mrs Wright. You will of course be paid by the estate for your services. Well, then, I'd better let you get on with your work.'

'Aye, don't let us make you late,' muttered Trease. 'You must have something far more important to do than hanging around here…'

Rebecca dug her father in the back and hissed, 'Father!' She knew Mr Drayton wanted to look over the house but found Trease intimidating.

'… Mr Drayton, sir,' Trease tagged on insolently.

'I trust I shall have the accounts I'm waiting for on my desk first thing the day after tomorrow,' Mr Drayton said acidly, dragging out each word. It made his long thin moustache wriggle about over his top lip and Tamsyn began to giggle. Loveday turned her smartly round by the shoulders and marched her away.

'We'll not stand much chance of keeping our jobs even if this major wants Trevallion if Mr Drayton tells him we're nothing but an uncouth, ill-mannered lot,' Joe said reproachfully when the solicitor had gone.

Jossy said nothing but his face showed he wasn't pleased with Trease.

Trease scowled and pushed off to the garage. Joe caught up with Loveday and they exchanged sympathetic looks for Rebecca. Rebecca went back to work suddenly feeling exhausted and heavy of heart. Why must her father always risk ruining everything?

When dusk fell, the work went on by lantern light. Jacky Jenkins' ancient fingers finally tired and two of his great-nephews turned up, one to escort him home, the other, Rebecca noticed with consternation, to share a few bottles of ale with the men. She hoped Trease would not see them. She left the few remaining men at ten o'clock and went home to sponge and iron Trease's chauffeur's uniform.

Joe put his final touch to the front of the house, ornate plaster tubs which he had scrubbed clean now containing cuttings of flowering shrubs. The shrubs were unlikely to take and grow in the pots but they might help to impress the Fiennes before they died off.

After taking a quick bite of supper, Rebecca left something on a plate for her father then made her way back to the big house to see if there was anything else she could do that night. One step outside the cottage door and she could hear Trease and Joe quarrelling, their angry words carrying all the way down to the creek on the still night air.

'I only had a couple!' Trease was shouting. 'What's the matter with 'ee? Always have to grumble, always on about bleddy something, you are, Carlyon. Why can't you just leave me alone!'

Rebecca tried to shut out the sound of Joe's angry retort and ran all the way up the hill to the two men and begged her father to come home and go to bed. 'It's best we all get some rest and start again at dawn,' she appealed to their tired faces.

'You get to bed!' Trease snapped. 'And don't always be telling a man what to do. This was all my idea, cleaning up the house and grounds, don't forget it, the pair of you. Anyone would think I was ruddy useless!' He snatched a lantern off a windowsill and stamped away.

'What was that all about?' Rebecca demanded.

'I'm sorry, Becca,' Joe replied with a long sigh. 'He bought a couple of bottles of ale off Royston Jenkins and he thought I disapproved of it.'

'Did you say something to him?'

'No, honestly, he's been getting more 'n' more prickly ever since Mr Drayton appeared. There's a lot riding on the outcome of tomorrow. I s'pose we're all a bit worried.'

'I just hope he doesn't get into one of his maudlin moods,' Rebecca said. 'It's a good job the pub's shut.'

She returned home, weary and dejected, and went straight to the cupboard where Trease had put the sherry bottle. It was still there, holding the same amount of liquid left from the morning. She breathed a mighty sigh of relief.

Trease came in a few minutes later. 'You off to bed?'

'Yes. Are you?'

He grinned and yawned. 'Reckon I'll sleep like a top tonight.' He kissed Rebecca, the first sign of affection she'd had from him in years, and she went to her bed full of hope again. A new master would breathe new life into the estate and hopefully into her father. Then perhaps instead of having to worry about the present she could consider her future, think about what she'd like to do with her life, decide whether to stay here in Kennick Creek or seek new pastures.

In the night Trease got up and took the sherry bottle out to his shed. Delving deep in a pile of oily rags, he pulled out a full bottle of whisky, the one he kept for 'emergencies'. A short time later both bottles were empty and he was moaning out words of lament, his face contorted with the pain of bitter memories and self-pity.

The arrival at the big house of Mr Drayton, a smart, honest and hard-working man, had reminded him of his own inadequacies and he had felt resentful. Now he felt angry, deeply, bitterly angry. What had given Drayton the right to come and check on what he and the other Kennickers were doing in preparation for Major Fiennes' arrival? What did he know about hard work anyway? He had never got his hands dirty fighting the blasted Germans! No, he had secured a cosy desk job for himself, everyone knew that.

Mr pansy-fingered Drayton had never married. He didn't know what it felt like to come back from war after you'd seen one of your closest mates drown in the sucking, oozing mud. To find that the beautiful wife you'd loved and cherished had run off with another man, a no-good spiv, and your little daughter was a virtual stranger to you, a constant reminder with her pretty dark looks of the bitch who betrayed you. He didn't know what it was like to fear for the future because his employer was dying a long, drawn-out, painful death. He hadn't felt the same way about Captain Miles anyway, just easy money in his pocket for him, watching over the estate and doing very little work for it.

Did he ever wake up sweating in the middle of the night with the sound of bombing and shelling and men's cries deep inside his head? He had never had to try to get the stink of death out of his nostrils. He had never had to share a latrine with dozens of others and felt the result of its previous use splashing all over his buttocks. He didn't know what it felt like to be hit by burning shrapnel and lose an eye.

No! Mr Drayton had a wonderful, cushy life. Did he ever feel the stiffness in his joints, a legacy from the horrific trench conditions? No! He was a healthy man. He had a good job, a nice little house in Truro, a dear old mother apparently to look after him.

And he had the bloody nerve to come checking on other people's work!

Trease put the whisky bottle to his lips and tried to drain one last drop of liquor out of it but without success. Howling in rage he threw the bottle at the roof of the shed and was forced to shield himself as it smashed and the splinters fell down on him. He got up from the pile of old sacks he was sitting on. He was feeling claustrophobic. He had to get outside. He tripped over the doorstep and hauled himself to his feet with a terrible curse. Then he stumbled about outside by the light of the moon.

Chapter 3

Rebecca rushed onto the platform of Truro railway station and looked anxiously through the milling crowd for the Fiennes family. Her heart was in her mouth. She'd heard a train pull out of the station as she'd bought her platform ticket. If she was late meeting them it might not only mean a bad start but the final straw in her hopes that she and her father would retain their home on the Trevallion estate. Not that her father cared. He couldn't possibly if what he had done last night was anything to go by.

She'd got up at the crack of dawn and was eating a hurried breakfast before starting work with Loveday at the gatehouse when Joe had burst into the kitchen with the terrible news. She'd wrapped her shabby dressing gown in tighter and held her throat as he told her in great anguish about the state he'd just found Trevallion House in.

'I'll kill your bloody father, I swear it!' he'd stormed.

'What makes you think—'

'For heaven's sake, Becca, who else would it have been? He must have gone off his blasted head!' Joe pushed past her and headed for the stairs. 'He's not up and about, is he?'

She shook her head numbly, knowing that Joe's suspicions were probably correct.

'He must have got drunk and went off his blasted head!'

She'd followed him as he'd raced up the stairs, filling the narrow stairway and making the bare steps tremble under his weight. 'Allen! Allen! Where are you? You won't get away with this, you swine!'

'Joe! Stop it!' Rebecca had wailed, clutching at his shirt.

They'd hurtled through Trease's bedroom door together. Trease was lying at an awkward angle stretched out over the bed. Joe snatched a handful of his hair and forced his head upwards. Trease's head lolled to the side, his eyelids too heavy to open and reveal his glazed eyeballs. He moaned. His mouth dropped open and Joe gagged on stale alcohol and threw him aside in disgust.

'Too damned drunk to even face up to his crime!'

Rebecca crept round Joe and straightened her father on the bed, putting his head carefully to the side. Then she turned to Joe with her face full of shame and guilt. 'Wh-what exactly has he done?'

'I'll tell you downstairs. I can't bear to look at that man another minute.' He left quietly, his head and shoulders hunched over in defeat.

Rebecca opened the windows wide to freshen her father's room, glancing at him briefly before going to her own room and pulling on some clothes. Downstairs, Joe had poured himself a mug of tea and was staring into it. She had to remove a lump in her throat.

'Well?'

'All the work that was done yesterday, all that effort and hard work, is ruined. Come and see for yourself.'

There was an unbearable feeling in her stomach as she had followed Joe's dejected strides up to the big house. She was desperate to have him tell her what her father had done, but the set of his broad shoulders forbade any more questions. She was Trease Allen's daughter, and up until now folk had felt sorry for her over his behaviour; now it seemed that Joe wanted her to share in her father's shame.

Even if he had told her what Trease had done, it wouldn't have prepared Rebecca for the shock and horror ahead. She stood outside Trevallion House, white-faced, staring numbly at the devastation. All the window panes had been dirtied with earth thrown at them. Plants and shrubs had been pulled up by their roots and shredded, their pieces tossed about and floating in the pond. The piles of grass cuttings were scattered everywhere. Huge pits had been dug out of the lawns. The heads of the beautiful rhododendrons were pulled off. The pots Joe had carefully cleaned and prepared had all been smashed. Trease had even chopped down a young tree and dragged it along the forecourt and dumped it over the steps. The biggest insult was the condition of the huge ornate front door. It had withstood generations of Trevallions, all weather conditions and many a drama. Trease had run the hunting knife Captain Miles Trevallion had given to him down it, gouging out deep pieces of wood; the knife lay abandoned on the doorstep.

With tears streaming down her face, Rebecca whispered, 'I'm so sorry. I must have been so tired I didn't hear a thing.' Joe pulled her close to him. ''Tis not your fault, Becca. There's only one person to take the blame for this, and I reckon he don't care a damn.'

His kindness and despair were worse than his anger and she sobbed in his arms. A gasp behind them made them unfurl and turn round. Loveday was staring at the house, her fingers clamped to her lips as if she was afraid she would scream and never stop.

Rebecca explained that her father had got drunk and was responsible and it was then she had realised he was incapable of meeting Major and Mrs Fiennes. 'What are we going to do?' she murmured feebly, all the hopes and expectations of yesterday completely drained out of her. 'What will the Major say? He might even get the police on Father.'

'Try to clear it up, I suppose,' Joe said glumly. 'Hope this new owner is an understanding sort of bloke.'

'Why did he do it? What got into Trease?' Loveday asked in a stunned whisper, putting her arm round Rebecca's waist in a supportive gesture.

Joe wanted to let off more steam but Loveday gave him a warning look. Fresh tears were scalding Rebecca's eyes and her shoulders were shaking as she tried to hold the sobs back.

'Well, never mind that now,' Loveday said briskly. 'We'd be better planning on what we're going to do to clear up this mess than standing around like this. We'll have to get help. I'll send Tamsyn to get the Jenkins.'

They adjourned to Loveday's cottage where it was decided she and Tamsyn, who was a capable child, would clean the gatehouse and prepare a lunch for the Fiennes, while Rebecca and Joe began the awesome task of trying to make the front of Trevallion in some small way presentable.

None of the men could be spared from the heavy work involved in clearing up to meet their new employer at the railway station, so Rebecca had been charged with this duty.

Now she was here on the station platform, she was overcome with an attack of nerves. She was late. On the way she had pictured herself standing about, walking up and down, rehearsing a suitable welcome, but she had not accounted for meeting Farmer Bocock in his big haycart in the lane and having to follow him slowly for over a mile. He was a stubborn old so-and-so and had flatly refused to move over to the side to let her pass. Now she was flustered, her mind blank one moment, a jumble of thoughts and words and explanations the next. What would she say about Trevallion anyway? If they asked questions about the big house, what on earth would she say?

A smartly dressed woman asked her if she had the time and with horror Rebecca realised how she was dressed in comparison, what she must look like. She had stayed helping Joe for so long that she had left the creek without changing into her best clothes. The leather of her old black boots was cracked and dusty, her clothes were shabby with a tear in her cardigan and the hem of her skirt was coming down. She was breathless and red in the face. She was about to meet a new mistress and she wasn't even wearing a hat. She pointed to the station clock and the woman thanked her, then Rebecca dug about in her pockets in a vain effort to find something to tie back her unruly hair with.

She looked anxiously at the two neat women serving at the stationery booth and decided they were too busy to be asked by an unkempt stranger if they happened to have a piece of ribbon she could use. She saw a discarded rubber band lying on the ground and pounced on it. She put the band between her teeth and had both her hands gripping her hair at the back of her neck when she became aware of some people watching her, and instantly, with flame-red cheeks and sinking heart, she knew who they were.

The lady, with a friendly smile on full red lips and brilliant blue eyes under her cloche hat, said, 'The station master informed us that you are from Trevallion.'

Rebecca thrust her hands down and fumbled the rubber band into her cardigan pocket. She didn't know what to say, whether to keep quiet or drop a curtsy. They were all looking at her: the stunningly elegant lady in a silk-chenille suit, casually holding a clutch bag, the gentleman in a wide hat and dark colours standing in a disinterested fashion slightly behind his wife, the boy, who had pushed his head round his father's side to see what was holding them up.

'Y-yes, yes, I have… I am. I'm here to collect you… th-that is if you are M–Major and Mrs Fiennes… My father couldn't come, he's unwell… he…' Rebecca wanted the station platform to open up and swallow her. She had never felt so embarrassed, so foolish, so unsure of herself. The boy was looking at her in utter contempt, and no wonder.

Mrs Fiennes extended a long, slim, gloved hand. 'So pleased to meet you,' she said in a silky voice that simply purred along with her graceful movements. 'And what a shame about your father. I do hope it is nothing serious. And you are?'

Rebecca's horrors were not yet over. She couldn't remember if in her haste she had washed her hands but she could hardly look down to see. She rubbed her hand furtively on her skirt and shook Mrs Fiennes' hand shyly, careful not to exert too much pressure.

'I'm Rebecca Allen, Mrs Fiennes. My father, Trease Allen, is the chauffeur, he's, um…' and she went even redder, 'got a liver complaint, left over from the war.'

'Oh dear, isn't that a shame, Alex?' Mrs Fiennes said.

He merely nodded. All Rebecca could see of Major Alexander Fiennes was the shadow of a dark face under his pulled-down hat, but she suddenly knew he was staring at her. He touched the hat to her, keeping his face unseen. 'Shall we go?' he said quietly.

Rebecca thought he'd addressed his wife but then realised he was talking to her.

'Yes, let's get on. I'm getting really fed up standing around in this horrid little place,' the boy snapped.

'Yes, yes, of course,' Rebecca said rapidly. 'I'll get a porter to—'

'All seen to,' Abigail Fiennes said breezily. 'Our luggage should be outside the station by now and waiting to be loaded into the motorcar. You lead the way, Rebecca.'

Rebecca gulped and said, 'Yes, ma'am,' and led the way as bidden. The boy pushed past her rudely and she followed him through the station building and out to the other side scowling at his back. He had inherited his mother's aquiline features and was tall, but unlike the Major, who was rather spare and rangy, he was broad in the body. Too much cosseting, thought Rebecca spitefully.

He stopped abruptly and Rebecca bumped into him. He turned on her and shouted, 'Can't you look where you're going!'

'Now, don't be rude, Stephen,' Abigail Fiennes called to him. Rebecca gritted her teeth; she had enough to worry about right now and didn't need nasty boys of about twelve years old adding to her problems. The brat was old enough to have acquired some manners by now.

Two porters were standing to attention behind two trolleys loaded with luggage, waiting for instructions.

'Where's the motorcar?' asked Stephen Fiennes, stabbing a finger at Rebecca as if he was accusing her of driving it to the station and stealing it.

As Major Fiennes didn't seem to be in charge, Rebecca looked appealingly at his wife. 'I can't drive a motorcar, Mrs Fiennes, and anyway Captain Trevallion wouldn't let any woman near his motorcars. I've brought a trap with me.'

The family and porters looked towards the trap and two patient ponies she indicated. The trap was a large square vehicle with four huge wheels and two tiers of seats, painted in blue and red with the Trevallion crest on it.

'I'm not travelling on that!' exclaimed Stephen Fiennes, stamping his feet and holding his arms up under his chin. Rebecca saw that along with his persistent scowl he had a row of tiny chickenpox scars over his left eyebrow. 'I'd feel really stupid.'

'The Captain designed it and made it himself,' Rebecca said hastily. Surely that ought to impress this young horror.

'It's perfectly charming,' Mrs Fiennes said, motioning to the porters to load all the luggage onto a horse-drawn taxicab. 'You can follow us to Trevallion,' she told its driver.

'Mother,' Stephen protested. 'We might be seen by someone we know, even down *here*.'

'Now don't be difficult, darling,' Mrs Fiennes returned, quite unperturbed. Rebecca could see this lady was completely in charge of all, she undertook. 'Get up in the front seat beside Rebecca. It's a beautiful day and we'll have a wonderful view of the countryside as we ride along.'

'I'm not sitting beside her,' Stephen shouted, tightening his stubborn lips and growing even redder in the face than Rebecca had been earlier.

'Well, sit beside me then.' Abigail included Rebecca and Major Fiennes in her next sentence. 'I'm sure the Major won't mind sitting up at the front, will you, Alex?'

The Major murmured in the affirmative. There was a gentle swish of silk skirt and the air was filled with a strong musky perfume as he helped his wife into the second row of black leather padded seats beside their truculent son, who sat forward with his elbows on his knees and his face held in the palms of his hands.

'W-would you like to drive, Major Fiennes?' Rebecca asked hesitantly, thinking that perhaps she ought to offer. Captain Trevallion had insisted on driving everywhere himself. He'd employed Trease to convey his guests.

'No, thank you,' Major Fiennes replied quietly, and he offered his hand to help her up, which Rebecca self-consciously accepted.

She headed the ponies back up the hill and on to the Falmouth road. After a short distance they turned off down a winding country lane between tall hedgerows. In the little hamlet of Porthoc some children out playing waved to them and were delighted when both Rebecca and Mrs Fiennes waved back. They went on past a tiny roadside Methodist chapel and were now deep in the countryside. Mrs Fiennes exclaimed at the wild flowers and rolling fields she could see up ahead and through the wide gateways. Stephen refused to look and the Major said nothing, only very occasionally turning his head.

Rebecca felt silly sitting beside him. He sat rigidly with his fists on his thighs, his long legs bent uncomfortably high at the knee. She stole a quick look at him. He was dressed very casually for a gentleman. He wasn't wearing a suit but a loose herringbone tweed jacket and a pair of trousers that were shiny at the knees. The top button of his white shirt was open and he wore no tie or gloves. His brown leather shoes were slightly scuffed and in need of a good polish. Rebecca had only been a little girl when Miles Trevallion went to war but she remembered enough of him to know he would never have arrived anywhere turned out like this.

The Major's hat was the most noticeable feature about him. It was wide and black and pulled down over his face, deliberately so, cutting himself off from everybody.

When she had seen what her father had done to Trevallion this morning, Rebecca had made up her mind to try to talk to Major Fiennes, to plead with him to keep the estate on and build it up again, even if he felt he must dismiss Trease and order them out of Allen Cottage. But if he never spoke, it was going to be very difficult.

'You handle the ponies very well, Rebecca,' Mrs Fiennes said.

'Thank you, ma'am. I've been around horses all my life. These two are called Ophelia and Hamlet. Captain Trevallion called all his horses after characters from Shakespeare's plays.'

'Did he really? How charming. There you are, Stephen, you'll be able to ride every day, and play in the creek. I'm sure you'll love the river, and there's bound to be someone there who can teach you how to row.'

Stephen was unimpressed and snorted, turning his head sharply away.

'What do you do on the estate, Rebecca?' she asked next. 'I understand your father is the caretaker of the big house. Do you help him?'

'No, Mrs Fiennes,' Rebecca replied uneasily. 'There's not enough work for both of us, I work on one of the estate farms, Verrian Farm, helping out the Kellow family.'

Rebecca suddenly sensed that Major Fiennes was looking at her. It made her feel extremely uncomfortable. This man would probably blow his top when he found out about Trease's crime. The trap jolted as a back wheel was lifted over a turnip that had fallen off Farmer Bocock's wagon earlier and her hair streamed over her shoulder in front of her. She glanced his way as she swept it back. Yes, he was looking at her. He had lifted his chin and she could see more of his face. Dark blank eyes and a gaunt face, made rather long and thin by lack of flesh, high cheekbones that stuck out a little, a substantial jaw in need of a shave. A little energy filtered into his eyes and he seemed to stare. It was unnerving and Rebecca turned quickly to watch the road. An instant later he looked away.

A few more bends, stopping and pulling in to the side to let a baker's van pass them, and then two tall granite pillars up ahead announced the turning into the Trevallion estate. Mrs Fiennes said, 'How thrilling.' Her son grunted and fixed his blatant blue eyes stonily on the floor of the trap. The Major said nothing and didn't move a muscle.

The ponies trotted elegantly down the short distance to the gatehouse. Joe, Loveday, Jossy and many other Kennickers were standing to attention in a straight line outside the front door. Tamsyn was fidgeting about and Loveday caught her by the shoulders and held her still.

When Mrs Fiennes saw the little girl, she declared, 'Look, Stephen, someone for you to play with.'

'I'm not going to play with a stupid small girl!' he snarled back and jumped down.

'Now don't be difficult, darling,' she called after him.

Rebecca was sure she would hear that lighthearted appeal often in the future – if she had a future on the estate.

Joe came forward and helped Mrs Fiennes down. The Major was already on the ground behind Joe when he turned. He stood smartly to attention and saluted.

'Pleased to meet you, Major Fiennes. I'm Joe Carlyon, the groom and groundsman of Trevallion, and I had the honour of fighting under the command of the late Captain Trevallion in the Duke of Cornwall's Light Infantry during the war.'

Rebecca jumped down from the trap and held the ponies still, watching her new employer to see if he was more forthcoming with another man.

'Thank you for being here, Carlyon,' the Major replied quietly.

Joe took it upon himself to make the introductions and then Loveday showed the family into the gatehouse. The Kennickers wandered away back to their homes, speculating on their future and the length of Mrs Fiennes' hemline – a good four inches above her ankles!

Joe helped the taxi-cab driver unload the luggage. 'Wonder what's in all these,' he grinned at Rebecca.

'Joe!' she hissed. 'I've got to slip down to the creek and change my clothes. I can't help Loveday serve lunch dressed like this.'

Joe looked her over and offered a typical male statement. 'You look all right to me.'

'I'm like a ragbag. They must think I'm a heathen or something.'

'Well, you'd better slip off now before you're needed again.'

She looked at the big man anxiously. 'Did you manage to do much clearing up?'

'Only the worst of it. It's still pretty bad. I'll do some more later.'

'Has my father showed his face yet?'

'No, thankfully,' Joe said tightly. 'The Major wants the trap left here until after lunch. I'll take it out of the way.'

Rebecca started quickly off down to the creek but Loveday ran after her. 'Becca! I've just shown Mrs Fiennes to her room. She wants to see you at once. She says there's a problem.'

Chapter 4

Neville Faull stood patiently on the red-paved doorstep of a large house in Melvill Road, one of the oldest thorough-fares in Falmouth. The house itself, standing back from a tree-lined pavement, was one of the oldest in the town, its outstanding features being several curious tall chimneys. Neville straightened his green silk tie, smoothed his short fair hair and knocked confidently on the green-painted door.

A maid, daintily built and clad in pale green except for a snowy white apron and lacy headband, answered the door. Her hand flew to her rounded cheek in surprise but she ushered him respectfully into the hall. She had not been surprised at Mr Neville Faull calling on her mistress; he was expected. She was simply surprised at how handsome he was and it made her blush and fidget with her headband. She had expected the solicitor to be middle-aged and plain-faced, quite unlike this man. He was in his late twenties, with a chiselled jaw, clear blue eyes, a thin neat moustache running along the top of a wide mouth which smiled often to show good teeth. Mr Neville Faull was a tall, elegant man with a muscular build under his perfectly tailored suit.

Neville appreciated the maid's flustered response to him.

'Madam said I was to show you straightaway into her sitting room, sir, if you'd be so kind as to step this way,' she said, blushing furiously under her long lashes.

He watched her quick agile walk with a smooth lazy grin on his face and allowed his thoughts to meander to what a thrill it would be for this sweet young thing if he was ever to stay overnight in this house.

The maid opened the double doors of the sitting room, curtsied low to her mistress inside and, after announcing Neville, quickly disappeared.

Neville walked to the middle of the room. He wore a well-rehearsed smile now because he had been warned that when he met this lady, who had written to his office and summoned him here, it would be hard to hide his revulsion of her. He succeeded but made a mental note to tell his latest love interest that he'd found it easier facing the Hun during the war.

'It was a pleasure to receive your letter, Miss Bosanko,' he said airily, kissing the lady's hand. He forced himself to press his lips to her flesh, taking care not to scratch himself on her sharp yellowed nails, then stood back a little and studied Susannah Bosanko with the same eye he'd used on her maid. He'd taken the trouble to find out all he could about Miss Bosanko and knew she would appreciate it.

Susannah Bosanko stared back at him through lashless slitted green eyes. She was in her ninetieth year but could easily pass for two hundred! Neville had never seen anyone so hideous yet peculiarly magnificent. Her appearance was one of emaciation; her face was a mesh of deep wrinkles with large drooping bags under her eyes and above them pencilled-in slanting brows. Her fallen throat was pulled back by an emerald choker. Her body was small and shrivelled. She had made an attempt to disguise her strange ugliness. Rouge was painted carefully on her hollow cheeks and a red wig swept up in Edwardian style sat on her head, looking decidedly top-heavy. Neville reckoned she was completely bald beneath the wig.

For all her apparent frailness, he sensed the old lady had an unusual energy pulsing through her and it was rumoured she'd never had a day's illness in her life. Her head suddenly came up sharply and Neville had to steel himself not to jump backwards. Her eyes were startlingly bright and perceptive.

'Sit yourself down, Neville Faull.' Her voice was low and gravelly; it had lost its richness many years ago.

He racked his brains to think of something complimentary to say. He'd heard that she'd prefer it to be seductive but there were some things even he wouldn't do to further a lucrative piece of private business.

He sat down, not too far away from her, and turned on his charm through his smile. 'This is a most pleasant room, Miss Bosanko.' He stroked his tie, held in place by a gold and single emerald pin which had cost him more than he could comfortably afford. 'I see that like me you have a penchant for the colour green.'

He was sure this was the right approach. The whole house was painted and decorated in tasteful shades of green. On every shelf and table and corner of the room were sweeping fern plants, the mantelpiece was graced with a green marble clock and jade ornaments. Even the piano was green. Miss Bosanko was clothed entirely in green in the latest Paris fashion down to her tiny emerald-buckled shoes.

'I think of the colour green as a symbol of eternal youthfulness, Mr Faull,' she replied. She was smiling back at him and Neville felt with a sick feeling in his gut that she was trying to be seductive. She lifted a claw-like finger and pointed to a discreet drinks cabinet. 'Pour me a gin and tonic, Neville,' she said, lowering her voice and leaning forward a little in her chair. 'I have no time for all this tea drinking. Help yourself to what you want, dear boy.'

Neville poured two gin and tonics and handed one to Miss Bosanko, trying not to appear in a hurry to get back to his own chair. 'In your letter to me you mentioned that you are interested in buying the Trevallion estate, Miss Bosanko.'

'That is correct, Neville. I hope I can trust you to be discreet.'

'Naturally.' He smiled over his glass. 'As a trustee I am concerned that only the best happens to the late Captain Miles Trevallion's property.'

Susannah Bosanko eyed him shrewdly. Neville Faull wasn't the only one to make inquiries in advance of this meeting. Apparently he wasn't as honest as his business partner and was continually looking for a way to enhance his cash flow, hoping to make a quick fortune.

'Naturally. What is this Major Fiennes like? Do you think he will sell?'

'He's a cold man, Miss Bosanko. Takes very little interest in anything or anyone. I went up to Berkshire a few days ago to meet him. You see I'd heard of someone interested in buying the house to turn it into a hotel. He wants to offer trips on the river, wildlife to the naturalists, that kind of thing. I will make a considerable commission if I succeed.'

'And what did the good Major say?'

'He said he wouldn't be making any decisions until he'd had the chance to look over the property. The very next day I returned to Cornwall to inform my partner that he would be journeying down within the week.'

'I see. And when does he arrive?'

'Today, Miss Bosanko.'

'Good. Then you can get to work for me immediately. You can forget the other buyer, Neville. I want you to offer the Major on my behalf, discreetly of course, ten thousand pounds more than the property's value or the same on top of any other offer he may receive. Your commission will be twenty per cent.'

Neville couldn't help whistling through his teeth. He knew Susannah Bosanko was very wealthy. She had set up canteens for embarking and returning troops in Falmouth during the war and had served in them herself She had supplied an endless stream of good-quality wool for the women of the town to knit socks, gloves, mufflers and scarves for the armed forces. But she'd also put her money into anything that would return a handsome profit, munitions, uniforms and coal. She was rich but Neville hadn't expected her to be so generous. He didn't care why she wanted Trevallion. For over two thousand pounds he'd do almost anything to get it for her.

'Come closer,' Susannah said, sending enticing signals across the room to him.

The rumours about Susannah Bosanko's prurience, even at her grand age, were probably exaggerated but clearly they were not entirely without foundation. He made his expression regretful. 'I'd love to stay longer, Miss Bosanko,' he said, 'but I'm sorry to say that I must attend a reading of a will at midday. As it is, I dropped everything to come here.'

'Don't come again unless you have some positive news for me,' Susannah ordered him stiffly. 'I hope it will not be too long, Mr Faull.'

Neville screwed up his courage to linger over her bony hand before he beat a hasty retreat. He brushed his hand over the maid's bottom as she showed him to the door, just to give him a feeling of normality in that department. Neville rubbed his hands together before pulling on his driving gauntlets. He had more than one reason to call often at Trevallion and while he was there he would further his tentative pursuit of a rather serious young woman living in its little creek.

Rebecca stood outside Mrs Fiennes' room flexing her hand as she tried to pluck up the courage to knock on the door. The door was suddenly opened.

'Don't be afraid to come in, Rebecca,' Mrs Fiennes said brightly, sweeping back inside the room. She went to the dressing table and picked up a perfume bottle, spraying her neck and arms. 'I heard you coming upstairs,' she said to Rebecca's reflection in the three-sided mirror. 'That's how I knew you were there. Oh, don't look so frightened, my dear. I'm not going to eat you. You've done nothing wrong.'

Rebecca couldn't help staring at the lady. She had taken her hat off to reveal ash-blonde hair cut short in a bob in straight sleek lines. Both sides were tucked in behind her small ears while she saw to her make-up, Rebecca found her voice at last.

'I'm sorry, Mrs Fiennes. Loveday said there was a problem.'

The gatehouse was basic and functional and Mrs Fiennes looked out of place in it, like an exotic hothouse flower in a gloomy garden shed. She should put her feet on Turkish rugs not worn linoleum. She was wearing a pale blue silk housecoat which complemented her fair colouring and sparkling blue eyes. She delicately stroked bright red lipstick along her bottom lip. Such a deep colour. Ira Jenkins would call it the mark of the Devil. Loveday would purse her lips but say nothing. Abigail Fiennes was going to cause a stir in the creek.

'It's only a tiny problem, Rebecca. Be a dear first and see if you can find my jewel case in one of the suitcases. The thing is, you're going to have to move into the fourth bedroom. The Major and I can't possibly stay here without a chaperone. You see, we're not married.'

Rebecca's jaw dropped. She straightened up from the suitcase she had opened on the bed and gaped at Abigail Fiennes wide-eyed. She knew people lived different lives in high society, but not married? And with a child? If that was the case, why did they need a chaperone?

Abigail turned round on her chair and caught Rebecca's shocked expression. She laughed loudly, putting long-nailed fingertips to her lips. 'Oh, don't look so horrified, Rebecca. I think there is a misunderstanding here. I was married to the Major's younger brother, Ralph Fiennes. He was a pilot during the war. He was shot down and killed,' she ended on a quieter note.

Rebecca made her face appear more normal. 'I'm sorry, Mrs Fiennes. We thought, we understood that, it said in the letter we had from Mr Drayton that you and the Major...'

'Then this Mr Drayton is obviously the one who got it wrong.'

'I feel such a fool,' Rebecca said, delving into the leather suitcase in search of the jewel case to hide her embarrassment.

'There's no need for that,' Abigail said, coming to her and pointing to a corner of the suitcase where the jewel box was to be found. 'You look so miserable, Rebecca. I think our arrival here has quite overwhelmed you.'

Rebecca took out a plain box, one made specially for travelling, and Abigail took it from her.

'I wanted this day to be special for you but everything has gone wrong.'

'In what way?' Abigail said sympathetically, returning to the dressing table and finding a small key in her purse.

'My clothes, for a start. I was so busy helping to get things ready I didn't have time to change. I'm sorry to have met you looking like this. I was just going to change when Loveday said you wanted to see me.'

Abigail looked Rebecca up and down slowly. 'Girls like you make me quite sick,' she said, but not unkindly. 'You would look good in whatever you were wearing, even a sack.' She sprang up, the quick movement no less elegant than her others, and began to scatter clothes all over the bed.

Rebecca stood frozen, wondering what Mrs Fiennes was doing and worrying about what it would mean to have to live under the same roof as the family. Her father could fend for himself but it would mean she would not be able to keep a close eye on him. She had a sudden horror of Trease coming out of his drunken stupor and arriving at the gatehouse, dishevelled and swearing and causing a terrible scene. He would be dismissed at once. They would be ordered out of their cottage and she would not be allowed to continue working on any of the farms on the estate. They would not be given a reference.

'There you go again, frowning as if you have all the burdens of the world to carry,' Abigail tut-tutted. She tossed a silver-grey low-waisted dress at Rebecca who caught it clumsily. Thinking that she was supposed to help Mrs Fiennes into it she hastily undid the hooks at the back and moved towards her new mistress.

'Hold it up,' Abigail said, frowning critically with her thumb under her chin and fingers on her cheek. 'It's not for me but for you.'

'Me?' Rebecca said stupidly.

'You can have it,' Abigail said dismissively. 'We're about the same build.'

'But I couldn't—'

'I'm having none of that. It doesn't suit me. I hate it. Can't think why I packed it, much less why I bought it in the first place. You'd be doing me a favour.' Abigail sat down and started to apply charcoal-coloured eyeshadow under her plucked pencil-thin brows. 'Well, go on, try it on. Mrs Wright said you are going to help her serve luncheon and you can't do it dressed like that. What's good enough for the creek is not good enough for the dining room.' When Rebecca still hesitated, Abigail added, 'If you're shy, go behind the screen.'

Rebecca wasn't ashamed of her underwear. What little money she earned she saved up and spent on items of good quality rayon – artificial silk – and her aunt who lived in Truro always gave her pretty lingerie on special occasions. She went behind the folding cane screen to gather her wits. There had never been so many abrupt changes and strange occurrences in just two days of her life. She had never dreamt she would be given a pure silk dress by a rich lady. It wasn't a good fit. Rebecca had a much smaller waist, and it hung like a bag there but was tight across the chest. Abigail Fiennes wore the sort of fashionable foundation garments that flattened her bosom. Rebecca took off her boots and stood in her bare feet. She would have to manage without stockings and hoped there would be enough time to send Tamsyn down to the creek to fetch her best shoes.

Mrs Fiennes had managed to dress herself and wore a crêpe de Chine pleated frockcoat, its hemline several inches above her ankles. Thank heavens the grey silk dress was not so short or Trease would have a fit. It might be the fashion to have plenty of calf showing but the Kennickers would never approve.

Nor did Loveday by the expression on her face when Mrs Fiennes entered the dining room. She hid her disapproval by raising her eyebrows at Rebecca in the lady's cast-off dress and Rebecca shrugged her helplessness at having to wear it. When they were in the kitchen, Loveday handed her a scarf to tie back her hair.

'Do I look awful, Loveday?'

Loveday considered her. ''Tis some strange to see you like this, the colour doesn't suit you, but no, you don't look awful. Pity you don't have more money of your own to spend on clothes. Tie your hair back and I'll make sure all the ends are tucked in. Tamsyn will be back in a minute with your shoes. Well, did you get the problem sorted out?'

Rebecca repeated what Abigail had told her about the family relationship.

'I see. Mind you, they hardly look one another's type, though most of they sort of people marry for money and position. That sounds like the Major and that boy coming down the stairs. I'll take in the fish and salad and you take in the peas and new potatoes.'

If Alexander Fiennes noticed Rebecca was wearing one of his sister-in-law's dresses he gave no sign of it but she felt him staring at her occasionally throughout the meal. He nodded to her and Loveday as they brought in the food and Abigail told them what he would eat and what he would not. The little he did take he ate in total silence.

This was obviously the norm at home in Berkshire because Abigail and Stephen talked as if he wasn't there. Rebecca couldn't help being stung by the boy's many disparaging remarks about the countryside and gatehouse. His mother asked him to at least look round the estate first before he made up his mind about Trevallion.

Now she could see the Major clearly, Rebecca had a good look at him. He was about thirty years old with a deathly pallor to his face. She thought it a desolate face and he seemed detached and preoccupied and vaguely restless. His hair was as dark as her own, short, but not neatly trimmed. His eyes were dark too, with a film drawn over them – deliberately so, Rebecca thought.

'That was an excellent apple pie, Mrs Wright,' Abigail said, throwing her napkin down, 'and the cream was delicious, so thick and smooth.'

'It came from one of the local farms, Mrs Fiennes,' Loveday said proudly, clearing away the dishes. 'Verrian Farm, where Rebecca works.'

'Oh, really? Isn't that interesting, Alex?'

'Yes, Abigail,' Alex answered, and as Rebecca looked at him to see if he really did think so he raised his eyes from the edge of the tablecloth he was picking at and glanced at her. 'Are we keeping you from your usual work, Miss Allen?'

'No, sir, not really,' she replied to the longest sentence she'd heard him say. 'Mr Kellow, he's the tenant of Verrian Farm, has given me permission to take time off for your and Mrs Fiennes' convenience.'

'Oh, she mustn't go back, Alex,' Abigail said in something that sounded like a plea. 'We need her here. I need her here. I can't possibly manage without Rebecca and Mrs Wright. Mrs Wright can look after Stephen too. That will be all right, won't it?'

'As you please, Abigail,' Alex said. 'I'll leave it to you ladies to make your own arrangements.' He added, in a tone that would not be argued with, 'I will look after myself. All that I will require are my meals and my room cleaned.'

'Good, splendid,' Abigail said, clapping her hands. 'You can bring in the coffee now, Mrs Wright, and a little later we will talk over the arrangements.'

'I will require the services of Miss Allen this afternoon,' Alex said stonily.

'Oh?'

Rebecca raised her brows but stayed nervously quiet. What did the Major want with her? Did he know about Trease's drinking and laziness and want to dismiss them both?

'I want to look over Trevallion House,' he said. 'She can drive me there and I shall get one of the cars out of the garage.'

Rebecca and Loveday exchanged looks of concern. They had been hoping the Major wouldn't want to go down to the big house so soon.

There was a model railway, once belonging to Miles Trevallion, in Stephen Fiennes' room and he couldn't wait to get back to it. Without waiting to be excused, he got down from the table and left the dining room. Abigail sighed then expressed the desire to retire and rest for the afternoon.

'My father has the keys to the big house, Major Fiennes. I will have to go home and fetch them,' Rebecca said, hoping to stall him.

'No need,' Alex said, looking directly at her and making her jump when he pulled something out of his pocket and plonked it on the table. 'I have my own.'

—

After much heaving and grunting, Joe had pulled the pine tree Trease had chopped down out of sight. He returned to the scene of the crime and shook his head at the bark and splinters left behind and went to fetch a broom. When he got back he was not pleased to see Trease there, bleary-eyed, smelling offensively and barely able to stand.

'What do you want?' Joe said acidly.

'Where's Becca?'

'Up at the gatehouse, doing your job.'

'She picked the Fiennes up, did she?'

'Aye,' Joe replied grudgingly, turning his back on Trease as he began to sweep up debris from the fallen tree.

Trease walked round him. 'Is Becca all right?'

'What do you think? What do you care? You've had that poor maid half out of her mind with worry since you got back from the war. You never stop punishing her for Nancy Ann leaving you.'

'Don't mention that woman to me!'

'I haven't got time for this. Get out my way, Allen. I've got work to do.'

Trease didn't want to get into another fight over his moods. He took his hands out of his pockets and tried to stand up straight. 'I'll, um, give you a hand, Joe.'

'You've ruddy well done enough,' Joe snapped.

'You need my help, Carlyon,' Trease said firmly. 'I made this mess and 'tis only right I help clear it up before the Major comes here. You'll have to forget how you feel about me for the time being.'

The two men worked in stony silence, careful not to get in each other's way. They brushed the forecourt clean and tried to cover the holes where the shrubs had been ripped up. About two o'clock Joe stopped and looked at Trease who was becoming increasingly unsteady on his feet from the after-effects of his drinking and lack of food.

'You best get back home,' he said gruffly. 'Wouldn't do for the Major to see you the way you are. Get a good meal inside you, tidy yourself up in case he wants to see you today. Becca has told him you're ill, with a liver complaint. Don't tell him a different story.'

'What's he like, the Major? Showing much interest?'

'Hard to say. He's very quiet but seems an agreeable sort of a bloke.'

'I'll be different now, Joe, I promise. We have a new master and we have hope for the future. I'll give up the drink. We'll make a go of this place, like the old days.'

Joe shook his head disbelievingly and said grimly, 'Do it for Becca's sake.'

–

Rebecca changed back into her old clothes and met the Major outside the gatehouse. He had brought the ponies and trap up to the front door and held out his hand to help her up then twitched the reins to begin the half-mile journey to Trevallion House. He had changed his mind about her driving the trap and she wondered why he still needed her. She watched him with a feeling of foreboding as he looked all around, up at the pale blue sky, down at the road which was in need of repair and at the neat verges Joe had cut, slowing down when the rhododendrons took over from the oaks, cedars and firs.

'Joe looks after them,' Rebecca said, feeling she couldn't allow her father to take the credit. 'There's over twenty varieties in the grounds, some are quite rare, I believe.' She gripped her hands together in fear of what he would think when he saw the ruined ones.

'So I understand,' Alex said briefly.

Rebecca wished he would open up and give a clue to his intentions for the estate but she knew it was asking too much at this stage.

She said, in a subdued voice, 'The big house hasn't been lived in since the Captain went to war. It's a bit run down.'

'I'm not expecting too much,' Alex replied.

That's a relief, Rebecca thought, and she had the comfort of knowing that Trease had at least looked after the garage and the motorcars. It might be something in his favour. Whichever car Major Fiennes selected, he would find it in tiptop condition for the drive back to the gatehouse.

Alex stopped the trap for a few moments to gaze at the top storey of Trevallion House, its walls glinting in the sunlight, its four rows of chimneys standing like silent guards at each end of the root Rebecca hoped he was impressed. She glanced at his face. There was no way of telling; he retained the same rock-hard expression.

They drove into the square courtyard and Alex brought the trap to a halt. He looked at the house and all around it for a long time. Rebecca felt her heart sinking down into her stomach. Much had been cleared up but there was still evidence of what Trease had done and it was obvious the damage was recent. Muddy pools had dried under the windows Joe had hosed down and the holes in the lawns and the scratches down the main door stood out like sore thumbs.

Joe appeared and nodded to the Major. He said nothing, believing an attempt at an explanation would only make matters worse. Better to wait for the Major to ask questions then he'd think of something to say.

'You can take the trap away, Carlyon,' Alex said, jumping down and taking the bunch of keys out of his pocket.

'I thought I'd show you around, Major Fiennes.'

'Miss Allen can do that,' Alex said shortly.

Joe's dismay at leaving Rebecca to bear the brunt of what was to come showed clearly on his rugged face. Alex moved away and looked in the nearest window. Joe shrugged his shoulders at Rebecca and climbed up on the trap.

Rebecca moved woodenly to the Major, who was standing in front of the damaged door. His dark eyes were travelling down the length of the deep scratches and suddenly they were resting, intensely, on her.

'Did you clean up the inside?' he asked quietly.

'Yes, me and Loveday Wright and several of the women from the creek and the farms on the estate. We've done the downstairs but we didn't have time to do anything upstairs.'

'From what I could see through the window, it looks immaculate.' He ran a thumbnail down one of the scratches on the door and said, slowly, 'And who was responsible for this?'

His eyes were on her again and Rebecca knew she had to tell the truth. She choked back the bile rising in her throat and her voice came out small and husky.

'My father.'

Alex sighed. What he said next was worse to Rebecca than an explosion of anger. 'Because of the drink?'

She gasped, her face as red as blood, and she could not look him in the face. He had obviously taken the trouble to find out all about the estate staff. There was no hope now of keeping Trease's alcoholism a secret. The Major must have been suspicious about Trease not meeting them at the station and now he had made her come down here with him to give them both their marching orders.

'Mr Drayton and Mr Faull have given me full information about Trevallion,' Alex said quietly. 'I know how much they value you and all the work you've done in your father's place.'

This did not lessen Rebecca's shame. Gulping, she said, 'It was the war, sir. He came home to find my mother had left us. It made him very bitter. I'll go to our cottage and get us packed up. I'm very sorry.'

She turned on her heel and began to run.

'Miss Allen!'

It was a command and stopped her in her tracks. She didn't turn round and his next words seemed to hit her one by one in the back.

'Don't take it upon yourself to make assumptions. Come back.'

Rebecca felt she had never made a bigger fool of herself. She retraced her steps and stood in front of Major Fiennes like a naughty schoolgirl.

'Yes, sir?'

'Although I've never visited Trevallion, I knew my cousin Captain Miles very well. I knew how much he cared about the estate and its employees. I know about your father and Joe Carlyon and Stanley Wright in particular. I received letters from Captain Trevallion during the war and he never doubted that any one of them would have given their lives to protect him. I visited my cousin several times during his invalidity. He couldn't speak, of course, but I know that somewhere inside him he was concerned for those who went to war with him. I know what war can do to a man. Many have come back and turned to drink. I am not about to throw you and your father off the estate.'

Rebecca was so relieved she could hardly speak for the emotion choking her. 'I'm s-sorry, sir. I spoke out of turn. I thank you for your understanding. I'll tell my father what you've said.'

Alex looked stonily at the door. 'I'll speak to him tomorrow. Now you go and collect your things and bring them back here in an hour and I'll drive us back to the gatehouse.'

–

Alex took only a quick look round the ground floor of the house. He wasn't much interested in it at the moment. He wanted to see the creek Miles had loved so much.

No one was about down by the water and he was glad of that. The last thing he wanted was company. The tide was coming determinedly up the Fal estuary, spilling over into the creek basin and filling it with emerald–green water, the colour given to it from the reflection of the trees that bowed down over its banks and the multitude of algae that flourished in it.

Alex looked at the few boats not out working, their names comfortingly familiar from what Miles had told him. Then his gaze rested on a section of the shore where a small tangle of seaweed, rope and birds' feathers lay. He watched the spot, fascinated as the water moved towards the tangle in smooth waves, the sound of their soft rush and fall like music to his ears. When it was completely submerged, he looked up and scanned the scene on the other side of the creek. In the meadow rising up from the trees, sheep were grazing, and above the meadow was clear blue sky, adorned with the odd puff of white fluffy cloud. It was a tranquil scene. It was peaceful here.

Birds were flitting about but Alex did not try to sift through the fog that was in his mind to recall their names. Miles had talked of them all; at the end of his life he wouldn't have recognised them either. A pity Miles wasn't brought here to sense the timeless peace of his home, Alex thought sadly.

He hoped this place would give him peace, peace to regain his right mind and be again as he was before the war, a place where his terrible nightmares would come to an end.

Alex shook himself Enough of that now. No brooding. He'd promised himself he'd try not to brood. He pushed his hands deep into his pockets as a positive action to prove to himself he was going to relax.

A movement caught his eye and he saw a large, scruffy dog ambling sheepishly towards him, its big brown eyes showing it was hoping to be welcomed and would receive some petting. Alex crouched down and whistled to it. 'Hello, boy. You're a friendly old thing. I wonder what your name is.' Alex turned the dog's collar round until he found a metal tag. A name was scratched on it. 'Motley,' he read aloud. He gave a short laugh. 'Me and you both, boy. You seem to like living here, and perhaps I will too.'

That night Rebecca sat in her nightie on the bed in the smallest room of the gatehouse. The air was hot and the house stuffy after its sudden use and she had pulled the windows wide open. A welcome breeze tinged with the smells of the river, fresh and clean with a hint of salt, ruffled the curtains and she breathed in slowly and deeply. The silk dress Abigail had given to her was on a hanger suspended from a high cupboard handle. She had worn it as she'd helped Loveday serve dinner to the Fiennes, a meal during which Abigail had chatted away gaily and the Major had hardly spoken a word.

He hadn't said much when she'd arrived back at Trevallion with a small bag of belongings, her best dress, change of underclothes, night things and a few toiletries. He'd taken the bag from her and put it in the back of the car, helping her to climb into the Mercedes, a long low-lined vehicle with a carriage body. His face was closed and gaunt and, Rebecca thought, very sad. She wanted to ask him what he'd thought of the house but knew it wasn't the right time.

Things were going to be difficult living in the gatehouse. There was the horrible boy to contend with, who never missed a chance to be spiteful; Rebecca had seen him push little Tamsyn away from him, shouting at her, 'Of course you can't play with the model railway!'

Rebecca had her own sink to wash her face, clean her teeth and rinse her smalls in, but she would have to share the bathroom. She hated the thought of standing in her shabby dressing gown, waiting her turn. What if the Major came out of his room to stand behind her? Apart from the embarrassment, was it manners to let him go first? Mrs Fiennes would, of course, spend hours and hours in there, but Rebecca thought it would be pleasant going in the bathroom after her and being swamped by the beautiful scents she would no doubt leave behind.

Still, things were not so bad. Her father wasn't going to get the sack and perhaps having a master again would encourage him to give up the drink and pull himself together at last. Mrs Fiennes was very friendly and had talked at dinner as if the family intended to stay down in Cornwall for the rest of the summer. A strange man Major Fiennes was, though. Quiet and somehow secretive but seemingly in charge of things.

She pondered on his sad face. Despite its emptiness, he was good-looking. Not that it mattered to Rebecca. There was only one man she was interested in. She took another deep breath of fresh river air and it came out in a long sigh. The real trouble with having to stay in the gatehouse was that she seemed so far away from Joe.

Chapter 5

The next morning Rebecca was dismayed to learn that she would not be able to help Joe with the horses. The Major liked to ride in the early hours and he had left word that he would exercise two of the horses himself before breakfast. Furthermore, Abigail made it quite clear that she expected Rebecca to be at her beck and call; Rebecca found herself in the strange position of being a lady's maid.

At least it meant someone would get a temporary job on Verrian Farm, she thought glumly as she put away the items of Abigail's huge wardrobe which hadn't been unpacked the day before. Abigail's clothes were bright and carefree, reflecting the move away from the drab and puritanical. Rebecca hung the dresses on scented padded hangers and carefully laid the filmy underwear in drawers. The many pairs of shoes went side by side at the bottom of the wardrobe. There wasn't enough space for everything; a lady of Abigail Fiennes' tastes needed a house at least as big as Trevallion to function properly. Rebecca could picture Abigail there, living comfortably and elegantly, entertaining the cream of the county, having house guests from upcountry. With a pang of foreboding, Rebecca could not picture Alexander Fiennes belonging in Trevallion House, not even in the Captain's study.

The Major went straight out again after breakfast, dressed in casual clothes, topped with an old cricket jumper. He took the car down to the big house. Rebecca wondered if he'd go down to the creek, if he would meet her father and, if so, what would be said.

Trease was as relieved as Rebecca had been that the neglect of his work, his drinking habits and the terrible havoc he'd wreaked on Trevallion were known to Major Fiennes. He'd broken down in tears when Rebecca told him that the Major had been understanding, that he hadn't lost his job and his home. He made her the same promise he'd made Joe, to give up drinking and to work hard to encourage Major Fiennes to keep the estate.

'How long do you think it would take before Trevallion is fit to be lived in, Rebecca?' Abigail asked, coming into the room and curling up in an armchair. She lit a cigarette in a long ebony holder and blew smoke delicately through her lips.

'Not very long,' Rebecca replied. 'Only about a week or so. It needs some paint and a bit of replastering, but it's not dilapidated. Just needs airing out and things put back in their proper places. It smells a bit musty upstairs but most things are in order. There's no electricity, I'm afraid. I'm sure Captain Trevallion would have had it put in if he hadn't been injured in the war.'

'Oh, I don't mind that. It was quite cosy here by lamplight last night and candles are so romantic, don't you think?'

Rebecca looked vague at the question. 'I suppose so.'

She wiped away the powder spills on Abigail's dressing table and gathered up her strewn-about jewellery, pretty brooches, rings, diamanté clips, bracelets, necklaces of pearls and sparkling stones and dozens of strings of beads, and put them back in their box. 'Would you like to lock this, Mrs Fiennes?'

'No, there's nothing of value in there and I'm certain I can trust you and Mrs Wright.' Abigail suddenly looked petulant. 'I wanted to go down to the big house with Alex but he flatly refused to let me go. He can be really stubborn when he chooses to be and is beastly about the things he abhors, like me smoking upstairs, so don't mention this.' She waved her cigarette in the air.

Rebecca was curious to learn all she could about Major Fiennes and with Abigail being so chatty she broached the subject. 'I take it the Major's not married, then?'

Abigail made a scoffing noise. 'A couple of girls got him close to the altar years ago but they didn't succeed. He likes his own company too much.'

'Has he always been quiet, if you don't mind me asking?'

'Oh, yes, but not like he is now. Well, the war, it affected him badly. He has turned in on himself. I'm hoping the change down here, the river, the milder climate and a new interest will bring him out a little.'

Rebecca was about to ask if she knew what he intended to do with the estate when Abigail murmured, as if to herself, 'I hope he will decide to keep Trevallion.'

–

Alex wandered about the grounds of Trevallion, noting repairs that were needed, the overgrowth of the orchards, the earth thrown into the pond that Joe and Trease had not had time to clean up the day before, the weeds on the pathways, a million and one little things that begged attention. The lawns at the back of the house had not been cut this year except for one small patch before Trease had lost interest. The grass there was already two inches high again and was scattered with daisies, a pretty sight but telling of the lackadaisical attitude of the man who was supposed to look after things here.

A narrow stream ran through the grounds and Alex walked over its small hump-backed bridge, its woodwork covered in layers of green algae. He passed a deserted dovecote and saw something glinting in the sunlight. He pushed aside some overgrown shrubbery and discovered a wooden bench. He set to work pushing back the bushes so he could read the brass inscription plate on its back. He rubbed at the film of dirt and read 'To My Beloved Harriet'. Alex was angry that the seat put here in memory of Miles Trevallion's fiancée had been included in the general neglect.

The sound of someone clearing his throat made him look round.

'Major Fiennes, sir,' Trease Allen said sheepishly, holding out his hand. 'I'm Trease Allen. 'Tis a pleasure to meet you. I'm sorry that I wasn't about to meet you yesterday, sir.'

Alex shook Trease's hand but his face was grim. He looked at the seat, part of it hidden again by the bushes that had fallen back round it. 'Are you responsible for this, Allen?'

'Um, yes, sir. I, um, meant to get round to it.' Trease hung his head.

'Don't make excuses, Allen, at least spare me that! Captain Treval-lion would despair at the state you've allowed this place to fall into. It's a great pity you are not diligent and caring like your daughter.'

'I'm very sorry, sir.'

'I don't want you being sorry either, I want you working. Damned hard! I want everything that you've neglected back in perfect order. I want you putting in every hour until the gardens and immediate grounds to the house are in immaculate condition. You are relieved of your duties concerning the house. I'll be putting someone else in charge.'

'Yes, sir. Thank you.' Trease had something in his hand and he held it out. 'These are the accounts of money spent on the house and gardens, sir, for the months January to March. Mr Robert Drayton said he wanted them on his desk first thing this morning. Shall I take them over to Truro before I begin work here?'

'No, I'll have them sent over. One of the Jenkins is going to Truro this morning, he can do it.' Alex took the accounts book and glanced through it. He saw the two sets of handwriting and guessed whose they were.

'Can I say something, sir?' Trease asked, twisting his cap round in tight fingers.

'If it's brief.'

'I just want to say that I'm glad the house 'as an owner at last, someone of the Captain's blood.'

Alex merely nodded. 'I suggest you make a start on clearing this bench and cleaning the memorial plaque.' He walked away, then stopped. 'Allen, I'm not against a man taking a drink, or even occasionally getting drunk, but I'm one hundred per cent against a man letting it get to him to the extent he damages beautiful property and leaves a young woman to shoulder his responsibilities.'

'Yes, Major,' Trease said contritely. He walked briskly towards the garden shed. He had work with a purpose now and lifted his shoulders as he carried tools back to the garden bench.

Alex wandered down to the creek and gazed at the boats which would soon be left stranded by the tide. Seaweed clung to their ropes at the point below the water level; the boats themselves were all in good repair. An old tyre from one of Miles's cars lay against the bank, put there for the children to play with, to sit on or use as a float. Further out where the creek flowed into the Fal he saw two mute swans and watched them until they glided out of sight. He strolled across the little beach of mud and shale, looked over Rebecca's boat, painted white with a blue strip round the top, not knowing it was hers, then looked further along the shore knowing that hidden from view was the boathouse where Miles had kept his boats. Alex went to it and there on the bench he found Jossy and Jenny Jenkins.

Alex took off his hat. Despite his stiff old limbs, Jossy jumped to attention. He lifted his battered flat cap but kept his pipe clenched between ivory-coloured teeth, his lips pulled back in his permanent smile. Alex introduced himself and bid Jossy sit down again. He found a pipe in his trousers pocket. He didn't light it very often and had no tobacco with him but Jossy was proud to pass him his tin. Alex sat on an upturned oil tub and listened attentively as Jossy told him of his life in the creek and the boats he looked after for Captain Trevallion.

'Was me who taught un how to sail, sir. He kept many a different boat in here. His favourite and mine was the *Lady Harriet*, although the *Iseult* is a fine motor cruiser. They'm both in the boathouse now. Captain Miles always sailed in the regattas. You'll have to come along to one, Major. My sons enter their working boat every year. That's their boat there.' Jossy pointed. ''Tis a gaff-rigged oyster-dredger, 'tis moored up for now because the dredging season don't start till October. They usually do very well racing un. Captain Miles used to sail the *Lady Harriet* against Pat Vincent. He's a St Mawes fisherman. They used to win turn and turn about. No one's been able to beat Pat since Captain Miles went to war. You should see the Captain's rowing gig, Major, 'tis a beauty.' Jossy eyed his new master keenly. 'Can't get around as much as I used to but I can still sail any sort of boat you care t'name.'

'We'll go out together soon, Jossy,' Alex promised. 'I want to sail the length and breadth of the river that Captain Trevallion loved so dearly.'

Jossy was delighted. 'Really, sir! I'll look forward to that.' Alex turned to Jenny Jenkins who had been listening with a cheery smile on her plump face. 'So you've lived all your life in the creek, Mrs Jenkins?'

'Aye, was a Grubb before I married. Mainly Grubbs and Jenkinses in the creek. I hope and trust you'll like it down here, Major. We'm simple folk and we care for our own, don't we, Jossy?' As Jossy agreed, she looked Alex over critically. 'A bit of good river air, some peace and quiet will do 'ce good. Put a bit of colour in 'ee, build 'ee up a bit.'

Alex grinned fleetingly. 'I hope so, Mrs Jenkins. Have you lived comfortably over the last few years?'

'Can't grumble. We'm practically self-sufficient, sir. Grow our own vegetables, trade for our meat on the farms. We country folk always have something to put on the table. We don't want for nothing nor hanker after anything.' She put a hand round to her back and made a face. 'Just have a bit of arthritis here and there. I've got this back today.' Mrs Jenkins always had a pain somewhere and this was how she referred to them, but it wasn't a grumble. She was a bright, hospitable soul who had a good word for everybody.

The old couple's friendliness warmed Alex's heart. He had not wanted to find the estate tenants subservient and suspicious of him, or distant and resentful because he came from 'upcountry'.

'Pity Captain Miles's boatbuilding had to be sold off,' Jossy said wistfully. 'It didn't even get the chance to get under way with the war happening. The Captain had such plans. We was going t'build some grand boats together.'

'What there was of it was sold to keep the estate going,' Alex explained. 'A pity though… Have the men got much work round here?'

'With so many being unemployed round the country, you mean?' Jossy removed his pipe from his mouth. 'There's some on the look-out, sir. They can get casual work on the farms during harvesting and suchlike but it's not the same as having something permanent. The only thing that's really looked up since the war is the oysterdredging.

With so many of our boys away fighting, the oyster beds had a long rest and their numbers built up.'

'I see. I might be able to help out one man looking for work. I want the big house put back to good working order and I need a new caretaker. Could you suggest someone who'd suit the job?'

'Aye, we could,' Jenny answered, looking at her husband for confirmation. 'Percy Gummoe. He's a nice young man who lives in the creek with his wife and they've had plenty of bad luck over the last couple of years. The job would be a Godsend to them. Percy'll do right by you, Major, won't he, Jossy?'

'You have our word on that, Major,' Jossy agreed.

Their enthusiasm made him smile. 'Perhaps you'd be so kind as to send him up to the gatehouse later in the day.'

'Be delighted to,' Jossy said, nodding his head. It would be good to go round Kennick Creek and tell their family and neighbours that the Major was having the big house 'done up'. It was a hopeful sign. Jossy mentioned some other local things he thought might interest the gaunt-faced young man. 'You a sporting man, Major? There's plenty of water sports throughout the year and there's a golf course and tennis courts in Truro. Me and my boys follow the football. My grandson Royston plays goalkeeper for Truro,' he ended proudly.

'I'll stick to the things that concern the estate for the time being,' Alex replied, gazing about him. He stayed another fifteen minutes chatting to the couple and was reluctant to leave them. When he did finally leave he felt optimistic that most of the other folk he would call on in the creek over the next few days would be just as amiable.

-

Stephen Fiennes found his way down to the creek soon after his uncle had left it. He explored the surroundings of Allen Cottage for a while and made up a game of pirates and smugglers in his head. He stood on the large white-painted rock he'd marked to hide his treasure under, unaware it had been put there on the bank so Trease and Rebecca could see where to moor their boats in the dark. There was still a little water lapping around Rebecca's boat, which he decided would make an excellent Spanish galleon. He climbed into it and played out his role as an English buccaneer stealing a Spanish ship's treasure.

Tamsyn was watching him from the bank with her big mongrel dog, Motley, given to her by Joe and so called after Joe had said the scrap of a puppy was 'the motliest little creature he'd ever seen'.

'You'd better get out of there if you don't want to get wet. The tide's coming in fast,' she called to Stephen to tease him.

Stephen whirled round, making the boat rock in the few inches of water. 'Go away! I don't want you here!'

'I aren't doing you no harm,' Tamsyn returned, stubbornly folding her arms. 'I'm warning you, the tide's coming in.'

'I know it is,' Stephen said crossly. 'I don't need a stupid girl to tell me something that's obvious.'

He clambered out of the boat and his boots squelched as he waded through water and mud to get to the dry part of the shore. He stepped into deep mud and promptly got stuck. He grunted and groaned as he tried to free himself Tamsyn came down off the grassy bank and stood on a firm stony piece of shore and laughed at him.

'Don't just stand there! Help me!'

'You'll be drowned in a minute,' Tamsyn called out.

'Shut up! Do something!' Stephen's face went dark with rage. The more he struggled, the deeper he sank and he began to panic. 'Help me!'

'All you have to do is put both hands on top of your boot and pull it out of the mud,' said Tamsyn calmly. 'Take a big step then do the same with the other foot.'

Tamsyn laughed again as Stephen followed her orders. When he was finally free of the sucking dark mud, seething with indignation, he ran up to Tamsyn and pushed her over. She fell with a thump on her bottom and cried out in surprise. Motley, who had been sniffing about the shore, barked at Stephen and rushed at him. The multi-coloured dog, with its broad body, narrow face, sharp nose and big teeth, looked quite frightening.

'Call that brute off or I'll get my uncle to shoot him!'

'You dare hurt Motley,' Tamsyn shouted back, scrambling to her feet. 'I'll tell him to bite your leg off.'

Motley danced about and barked, not sure whether this was a child's noisy game or if his young mistress was being threatened.

'Motley! Is that its name? It's a stupid name for a stupid, stupid dog!'

'There's no need to be so horrid. There's no other children our age in the creek so we might as well be friends. Come on, I'll show you my hideout.'

Tamsyn was too young to be aware of the mounting anger growing inside Stephen's head. She made to skip away, sure that he would follow her, but he grabbed her by the shoulders and yanked her back to face him. Holding her tightly, he shook her violently.

'Stupid, stupid girl! I'm the son of a gentleman, an officer of the Royal Flying Corps, and I don't play with stupid common little girls!' He pushed her away violently and this time Tamsyn was hurt.

Motley was making a loud din as Stephen surveyed the sobbing girl coldly. Suddenly a harsh voice broke through the noise and the dog was ordered to be quiet. Joe Carlyon marched up to Stephen Fiennes, his face furious and as hard as granite. He took Stephen roughly by the shoulder and boxed the boy's ear.

'You little brute!' Joe said furiously, picking Tamsyn up in his arms.

'How dare you touch me,' Stephen said icily through his teeth, fighting to hold back tears. 'My uncle will dismiss you for this. He'll have the police on you. I'll make you pay!'

'Major Fiennes isn't far away. Just round by the boathouse if you want him, Master Stephen,' Joe said coldly, cuddling Tamsyn in his big arms. 'I'm sure he'll be very interested in the reason why I clipped your ear. Hurting a little girl, half your age, you ought to be ashamed of yourself, boy! Go on then, round to the boathouse. We'll come with you.'

Stephen's chin trembled as he saw he was in no position to play the outraged nephew of the new master. He was humiliated again and he hated it. He took his hand away from his red ear and stalked off.

'Where are you hurt, my handsome?' Joe asked the child, so precious to him as Stanley Wright's only legacy to the world.

Tamsyn had stopped crying. ''Tis all right, Uncle Joe. Just a sore backside and shoulders.' She snuggled in closer to him. 'But I never knew people could be so horrible.'

Chapter 6

The following day Alex agreed to allow Abigail to go down to the house with him. Rebecca had to drive with them, sitting self-consciously in the back seat of the car and hoping that none of the Kennickers would see her. It was exciting to travel in the Mercedes but it seemed almost a scandal not to be walking the half-mile. Alex had planned to walk but Abigail, dressed up as though she was going to a high social function, wanted to arrive in style, even though there was no one there to receive her.

Rebecca felt uncomfortable in her new elevated position and Abigail seemed to be reluctant to let her out of her sight. Rebecca missed the informality of her riding breeches, boots and old blouses and baggy jumpers. It was a pain to have to dress up, to pay extra attention to her hair and wear her only pair of high-heeled shoes, the ones Loveday had encouraged her to buy in Truro on a shopping trip, to be more feminine. Rebecca had thought the black-leather, one-bar shoes would only see the light of day on Sundays to church. Their two-inch heels made her much taller than Abigail and somehow that didn't feel right. At least Abigail didn't insist she wore a hat.

Rebecca was glad that Stephen did not want to come with them. He stayed at the gatehouse, moodily saying he had plans for the model railway. Tamsyn had not come to the gatehouse with Loveday that morning. She had insisted she wanted to stay in the creek with Motley, who wasn't allowed near the gatehouse, and she had been left under the watchful eye of Ira Jenkins.

'How magnificent,' Abigail breathed sincerely as the big house came into sight. It wasn't a quarter as big as the Fiennes' family house she lived in in Berkshire, but it had a quiet dignity, a sense of history merging with an inviting warmth.

She was out of the car and hurrying to the front door before Alex was. 'Oh, do hurry up, Alex. I can't wait to see inside. Who knows what secrets the house is harbouring after being empty for so many years? Come along, Rebecca!'

Alex offered Rebecca his hand with a sigh at Abigail's impatience. It seemed he often found her irritating. He unlocked the big door, which opened quite noisily and was a little hard to push. 'I'll have to get Percy Gummoe, the new caretaker, to oil the hinges,' he told Rebecca.

'Don't hog the girl, Alex,' Abigail said crossly, taking Rebecca's arm and sweeping her into the hall. 'You take the lead, my dear. You know the way around.'

Rebecca rearranged her startled face into one of serious intent and led the way to the drawing room. The room was painted white and a warm rose-pink. It needed fresh coats, but looked serene and inviting. The sun was shining in through the French windows and the vases of roses and carnations she had put there were still fresh and gave the room a heady fragrance, masking the musky smell that the lavender polish and beeswax had failed to eliminate. The top windows were open. The Major must have done that yesterday, Rebecca mused. As Abigail floated about the furniture, picturing herself entertaining guests, Rebecca looked round and realised the Major was not with them.

Alex had made straight for the study but stopped first to greet Percy Gummoe who was coming along the corridor from the kitchens.

'Momin' to 'ee, Major. Been having a look round upstairs?'

'No, I've only just arrived with Mrs Fiennes and Miss Allen.'

'Oh? Strange. Could've sworn I heard someone walking about upstairs. Oh, well… Can I get 'ee something, sir?'

'No, thank you, Percy. I've given you a list of jobs you can get on with and I'd appreciate not being disturbed.'

Alex closed the study door behind him and left Percy Gummoe scratching his head. He went back to the kitchen to fetch his tool bag.

He was happy today, after being out of regular work for the last two years and he and his wife losing their only child in infancy, but he did not whistle as he usually did when in good spirits. Trevallion's ghost was rumoured not to like it.

'Wouldn't it be wonderful bringing the ladies into this room after a dinner party?' Abigail said. She was admiring the silver-framed photographs of past Trevallions; they had such a stately air about them. Holding her hands together in front of her flat chest, she walked about the room.

'We could stroll outside on fine summer evenings.' Her voice was low and soft, without the hint of mockery that it usually held. Plans were busily forming behind her brilliant blue eyes.

Rebecca thought her perfect in this setting. She belonged here, in her impeccably tailored clothes, worn so well over her slender figure and shapely arms and legs. She could be the rightful lady of this house if she married her brother-in-law.

'This is much nicer than any room in Carsham Hall, the ancestral home of the Fiennes where I usually live. It's not so grand, of course, but it's so much more comfortable, so friendly. I must take you to Carsham Hall one day, my dear, so you can see the difference.'

Rebecca frowned. She would not follow Abigail everywhere she had the whim to take her.

Abigail went to the french windows to see if the house had a tennis court outside and was disappointed not to find one. 'Who's that man out there?' She screwed up her face with distaste, which would have upset Rebecca if she'd witnessed it. 'Working on the gardens.'

Rebecca came to look. Trease was hard at work rolling the mown lawns. He was proud to see his daughter all dressed up and inside the big house and took off his cap and bowed to them.

'It's my father, Mrs Fiennes, Trease Allen.'

'Oh, really?' and boredom was in Abigail's eyes. A moment later the glint of amusement was back. 'Tell me, Rebecca, which rooms is the ghost supposed to haunt?' Rebecca was picking up fallen rose petals from a table. She scattered them over the logs laid in the fireplace and thought carefully before she answered.

'Oh, come on, Rebecca. Don't be mysterious. I overheard Mrs Wright talking to the farm boy who delivered the eggs this morning. He wanted to know if we'd been told about the ghost and Mrs Wright told him off quite roundly for mentioning it. So there must be something in it for the woman to let off so much steam.'

'I don't know what to tell you really. You can't get anyone to talk about it, especially the older folk. All they say is that it's better for people not to know. Of course it's common knowledge that Mr Roland Trevallion, he was Captain Miles's grandfather, hanged himself here about sixty years ago, and it must have something to do with him. It's probably just old rumours.' Rebecca didn't want anything to put the Fiennes off the house. 'I don't think there is a ghost.'

'A hanging? How interesting. I didn't know anything of that sort had happened here. I bet Alex knows about it but of course he wouldn't mention it. What happened to Roland Trevallion to make him hang himself? A broken love affair?'

'As far as I know it's said he was afraid of being ruined in the mining slump, he couldn't take the shame and hanged himself.'

'Where?'

'In the cellar.'

'How divine. Let's go at once and ask Alex for the keys.'

'But Mrs Fiennes, it's cold, dark and dusty down there.' Abigail wouldn't be put off. 'Who cares about a few old spiders? Anyway, we can change our clothes,' and she went off in search of Alex. She tried a couple of rooms before she found him in Miles Trevallion's study.

Alex was sitting at the desk, leafing through papers and writing in a notebook. He looked annoyed at Abigail's interruption.

'We need the keys, Alex,' she said, grasping the bunch of keys sitting on the desk.

Alex closed his big hand over hers and snatched them away ungraciously. 'All the doors in the house are unlocked,' he grunted.

'Even the cellar?' Abigail purred.

'I'm not having you groping about down there in the dark.'

'But Rebecca and I want to go ghost-hunting.'

'I'm sure Miss Allen doesn't want to do anything so useless and foolish, Abigail.'

Certain that the Major wouldn't appreciate being disturbed, Rebecca had only peeped round the door and at the sound of his impatience she retreated out of sight. She heard Alex continue crossly, 'Look upstairs then walk back to the gatehouse or down to the creek and leave me to get on with some work in peace.'

'Crosspatch,' Abigail grumbled. 'Why can't I drive back?'

'Because you're a terrible driver and the walk will do you good.'

As Abigail turned to go, she noticed the portrait of Harriet Bosanko. She walked over to it and gasped in wonder. 'How beautiful. Is this the woman your cousin was engaged to?'

'Yes.'

'Did you ever meet her?'

'Just once. Miles brought her up to Carsham Hall. I fell in love with her, like every man who ever set eyes on her.'

'Really?' Abigail stared at her brother-in-law. 'Well, that's the first time I've ever heard you admit such a thing, Alex.'

Alex banged the desk with a clenched fist. 'If you please, Abigail, I want to get on!'

Out in the corridor Rebecca jumped as Alex's fist hit the desk. The Major was obviously angry with himself for dropping his guard. Abigail slammed the study door.

'There,' she said angrily to Rebecca, 'perhaps he will get on better if he feels shut off from the rest of the world. Goodness knows that's how he's lived since the war.'

She rallied almost at once and linking her arm through Rebecca's led her towards the curving stairway. 'How tragic, the story of Harriet Bosanko and Miles Trevallion, but how wonderful to be remembered as a woman whom every man fell in love with,' she said as their shoes tapped over each step. When they reached the top of the stairs, Abigail looked at Rebecca closely. 'Are you walking out with anyone, Rebecca?'

Rebecca thought of Joe and blushed. 'No, of course not.'

'Why "of course not"? You're very attractive.'

'Am I?' Rebecca headed for the nearest bedroom. No one had told her so before. Her father had never said anything of the sort, nor Loveday. The creek women had given her only the usual teasing a single girl received, and Joe, most important of all, had only ever complimented her on her hair.

Abigail tapped her on the shoulder. 'Have you no idea yourself how you look?'

Rebecca tried not to show her irritation. She was unused to people touching her or asking her personal questions. 'Young men don't exactly beat a path to the creek to see me, Mrs Fiennes.'

'And I can tell you why. Turn round.'

Rebecca obeyed, feeling embarrassed and vexed. Why couldn't they just get on with looking over the house? Abigail stroked her cheek and tilted her chin and gazed into her eyes.

'You look far too serious. It puts up a barrier and I'm sure many a young man interested in you is put off from asking you out.'

'I have been asked out,' Rebecca said defensively.

'How many times?'

'Lots, by Royston Jenkins from the creek, one of the local farm hands and,' Rebecca couldn't help saying rather proudly, 'even Mr Neville Faull, solicitor and trustee of the estate.'

'That wolf! You mustn't go out with him, Rebecca, whatever you do. He came up to Carsham Hall to suggest to Alex he could get a good price for Trevallion if he chose to sell it. I had a terrible time keeping him away from the maids and he even propositioned me. You just put a smile on your face and keep to the local young men.'

Abigail wanted to move on, afraid the girl's clear eyes would see through her pretence that Neville Faull's proposition had failed. In fact she had been a willing participant in the flirtation and seduction; Faull had not had to try too hard. She was sure he would be discreet about their affair, particularly if he wanted to persuade Alex to sell this little estate. She hoped so; she couldn't afford to upset Alex. At least with Alex making it plain to the solicitors that he didn't want to talk about estate business for several days she wouldn't have to face Neville Faull for a while.

Abigail had more reasons than Rebecca to hope Alex would keep the estate, not for himself, but for her and Stephen, to give Stephen an inheritance. When Ralph had died he'd left her nothing, only gambling debts, which, thankfully, Alex had paid off. Since then she had lived at Carsham Hall on a generous allowance from Alex. The ideal solution would be to marry him; she couldn't have any more children and Stephen would be heir to a vast manufacturing fortune and several properties, in Berkshire, London and overseas. But Alex wasn't interested. She had asked him point-blank and he had turned her down in a similar manner. If he wanted a wife he wouldn't choose a woman with a reputation, colourful, wanton and untrue.

Abigail had enjoyed herself rather too much during the war. Unfortunately for her a jealous wife had made it public, then others had climbed out of the woodwork to point an outraged finger. Ralph Fiennes might have been a gambler but he was away fighting for king and country and his wife had brought public disgrace on herself and his name. She had found herself ostracised by the social circles she moved in. Her only hope now was to gain Trevallion for herself and her son, to have this out-of-the-way estate to play the lady in, her own domain, no matter how small. She wanted Alex to agree to this then go back to Berkshire and leave her to it; she would work hard to make sure that Stephen never learnt of the stain she had brought on the Fiennes name.

Abigail was impressed by the bedrooms, marking out one for herself and one for Stephen. The bathrooms she found satisfactory, though she would have to have something done to make hers more feminine. In one of the attic rooms with a skylight Miles Trevallion had installed a giant telescope for star-gazing but Abigail gave it only cursory attention. Rebecca next showed her the servants' quarters and there the tour ended. Abigail refused to go to the kitchens, saying she made it a policy never to visit one.

Rebecca was encouraged that Abigail liked the house so much. When they parted, Abigail back to the gatehouse and she to Allen Cottage to make a meal for her father, her hopes were lifted high to see Trease still working hard in the gardens, now tackling the azaleas. The study door remained closed.

Alex had been reading the entries in a little booklet he'd found in Miles's desk when Abigail had interrupted him. The booklet contained Miles's hopes for the estate when he got back from the war and the poignancy of them had torn his heart. He couldn't concentrate now. Trust Abigail to turn her opportunity to look over the house into some sort of silly adventure. He intended to look over the house himself but wouldn't do so until his sister-in-law left.

He got up and looked at Miles's portrait. Miles had loved Trevallion; he wouldn't have wanted a silly female tripping all over it, exclaiming dramatically at this and that, making pretentious plans for it and not taking it at all seriously. Alex hadn't looked over much of the house yet but he could sense its appeal. There was nothing grand about it, in the way of the big mansions which were built purely for show. It was a family house, a home, built on simple lines for one generation to follow another, a place where its children could enjoy the quiet and picturesque setting as they grew up, a place to look forward to coming home to from wherever they roamed. Miles had been part of the Trevallion line, part of its continuity. He had belonged here. Alex was his cousin but he felt like an interloper here.

Damn it, why was life so cruel! Miles had known exactly what he'd wanted to do with his property. He'd been making plans for a boatbuilding yard along its shores. Now that would never be – unless Alex himself took up the idea. He felt a stab of pain in his temples and rubbed his head. Was that what Miles would have wanted him to do? Was he up to it? He had barely taken an interest in his own business concerns since coming home after hostilities had ceased.

For a long unnerving moment Miles's face in the picture seemed to be glaring at him. The cold clammy feeling Alex had come to fear, a sort of numbness that made him feel he wasn't part of his surroundings or the world of the living, swept over his body, invading every cell, vein and nerve. It felt hot and stuffy in here. He began to sweat profusely. His legs were trembling. He couldn't breathe. He had to get some air. He groaned as the heavy gloom settled over him like a huge suffocating black cloud. He tore across the room and rushed out of the house.

Rebecca was surprised to come across the Major down by the creek. He was standing on the bank, his hat pulled down over his face, his back stiff, his head sunk down on his chest. Rebecca would have left him alone but she noticed there was blood on his hand. She moved up to him and looked under his hat brim.

'Major,' she said softly.

He looked up but did not realise she was there. He stared straight ahead as though into the past, seeing haunted memories. He was muttering to himself. She listened. She couldn't make out what he was saying at first. Then it became apparent that he wasn't speaking to himself but to someone he couldn't see. His voice rose.

'No, no, you mustn't go.' He shook his head and his words became anguished. 'It's not safe. You won't come back.' He was trembling all over and Rebecca was alarmed.

'Major, are you all right?' She touched his arm, shook it, but he had no notion she was there.

'My God, don't!'

The hand that was bleeding shot out and gripped a hazel bush. He squeezed it tightly and ran his hand up and down it, moaning, tearing off the leaves and damaging his hand further.

Rebecca caught his arm and tried to wrench his hand away. His eyes were glazed over and she thought he was in a drunken fit.

'No! No! You mustn't go! Come back! You'll all be killed! We'll all be—'

'Major, stop it! Wake up! What are you doing?' Rebecca cried desperately.

He came out of his living nightmare with a start. 'What? Oh, Rebecca, I... I'm sorry.' His face was deathly white, his eyes seemed too big for his face as he came fully to and realised where he was.

'You're bleeding,' she said gently. She was quite used to dealing with Trease after a drinking bout, although she was sure now that this man had not touched a drop. He had been terrified and full of despair. 'Come to the cottage and I'll bathe your hand.'

She tried to lead him but he wouldn't move and stared with horror at his hand. 'No, no. I'll see to it. I'm sorry. Please,' he appealed to her, 'don't say anything.'

Then he rushed past her, leaving her alone on the bank.

Chapter 7

Alex didn't appear for lunch or come down to dinner that night. After collecting a bowl of hot water, a bottle of antiseptic and a bandage, he locked himself away in his room. He pulled off his shirt and sat bare to the waist, gazing sightlessly out of the window, not taking in the scenery of trees, hedges and sheep quietly grazing in a patchwork of fields. He cried out when he put his torn hand in the hot water, made a cloudy white by the antiseptic, the steam rising and filling the room with its sharp clinical smell. It was agony, but he welcomed it; it was only right that he should suffer. He deserved it.

He had no right to be alive, to be fit, strong and healthy, to have all his limbs, his full sight, his hearing. He should have died with his men, the men he had ordered over the top of the trenches. The order had come via the field telephone: it was the turn of his unit to go. He had passed on the order even though he knew, and his men knew, it was certain death, but not one of them had dreamt of disobeying.

Alex, Georgie Gilbert, Jimmy Clark and Cyril Dawkins had reached the machine-gun post. Alex had looked at Georgie and nodded. Georgie took out a hand grenade, pulled the pin and counted to four. Then he threw it into the enemy's nest and the men hit the ground with their hands over their ears for the explosion. They were on their feet before the screams within had died away, Alex putting his gun through the slit and emptying it.

Alex and Georgie grinned grimly at each other but the next instant they saw that young Jimmy Clark was lying in a bloody heap behind them. Alex went to him but Georgie grabbed his arm. He shouted above the din, 'Leave him sir, he's dead!'

71

A quick glance round and Alex could see all his men were down. Cyril Dawkins' head was buried in the thick, black, oozing mud. There was just him and Georgie Gilbert left. Then Georgie took a bullet in his back.

He keeled over onto a solitary leafless bush that had withstood the barrage. Alex cried out in anguish. He grabbed Georgie's gun and turned back to face the battle, running, the gun blazing, shouting, cursing, promising Hell to those who had killed his men. A shell exploded in front of him and he was tossed into the air.

It was his turn now, he would join his men, perhaps see them somewhere in the next world. They had all done their duty, and blessed oblivion was their reward. No more pain of bursting lungs as he ran charging the enemy, no more grisly sights of those who had once been. He was to be one of them now, dead, gone, another casualty, one more among the many millions dead. Gone now, to be mourned, honoured and remembered like the others for giving the ultimate sacrifice.

But he had woken up. In a tent, a field hospital, with a big bandage round his head. His head thumped, gave him no peace, kept him awake to listen to the moans and agony of others. When they took the bandage off he expected to find half his head blown away but there was just a bad cut and swelling.

'You were lucky, Major. Just a shell passing too close, knocked you off your feet, shocked you.'

'Where are my men?'

'I'm very sorry, they didn't make it, only you. You were lucky.'

'But I should be dead!'

'You brought a man in with you but sadly he died. Never mind. You did your best.' Alex couldn't remember picking up Georgie Gilbert. After the explosion he must have come to and noticed Georgie was still alive. Somehow he'd got them to safety but Georgie had still died. And Alex wished he had died.

He went back to the war and took over a new unit, but his behaviour was erratic and foolhardy. He was considered a danger to the men, and on medical grounds was quickly pulled back from the front line and put in an office job. He ranted and raved about it but his superiors would not change their minds. He was sick to the gut at being bound to a desk while Sir Douglas Haig, the commander-in-chief of the British forces, was delivering a message to all ranks: 'Every position must be held to the last man... each of us must fight to the end.' Alex was ashamed, despite being battle-honoured, and he hated to be continually told he had 'done his bit', that 'you'd be allowed to fight, sir, if you were fit'. He wasn't fit to command but he felt he was fit to fight. His superiors did not see it that way. Any man in the noncommissioned ranks would have had to fight, would have been expected to fight whatever their condition. Alex hadn't wanted a damned medal. He'd wanted to fight again and die.

He snatched his hand out of the bowl of water, knocking it to the floor and breaking the thick glass. He watched the growing puddle, the water spreading across the rug, seeping over onto the linoleum like the bloodied black mud of the killing fields.

'I should be dead,' he groaned in despair.

Ralph, his brother, had been shot down in his aeroplane. He had died in the same horrible way as his men. If only he could change places with his brother. Ralph had been something of a wastrel but he had been a family man. He should be here now, looking after his family, instead of Alex.

He held up his torn hand, made white and puffy by prolonged immersion in the bowl of water. It was numb for a while then began to sting. He flexed it and it began to bleed. He watched the droplets form and grow till they ran in tiny rivers, gathering at his wrist, and dripped, very slowly, one full red drop at a time, onto the floor, mingling with the water, turning a strange pink.

He brought his hand close to his face to study it. The flesh on each finger was shredded, some of the rips on the palm needed a couple of stitches. But it didn't matter, nothing did. Such a little thing. A few cuts, a little pain. Not with all his men dead.

All he'd got from the war was a few hours of unconsciousness and an excruciating headache, like the one that had precipitated the living nightmare, the act of masochism down on the bank of the little creek. The act Rebecca Allen had witnessed with her huge sympathetic eyes.

Alex picked up the bandage and bound his hand, round and round, in careless fashion. Now he wanted to sleep, to seek oblivion and be rid of one more wretched day. He reached for a whisky bottle, unscrewed the top with his teeth and spat it out. He drank steadily, feeling the spirit burn into his guts, warming his vitals, scourging his soul. When the bottle was empty, he climbed somehow onto his bed, stretched out and, with the room spinning, closed his eyes. Before the whisky did what he longed for, he thought Rebecca Allen had come into the room, sat on the bed beside him and was stroking his face, gently, soothingly. He put out his hand but felt nothing, it was only an illusion. Alex grinned, a silly sort of smile; he'd asked the girl not to say anything, at least he could trust her.

—

Much later, when she was going to bed, Rebecca knocked on Alex's door and called softly to him. There was no answer but she did not expect one.

Abigail had made her sit and play cards all evening. She was still peeved over Alex's bad temper in Trevallion House. 'I can never get him to take cocktails with me, he finds them a crashing bore,' she'd said, 'but when he's in one of his moods he shuts himself away and gets drunk. I hope he wakes up tomorrow with a terrible headache.'

'Does he often get drunk?' Rebecca asked, trying to sound casual.

Abigail raised her eyebrows and smirked. 'Doesn't every man?'

But Abigail had not seen her brother-in-law in the creek, off in a kind of trance, tearing his hand on the bushes.

When Abigail had retired, declaring the 'sea air from the creek makes me so terribly, terribly sleepy', Rebecca had fetched the spare set of keys from the kitchen and gone to Alex's room. She unlocked the door and slipped quickly inside, closing it silently behind her.

She could just make out his figure, lying on the bed, breathing heavily in a drunken stupor. The room reeked of whisky and anti-septic. It was a sickly combination in the hot night and Rebecca opened the window. Then she went to the bed and looked down at the pitiful figure lying there.

Alex's features were twisted in pain, emotional pain, and Rebecca felt a catch in her heart for him. Trease had got drunk often enough to drown his self-pity. With this man there was something more than that. One thing she was sure of was that Alex Fiennes had something very terrible on his mind.

She mustn't wake him. That would be cruel, to leave him to endure the long night with whatever was hurting him so much. She touched his shoulder. It was hot and he was sweating profusely. She took a towel off the back of a chair and gently rubbed him down, his neck, back, shoulders and arms, patting gently near his bandaged hand. Then she felt his skin to make sure he was dry. He didn't come round, but sensing someone was trying to bring him comfort he snuggled down and breathed more easily. Not wanting him to get chilled, Rebecca covered him with a spare blanket from the top of the wardrobe.

She took off his shoes, placing them where he wouldn't stumble over them the next morning. It was then that she noticed the broken glass of the bowl, which would be even more dangerous to him. She carefully collected up all the pieces, placed them in the wastepaper basket with the empty whisky bottle and crept downstairs to dispose of them so no one would know about them.

She returned the wastepaper basket to the room and gazed down at Alex. He was sleeping more peacefully, his body rising and falling in a steady rhythm. She stroked his hair, damp and dark and curling at the nape of his neck. Then before leaving for her own room and locking the door behind her, she whispered goodnight to him.

Chapter 8

Stephen Fiennes got up early the following morning for his breakfast. He wolfed it down while complaining to Loveday that he hated his egg unless it was boiled for exactly three and half minutes, that the toast was burnt, the marmalade too sickly-sweet, the tea too weak, and he didn't want to drink any beastly milk. Loveday was angry at first and resolved to speak to Mrs Fiennes about her son when she rose, probably a good two hours later, but when she saw the dejected slope of the boy's shoulders and his hangdog expression as he climbed the stairs to play with the model railway she found herself following him to his room.

'What do you want?' he said crossly as she entered.

'I was just wondering if you're going down to the creek today, Master Stephen,' she said, stepping over the railway track he had running all over the floor and beginning to make his bed.

'No, I shouldn't think so for a minute,' Stephen replied in a superior tone.

'That's a pity, it's going to be such a lovely day and the creek is just the sort of place for a boy to have adventures in.'

'Do you think so?' Stephen said. He was genuinely interested. It had been boring staying in the gatehouse yesterday. He wanted to explore more of the creek but was ashamed of hurting Tamsyn. He was still smarting at having his ears boxed and wanted revenge on Joe but didn't want to face him so soon.

'My husband lived all his life in the creek, before he went to war. He used to tell me about the games he used to play.'

'What sort of games, Mrs Wright?' the boy asked, suddenly finding his manners.

'Oh, smugglers, pirates, boat races, that sort of thing. The sort of games you can only play if there's water. I know you can swim, your mother told me you've won medals in school on sports days, so you shouldn't come a cropper.'

Loveday turned down the thin summer coverlet and looked at him. His sturdy face was deep in thought.

'That sounds like a lot of fun. It's a pity there's no boys to play with here.'

'You could always play with my Tamsyn. She's got her own little camp. I'm sure she'll be glad to show it to you. I can't get her away from the creek these days. She wants to spend every minute of the summer there.'

Stephen's face took on its sulky look again.

'What is it?' Loveday asked kindly, almost putting her hand out to the unlikable boy. 'Has something upset you?'

'Hasn't Tamsyn told you?' he said, with a note of challenge in his voice.

'Told me what? Has she done something to upset you?'

'No,' Stephen said abruptly, going back to the train set. 'I upset her.'

'Do you think that's why she refuses to come to the gatehouse with me?' Loveday asked.

'Probably.'

'Tell me what happened, Master Stephen,' Loveday coaxed. 'Tamsyn doesn't tell tales. I'm sure you can make it up and there's no reason why you shouldn't both have fun down in the creek.'

Stephen got up and stood in front of Loveday. He wasn't afraid to own up to what he had done. 'I got stuck in the mud and Tamsyn laughed at me. I was furious, even though she told me how to get myself out. I was out of order and pushed her over, twice. I'm sorry. The second time she was hurt.'

Loveday breathed in heavily through her nose and held her lips in a tight line. She could easily imagine this boy being a bully, but at least he'd had the courage to admit it and he seemed sorry. She had to give him credit for that.

'I see. Don't you think you ought to tell Tamsyn you're sorry?'

'Yes, I do.' Through the open doorway Stephen saw his mother, dressed in a floating negligée, tripping to the bathroom. A dark look passed across his face. He'd had an idea. Suddenly he grabbed Loveday's hand and blurted out, 'I want to say I'm sorry to Tamsyn, honestly I do, Mrs Wright. But I'm afraid to go down to the creek again.'

'But why on earth is that, Master Stephen?' Loveday said, placing a hand on his broad shoulder.

He shocked Loveday by throwing himself in her arms. 'Please don't make me go down there, Mrs Wright. Ask Tamsyn to come here and I'll apologise to her and let her play with the train set. If I go there he'll get me!' Stephen wailed.

'Who will?' Loveday was most alarmed.

'That big man, the one who looks after the horses, the one called Joe. He saw me push Tamsyn over and he beat me. He shook me and thrashed me and he said if I hurt her again he'll drown me in the creek and make it look like an accident! Oh, please don't make me go down there while he's there. He'll hurt me, I know he will.'

Abigail came hurtling into the room. Loveday looked up from the clinging boy and was about to say she couldn't believe Joe would do such a thing, but Abigail's cold-blooded fury stopped her.

'I heard it all, Mrs Wright. It's a pity the Major went out early to visit one of the tenant farms or I'm sure he'd thrash Joe Carlyon and march him off the estate. No one treats my son the way he did and gets away with it. Look at him,' she pulled Stephen to her own bosom, 'he's terrified out of his mind. I'll see Carlyon at once. Find me something to wear, will you? Rebecca's not here, she's been allowed to exercise one of the horses this morning. I'll have my breakfast when I come back.'

Abigail put on her make-up, a smart light skirt and blouse, a low-heeled pair of shoes suitable for walking and a small hat and tied a silk scarf round her throat. Alex must have ridden to the farm because the Mercedes was outside, but Abigail knew she wasn't in a fit state to drive in her rage. She half strode, half ran down the road to the creek, giving a curt good morning to Ira Jenkins who stared after her. Following Loveday's instructions, she found Joe Carlyon's cottage. It was still early in the morning and Loveday had reckoned Joe would be home for his breakfast round about now.

Abigail marched up to the door, which was wide open, and went straight in. Joe was in the little kitchen sitting at the table, pouring tea from a large brown teapot into a mug. He jumped up in surprise, the teapot still in his hand.

'Mrs Fiennes. Is anything wrong?'

'That, you great clodding ox, you may well ask!' she hurled at him.

Joe put the teapot down and blinked at the lady who was shaking with rage.

'How dare you, Joe Carlyon! How dare you touch my son? I'll have you dismissed for what you did to Stephen. Beating him, thrashing him and threatening to drown him in the river. You big brute! You wretched beast! How dare you touch a child like that. Well? Haven't you got anything to say for yourself?'

Joe looked at Abigail calmly. He was prepared to face her and the Major over his punishment of Stephen and wasn't surprised at the inaccuracy of the boy's account. He said, 'Only that your son is a liar as well as a boy who likes to push little maids and hurt them, Mrs Fiennes.'

'What? I...' Abigail's face was as red as her lipstick.

'You owe me an apology,' Joe said. 'Is that what you're trying to say? I only boxed the boy's ear, and not as hard as I would a boy from the creek. Tamsyn is very special to me. I saw her father fall and drown in mud because he missed his footing on the duck-walk in the trenches. When I got home and realised he had a daughter, I vowed I would look after that child, with my life if needs be.'

Joe had succeeded in taking the wind completely out of Abigail's sails. Like a ship foundering out of its depth, she sought a harbour, finding it by sinking down on the nearest chair.

'You would agree your son is capable of lying, wouldn't you, Mrs Fiennes?'

'Yes,' Abigail admitted numbly. She didn't have to think too long and hard about it. Stephen had always been a spoiled, difficult child, but he had grown much worse since his father's death. He had turned to his uncle for male companionship, as someone to look up to, but Alex had not been able to respond to the boy's hero worship. Hurt at the rejection, Stephen now despised him.

'I'll deal with Stephen when I get back to the gatehouse. Please accept my apology, Carlyon.' Despite having been put so firmly in her place, Abigail rose gracefully. 'I'll leave you to get on with your breakfast.'

'I accept your apology, Mrs Fiennes. I'm sure your son will learn to play fair and square, given the right sort of encouragement. Can I offer you a cup of tea?'

Abigail was suddenly struck by the physical attributes of this big muscular man. He was a handsome brute, all muscle and sinew and male sexuality. She accepted his offer immediately. After all, she didn't want to be on bad terms with any of the creek people. If they liked her, it would impress Alex and might help him to decide on Trevallion's fate in her favour.

She sat down again, elegantly crossing her legs and perkily turning up her toes. Joe excused himself and disappeared briefly into the only other downstairs room. He brought back a cup and saucer.

'See that?' he said proudly. 'Know what that's made from? Real Spode-Copeland ware, made locally. Captain Trevallion gave that to my mother on her fiftieth birthday, for all the work she'd put in at the big house over the years.'

'It's lovely,' Abigail purred, tracing a red-varnished fingernail round the cup's rim. 'Floral-patterned, my favourite. Your mother must be very proud of it. Where is your mother?'

'Oh, she passed on years ago, just before the war ended, and Father went just after. There's just me here now. I'm the last Carylon hereabouts.'

Abigail held up her hand to the cup and saucer. 'This must be very special to you, Joe. I wouldn't dream of using it, it wouldn't be right. Please use another cup.'

Joe smiled and took the cup and saucer back to its special place on a built-in shelf beside the fireplace in the sitting room. He put another mug on the table and filled it with strong tea and milk from a tall blue and white jug. Abigail helped herself to sugar.

'Are all the cottages in the creek like yours?' Abigail asked as Joe sat down and ate his cold eggs and bacon.

She looked around, at the low-beamed ceiling, the built-in cupboards either side of the hearth, the little Cornish range inside the black fireplace which was topped with a high, wide mantelshelf The windows were made up of small square panes, the walls were thick and uneven. One shelf held a green glass fishing-net weight. A Bakelite ashtray sat in the middle of the table. Joe had been a bugler in the army and his dented bugle was hanging on the wall.

'Aye,' Joe replied, gulping down tea. 'More or less, some are smaller, some bigger.'

'What is Rebecca's like?'

'A bit bigger than mine. She keeps it nice.'

'I can't imagine her keeping it any other way. She's a rather quiet girl, seems sad most of the time. I suppose she hasn't had much of a life with that drunken father of hers. I saw him briefly; I must say Rebecca doesn't favour him in looks at all.'

'She's like Nancy Ann, her mother. She was a real beauty, but needing her freedom. She walked out on Rebecca when she was a little girl, left her with Loveday and never came back.'

'How awful, the poor girl. I know I don't see much of Stephen, he's away at boarding school most of the time.' She thought about her reputation. 'But whatever I may be criticised for, I would never desert him.'

'He'll be all right,' Joe said. 'Perhaps a few weeks round the creek will sort him out a bit.'

'I hope so. I don't want to foster bad feelings among the people here.'

Joe rose and put the dishes in the sink where they would stay until his work was finished now that Rebecca wasn't available to come and wash up for him. A glance round the kitchen showed how untidy the room was getting. 'I suppose we all get to rely on Rebecca. Nothing but work for her, hardly fair.'

'Well, I'll have to do something to cheer her up. Take her on a shopping trip into Truro.'

'Aye, I reckon she'd like that.'

'Thanks for the tea, Joe,' Abigail said softly, gazing directly into his eyes, 'and the chat. I must find little Tamsyn now and arrange for Stephen to tell her he's sorry for what he did. I'll see you around the estate, I expect.'

Abigail also wanted to see the woman she had greeted so curtly a short time ago. She must have appeared very rude to whoever she was, and that wouldn't do. She didn't want the Kennickers to think she was stuck up. If she could get them to like her, things would be easier with Alex.

She found Ira Jenkins sitting outside her cottage on the wide doorstep singing hymns as she shelled peas from a huge enamelled bowl. Tamsyn was helping her. She jumped up and dropped a curtsy, looking as if she was about to hare off. Ira struggled to shift her bulk.

'Oh, please,' Abigail said in the friendliest of tones, 'don't trouble yourself on my account, Mrs... Hello, Tamsyn, dear. I've come to talk to you.'

Tamsyn set her small chin high, tightened her features as much as she could and clenched her fists at her sides. She looked as though she wanted to charge Abigail and knock her off her feet. Abigail was very sure of herself where other adults were concerned, men especially, but she had very little experience of children. Tamsyn's stance and attitude were most disconcerting.

She looked uncertainly at Ira Jenkins for a moment then said to the recalcitrant little girl, 'I have come to say sorry about Stephen, about his bad behaviour towards you. He's very sorry and he wants to tell you so himself.'

She expected, hoped, Tamsyn would say something in return but she just kept up her penetrating stare.

Ira Jenkins' eyes were fully on Abigail, amused at her discomfiture. She was ready to come to Tamsyn's defence should the lady take on a temper like her son.

Abigail swallowed and tried again to break through Tamsyn's obstinacy. 'Will you come with me now, Tamsyn? To the gatehouse and see Stephen? I'm sure you can make friends and play happily together. I think your mother would like you both to be friends.'

Tamsyn moved her head very slightly to the side, as if she was thinking. Ira Jenkins tapped her arm; she wasn't sure the lady would stand for much more cheek.

'If you like,' Tamsyn said, but most of the fire stayed in her eyes.

Abigail thought she ought to put her hand out to the child but couldn't bring herself to do it. She noticed what looked like clouds of white at the side of the cottage and saw it was washing billowing on Ira Jenkins' washing line. She pointed to it. 'How pretty.'

''Tis for my niece, Margaret. She's getting married in a fortnight's time to Archie Magor, the grocery shop assistant. Be at Kea church, All Hallows, even though her man is chapel. It was my mother-in-law Jenny's wedding dress and veil. Lilian, her daughter, wore it and so did I when I married her brother Matt. Now Lilian's daughter Margaret wants to carry on with the tradition.'

'How absolutely wonderful,' Abigail said. 'In two weeks' time, you said? I must meet the bride and do something for her.'

'I'm sure that will be very kind of you, Mrs Fiennes,' Ira said and formally introduced herself.

The two women, having nothing in common but eager to be on good terms for the future good of the estate, chatted amiably for several minutes about the forthcoming wedding, while Tamsyn, who was planning to be difficult with Stephen if he really did say he was sorry to her, grew fidgety.

'Now then, Tamsyn,' Abigail said at last, 'shall we go and see that son of mine?'

Chapter 9

While his sister-in-law was trying to charm Tamsyn, Alex rode to Verrian Farm, the nearest one to Trevallion and the largest on the estate, consisting of about one hundred acres. Frank Kellow and his sons Leslie and Clifford grew cereal crops and kept a flock of fifty sheep. Alex hitched Polonius to a gatepost and Frank, who had been saddling his own horse, came over to him, scattering his hens.

'Major Fiennes, how good of you to call. Pleased to meet you, sir. I'm afraid you've come at a rather hectic time. District nurse is here. My boy Leslie's wife is about to give birth to our first grandchild. My wife's a bit busy but I'll make 'ee a cup of tea if you'd like to come inside.'

Alex smiled, just a little, which lessened the dark circles under his eyes. 'No tea for me, Kellow, and I think it would be best to leave the farmhouse to the women at the moment. I hope there will be some good news before I go.'

'Might take a bit of time, these things do. But the good Lord willing, 'twill be all over afore the day's out. The first one 'tis reckoned t'take a bit of time. We're hoping it will be a boy and we'd like to name him after Captain Miles.' Frank looked at Alex as if for his permission.

'My cousin would have been very proud.'

Frank Kellow looked proud. He was also nervous for his son and daughter-in-law and was glad to have the new owner of Trevallion here to take his mind off his coming grandchild. He was stout of build like his wife and stout of heart, honest and religious, a man well liked in the community.

'If it's not inconvenient, I'd like to look round the farm,' Alex said.

The two men spent most of the morning riding round the farm, looking over the crops and sheep. They rolled up their sleeves and let the sun tan their skin. The fresh clean air helped to shift Alex's headache, the dull throbbing ache of a hangover. They stopped at the top of a sloping field that looked down over the River Fal, sharing it with some sheep. They watched the pleasure steamer *River Princess* on its way to Falmouth and a smaller craft going in the opposite direction to Truro.

'I'm going to take a trip on the river this afternoon with Jossy Jenkins and his sons,' Alex said. 'It's years since I've been out on a yacht. I want to see Malpas and Roundwood, Flushing and Mylor, all the places Captain Trevallion used to talk about.'

'You want to sail down to St Just-in-Roseland,' Frank replied. ''Tis some pretty there. Has the most beautiful church and churchyard in the world, 'tis full of tropical plants and full of history.'

'How's life been treating you, Frank?' Alex asked, sincerely wanting to know.

'Aw, well enough, sir. Lost a boy in France backalong… the missus don't like t'talk about it. But the farm's jogging along all right, got nothing to grumble over and we farmers have kept our prices down while most other things have doubled.'

They got down off their horses and Frank took his crib bag off his saddle and offered Alex the open box full of thick-cut ham and pickle sandwiches.

'Go on, sir. I've got plenty.' He patted his wide girth and grinned. 'The missus is afraid I'll waste away.'

Alex realised he was ravenously hungry and gratefully took one of the sandwiches. He tapped his lean chest. 'I suppose I could do with putting on a bit more weight. I always seem to forget to eat.'

'Good country fare's what you need. Will set you up proper.'

'Loveday Wright is a good cook,' Alex said, having just realised it. He made a mental note to compliment her on it.

'I don't doubt that.' Frank looked at the Major meaningfully. 'There's some good people on the estate. Folk who've lived here for generations.'

'I don't doubt that, Frank,' Alex replied at once, returning the look. He wiped an insect off his cheek and grimaced at a spot that stung.

'Cut yourself shaving, did 'ee?' Frank said, eyeing the sore spot and bandaged hand as he bit into a giant slab of saffron cake.

Alex touched the cut gingerly. 'Yes, my hand wasn't too steady this morning.'

Frank nodded and ate his cake; he knew how to mind his own business.

Alex liked being in the company of another man who wasn't quick to make judgements. 'Had a drop too much,' he explained.

'Took us all ways,' Frank said, and they knew they were in rapport over wartime experiences. It gave Frank the courage to ask a personal question. 'I was wonderin'. Left your business to come down here, have 'ee?'

Alex nodded over a mouthful of sandwich. 'My family's been in banking and manufacturing for years. The managers didn't seem to miss me during the war so I just left them to get on with it again. I haven't been able to settle since the war, Frank. It's not what I want, sitting in an office in a dark suit and stiff collar all day long. I get restless, impatient.' He grinned at the peaceful river below them. 'They were probably glad to see the back of me.'

'Some men aren't meant to be indoors,' Frank said simply. When they got back to the farmyard Clifford Kellow took the horses and Frank had a quiet word with his other son, Leslie, who was pacing up and down the yard with the farm collie following on his heels.

'Be better if 'ee got on with a bit of work, boy,' Frank said knowledgeably. 'I didn't hang about here when you and your brother were coming into the world.'

'I left the haymaking to check on things, Father,' Leslie said in a nervous voice. 'I was going back but things have speeded up a bit.'

Frank elbowed his son in the side and inclined his head towards Alex. Leslie stopped dead and stared at him.

'I'm sorry, sir. Me head's been so filled with Gwen and the baby coming I didn't see you there.'

Frank formally introduced Alex to his two sons then he and Leslie went to the front door of the farmhouse to listen. Clifford joined them and Alex was touched at the family picture, envying their closeness and the coming child who meant the family had a future as well as a past.

'I heard something,' shouted Leslie. 'Gwen! Are you all right?'

'Shush!' Frank ordered.

Alex found himself coming up behind the other men. 'What's happening?'

Frank looked at him but his ear was straining for sounds. They heard Gwen groan and then there was silence. Leslie moaned and walked into the yard. Alex put his hands in his trouser pockets hoping to find a stray cigarette. He smoked occasionally and knew expectant fathers were helped through their ordeal by a cigarette. He came up empty-handed and Frank, knowing what he was looking for, shook his head. It would have been an unwanted gift anyway.

'Have you enough help here now that my sister-in-law has commandeered Miss Allen?' Alex asked, to break the tension. He knew the farm had taken on another farmhand but the conversation would help pass the time. He didn't want to leave before he knew the outcome of the birth.

The four men talked about the farm, the creek and the weather as they paced about, one or other of them stopping abruptly every now and then because they thought they'd heard a baby's cry.

Leslie kept taking off his cap and scratching his head and putting it back on again. Clifford chewed on a piece of straw. Frank patted the dog's head. Alex rubbed his sweaty palms down his trousers and wished he could think of something new to say. He had exhausted all the things he'd said to the men in the trenches when they'd received word from home that there was to be an addition to the family, or when the birth was imminent and there was no way of knowing what was happening at home.

The women upstairs, Gwen, her sister Doris who had come for the confinement, Mrs Kellow and the district nurse didn't know Alex was out in the yard and seemed to have forgotten the men altogether. No one appeared to tell them lunch was ready and with the birth apparently so close Frank Kellow was too nervous to step over the threshold and make a pot of tea in his own kitchen. The waiting went on.

It was nearly two o'clock when Leslie jerked his head to the bedroom window. A baby's cry was heard across the length and breadth of the yard. The men let out a cheer and Mrs Kellow put her head out of the window.

''Tis a boy, Les! She's done 'ee proud.'

Leslie Kellow, his face abeam, eyes streaming tears of joy, went round his father and brother and Alex pumping their hands. The collie barked, joining in the commotion.

'The next generation,' Frank Kellow said, wiping a tear from his own eye. 'Praise the Lord.'

A few minutes later the men were allowed in the house. Leslie rushed up the stairs to see his wife and son. Mrs Kellow and Gwen's sister were thrown into a flap to see Alex there.

'Here all the time, Major, and I never knew it,' Mrs Kellow said, sending Doris to fetch things from the larder. 'What must you think? Father, why didn't you invite the Major in and offer him a drop of that port we got left from Gran's funeral?'

'Don't pay any special attention to me, Mrs Kellow,' Alex said, leaning back comfortably in the chair he'd been seen to. 'It's me who's overstayed my welcome, but I wanted to stay on to find out about the baby.'

'You're welcome here any time, Major.' Mrs Kellow was taking a good look at him as she talked, and she didn't stop working. In minutes she and Doris had a meal of pies, cheeses, crusty bread and fresh salad vegetables from the garden on the table. 'You will stop for a bite, Major?'

'I'd love to,' Alex said with relish. Glancing at his watch he saw there was a whole hour before he and Jossy were to launch the *Iseult*. He ate more that day than he had in a whole week for the last eleven years, tucking in, relaxed, perfectly at home with this family.

Leslie came downstairs proudly displaying his baby son, wrapped up cosily in a lacy shawl that had been wrapped round generations of Kellows.

'He's grand, isn't he, Mother?'

'Aye, he certainly is, and a Kellow to the last bit of un.'

The proud grandfather and uncle had a good look then Leslie presented his son to Alex. ''Twas an honour to have you here with us this day, Major.'

'I feel honoured to have been here and part of such an intimate and wonderful family occasion,' Alex said.

'We'd like to name him Miles if you have no objections, sir.'

'Of course not. As I've told your father, Captain Trevallion would have been very proud.'

'The missus, Gwen, she was wondering, if you don't mind, sir. Would you choose a name for him?'

Alex thought about it. A lump came to his throat as he said, 'George. After someone I knew.'

Mrs Kellow clapped her hands. 'The King's name. A fine solid name. Thank you, Major.'

'Miles George Kellow,' Alex said. Now that a little bit of life seemed to have returned to Georgie Gilbert, he felt he could hold the baby, something he had never done or wanted to do before, not even Stephen. He held out his arms. 'May I?'

Leslie Kellow looked fit to burst with pride to see his son, his firstborn, held so firmly and lovingly by the estate's new owner.

The district nurse came down the stairs and tut-tutted. She was only impressed with the aspects of her job at that moment. 'This will never do,' she said chidingly, taking Miles George from Alex's arms. 'Back to mother at once for you, young man.'

Mrs Kellow and Doris went upstairs and, as Alex was about to leave, the nurse returned with her bag. 'Just a minute, Major Fiennes,' she said in a professional voice. 'I want to take a look at your hand. That bandage is filthy!'

'It's nothing,' Alex said firmly, making for the door.

'Then it won't hurt to let me look at it, will it?'

Alex's face closed over. 'I'm going now,' he said stubbornly.

Maisie Uren was trained in midwifery and had been a general district nurse for eight years; she had passed all her examinations with high marks and had a certificate from the General Midwives Board to prove it. She had nursed patients of every age, social standing and temperament. She was a single-minded woman dedicated to her career and the parish and no one would put her off when she was about her business. She was tall, slim, firm-figured, had no-nonsense features that could overcome the hardest opposition, eyebrows that could dismiss a misfit with one decisive lift. Her uniform was immaculate, her brown hair tied up in a simple bun with not one hair out of place. Nurse Uren stood, her back erect, hands clasped with thumbs on top, waiting for Alexander Fiennes to obey her.

Frank Kellow was so sure that he would he put a chair out for him to sit down for the examination.

'Can I fetch 'ee anything, nurse?' Clifford asked.

But these people had not met Alex Fiennes before. In a cold voice, he said, 'When and if I want my hand looked at, Miss Uren, I'll send for you. The estate has paid its master's subscriptions over the years and I will decide when I will make use of the medical treatment it entitles me to. Good afternoon to you all.'

–

Alex recalled the shock on Nurse Uren's face, with wry amusement. Robert Drayton had mentioned her in his letters, saying she was good and efficient at her job, and worked tirelessly to better the lot of the folk on her patch, but was something of a battleaxe. Alex wasn't worried about her sort.

He still felt something of the Kellow family's closeness, the sharing in a special event. But as he trotted along and got closer to the estate the old familiar loneliness of his later years assailed him again. He had come down here to wind up Miles's affairs, not a hard task as Miles had always worked methodically and the trustees had done an excellent job since his incapacitation. Trevallion was beautiful, but it still belonged to Miles.

As he turned into the driveway he met Rebecca coming out on her bicycle.

'Good afternoon, Major,' she said, stopping with a foot resting on the top pedal. 'Have you had a good look round?'

She was still wearing her riding breeches from the morning and her hair was free. She was in a happy mood. It was good to be in her comfortable old clothes again and she'd had the chance to be close to Joe. Alex dismounted, moving close to her.

'I've been to Verrian Farm,' he said.

'That's where I'm going now. Young Mrs Kellow, that's Matt and Ira Jenkins' daughter Gwen from the creek, is expecting a baby any day now and Mrs Fiennes has given me permission to go and see how she is. Mrs Fiennes, by the way, has gone out to lunch with the vicar's wife and is spending the afternoon at the Ladies' Guild. The invitation came this morning.'

So that explained the return to her usual clothes. Alex admired people who weren't afraid to be themselves, who didn't put on airs and graces, as Rebecca might have done given the amount of clothes Abigail kept giving her and embarrassing her with.

He said, 'Mrs Kellow gave birth to a son about an hour ago.'

Rebecca's face lit up at the news. 'That's wonderful! Leslie and Mr Kellow had their heart set on it being a boy to keep the family name going. I'll still go, they won't mind me popping in for five minutes.'

Alex could see the feeling of continuity and caring among these people who worked on the estate. He tried to capture some of it, to help shake off the feeling of coldness and loneliness that seemed to be his lot.

'Becca, I want to thank you.'

'Oh?'

He gave her a rare and quiet smile. 'For last night. Clearing up the room. Not saying anything to Mrs Fiennes.' Rebecca was glad he seemed to trust her. He had called her Becca, like her father and those closest to her did. She didn't mention his clumsily bandaged hand. He was a grown man, in charge of her life now as well as his own and didn't need to be badgered over something he would see to himself if it was needed.

She smiled and nodded. 'I'll be getting along then. I'll be back to help Loveday with the dinner.'

Alex smiled back and watched her ride away to share in the Kellows' joy. 'We must ride together one morning,' he called after her.

Chapter 10

Stephen and Tamsyn were standing outside Trevallion. It was dusk and they had just seen Percy Gummoe lock up and leave.

Stephen looked at Tamsyn. 'How do we get in?'

'Why ask me?' she replied gruffly.

She had been difficult with Stephen all day. She had accepted his apology but only after she'd made him say it twice. Then she had smirked as his mother had given him a dressing-down in front of her. Stephen wished there were boys of his own age in the creek, he felt embarrassed to be seen about with a little girl. He was exasperated with Tamsyn now but determined not to show it. In fact he had made up his mind to tolerate her by pretending she was a boy. He called her simply Tam. He'd once had a male Scottish terrier called Tam. The girl seemed quite tough, he didn't think she'd cry every time he got rough with her, so it wasn't difficult to think of her as a boy.

He said in a patient voice, 'Because I assume that over the years you and the other children in the creek have found a way into the house to play in it.'

'I haven't,' Tamsyn said stubbornly. 'There's a ghost in there and if anyone goes inside it'll get them.'

It was Stephen's turn to smirk. 'Don't be ridiculous, Tam. My uncle, my mother, that man Gummoe and Rebecca have been in there and no ghost has got them.'

'Doesn't mean there isn't a ghost, doesn't mean it won't get them.'

'Are you afraid?' he challenged her. Her answer was totally unexpected.

'Yes, I am. And before you laugh at me, Uncle Joe said he was scared during the war, that it's right and sensible to be scared in the face of danger.'

Stephen gave a long sigh. 'But the danger in the war was real. There's no such thing as ghosts. It's something people make up to be cruel and frighten others with. Perhaps to keep them away from something, like the location of a smuggling run or hide.'

Tamsyn tightened her face against his persuasion. 'I thought you said we were going to play smugglers anyway. I'll have to go in for my supper soon and Motley will be fussing for me.'

'Oh, Tam! Look, we'll play smugglers tomorrow. I want to look around the house now, just for a few minutes, that's all. It'll be exciting, I promise you. I'll look after you in there. I won't let anything happen to you.' Tamsyn shook her head so he threatened her. 'If you don't come with me then you can't be in my gang. Anyone who joins a gang where I come from has to do something exceedingly brave for their initiation and this can be yours.'

'My what?'

'Your way into my gang. You do want to be in it, don't you?'

'Yes…'

'Well, come on then before Mrs Jenkins calls you.'

Tamsyn reluctantly followed Stephen to the huge front door. A quick scout around showed Stephen there was no way in at the front and he led Tamsyn round to the back of the house. The tall cedar trees swayed in the evening breeze and cast long dark shadows. Tamsyn wanted to hold Stephen's hand but knowing he wouldn't like it she clenched her fists and followed close on his heels. He pushed at the two back doors and rattled the windows.

'Everything's locked up,' Tamsyn whispered behind him in relief. 'We daren't break in.'

'One of the kitchen windows shook when I touched it. The latch is loose. I think I can get it to move and the window open. Then we can climb inside.'

Tamsyn held her breath and her stomach did a backward flip when Stephen got the window open. Trease had left a wheelbarrow close by. Stephen wheeled it under the window and climbed into it to give him the extra height to get in through the window. With his head and arms hanging out, he beckoned to Tamsyn.

'Climb in the wheelbarrow and give me your hand.'

With a mighty gulp she obeyed and the next moment Stephen had hauled her up and through the opening. He was kneeling on the wide scrubbed draining board and when Tamsyn was beside him he lifted her to the floor. She made a frightened protest and as he jumped down beside her he took her hand.

'Shush. I've told you there's no need to be scared. I'm your leader and will defend you with my life.'

Tamsyn clutched her leader's hand tightly; nothing would have made her let go.

There was just enough light stealing in through the windows for them to see to move about but everything in the kitchen looked big, dark and looming. Stephen led them out of the room, through the short corridor and into the hall. The stairs seem to rear up in front of them and Tamsyn imagined all sorts of horrible creatures rushing down at them.

'Can we go back now?' she whispered shakily. She was clutching the back of his shirt.

'We'll just take a quick look upstairs,' Stephen said bravely, but her fear was infectious and his heart was thumping wildly.

'No!' she protested, yanking back on his hand and shirt. 'We'll be got for sure if we go up there.'

'Just to the top of the stairs then. We can't back out now.'

'But Stephen…'

Stephen didn't think he'd prove himself much of a leader of their gang of two if he turned tail and ran now. It was all right for Tamsyn to show she was scared, she was after all only a small girl however hard he might pretend otherwise, but he had to show her he was almost a grown man and scared of nothing.

'You either come with me or go back by yourself, Tam,' he hissed through the gathering darkness.

Too afraid to leave him, Tamsyn followed his steps up the stairs, clinging on to him. At the top he could just make out her staring eyes.

'So far so good. See, there's no one here but us. Listen, you won't hear anything but our own breathing.'

Tamsyn was too scared to look around and she didn't want to concentrate on listening either. She was sure that any moment now they would hear the most horrendous screams and groans and a huge white monster would loom up from somewhere and get them.

'I… I want to go back…'

Stephen ignored her fear and walked round the landing, trying to fight down his own growing panic as he studied paintings and furniture in the gloom. A small scratching sound was heard from an undetermined part of the house and Tamsyn gave a small scream.

'What was th-that? Oh, Stephen, I want to go home,' she wailed, running round him and clamping her face to his chest.

Instinctively he put his arms round her. 'Be quiet, Tam,' he whispered in her ear.

They stayed rigid, listening. There was a scurrying noise and they both jumped. 'It… it was only a m-mouse,' Stephen stammered. He took a step back to the top of the stairs, taking Tamsyn with him. They moved gingerly, one step at a time, picking up speed with each one.

The grandfather clock in the hall chimed the half-hour and the sudden noise made the boy and girl jump and quicken their pace. A clock in one of the bedrooms joined in and there was a sudden big bang which seemed to come from behind them. The open window in the kitchen creaked as a breeze caught it. There seemed to be noises all around them, getting closer, coming for them. Stephen grabbed Tamsyn's hand and they ran down the steps, through the hall, the corridor and into the kitchen. Gasping for breath, Stephen threw Tamsyn up on the draining board. She needed no encouragement to scramble through the window and jump down into the wheelbarrow. She waited just long enough for him to join her then they were running as fast as they could away from Trevallion House.

Jossy Jenkins cut the engine of the *Iseult* and Alex leaped ashore from its sharp bow with the mooring rope to help guide the boat, a locally built motor launch, into the boathouse. He'd enjoyed the excursion with Jossy and his son Victor, who did oak barking for the tanning trade and oysterdredging in the winter for a living, and he was feeling light-hearted. It seemed days, rather than hours, since he'd been at Verrian Farm and joined in the elation at the birth of Miles George Kellow.

Watched by a bright-faced gathering of Kennickers, the *Iseult* and its three-man crew had slipped out of Kennick Creek in the mid-afternoon and was soon out in the main course of the River Fal, all set to explore some of the estuary's eleven winding miles. They passed the point where the merging waters of Lamouth and Cowlands Creeks united with the river and soon after that passed Church Creek with its jackdaw-infested fifteenth-century church tower.

Victor didn't speak much but Jossy eagerly told Alex about anything of local interest. 'I like the services in the old and new Kea churches, sir. Worshipped in 'em, man and boy, and sang in the choir. The vicar, he lost his son in the war. There's a little mission church, built in the last century, standing behind that ruined tower we just saw. Back there in Cowlands Creek you'll find the little village of Coombe. 'Tis some pretty and famous for its plums.'

'Ah,' Alex smiled. 'The famous Kea plums. I know about them, in fact I've tasted them. Mr Drayton used to have some sent to Captain Trevallion every year in the nursing home. I understand that they're part of the local livelihood and people come for miles around to buy them.'

Jossy handed the boat's wheel over to Alex. 'I've ate Kea plums every year of my life. It was nice of Mr Drayton to think of the Captain like that.'

On the other side of the river was the vast Tregothnan estate of Lord Falmouth and its magnificent castellated mansion. When they sailed past Tregothnan's boathouse, the boatman stood up straight and saluted the Trevallion flag.

Here and there on the shore children enjoying the school summer holiday waved to them. Some were swimming, some shrimping, others were out in small rowing boats.

Alex felt his tension ease as the salt air reached his lungs, the fresh breeze sifted through his hair and cooled his skin. He tossed aside his hat and opened the top buttons of his shirt. He felt free like this, free from the restrictions and expectations of society life, free to be himself. He thought of Rebecca and how good it would have been to have her here too.

They sailed into the Tresillian River, one of the many waterways which fed the Fal, passing St Clement village where men tarring a boat waved to them, and on past Pencalenick. As it was a full tide they were able to reach the picturesque old village of Tresillian. That was as far as they could go and they turned back at the river's ancient bridge which stood adjacent to the impressive gatehouse of the Tregothnan estate. Alex watched the slow-moving traffic on the main road to Truro on the other side of the attractive village cottages. Then he looked down at the freshwater channel lapping round the boat. The mudflats, mostly covered by the tide now, provided a habitat for a wide variety of water birds and Alex lifted the binoculars round his neck to spot, among other birds, mallards, oystercatchers, curlews and sandpipers.

Retracing their passage, they entered the Truro River, passed through Malpas and sailed on to Calenick Creek, just south of Truro. For centuries it had housed a corn mill and a tin-smelting house, the chimney of which was still standing. The tidal mudflats and salt-marshes, flanked by an ancient semi-natural woodland, were a paradise for water birds, including some wintering wading species.

There was a spot near the village where until about the time of the Great War there'd been a boatbuilding yard. Its history lent much to the tranquillity of the creek and Alex, Jossy and Victor went ashore there to eat their sandwiches and drink from their flasks of strong tea. A couple of locals were enjoying the quiet and Alex chatted to them about the boatbuilding.

They sailed back down the creek and on to Truro. They didn't disembark but stayed close to Newham to admire the impressive view of the city's three elegant cathedral spires. Once more they turned to retrace their passage and Alex asked Jossy to stop a moment so he could talk to some boatbuilders at Sunny Corner. Then they made their way to Malpas and moored up near the ferry where the waters of the Truro and Tresillian rivers converged. They crossed the jetty and walked up the steep ferry-slip to the Park Inn where Alex paid for a round of drinks. Then it was time to head for home.

'I can't remember when I last enjoyed a day out so much, Major,' Jossy said, grinning as he lit his pipe. He tapped the side of the boat. ''Tis years since the old girl's had a good outing.'

'It clears the head, clears the lungs and clears the mind,' Alex said, smiling back from the wheel.

Jossy looked at the banks each side of the river, screened by woods. He said rather slyly, 'The oysters'll be spawning now. If you stay till October you'll be able to eat local oysters, sir, when the dredgers start work. 'Tis said the Romans put 'em in the river. You can have a thousand for half a crown. Boats d'come from all over, St Mawes, Porthleven and Fowey, to dredge the river. And the French come over to buy our local oysters and you know how particular they are about their food.'

'I've tasted the local oysters, Jossy,' Alex said quietly. He met the old man's shrewd eye. 'And I daresay I will again.' Jossy crammed his pipe in his mouth, satisfied.

At the end of the day, as Alex helped moor and tidy up the *Iseult*, he was satisfied too. He looked up as he heard a sudden shrill of excited voices and a clattering of shoes. To his surprise he saw Stephen and Tamsyn holding hands and running towards Ira Jenkins' cottage as if for their lives.

Chapter 11

Rebecca was helping Loveday in the kitchen of the gatehouse. She was washing dishes while Loveday chopped beef into cubes at the table. They were discussing the events of the day before.

'I think things might be working out all right,' Rebecca said, wiping a dishcloth over the same plate for the twentieth time.

'Why do you keep saying that?' Loveday said, unconvinced, as she cut off a piece of fat and put it aside for Motley.

'Well, take yesterday. Master Stephen apologised to Tamsyn and they played quite happily with Captain Miles's model railway and down in the creek. They were even late getting back to Ira's for Tamsyn's supper.'

Loveday chuckled. 'Tamsyn made the boy repeat the apology and then Mrs Fiennes gave him what-for afterwards. He won't be too quick to push her around in the future.' Then she frowned. 'I'd like to know what they got up to though. Tamsyn was restless all night and said she had bad dreams.'

'Probably some silly game or other that got her imagination going. But the point I was making is that the children are getting along with each other now. And Mrs Fiennes went to tea with the vicar's wife and said she got on famously with the Ladies' Guild. I really think she wants to settle here. As for the Major, I was amazed when I heard the full story from the Kellows about how he stayed in the yard with the men while they were waiting for Gwen to deliver her baby. They reckon he was nearly as worried as they were until they heard the baby cry. I saw the Major in the lane and he told me Gwen had given birth to a boy but he didn't tell me he'd said that Captain Miles would have been proud to have it named after him, or that he chose the second name, George.'

'Well, you'd hardly expect him to tell you everything, Becca. He's your master and is as closed-minded as they come.'

'You're missing the point again, Loveday,' Rebecca said, drying her hands and facing her friend at the table. 'The Major was interested enough in the Kellows and the baby to stay for the birth and choose a name, one that the Kellows believe belonged to a wartime friend of his. It means the Major is beginning to feel at home.'

Loveday looked thoughtful. 'Perhaps, but I think 'tis still too early to say for sure.'

'Well, at least it gives us some hope,' Rebecca said, getting exasperated. Loveday Wright couldn't see anything if it didn't happen under her nose.

A noise by the door made them look up. It was Alex and both women flushed, hoping he hadn't overheard them talking about him.

'Mrs Wright, are you making pasties?' he asked, giving them both a rare smile.

'Yes, Major. Don't you like them?'

'I like them very much. I used to buy one at a baker's in Truro every time I visited Captain Trevallion. Can you make me a really big one? And send it down to the big house when it's cooked, please? I'm going to spend the morning there. There's wine in the cellar but could I have a flask of coffee to take with me, say in ten minutes, please?'

'Certainly, Major.'

'There's another reason to believe things are looking up,' Rebecca said as she made the flask of coffee. 'He complimented you on your cooking last night.'

'He's generous too. He's paying me a handsome wage for this work, it's much better than when I was taking in sewing. It means I'll be able to buy Tamsyn a new pair of shoes for the wedding.' Loveday went on cutting the pasty beef. Then she made a statement that Rebecca never thought to hear pass her lips. 'Some handsome when he smiles like that, isn't he?'

Alex unlocked all the drawers of the desk and those of a tall filing cabinet in the study and turned everything out on top of them. He put letters and documents into order of importance to correspond with the list of business he'd received from Robert Drayton. Anything personal of Miles's he put aside, after examining it poignantly and sadly. Miles had secured stocks and shares in several companies, some that Alex had recommended to him himself. Some of the companies had gone out of business during the war, others were thriving. The farming and sheep rearing of the estate were only small beer against the other concerns Miles had successfully run to keep his beautiful home and small piece of land functioning well. Alex had to make a decision about what to do with each concern.

He worked until mid-morning then turned his attention to the file he had found on his first visit to the study, the details of the concerns of past Trevallions. He was in no particular hurry to wind up Miles's affairs, to decide the future of the house and estate, to leave Cornwall.

He studied maps of old mine workings once belonging to the Trevallions. There had been some on the north coast, at the far west of Cornwall, and nearer to home in a small village called Chacewater. Study of old documents revealed that Roland Trevallion had over-stretched his means. There had been no capital with which to keep the family properties by the time the bottom had dropped out of the coppermining industry. Other land and the houses owned at Truro had been gradually sold off, until only the house Alex was now sitting in was left.

After Roland's death his son Vyvyan, Miles's father, had made enough money through the tenant farms to keep Trevallion as a going concern.

Alex was puzzled over a discrepancy in the accounts of sales of mining property and began to pore over an old map.

Rebecca brought his lunch at exactly one o'clock. A pasty, as big as he could possibly manage to eat, was wrapped in a tea towel to keep it hot and Loveday had sent down a bowl of strawberries and clotted cream for dessert.

'Here you are, Major. Loveday said—'

'Come here, Becca,' he said, not listening to her, beckoning with his hand.

She put his lunch down on top of a pile of scattered papers and walked obediently to his side.

'There,' he said, pulling her closer and pressing a finger down hard on what he been studying under a magnifying glass on the desk. 'What do you make of that!'

Rebecca was taken aback by his unexpected exuberance and the fact that he had her imprisoned by the arm, but she looked at a large piece of badly creased and faded parchment he had spread out over the desk.

'Um, it's a map of Cornwall, isn't it? An old one.' Somehow he seemed to expect her to know exactly what he'd found that was causing him so much excitement.

'Yes, it's a map. But see there?' He pointed to a spot near the coastline.

She nodded, still puzzled.

'It's the site of an old copper mine called the Wheal Fortunate.' Alex pointed to other old documents he had scattered about. 'I've been studying these and from what I can make out this little mine and the scrap of land it stands on was never sold by any of the Trevallions. It was probably so small that when the lodes ran out, long before the slump in the eighteen sixties, it was just forgotten. And from what I can gather, there was a house built in the area. One of Miles's forebears, a crotchety old character by the name of Aristotle Trevallion, had it built there because the sea air was good for his lungs. From these documents it appears the house wasn't very grand, and it had its roof ripped off in a gale. The house seems to have been forgotten and is probably gone now but there's no record of the land it stood on being sold. If that's so, it belonged to Miles and he probably never knew of it.'

Rebecca leaned closer to the map, taking in the area under and around Alex's finger. 'There all that time, well, the ruins anyway, and no one knew. It's near Perranporth, on the other coast. It's very wild and beautiful on those cliffs.'

'I'm going to take a trip there to see what I can find.' Alex leaned over the map, his nose practically on the spot he was so excited about. He did not realise he had pulled Rebecca with him. 'I never thought I would come across something like this.'

Their shoulders were touching, they were almost cheek to cheek, but he did not seem to notice the closeness he had contrived. Rebecca straightened up and moved away from him slightly.

'Brought my lunch, have you?' he said absentmindedly.

She had been wondering what he would drink with the pasty as he had not asked for another flask, then she saw he had been down to the cellar and brought up a crate of wine. A crate! She knew it was more convenient than popping down to get a bottle or two every day but she hoped he would not dispose of them too quickly, or let her father see them. Trease had made remarkable progress with the gardens and was the happiest she had seen him in years. She didn't want alcohol getting the better of him now.

Alex selected a bottle of white wine and searched about for glasses.

'I don't think Captain Trevallion ever took a tipple in this room,' she said quietly.

He did not miss the hint of disapproval in her voice and surveyed her with mild amusement. 'I was going to ask you to share the bottle with me. Help me celebrate my curious little find.'

'Then it's a good job Loveday didn't bring down your lunch – well, dinner we call it. She doesn't approve of anyone drinking unless it's one on Christmas Day.'

'A good job? You talk differently too, as well as having different names for meals.'

Rebecca wasn't sure if he was making an observation or poking fun at her.

'I'll get you a glass, Major, from the drawing room. Thank you for the offer of the drink but I have to get back to the gatehouse. Mrs Fiennes wants me to go shopping with her in Truro.'

'You're not cut out for that sort of thing, are you?' he asked seriously, knowing how tiresome Abigail could be.

'I don't mind,' Rebecca said. With the fate of the estate in this man's hands, she was not about to whinge.

He smiled at her for a moment. 'You are a most graceful liar, Becca. I've been meaning to speak to you about your wages. You earned much less than a shop assistant on Verrian Farm but now you're doing two or three jobs at the same time as well as looking after your father. I propose to pay you two pounds ten shillings a week.'

'That is very good of you, Major.' Her eyes were wide at his generosity.

When she came back with a wine glass she found him scrabbling about on the floor. 'I knocked over a pot of pens,' he explained.

Becca smiled down on his dark head. He couldn't see her, he was facing the other way. She thought what a strange man he was, quiet and moody most of the time, but kind and understanding. Understanding of her father's heavy drinking, and her preference for a simple country life working on the farm rather than being dressed up as his sister-in-law's companion.

'Hello, what's this?' he said, tossing away a pen that had rolled next to the chest. 'There's something under here. Two finds in one day?' He pulled out the mysterious love letters signed S.B.

—

After lunch Rebecca and Abigail were driven by a very proud Trease in the Spyker into Truro. He had shed some of his slack puffiness with the hard work he had put in over the last three days and looked quite fit and sleek in his blue and grey chauffeur's uniform. Rebecca was wearing one of the dresses Abigail had given her and now that she was this close to the city she felt some of the importance and sophistication Abigail emanated; she hoped she would see lots of people who knew her.

Rebecca's hopes were realised; they received many curious looks and some people stopped to gossip and be introduced to Mrs Fiennes. Abigail was impatient to get into the shops and launched Rebecca through the doorway of every shop that sold or made ladies' clothes. When she told Rebecca she was going to buy her a hat for the Jenkins' wedding, Rebecca tried to protest. It fell on deaf ears. Abigail saw a lovely picture hat, ideal for a special occasion, in a shop in Cathedral

Lane. Just right for Rebecca, she said, whose wealth of hair wouldn't sit under a cloche hat.

Abigail was impressed by Truro's shops, which were mainly owned by local traders, and she thought its cathedral absolutely splendid. Rebecca told her that as a child she had often stayed with her uncle and aunt in St Austell Street, which was not far from the cathedral.

When the shopping, including a lacy negligée set for Margaret Jenkins' honeymoon, was safely in the Spyker under Trease's watchful eye, Abigail declared that her feet were aching and her throat was dry and it was time for afternoon tea. She ordered Rebecca to take them to the Red Lion Hotel, the city's leading hotel and the best place to meet people of consequence. As they walked along Boscawen Street, a tall well-groomed man in a dark suit lifted his hat and smiled charmingly at them.

'Mrs Fiennes and Miss Allen.' Neville Faull stretched out his hand, lingering over Rebecca's fingers and Abigail's eyes. 'How good to see you again, Mrs Fiennes. I hope you enjoy your visit to Cornwall and the Trevallion estate as much as I did the visit to your beautiful home in Berkshire.' Neville Faull stood out like a god of Scandinavian legend against the backdrop of simple shops. He was elegant in manners and dress. He smelled of expensive tobacco and exotic aftershave.

Abigail looked straight back into his shameless eyes and said huskily, 'I hope I do indeed, Mr Faull. Already I can tell you I am quite taken with Trevallion and its little creek.' She touched Rebecca's arm. 'I can understand why Rebecca loves it and is so strong and healthy looking.'

After that remark, Neville Faull took his time looking Rebecca over. In reality it was only a few seconds but she knew he'd taken in every detail of her appearance, her smart clothes, high-heeled shoes, her hair tamed in a twist Abigail had told her how to do, pinned under a wide-brimmed hat Abigail had insisted she wear. Rebecca had added a tiny touch of colour to her face from the cosmetics Abigail had given her. Before today, Neville Faull had only seen her in her riding clothes.

'You have had a marvellous effect on Miss Allen, Mrs Fiennes, but then Miss Allen is a most attractive young lady anyway. I shall not detain you, I'm on my way to the rural council chamber for a meeting. I hope, when the Major permits, to see you both on the estate shortly.'

He lifted his hat again and walked away. The two women watched him. Rebecca was flattered by what he'd said and Abigail was thinking what a great pity it was to have to present and keep up a moral front for Alex if she was to gain the estate for herself and Stephen. She and Rebecca looked at each other, smiled their mutual appreciation of the man who'd just left them, and carried on to the hotel.

'Are there many men like him about this area?' Abigail said lightly. She was curious to know.

'No one quite like Mr Faull,' Rebecca replied, taking another appreciative look at Neville Faull's impressive back.

'He is attractive, but as I've told you before, Rebecca, he can't be trusted. I can't speak about his professional manner or his dealings in his position on the rural council, but you keep your distance.'

'If he asks me to go out with him again I won't accept.' This was true. Rebecca had designs on Joe Carlyon.

'Good, I'm glad to hear it.'

As they stood outside the elegant entrance to the Red Lion Hotel, Abigail knew there would be only one reason why a man like Neville Faull would ask out an inexperienced girl like Rebecca. Abigail couldn't afford to upset Neville Faull. If she did he might spill the beans about his affair with her, but she wasn't going to stand by and allow him to seduce Rebecca either.

Chapter 12

Since Stephen Fiennes had arrived at Trevallion he had longed to go riding but having had his ear boxed by Joe Carlyon he was reluctant to ask the groom to saddle a pony for him. After the first week, however, he screwed up his courage and made his way to the stables, taking Tamsyn and her dog along with him. He didn't care if people saw him as a spoiled brat but he didn't want to be thought of as a bully. The estate folk had turned out in force to go to church on Sunday, hoping to meet and impress their new master and mistress and Stephen had made sure that he'd behaved like a perfect gentleman and that Joe had noticed. Because his uncle had been reluctant to be drawn into long conversations and had refused all offers of social contact, Stephen had made a good attempt in his stead, even delighting the vicar by suggesting he might be prepared to join the choir.

Stephen felt he had proved that he could play sensibly with Tamsyn and he hoped Joe would say no more about him hurting her. Stephen took charge of all their games, however. He was Captain Redbeard, Tamsyn only a pirate. He was King Arthur, she only a humble knight. He was commander of the fleet, she only an ordinary seaman. Tamsyn was quite happy with this; after all, she had Motley who growled at Stephen every time the boy came near him.

Joe was in the stable yard grooming Polonius, the horse Alex usually rode, when the two children approached him. 'What can I do for you two, then?' he murmured, keeping his eyes on his work.

'Stephen wants to ride,' Tamsyn piped up.

'I can speak for myself, Tam.' Stephen was careful to keep the anger out of his voice but it carried a haughty tone. 'If you please, Carlyon.'

'Your mother's told me you can ride well,' Joe said, carrying on with the curry comb as if he had no interest in the boy. 'But she also said I was to go with you, at least at first. She doesn't want you getting lost.'

There was no outburst, just a scowl. 'Fair enough,' Stephen said.

'Can I come?' Tamsyn pleaded. 'Motley will be good and stay here.'

'Well, it's not really up to me, Tamsyn,' Joe said, looking at Stephen with raised eyebrows. 'Can she?'

Stephen smiled widely at Tamsyn and said, very sweetly, to Joe, 'Of course she can.'

'You'll have to run and ask your mother, Tamsyn,' Joe said, trying to figure out Stephen's true mood.

'Ohhh. She's gone over to Verrian Farm to look at the new baby. I'll run and ask Mrs Jenkins, she's looking after me.'

'No, you can't do that. It wouldn't be fair to put the responsibility onto Mrs Jenkins if you were to fall off or something.' Tamsyn looked very disappointed and Joe was surprised when Stephen offered a solution.

'She could ride in front of you though, Joe. That wouldn't hurt, surely?'

'Can't see your mother objecting to that.' Joe thought that perhaps the boy wasn't as bad as he first thought but the main reason Stephen wanted Tamsyn to come along was so he could show off to her how well he could ride.

They trotted along the lanes, Joe on Polonius with Tamsyn happily tucked in front of him and Stephen sitting importantly astride Hamlet. Then Joe took them through the woods, down a well-trodden path beside a stream. Stephen spotted a butterfly drinking water at the edge of the stream and jumped down off his pony.

'What are you doing?' Tamsyn asked.

'I'm going to catch this butterfly to add to my collection,' he informed her curtly.

'Don't you dare! That's cruel,' Tamsyn called back, wriggling down beside him. 'That's a painted lady. It's beautiful, all insects are beautiful and they should be seen alive, not pinned dead on boards. Captain Miles never captured butterflies.'

'How do you know?' Stephen demanded. 'You never knew him.'

'Uncle Joe said the Captain was a kind man so he wouldn't have done anything cruel.'

Tamsyn looked at Joe for confirmation and Stephen began to feel ashamed. 'I wasn't really going to touch the stupid butterfly,' he said harshly. He mounted his pony and as Joe lifted Tamsyn back up in front of him he stole a look at the butterfly and admitted to himself that it was indeed a beautiful creature and probably looked best when seen in its natural habitat.

They trotted on, stopping at a spot which overlooked Kennick Creek. The tide was fully in and the waters lapped and sparkled up to the high bank. Joe tethered the horses to an oak tree and sat down with a cigarette while the children pulled off their shoes and clothes down to their underwear to swim. Stephen was an excellent horseman but Tamsyn was a much better swimmer. They splashed and played about, pretending to be saboteurs, swimming out to sea from Falmouth Bay to plant explosives on a German submarine.

'German submarines used to hide themselves just outside Falmouth Bay, even around the Manacles, a group of very dangerous rocks,' Joe told them when they were out of the water and getting dressed. 'There used to be warships moored up in the river. Times are more peaceful now and very soon there'll be the regattas. You'll enjoy them, Master Stephen, won't he, Tamsyn?'

'You will, Stephen,' Tamsyn agreed. 'You'll be able to watch Joe row. He wins nearly all the races.'

Stephen ignored Tamsyn and flopped down beside Joe. 'Will you teach me how to row?'

'If I've got the time. You could always ask one of the other men in the creek, they're all good boatmen.'

'I might do that,' Stephen said haughtily. But he really wanted Joe to teach him. He asked the groom what every boy asked every man. 'What did you do during the war, Joe?'

'I went to fight with Captain Trevallion. We were at Passchendaele. In fact we weren't that far from your uncle.'

'Were you really brave?'

'I don't think so. I just did my duty like every other man.'

Stephen was very serious. 'What happened to Captain Trevallion? Was he blown up?'

'The Captain's injuries were caused by a mine exploding next to him,' Joe said grimly. 'He suffered very much.'

'My father was an ace pilot before he was shot down,' Stephen said sadly and proudly. 'Uncle Alex was blown up during the war. He didn't get hurt much but he came back a real misery. I hate him!'

Tamsyn sucked in her breath and looked at Joe, expecting him to tell the boy off. Stephen looked angry and sulky but Joe could see he was also very sad.

''Tis best not to say things like that, Master Stephen. Major Fiennes lost all his men during the war. He told me about it. It's affected him very badly. I'm sure he doesn't mean to be miserable.'

'He doesn't even speak to me,' Stephen said, his voice dropping. 'He found an old map in the study of the big house and all he wants to do is lock himself away down there and look at the silly thing!'

'Well, some men are uncomfortable with children, they can't get used to them. Go on trying to talk to him, take an interest in the estate, give him a chance to come round. But, if you like, I'll take you out on the river, you and Tamsyn together, mind. Becca will lend us her boat.'

Stephen seemed satisfied with this, but persisted, 'You will teach me how to row?'

'I'll see.' Joe left it at that. He dug in a pocket and took out a bag of humbugs and offered them to the children. He thought he might have done some good in suggesting Stephen take an interest in the estate, but he had not missed the wistfulness in the boy's voice.

–

Rebecca had gone to Truro again with Abigail that morning but had the afternoon off to tidy up Allen Cottage, see to her father's laundry and cook him a meal. She didn't change her clothes before she left the gatehouse but carried her old ones down to the creek with her. After putting the washing in to soak she went outside and looked about to find Joe. She wanted him to see her all dressed up.

She found him further along the creek, helping Jossy Jenkins and some other men to wash down and spruce up the *Lady Harriet*. Joe waved to her and shouted 'Hello' and then ignored her as he got on with his work. Rebecca went back home, feeling dejected.

Her father was there, rooting about in a box of odds and ends he kept in the bottom of the cupboard under the stairs.

'Hello, Dad,' she said to his crouched-over figure. 'What are you looking for?'

'A tiny little spanner, no bigger than a woman's nail file. Seen it lying about, have 'ee? I've given the Spyker a thorough overhaul now I've had her out a bit and there's a difficult nut underneath her chassis.'

Rebecca looked in the usual places for small items of lost property. On the mantelpiece, in the drawer of the kitchen table, in an old tea caddy on the windowsill by the sink.

'No luck?' Trease said from behind her.

'Sorry,' she said, turning round.

'What the hell!'

'What's the matter?' Rebecca cried as her father lunged at her.

'What's that you've got on your face?'

'It's just a bit of make-up, a little powder and a smear of lipstick, that's all.'

'That's all! Made up like a tart and you say that's all? Just what are you trying to do to impress Major Fiennes into staying on here? Dress up like a tart and give him what every man wants?' Trease was shaking with rage. He pushed Rebecca until her back was against a wall and stood close in front of her.

'It's only a little bit of make-up, Dad,' she appealed to him. 'For goodness sake, calm down. Mrs Fiennes gave me some cosmetics and I'm simply trying them out.'

'That women's a whore, she's got it written all over her face. Course she would give you powder and paint. She wants to turn you into what she is and you, my daughter, are willing to let her. What will the other women in the creek think? They don't plaster muck on their faces.'

Trease's hand shot out and grasped Rebecca by the throat. 'You're turning out like your mother! Doing yourself up in fine clothes and making eyes at any man who comes along!'

'Dad, stop it!' Rebecca cried out fearfully. 'Let me go, you're hurting me.'

'Hurting you? I haven't started yet.'

Trease drew back his hand and smacked Rebecca heavily across the face. She screamed and he dragged her across to the kitchen sink where his clothes were soaking and dashing his hand into the soapy water he splashed some over Rebecca's face. She screamed and struggled but her father wouldn't stop, shouting obscenities at her, rubbing the water into her face, hurting her. Soap got into her eyes, she breathed it in through her nose, she tasted it on her tongue, she choked and gagged and tried to catch her breath.

She was dragged away from the sink and Trease grabbed a towel and thrust it against her face. 'I'll rub this paint off you!' he shouted wildly. 'I'll have no whore under my roof. You either change your ways or out you go like that bitch, your mother!'

Rebecca pleaded with him to stop but Trease started to tear the clothes off her body. 'You'll wear your own clothes from now on or I'll take my belt to you!'

Trease was suddenly yanked away from Rebecca and she pulled the tatters of her dress up to cover herself. Shaking and crying, she watched Joe manhandle her father outside the cottage. Jenny Jenkins came in and put her ample arms round her. Rebecca clung to her while Trease and Joe shouted at each other outside.

'What happened, my dear?' Jenny said gently, smoothing Rebecca's hair away from her face and holding her close. 'We could hear you screaming and your father shouting at you all round the creek.'

'He… he just went mad… because I put some lipstick on.' She buried her face against Jenny's shoulder, sobbing. 'He said I'm like my mother.'

'Never mind, child. You're safe now.' Jenny reached for a cardigan hanging on a chair and put it round Rebecca's shoulders. She had seen the bruises and scratches on Rebecca's face and body and was furious.

The shouting outside went on and Rebecca pushed herself away from Jenny. 'What are they doing out there? Why don't they stop?'

The other women from the creek came into Allen Cottage and stared in disbelief at what they saw.

'You stay here with us, Becca,' Lilian Grubb said soothingly. 'Let the men slog it out between them.'

'You mean they're fighting?' Rebecca wailed. 'Joe and my father are fighting?'

'It's been coming for years,' Ira Jenkins said, making for the chair where Rebecca had put her old clothes. 'Joe will teach your father he can't treat you like this. Come and put your own clothes on.'

Rebecca heard her father howling in pain and, despite the women's attempts to stop her, she went hurtling out of the cottage. Trease was getting to his feet and Joe was about to thump him again.

'Stop it!' Rebecca shouted at them, but to no avail. Years of dislike and brooding feelings had overflowed into hatred and no one was going to stop them now.

The men watching gasped at the sight of Rebecca, battered and bruised, in ripped clothes.

'Beat the lights out of un, Joe,' Jossy Jenkins shouted. The respect he had for Rebecca and the years of disapproval he'd felt at her father's treatment of her made him, like the other men, want the outcome of the fight to be in Joe Carlyon's favour.

'Stop them!' But Rebecca's appeals fell on equally deaf ears.

She saw the Major coming down the hill and ran as fast as she could to him.

Alex was shocked by her appearance. He caught her arms and tried to get her to calm down. 'What's going on? I came down to see what the shouting was all about. Who did this to you, Becca?'

'You've got to stop them, Major,' she cried, trying to wrench herself away from him. 'Tell them to stop, they'll listen to you.'

Alex looked into her anguished eyes and said clearly, 'Who hurt you, Becca? Who did this to you? Your father?'

Tears trickled afresh down over her face. She nodded wildly and tried to force Alex towards the lighting men. He pulled the cardigan round her to cover her bare skin and held her against him, tightly, so she couldn't move.

'It's better to let them fight it out,' he said grimly over her head, looking hard at Trease. There was no doubt who he wanted to win.

Rebecca managed to turn in his arms but he kept his hold on her and she watched in horror as Joe and Trease hammered their fists into each other. There was blood on their faces and hands, their shirts were torn, their clothes dirty from contact with the ground. Trease took a blow in the stomach and exhaled a loud breath, badly winded. 'Please, do something,' Rebecca whimpered.

'Stopping them now wouldn't serve any purpose,' Alex said quietly. He shook his head at the women who were motioning to him to let Rebecca come to them. He knew she would run straight into the fight and probably get hurt again.

The fight ended when Trease was laid out, semi-conscious, on the ground and Joe stood over him, panting, his fists curled ready to start again if need be.

Rebecca gulped back a sob. It was ironic that the man she had put the make-up on for had been the one to beat her father for being cruel to her over it.

Alex relaxed his grip and held her gently. Joe came to her.

'I'm sorry, Becca. It had to be done.'

She swiped his hand away, the one he was going to put on her shoulder in a comforting gesture. 'Why did you have to beat him like that? Because the rest of you decided it was right? It wasn't what I wanted. None of you cared about what I wanted.'

'Dear God,' a soft voice breathed from behind the gathering. 'Rebecca, my dear, what's happened to you? Alex, what's going on?'

'Let me go,' Rebecca hissed at Alex and when he did she turned and faced him angrily. 'You could have stopped the fight. Why didn't you? Is it because you like fighting, to see men at war? That was all over years ago and it's time you learnt it. I don't care what you do with the creek or with Trevallion. I'm sick of worrying about it all.'

She ran straight to Abigail who, after giving the others a cold hard stare, led her away.

'What was that all about?' Abigail asked gently as she bathed Rebecca's scratches and bruises. She'd helped Rebecca out of the ripped clothes, into her nightdress and into her bed in the gatehouse. Loveday had been ordered to bring hot sweet tea and Rebecca stared into the steaming cup.

'I'll tell you one thing, Mrs Fiennes,' she said bitterly, the attack by her father, the fight, her failed appeal to Alex to stop it and Joe ignoring her milling feverishly round in her brain. 'I think I could quite easily leave Kennick Creek and never come back.'

Chapter 13

Miles Trevallion stood at the end of Alex's bed, the glow from the moon behind him making him stand out eerily in the darkness. Alex stared at him, closed his eyes, opened them again and found his second cousin was still there looking at him from huge, dark pain-filled eyes.

'Miles,' Alex whispered, 'what are you doing here?'

'I don't want you to have Trevallion.' Miles Trevallion's voice echoed like the boom from a cannon through the dead of night.

'But the others you mentioned in your will all died too, in the war, none of them came back. I'm your next of kin, that's how the property came to me.'

'I want the people of the creek to have Trevallion, not you,' Miles said accusingly. He came closer, up to the top of the bed where Alex was sitting in just his pyjama bottoms, his body rigid with his knees drawn up.

'You can walk,' Alex gasped, having just realised that Miles had his two legs. 'You can talk,' he added, seeing that Miles could hold his head upright, that there was no drooping mouth constantly open and dribbling, no rolling of unfocused eyes, that Miles was perfectly sensible.

Miles's eyes burned into his. 'I brought my men back home, I want them to have the creek, Trevallion, the whole estate. It's not yours, Alex. It doesn't belong to you. It never will.'

'I haven't made any plans for the estate, Miles,' Alex said meekly, wiping at the sweat on his brow. 'I only came down here to settle your affairs, to see what can be done for the best.'

Miles pointed a finger. 'You didn't bring your men back with you, Alex.'

'I didn't want them to die, Miles,' Alex protested. 'I had to follow orders. I wanted to die with them. I didn't want to come back alone. I didn't, I swear.'

Miles stabbed his finger in Alex's chest. It hurt, it burned. 'You should have brought them home. I did. I brought mine home.'

The finger was lifted and pushed into Alex's forehead. It drove a hole between his eyes, hot and burning, boring into his skull.

'No! No! I didn't want to leave them!'

Arms were put round him and Alex fought them off, wildly, madly. Someone cried out. There was a voice different to Miles's and he came to with a jolt.

'Major, please, you're hurting me.'

'What? Who is it? Oh, Becca, is that you?'

'Let him go, Rebecca,' came Abigail's scathing voice. 'He's had a nightmare, that's all. Go back to bed.'

Alex clung to the warm body close to his, soft and smooth in flimsy clothes. In mortal fear he held on to his source of comfort. The lantern was lit and he hid his face in the softness, the gentle contours, his eyes unable to stand the light. A soothing hand stroked his hair.

'Don't leave me,' Alex moaned into the silky dressing gown.

Abigail put the lantern down and roughly pulled Alex's head away from Rebecca's body. 'Oh, just look at him. He's been at the drink again and woken up the whole household. I'll go and tell Stephen not to worry, although he's quite used to his uncle disgracing himself in this way. I've got a beastly headache now, thanks to him. Are you coming, Rebecca?'

Alex held her tighter and whispered, 'Please stay.'

Rebecca could tell he hadn't been drinking and she could feel his fear as he clung to her. She shook her head at Abigail.

'Please yourself, but I think it's pathetic. When I've looked in on Stephen I'm going to take a sleeping pill. You can stay up all night with him for all I care.'

Abigail swept out of the room, closing the door behind her with a bang.

Alex stayed as he was, his legs on the bed, his upper body twined round Rebecca's. She reached past him and opened the top drawer of a chest of drawers, took out a handkerchief and wiped the sweat from his neck and the side of his face. When his breathing had become regular and the fear had almost gone, he raised himself and looked at Rebecca in the lantern light.

'That's the second time you've come to my rescue. I'm grateful, Becca.'

Rebecca's dressing gown, one given to her by Abigail to sit up in bed in after her ordeal with her father that afternoon, was damp where his head had pressed into it. It was a hot night but she felt cold and shivered.

'Were you dreaming?' she asked tightly. She hadn't forgiven him yet for not stopping the fight between Joe and her father.

Alex took the handkerchief and wiped his neck and face. 'Yes. It was about Miles Trevallion. He was standing there.' He pointed to the end of the bed. 'He came to me and bored a hole right through my head. I could feel my brains spilling out over the bed.'

Rebecca shuddered, more at the distress in his voice than because she was feeling cold. She couldn't go on feeling hard-hearted towards him. 'That must have been terrible for you.'

'You're cold…' Alex lifted the top bedcover. 'Here, wrap this round you. Stay and talk to me for a while. I'm sorry to ask but I don't want to be alone. Please, Becca, Abigail won't know, she sleeps heavily for hours when she takes those pills.'

Rebecca looked at him closely. She'd been about to return to her own room. It wouldn't be prudent to stay here alone with the Major but Mrs Fiennes would soon be asleep and he wasn't in a fit state to be amorous; if he did try anything, he'd get the lantern across his head. Rebecca decided it was a small risk to take, and at that moment she also needed someone to talk to and keep her mind off her worries. Abigail had been very kind after the fight, but she had used the opportunity to berate men in general and talk about some of her own disastrous love affairs. She had been oblivious of Rebecca's need to be alone, she didn't realise that Rebecca would sit up all night reliving the shame and humiliation her father had subjected her to, to wonder what to say to him when she saw him next, to worry that he would go on a drinking binge.

Rebecca wrapped the bedcover round her shoulders and sat on the end of Alex's small single bed.

'Sometimes I think I'll go mad,' Alex whispered. 'I'm sorry about today, sorry I upset you. I should have stopped the fight for your sake.'

'I'm sorry about what I said to you,' she whispered back. 'I didn't mean it. I was just lashing out.'

'People say a lot of things they don't mean in the heat of the moment. I wonder what Miles meant, why he said—'

'It was just a dream,' Rebecca gently reminded him.

Alex carried on talking as if he hadn't heard her, as if Miles Trevallion was actually alive with all his limbs and faculties and had spoken in accusation against him 'He said he didn't want me to have Trevallion. That he'd brought his men home and he wanted them to have it. He must have meant Joe Carlyon and your father. He said I should have brought my men home too.' Alex's eyes filled with tears and Rebecca moved closer and reached out to him. He pulled her to him and she was holding him again. 'I wanted to bring them home, and not just two of them, all of them, Georgie Gilbert, Jimmy Clark, and Cyril Dawkins and the others. So many times I've wished I'd died with them. Oh God, Becca, what am I going to do?'

He gripped a handful of her hair and wept. Rebecca cried too, silently. She cried for those who had died in the war, for the pain of those who'd come back, of the once proud and happy man who had beaten her in a rage as if he hated her, for her loneliness and uncertain future. And she cried for the man she held in her arms, who had no hopes or dreams, only shame, guilt and despair, and who didn't want to live at all.

'Are you all right?' Alex said softly when their tears were spent and dried.

'Yes, are you?'

'I feel better now, thanks to you.'

Rebecca let him go and shifted herself so they were sitting closely side by side.

'What sort of man was Georgie Gilbert?' she asked. 'Was he the one you named the Kellow baby after?'

She looked at his face and found he was softly smiling. 'Georgie was a human tank. A very big man with a big sense of humour, rather naughty humour at times. I wouldn't like you to have heard the sort of things he used to say, but then it wasn't meant for a woman's ears. If there was a wall in front of him and he couldn't go round it, he'd walk right through it. He loved life in the regiment and would have fought to the last drop of blood to save the lives of the rest of us. I'd promised him a job at the end of the war or when he chose to leave the army. I wanted to have him near me. I miss him badly.'

'He sounds like a loyal friend.'

'He was,' Alex said.

'And I'm sure all the others were too.'

'Yes.'

'You asked me what you could do, Major. You could stop mourning the death of your men and do something positive, something worthwhile to make them proud of you. They wouldn't like to see you like this, would they?'

'No, I suppose not. Call me Alex, seems silly to be calling me Major. You're my friend, Becca.'

'Very well, I'll call you Alex, but there's no "I suppose not" about it. Georgie Gilbert used to walk through walls, remember. He wouldn't have allowed anything to flatten him.'

'I take your point,' Alex said huskily. 'Got any more suggestions?'

'Yes, you could get on with sorting out Captain Miles's affairs and decide what to do with the estate. There's a lot of people on tenterhooks wondering about their future.'

'You included?' He gently touched the ugly bruise left on her cheek by her father's hand. 'You didn't mean what you said about wanting to leave and never coming back, did you, Becca? Abigail was very angry on your behalf and told me what you'd said. She said she'd never forgive me if she lost you because of something I did, or rather didn't do.'

Rebecca was quiet for a moment, then she said, 'I don't know how I feel right now. I'm all numb inside. Let's not talk about me. I'll sort myself out. It's you I'm more concerned about. You said that Captain

Trevallion accused you of not bringing your men back with you. It sounded as though in your dream he was horrible to you, but you got on well with him, didn't you?'

'Always. We went to university together and kept in touch. Then after he was brought back from France and put in the home in Truro I came down to visit him at least three times a year. I was there when he died.'

'That proves that whatever you think happened was just a nightmare. Captain Miles wasn't horrible to anyone that I know of.'

Alex gave a tiny laugh. 'You're such a comfort to me, Becca... I first saw you at Miles's funeral. You're easy to remember with your beautiful long black hair.'

'I don't remember seeing you there,' Rebecca said, looking at him closely in the lamplight. 'Or Mrs Fiennes.'

'Abigail refused to go and I kept a low profile.'

'Hidden by a big hat probably.'

'Probably,' he laughed softly. He hugged her to him. 'I always feel so much better when you're around.'

'I'll have to go,' Rebecca said, crushed against his chest.

'No, don't do that. Turn out the lantern and let's go to sleep... you can trust me.'

'Major! Alex... How can you make such a suggestion? As it is I don't know how I've had the nerve to stay here for so long.' Rebecca was halfway off the bed but stopped when Alex gave an anguished groan.

'Please, Becca,' he begged. 'I swear I won't try to do anything. I just need you to be here.'

She wavered between her outrage, although this was mostly for show because she did trust Alex Fiennes to keep his word, and the note of despair in his voice.

'I'm sorry. I have no right to put you into such an impossible situation,' he said in a small haunted tone and the sincerity in the apology made her decide to stay with him.

'All right, I'll stay a bit longer but I'll have to go long before daylight. If Loveday were to see me coming out of your room in this dressing gown she'd be rightly shocked.'

They lay down, side by side, with the top bedcover over them. It was strange to Rebecca, being this close to a man. She'd imagined the only man she'd ever lie with in bed would be her future husband. But after today's scene she felt her interest in Joe Carlyon waning.

–

Rebecca woke at dawn. Alex's arms were about her and she was embarrassed that she had fallen asleep in the warmth of being close to him and had stayed so long. She pushed his arms away from her and slid off the bed.

'Did you sleep well?' he whispered.

She was horrified he was awake. She didn't look at him but edged towards the door. 'Y-yes. Did you?' Last night it had been dark, with only the lantern light to show her in her flimsy nightclothes. She hoped he wasn't looking at her.

'Not really but at least I had no more horrible dreams.'

'That's good. I really must go, before Loveday arrives. Good morning, Major.'

'Becca,' he said her name firmly and she hoped he wasn't trying to detain her.

'Yes?'

'It's Alex, remember.'

'Alex then,' she said, reaching for the door handle. 'But only when no one else is about.' She didn't want to provoke any gossip in the creek.

Chapter 14

Joe popped his head round the kitchen door and was met fully with Loveday's disapproval.

'Rebecca's not here,' she said tartly as she stoked up the range fire. 'I daresay she'll be here any moment to help me with the breakfasts. Come to say sorry, have you? I should think so too. Trease was cruel to Becca yesterday but there was no need for you to go fighting like that with him. That only upset the poor girl more.'

'If you'll only let me get a word in edgeways, Loveday, yes, I have come to tell her I'm sorry,' Joe said, creasing up his face as he stood about uncomfortably. 'I feel terrible about what happened yesterday. She'd been down to the shore to wave to us men a few moments before Trease attacked her and she looked so happy then.'

'Poor maid.' Loveday heaped tea into the teapot. 'She was only trying to please Mrs Fiennes. Mrs Fiennes would be offended if she didn't make the effort to dress herself up a bit and wear the clothes she's been giving her. After all, Rebecca's not just a farm girl now. She has a bit of a position and both the Major and Mrs Fiennes seem to like her. We ought to remember that. They won't be so keen to stay on here if they think the Kennickers beat their womenfolk and two of their employees are always ready to fight. All our futures are riding on what the Major decides to do with the estate. Trease ought to remember that, and you, Joe.'

'Don't worry, Loveday. I won't let anything like that happen again. How much longer do you think Becca's going to be?'

'I told you, any moment now,' Loveday said a little impatiently. 'But I think it's better if you wait outside and let me tell her you want to speak to her.'

Loveday was looking down over her nose at him and Joe knew he had no option but to retreat from her domain.

A short time later Rebecca appeared in the kitchen wearing her own clothes.

'Ah, Becca. Joe's waiting outside to have a word with you,' Loveday told her, smiling kindly.

'I'm too busy,' Rebecca said, tying an apron round her waist.

'Oh, don't be like that. He's most anxious to see you. I've already given him a piece of my mind and he feels terrible about yesterday.'

'I can't, Loveday. Not yet, you tell him that.'

Loveday could see Rebecca meant what she said. She patted her arm. 'I understand how you must be feeling. That fight yesterday was absolutely disgusting and so was your father's behaviour towards you before it. The creek folk were really worried about what the Major would think but he took it well. He's a strange man in some ways. Oh, well, no good standing about like this. I'd better get on with the breakfasts. I'll nip outside and tell Joe you don't want to see him right now.'

When she came back, Loveday asked Rebecca conversationally, 'Did you hear the rain last night?'

'Rain?' Rebecca frowned, going to the larder to fetch the marmalade and sugar bowl.

'Didn't you hear it? Goodness me. You must have slept well.'

Rebecca kept her face inside the larder, glad that Loveday hadn't arrived early this morning.

Tamsyn trotted into the kitchen. 'Captain Redbeard wants to know when his breakfast is going to be ready. It's too wet to play down in the creek and he wants to build a new track for the railway.'

'Tell Master Stephen in about fifteen minutes,' Loveday said, smiling as she cut the rind off rashers of bacon.

Tamsyn ignored Rebecca, giving her an odd look before running off.

'I'll have to speak to that little madam,' Loveday said crossly. 'I'm not having her taking on Master Stephen's ways.'

'Leave it be,' Rebecca said quickly.

Rebecca's worry that Stephen knew she had spent the night in his uncle's bed and had told Tamsyn was horribly realised when the boy came up to her in the kitchen after breakfast and said loudly, 'Did you enjoy sleeping with Uncle Alex last night?'

Rebecca was getting a tray ready for Abigail and nearly dropped a cup and saucer but it was Loveday who exclaimed shrilly, 'Master Stephen! I'll thank you not to speak to Rebecca like that. How dare you say such a thing? I'll tell your mother and I'm sure she'll punish you for it.'

Stephen made a smarmy face and pointed a finger at Rebecca who stood with her face burning. 'She was in my uncle's room last night. She can't deny it.'

Her eyes agog, Loveday switched her attention. 'Rebecca?'

'Master Stephen's right. I was in Major Fiennes' room last night and so was Mrs Fiennes. The Major had a terrible nightmare and we both went in to him. That's all there was to it.'

'You see, Master Stephen,' Loveday wagged a finger at him sternly. 'You mustn't jump to conclusions. You must apologise to Rebecca at once.'

Stephen went over to Rebecca. She put the cup and saucer down on the tray, shakily. She looked him straight in the face and he could see she was furious.

'I'm sorry,' the boy said, with an unrepentant grin on his face. 'It was beastly of me to think—'

'Yes, it was,' Rebecca said coldly, hating every inch of his fair face.

'That's that then,' Loveday said, making to leave the kitchen. 'The Major's back from his ride. I'll make sure the table's laid up for him.'

When she'd gone, Stephen grinned wickedly at Rebecca and took a hairgrip from his pocket and held it up in front of her eyes. 'As soon as Uncle Alex had gone riding I went to his room. I found this in his bed. My mother has short hair and anyway she would never use anything so plain and ugly.'

Rebecca snatched the hairgrip out of his hand. 'It must have fallen out of my hair when I shook your uncle to wake him. Why are you trying to make trouble for me?'

'Only teasing,' the boy said. 'I knew you wouldn't do anything wrong with Uncle Alex, he's quite dead where women are concerned.'

Rebecca clenched her hands, they were itching to smack his face. 'You shouldn't say things like that, Stephen Fiennes.'

He was pleased with the reaction he'd got. He laughed. 'I'm going to keep an eye on you.'

Loveday came back and Stephen swept past out of the room, grinning broadly.

'Are you all right, Becca? You look quite shaken,' Loveday said.

'How old is that boy?' Rebecca demanded.

'About thirteen. Why?'

'Well, he's a bit too grown-up in some of his ways,' Rebecca said, banging things on the tea tray.

'These rich folk have got no manners and a lot of them haven't got any morals either.' Loveday dropped her voice. 'I don't like to say it but the boy's mother seems a bit... well, you know what I mean.'

'The Major's not like that,' Rebecca said emphatically. 'He's a man of honour.' And who knew that better than she.

Abigail was sleeping when Rebecca entered her room with the breakfast tray. She woke up grumpily, sipped a cup of tea, refused to eat anything, complained of having a headache and ordered Rebecca to Stephen's room to tell the children not to play so noisily. Rebecca did so and Stephen swore at her.

'Captain Redbeard!' Tamsyn exclaimed, clamping a hand over his mouth. 'You shouldn't use that word.'

'I'll say exactly what I like,' Stephen scowled, thrusting Tamsyn's hand away. He turned his back to Rebecca and continued to lay railway track against the skirting board under the window on the wooden floor.

'Oh no you won't, young man,' Rebecca uttered with quiet deliberation. She stalked through the railway and caught the boy by the shoulders. 'I will not be spoken to like that by anyone, particularly a tiresome little boy. Do you understand?'

Stephen struggled and the track was sent scattering. Then he held his body stiffly, set his mouth in a hard twisted line and stared into

Rebecca's eyes. At his boarding school he could outstare anyone. It made him feel superior. He had even reduced other boys to tears doing it. He would show this menial her place.

'Say you're sorry, Stephen,' Tamsyn shouted, jumping about.

Rebecca did not waver under the boy's contempt. He was tall for his age and she sensed he was strong, but she would not let him get the better of her. She wondered how long she would have to stay like this before he lowered his eyes when a harsh voice broke the spell.

'You had better apologise to Miss Allen this instant, Stephen, or I shall see to it that you are punished severely.' It was Alex. He stood in the doorway, the look in his gaunt dark eyes a lot more unnerving than the boy's.

Rebecca kept her eyes on Stephen and was satisfied to see him look guilty. He looked down and she took her hands from his shoulders. Stephen swung round to face his uncle and put on a contrite face.

'I'm sorry, Uncle Alex. I'm afraid I forgot to be a gentleman and I swore in front of Miss Allen and Tamsyn.'

Rebecca moved over to Alex. She might be a servant in this house but she was not going to be treated like some worthless lackey. She wasn't surprised to see a look of blatant spite on the boy's face.

'Do forgive me, Miss Allen,' he said sickeningly sweetly, and with practised ease. Then he repeated it to Tamsyn. 'I'm really very sorry.'

Tamsyn tittered but Rebecca couldn't trust herself to speak.

Alex cautioned his nephew. 'You'd better not let me hear you be rude to anyone again while we're here.' He gave Rebecca a brief smile. 'I'm off to the coast at Perranporth. The weather should clear up in an hour or so and I'm going to look over the property I found on the old map.' He motioned her outside the room. 'Your father will be bringing up the car for me. It might be a good time for you to speak to him.'

Before Rebecca could reply, Stephen pushed his head round the door and asked meekly, 'Can I come with you, Uncle Alex, to the coast? Please say I can. I promise to be good.'

Alex was taken aback. He hesitated and found Tamsyn looking up at him round Stephen's body, her face shining and hopeful.

'I've been stuck on the estate ever since we arrived here,' Stephen pleaded.

Alex looked at Rebecca for help but she was too absorbed in thinking about Trease and what she would say to him.

'Well, I, um, don't know,' he said helplessly.

At that point Abigail charged out of her room in her negligée with a hand over her brow. 'For goodness sake, Alex, take the boy with you! It won't hurt you for once. All this noise! I can't stand it. Really, Rebecca, you know I've got a bad headache and yet you allow the children to go on making a terrible racket.'

'I'm sorry, Mrs Fiennes,' Rebecca said, taking Tamsyn's arm and pointing the child towards the stairs.

'But I want to go to the coast with Master Stephen. I've never been to Perranporth before,' the little girl wailed, pouting her disappointment.

'Yes, I want her to go too,' Stephen said softly, surprising Rebecca.

'But I want to explore an old mine works and a dilapidated house. I can hardly do that with two children round my neck,' Alex protested. 'And I don't know anything about children.'

'Then take Rebecca with you!' Abigail snapped. 'Just get out of the house, all of you. Mrs Wright can look after me, not that I shall need her. All I want to do is sleep!' She moaned and held her hand to her head. She really did look in pain, Rebecca thought.

'Will you come?' Alex asked Rebecca, glancing at his furious sister-in-law and the hopeful children uncertainly.

'Gladly, Major,' she replied, a little acidly. She would be grateful to get away from the estate and some of the people on it today.

'Thank goodness that's decided,' Abigail said impatiently and flounced back into her room.

As they walked side by side down the stairs, Rebecca noticed Alex rubbing his bandaged hand. She wrinkled her nose. 'You ought to put a clean bandage on that. It smells terrible.'

'Yes, ma'am,' he grinned. He looked at his bandaged hand. 'You haven't mentioned it before. Abigail has and Mrs Wright. The district nurse was mortified because I refused to let her look at it.'

'The way I see it is you're a grown man, quite able to attend to things like that yourself. Anyway,' she added sadly, 'I learned long ago not to make a fuss with my father.'

'I'm sure he is very sorry about what he did to you yesterday, Becca. Deep down he loves you, I'm sure.'

'He was all right until the war. He came back so bitter. I don't think he's ever accepted that my mother left us. He used to be handsome and proud. I loved him so much when I was a little girl.'

'Every man came back different from the war,' Alex said quietly. 'Your father was angry because you've been wearing the things Abigail has been giving you. They're not for you and you don't need make-up to make yourself beautiful. I'm going to give you some money to buy new clothes for yourself, things more in keeping with the way you are.' When she tried to protest, he added firmly, 'You've done years of unpaid work on the estate. You've earned it.'

They were at the bottom of the stairs. Before someone could come and see them enjoying their new friendship, she said, 'Thank you, Major,' and headed for the kitchen.

In double-quick time Rebecca and Loveday packed a picnic hamper and carried it between them out to the Spyker, which Stephen and Tamsyn were already sitting in, Stephen in the front, Tamsyn in the back as befitted her status as Captain Redbeard's sidekick. Trease was standing sheepishly at the rear of the car, his face cut and bruised from the beating Joe had given him and his complexion blotchy from a night's drinking. He took the hamper from the two women and lashed it to the running board. Loveday gave him a full disapproving look with her nose tilted high. Then she kissed Tamsyn, warned her not to take off her sun bonnet and to behave herself, and went inside.

'Becca.'

'Yes, Dad,' she replied tonelessly.

'How are you?'

'I'm going with the Major and the children to the coast.'

'Aye, I know.' He looked up at the sky, gradually casting away its rainclouds and turning from grey to a pale blue. 'Be a nice day later on, do you good. Look... I... about yesterday. I don't know what came over me... I...'

Rebecca felt the hurt and shame coming over her again and Stephen was listening gleefully. 'Let's just forget it, Dad,' she said briskly. 'You won't find me wearing make-up again. I'll be down to the cottage later in the day.'

Alex joined them, waited a moment to see if they had anything more to say, then said quietly to Rebecca, 'Shall we go?'

He beat Trease to it and helped her in next to Tamsyn on the back seat.

'I'm some sorry about yesterday, sir,' Trease blurted out. 'It wasn't right for you to see such a spectacle.'

'It's not me you should be apologising to,' Alex retorted harshly. He took Trease roughly by the shoulder and hauled him out of earshot of the others. 'I abhor a man taking his fist to a woman, and let me tell you this, Trease Allen, if you ever lay a finger on Rebecca again I'll beat the living daylights out of you myself!'

Trease blinked at the Major's passion. 'Y-yes, sir. I can't tell you how bitterly I regret what I did. I swear it will never happen again.'

'It had better not. How could you believe for a moment Rebecca's that sort of woman?'

'I know, sir. I'm ashamed. Becca will never be like her mother. She's a good girl and has always looked after me.'

'And always done your damned work. Well, things are going to be different in the future.' Alex let Trease go and continued in a less angry voice. 'There will be four new men starting work today. Two gardeners, a woodsman and a roadmender to take care of the drive. Later there'll also be a mason and a carpenter working in the big house. That will allow you and Carlyon to get back to your original duties. I've told Carlyon myself. I'm sure at this moment he wouldn't appreciate the news from you.'

Trease's face changed from contrition to delight. This news raised his hopes. 'Thank you, sir. I'm at my best when I'm busy round the garage.'

'Don't let me down again,' Alex warned before going to the car.

Trease gave Rebecca a big smile and waved cheerfully before heading off back to the creek. She was puzzled by this until Alex got in the driving seat and explained what he'd said about the new workmen.

'Are you ready for the off?' he asked the two children. They replied they couldn't wait to get there. 'And you?' he asked Rebecca.

'Yes, Major,' she replied rather grimly.

'I think your father really is sorry,' he said to try and lighten her mood.

Stephen twisted round in the front seat and stared at her.

She stared back stonily and he actually blushed. Then she caught sight of Joe on one of the horses, watching from a distance. She could hardly bring herself to think about Joe, the man who had fought with her father because she had been wearing powder and lipstick in the hope he would notice her at last. But you had to be a horse or a boat or a lazy stretch of river for Joe Carlyon to notice you. She didn't want to hear his apologies, not yet.

She said blandly, 'I've heard too many sorries for one day. Let's just get away from here and enjoy the day out.'

Chapter 15

A knock at the gatehouse door later in the morning revealed Mr Robert Drayton on the other side. He lifted his hat to Loveday who politely asked him inside and showed him into the sitting room.

'I'm afraid if you've called wanting to see the Major, Mr Drayton,' she said, 'he's gone out. Taken one of the cars and Master Stephen, and very kindly my little girl Tamsyn, with him. And Miss Allen, too, to supervise them. Gone to the coast he has, round Perranporth way. From what I could make out the Major's found an old map or something, has become quite excited about it by the look of him.'

'Indeed?' Mr Drayton pondered on this. 'How interesting. Have you any idea what he found concerning this map?'

'I don't know,' Loveday replied, edging towards the door. She was never inclined to gossip and felt she had disclosed too much of the Major's business already. 'I'll go and see if Mrs Fiennes will come down to see you. She's resting with a headache at the moment.'

'Oh dear, I am sorry to hear that. Please do not disturb her. I have some letters and documents I would like to leave for Major Fiennes' attention. I will leave a note for him. Perhaps I could sit at the desk and write it, if that is convenient, Mrs Wright.'

Loveday liked and respected the mild and pleasantly mannered Robert Drayton. 'Please do, Mr Drayton. If you'd like to put the correspondence on the mantelpiece next to the clock, I'll see the Major gets it the moment he comes back.'

'How kind.' Mr Drayton smiled shyly. He seemed a trifle breathless today.

'Um, I wonder… could I get you a cup of tea, Mr Drayton?'

'That would be most welcome, Mrs Wright. I have had a trying morning and came out of the office in rather a hurry.'

Mr Drayton flushed a little and pulled a chair out clumsily from the desk before seating himself Loveday noticed he wasn't quite so well turned out today. His severe dark suit needed brushing down, his collar needed more starch. She hadn't seen him before without his hat. His thin colourless hair was not quite tidy. Worry lines were evident among his naturally pale and unremarkable features, ageing him rather more than his forty-seven years. As he took writing paper from his black leather briefcase and a fountain pen from an inside coat pocket, Loveday thought he looked hungry and like most women with a mothering instinct she did not like to see it. And he had been so kind, allowing her to go on living in the creek after Stanley had been killed.

'Um, it's nearly midday,' Loveday said hesitantly. 'Could I make you a sandwich or something? It will be well past dinner time when you get back to Truro.'

Mr Drayton looked astonished and Loveday wondered if few people paid him any kindness. She knew that Mr Neville Faull denigrated his affability and had been heard to scoff at his partner in public.

'I... I... couldn't possibly put you to any trouble.'

'It's no trouble,' Loveday said firmly, straightaway leaving for the kitchen.

When she brought in a tray ten minutes later Mr Drayton was on his feet putting a bundle of letters held by a rubber band next to the clock on the mantelpiece. He managed a stronger smile than usual.

'This is very kind of you, Mrs Wright. I cannot tell you how much I appreciate it.' He blushed furiously.

Loveday did not retire as she usually would have done. 'I do hope you are quite well, Mr Drayton.'

'N-not me, Mrs Wright. It's my mother. She's been unwell of late. It's her chest. She's always been of a strong disposition but recently she developed pleurisy and pneumonia. She was very ill but thankfully is over the worst now.'

'I am sorry to hear that,' Loveday said sympathetically, laying out a meal of thinly-cut ham sandwiches and seedcake and a pot of tea on the table. 'I don't suppose you've been eating properly.' When she thought about that remark later she didn't know from where she'd got the neck to say it. But Mr Drayton had looked so forlorn and he seemed appreciative of the attention she was giving him.

'I'm afraid Mother doesn't like anyone but me tending to her. It's so worrying when I'm busy at the office or at a meeting I must attend.'

'Of course it is.' Loveday studied the items on the table. 'Let me take this back and cook something for you. It won't take long.'

'Oh no, no. I really appreciate what you've done, Mrs Wright, but I haven't time to stay long.' He smiled at her but then the harassed look returned and he struggled to regain his professional demeanour. 'I've put the correspondence on the mantel for Major Fiennes as you suggested. I would like him to see it as soon as possible. There's nothing there you need bother Mrs Fiennes with.'

'I'll leave you to eat then,' Loveday said, closing the door gently behind her.

–

When they emerged from the lanes and were on the main road heading towards Truro, Stephen, tired of craning his neck to speak to Tamsyn and wanting his next adventure to be for her ears only, asked his uncle to stop the car so he could exchange places with Rebecca. Alex smiled at Rebecca when she was sitting next to him and asked her to look at a roadmap and help him find the way to Perranporth.

'I know the way,' Rebecca said as they resumed their journey.

'You've been there before? I thought you'd spent all your life in the creek and ventured only as far as Truro.'

'I used to stay with my uncle and aunt in Truro as a child and they sometimes took me to Perranporth on Bank Holiday outings. It's beautiful, so much golden sand and tall dunes. It felt like paradise to me then.'

'I didn't know you had relatives in Truro.'

'Uncle Bert's my mother's brother and Father won't have anything to do with him.' She perused the map with a rather cheeky grin on her face. 'I've been to Falmouth and other places too, on the boats, many times.'

Alex grinned back. 'Yes, ma'am. I stand corrected.'

'Sit corrected,' Stephen corrected him and they all laughed.

The road was busy for the holiday season when they entered Perranporth via Liskey Hill, becoming quieter after they'd driven through the village and were climbing the steep, winding St George's Hill. The road levelled out and when the children turned their heads they could see the tall sand dunes towering over the beach. They exclaimed excitedly and extracted a promise that they would be allowed to go beaching afterwards and have an ice cream. Alex asked Rebecca to look at a piece of paper he handed to her. He had meticulously copied and enlarged the small stretch of coastline he was interested in, marking the spot where the mine ruins were with a big black cross.

He tapped the cross. 'That's what we've got to find.'

'Is it a treasure map, Uncle Alex?' Stephen asked loudly, wanting attention. He craned over the seat and breathed down Rebecca's neck and she leaned away from him.

'Not the kind you mean,' Alex answered. 'It's between here and Cligga Head.'

'It's not far,' Rebecca said. 'There's a cottage up ahead. We could stop and ask there.'

Stephen loudly and rudely declared that to ask for directions would spoil the adventure of it.

Alex ignored him and pulled the car up outside the wayside cottage. He and Rebecca got out and walked to the garden wall. An old man tending his garden straightened up and came to lean over the wall.

'Fine lookin' car you got there,' he said in a thick accent that Alex could barely understand.

'We're looking for some old mine workings.' Alex showed him his home-made map. 'Do you happen to know if we're close to it, please?'

'Aye, you're nigh on top of it,' the local said, nodding his head sagely over the map and smiling to reveal toothless gums. 'Just go a bit further on, round the next bend and —'

'And you'll see an old gate hanging off its hinges,' butted in the old man's wife who had come out of the cottage to join them. ''Tis there you'll find the beginning of an old track.'

''Tis rough and overgrown. You won't be able to take your nice car down there,' her husband said.

'Just keep going and you'll come to a little headland and there's some bits left of old buildings and the beginnings of the chimbley. 'Tisn't much but you can't miss it. I used to play there as a child,' the wife said.

''Tis awful dangerous, you'll have to be careful. If you fall down the shaft you won't stop for hundreds of feet,' the husband warned.

'Thanks for your help,' Alex said, holding out his hand and smiling. Rebecca knew he had understood only half of what the old couple had said.

The old man shook his hand with a toothless grin. 'Dick Penhallow and this is my wife Nora. Call in any time you're passin'.'

'Thank you. I'm Alexander Fiennes.'

Dick Penhallow had been staring at him. 'Not local then?'

'No,' Alex admitted, feeling somewhat guilty. He knew a lot of Cornish folk were possessive about their county and didn't like foreigners owning parts of it.

Before Alex could say anything else, Nora Penhallow said warmly, 'What a lovely family you have, Mr Fiennes. Pretty children and a lovely wife.'

Alex's jaw dropped but he decided it would take too long to explain their true relationship. 'Well, thank you very much,' he said rapidly and bustled Rebecca back to the car.

'What did they say?' Stephen demanded.

'I'm not sure,' Alex said drily, thinking about Nora Penhallow's assumption that Rebecca was his 'lovely wife'. She was too young to be even Tamsyn's mother. But she was certainly lovely.

They stopped beside the broken gate Nora Penhallow had spoken of and the children piled out. Alex took the hamper off the running board and shouted after them to go no further than a few paces in front where they could be seen clearly. Rebecca took off her hat and tossed it on the seat. She hated anything on her head and scowled at it sitting there.

'The sun's hot,' Alex cautioned.

'It's how I like it,' she returned breezily. 'Shall I help you carry the hamper?'

'I've not had that much soft living,' he said with an element of hurt male pride.

She made a face at him and they strode off after the children through the thick overgrowth of long stringy grass, heather and brambles. They followed a tall manmade hedge where contented Fresian cows chewed the cud on the other side, then the path veered off and soon the first rubble of the long neglected mine buildings came into view, with the sea stretching out in the distance. Alex gave a gasp of excitement and Rebecca glanced at him.

'I don't want the children going anywhere near the ruins, Becca. We'll take a wide detour where you can sit and watch the sea. Will you stay there and watch them? I'm sure Tamsyn is a sensible little girl, she hasn't drowned herself in the creek. I'll tell my obnoxious little nephew he mustn't follow me and should stay in sight of you on pain of death.'

They stopped several yards back from the cliff edge, standing two hundred and fifty feet above miles and miles of roaring Atlantic Ocean, where ships of every century had foundered. The cliffs were coloured in reds, oranges, purples and blues, bearing patches of lichen and wild flowers, bird's-foot trefoil, squill, thrift; and bird life, kittiwakes, herring gulls, guillemot and fulmar. They could see Perranporth beach, two miles of fine golden sand stretching away from the Towans, exposed now all the way to Penhale Point at low water. Holidaymakers were sunbathing or swimming in the ocean, children were playing and paddling, a few dogs were running about, a scene of fun and relaxation. To the west, Cligga Head, where copper-mine works battered the landscape but gave rise to gaunt but majestic-looking engine houses, obscured the view of St Ives Bay and beyond. A little landwards rose the ancient cairn of St Agnes Beacon.

'Magnificent views,' Alex said in an awestruck voice, passing his binoculars to Rebecca. He pointed to the sea. 'Look there, you can see a basking shark.'

'There's so much to see on this coast,' she agreed.

When Stephen and Tamsyn had looked through the binoculars, Alex gave them a small radius within which they could play, the centre being the spot where Rebecca would set up the picnic things. Stephen seemed quite happy with the arrangement and as Alex backtracked to the old mine workings Rebecca sat on the blanket, feeling at peace. She watched the children playing. It was a noisy game with plenty of death threats and bloodcurdling talk drifting towards her on the keen wind but she could see they were perfectly happy.

The children had munched their sandwiches, pies and cake and were off playing again when Alex returned. He flopped down beside Rebecca and she handed him a flask cup of black bitter tea.

'I'm afraid it's a bit stewed,' she said.

He drank it down without noticing and took a sandwich from her, chewing thoughtfully without tasting it.

'What did you see?' she ventured, breaking in on his thoughts.

'There's nothing there really,' he said dreamily, leaning on an elbow and gazing at the sky. 'It's been deserted for over a hundred years, absolutely mined out. It was a poor prospect right from the start.'

'You seem to like it,' she observed.

'There's something magical about it, Becca,' he said fervently. 'It may be just an old pile of rubble but it's timeless, mystical. It's a thrill to think I own it, my own little spot of Cornwall.'

Rebecca felt her heart sinking. Did he not want the estate? He never seemed enthusiastic about it. 'You own Trevallion,' she pointed out sharply.

He looked at her. 'I know. Why say it like that?'

'You don't seem to care about it.'

He moved closer to her and pulled on the tip of a black tress of her hair. 'After what you said yesterday I began to think that you don't care that much about it.'

'I do care about it, Alex,' she said, staring back at him. 'Don't you like it?'

'Not as much as here. Don't worry, I won't do anything that will leave you out in the cold. You're my friend.'

'That's very comforting but what about the others?' She was going to say more but he looked away and seemed to have switched off, like the way he was when she'd first met him.

'The house is not far from here, just a bit further along the coast. There won't be much more left standing than the mine. I'll take a look at it another day. I mustn't forget I promised the children time to play on the beach and an ice cream. They seem to be enjoying themselves. Have you got another sandwich? The sea air makes one hungry.'

Rebecca sighed and passed him a sandwich then watched him as she nibbled on a piece of yeast cake. He might be scared and distressed when he had bad dreams and was haunted by his war memories but at other times he was in control and could turn on any mood he wanted to. Why wouldn't he say what he intended to do with the estate? She wasn't intimidated by him, however, and asked him again.

'Haven't you decided what to do with the estate yet, then?'

Alex leaned round her and helped himself to a piece of chicken pie. He was very close and looked straight into her eyes. 'No.'

It was said in such a way that she knew it was all he was prepared to say.

'That's all I wanted to know,' she muttered, her eyes blazing.

Alex laughed. 'Oh, you're lovely,' he said, sitting upright to eat.

Rebecca glanced across at the children to make sure they were still there, safe and sound. 'Don't patronise me,' she said crossly.

'Well, well, well. Don't say I've got another militant modern-day woman like Abigail on my hands.'

'What does that mean?'

'Some of you women seen to have lost the ability to know your place since the war.'

'Well, of all the…' Rebecca was astounded and outraged. 'Some of us weren't content to be humble marriage fodder before the war either, Alex Fiennes!' She swung her head round, sending her hair across his face.

'I was only teasing. Rebecca?'

She swung back, almost bumping her face on his chin. He made a funny face at her and fell on his back laughing hysterically. When he wiped the tears away she was looking down at him wryly. She shook her head. 'Just like a little boy. Now I know where Stephen gets his spoiled brat ways from.'

'But we are friends?' he said, grinning.

She smiled back. 'Yes, of course, and it's good to hear you laugh like that. And,' she pointed towards his bandaged hand, 'as your friend I demand to see that hand of yours. It smells terrible. I should think it's about ready to fall off by now.'

He held it up. 'Go ahead.'

With distaste written clearly over her face, Rebecca gingerly unpicked the knot of dirty bandage and unwound it from his hand. She was afraid of what she'd see underneath, but there were only healing scratches on his fingers and a clean piece of lint in the middle of his palm. The skin round it was clean and healthy. She looked at him questioningly and he grinned.

'I've been cleansing it in salt water every day. Did you think I'd risk getting an infection and having the formidable Nurse Maisie Uren after me?'

'But you shouldn't have kept that filthy bandage round it,' Rebecca asserted.

Alex became serious. 'When you've seen the horrific injuries I have and men lying injured in mud and filth you don't make a fuss over such a little thing. I'm glad you didn't have to see those sights.'

'Like Captain Trevallion?'

'Especially Miles.'

'I was about eleven when I last saw him. He was on leave at the time. He threw a big party for the estate on Trevallion's lawns. He was such a handsome man, and kind and caring. The women cried for a week when we heard news of his injuries. We didn't know they were so serious. We all hoped he'd recover from the head injury and come home and run Trevallion from a wheelchair. He would have had the strength and determination to do it.'

Alex looked up at the sky and said in a small voice, 'I suppose your father and I don't rate very highly to you, Becca. Neither of us have coped well.'

'Don't say that,' Rebecca told him sharply, drawing his dark eyes to hers. 'You're a man of honour, I can see that. You and my father lost so much during the war. I don't blame either of you for anything.'

'But you admire Joe more for the way he's coped?'

She frowned at the thought of Joe Carlyon. 'No, not really. Joe may not have turned to drink and he works hard, but he has a coldness about him. I think he's afraid to love, to show his emotions, unless it's something like yesterday when he found an excuse to fight my father.'

'Is that how you see it?'

'Yes.' Rebecca turned to check on the children's whereabouts again.

Alex sat up beside her. 'Do you think all men are brutes then?'

'No, of course not.' She smiled at the question.

'What then?'

'I don't know. I don't know much about them really.' She took a clean napkin from the picnic basket. 'You'd better put this round your hand.'

'Thanks.' When he'd done it he said, 'I'm going somewhere else tomorrow of interest to me. Remember those letters I pulled out from under the chest in Miles's study?'

'Yes,' she replied, full of interest. She had not told Alex that Tamsyn had found them while they were cleaning the room. She was very curious about them.

'They were signed S. B. I've done some investigating, well, pulling out old papers and things, and I kept coming across the name Susannah Bosanko.'

'Bosanko? That's the surname of Captain Miles's fiancée, Miss Harriet.'

'Yes, and Susannah Bosanko was – is, apparently – Harriet's great-aunt. I mentioned her name to Jossy Jenkins and he reckons she's still alive. She lives in Falmouth and must be about ninety years old now. She never married, and, most interesting of all, was an old flame of Roland Trevallion's.'

'Roland? The gentleman who hanged himself and haunts the house?'

'The very same. Jossy and I are going to take one of the boats to Falmouth tomorrow and I'm going to look her up.'

'I almost wish I could come with you,' Rebecca breathed, wild thoughts running through her imagination as to what the relationship between Susannah Bosanko and Roland Trevallion must have been for her to write such intimate love letters.

'You'd be welcome to come but I can't see Abigail dispensing with your services for a second day.'

Stephen and Tamsyn, who had been running about and creeping through the clifftop growth playing smugglers, were walking towards them.

'I was about to call to them,' Rebecca said. 'They look hot and tired.'

'Come on,' Alex said, putting things back in the picnic basket. 'Let's go down into Perranporth and I'll treat my "family" to an ice cream.'

Chapter 16

Abigail was strolling along the creek, trying to lift the remnants of the headache with fresh air and exercise. She kept away from the cottages, not wanting to speak to anyone. It was a quiet afternoon and she was glad that no one was about. Insects and butterflies flitted among the grasses and wild flowers, the sun was pleasantly hot. The tide had filled the creek and boats bobbed gently on the water. A shelduck was shovelling its beak horizontally into the fine surface mud of the last part of the beach left uncovered by water to extract small organisms. When it looked up it made a rasping call, as if it was chattering to someone, then went back to looking for the rest of its meal. Two elegant swans were swimming into the creek – Abigail had heard about this particular pair. They were called the Trevallion's swans and if Alex would only allow her and Stephen to have the property they would become *her* swans. She could see herself writing to old acquaintances, the few who knew nothing of her reputation, casually mentioning her swans. If only…

After a while she walked up through the woods towards the big house. She knew the doors would be unlocked because Alex had told her about the workmen. She was pleased he was having work done on the property and hoped it was because he'd decided to keep it rather than to make it a more attractive purchase to any prospective buyer. She wanted to take a long look at it, to plan changes of her own if Alex said she and Stephen could have it. Why wouldn't he tell her what he was going to do, even if it was only one stage at a time? It affected all their futures.

She frowned, the angry thoughts making her head thump. When she neared the house she could hear hammering and banging and promptly turned back, deciding to find a quiet nook by the river to sit and try to relax and make her plans with her eyes shut. She'd go to a little spot where Stephen and Tamsyn played. She had seen them there from a distance and thought she could find it.

She was successful, following the steps down through the woods, but as the trees thinned out near the water's edge she caught sight of a figure, a man, and cursed under her breath. Now she would have to try somewhere else. Tamsyn's dog was with the man and he called to it. Abigail realised it was Joe Carlyon. Now that was different. She smiled to herself. She admired his broad shoulders and muscular arms, his dark curly hair and tough tanned hands – there was more than one way to cure a headache.

'I hope I'm not disturbing you, Joe.'

With Motley racing about for sticks he was throwing, Joe had not heard her approach. 'Mrs Fiennes. Good afternoon. Out for a walk?'

Abigail massaged her brow. 'Trying to get rid of a headache actually.'

'That's a shame. A nice quiet sit-down by the river should help.'

'Yes, that's why I'm here.'

'I was just taking a short break to play with Motley. I'll leave you to it.' He called the dog to him so it wouldn't bother the lady.

'Don't let me drive you away,' Abigail purred. 'If you have the time I'd like to hear a little history of the creek. I've quite fallen in love with it.'

She sat down on the dry warm grass, stretching out her long slim legs, letting her skirt rise towards her knees, slipping her cardigan off her shoulders. She threw back her head to let the sun warm her slender throat then she turned her head slowly to look at the groom.

'Have you always lived in the creek, Joe?'

'Aye, my family goes back four generations.'

'Really? Nearly as long as the Trevallions.'

'That's right, Mrs Fiennes. But I'm the last Carlyon now.'

Abigail watched him flexing and tightening his huge hands, something he did often. 'Perhaps you should consider getting married, Joe. Have children to carry on your name.'

He shook his head. 'Never seem to have the inclination.'

'Oh, nonsense. A man like you must have had plenty of adoring females throwing themselves at his feet. You must be tempted.'

Joe looked at her pouting red mouth, the lips slightly parted with her wet pink tongue sitting provocatively on the lower lip. He knew she was flirting with him and he didn't mind one little bit. He admired her physical attributes as much as she did his. He knew what sort of woman she was, doubtless he wasn't the first servant to receive her attention in this way. 'I've not been tempted so far... and why should women throw themselves at me?'

Abigail shrugged demurely. 'You're an attractive single man. There must be some young woman who has her sights set on changing that status.'

Joe sat down facing her, making Motley sit close beside him and caressing her neck. 'There's none that I know of.'

'What about Rebecca?' Abigail said, mentioning the first young woman who came to mind, unaware that she had spoken unwittingly near the truth.

Joe laughed. 'Becca's like a niece to me and she's not interested in men anyway.'

'It's a pity there's no suitable young man, honest, ambitious, well set up for her. I'm afraid I probably upset her this morning,' Abigail said, changing tack, as she recalled the girl's angry face when she'd shouted at her outside Stephen's room. 'I was unnecessarily short with her. She hasn't had a good time of it since we arrived here.'

'She refused to speak to me this morning when I wanted to tell her I was sorry for fighting with Trease yesterday,' Joe sighed. 'Seems a lot of us have reason to say sorry to her.'

'I hope we don't drive her away from the estate.'

Joe frowned. 'What makes you say that, Mrs Fiennes?'

'Well, you've known her for so long that you probably take her for granted, perhaps you haven't noticed what a strong-minded young woman she is. She may not be content to stay here all her life. One day she might decide to spread her wings.'

Joe frowned again. 'I hope not. Couldn't imagine the creek without Becca.'

'At least she's having a day out with the Major, perhaps that will cheer her up a little.'

'Aye, hope so, but Becca's not one to bear grudges anyway.'

Abigail turned over on her side, running her hand down over her waist and hips, letting it rest on her thigh. 'You must be glad to be back doing your proper job.' She was pleased that Joe's eyes had followed her hand and rested upon it.

'I am, but it would be even better if I knew it was permanent.' He raised his eyebrows at Abigail.

'Don't ask me, Joe. I'm afraid my future lies at the whim of the Major as much as yours does, and it's no good me asking him. He's always been reluctant to tell me anything.'

'At least the Major looks better for the few days he's been here.'

'Perhaps, but he's still troubled by old memories. I was hoping...' Abigail hesitated, then she thought it wouldn't hurt to confide in Joe and tell him some half-truths about her hopes. 'I was hoping that down here he would be able to put it all behind him and make a fresh start. If Trevallion made him forget those terrible memories then he'd stay on here and Stephen and I could start a new life too. But he had another bad night last night. It was a good thing Rebecca was there. She's the only one who seems able to calm him.'

'Well, we'll have to pin our hopes on her then.'

'It looks like it.'

Joe made to go. Abigail looked disappointed. He crouched down and looked at her closely. 'I'd invite you to my cottage for a cup of tea but it would cause gossip.'

'Thank you for the thought,' she said, running her eyes over the strong hairy chest she could see inside his opened shirt, the red marks left from his fight with Trease exciting her.

'Perhaps some other time, Mrs Fiennes.'

Abigail gave him a long lingering look. 'Perhaps...'

—

Abigail watched Rebecca's serious face in the reflection of her dressing-table mirror.

'I'm terribly sorry that I shouted at you this morning, Rebecca,' Abigail said, toying with the multitude of cosmetics in front of her. 'I had such a dreadful headache, you see. The noise of the children playing was going right through me. And then I heard you and Alex raising your voices as you reprimanded Stephen followed by the silly fuss about who was and who was not going to Perranporth, well, I'm afraid I lost my temper.' Abigail pouted slightly and put on her most appealing look. 'Say you forgive me.'

'Of course I do, Mrs Fiennes,' Rebecca said, feeling embarrassed by this. She met Abigail's reflection in the mirror. 'I'm just sorry we all disturbed you.' She smiled and Abigail felt she might get some information out of her now. Rebecca could be rather formal and tight-lipped.

'You are sweet. I went for a walk down in the creek and the fresh air did wonders to clear my headache away. It was quiet and peaceful there. It got me thinking though. What do young people like you and unattached people like Joe Carlyon do for a social life living in such a quiet place as this?'

'Oh, there's lots to do,' Rebecca said, waiting patiently for her mistress to choose which fragrance she would wear tonight. 'There's church and some people sing in the choir so there's choir practice. There's the cinema in Truro, people go there occasionally. There's friends and family to visit. Soon there'll be the regattas on the river, they're really popular and that means rowing and sailing practice. There's the pub just up the river, of course. Some of the men, including Joe, go there perhaps two or three times a week.'

'Joe tells me he's the last of his family,' Abigail said, picking up a frosted glass bottle labelled *Le Fleur.* 'I can see he works very hard. Who cooks and cleans for him?'

'Loveday and I used to take turns, but apart from the occasional meals Jenny or Ira Jenkins cook for him, Joe usually does it for himself,' Rebecca replied, carefully spraying Abigail's wrists and neck with the perfume.

'Oh, he must be cross with us coming here, taking you and Mrs Wright away from him.'

'Joe doesn't mind,' Rebecca said, reflecting on how much things had changed since the Fiennes' arrival on the estate. 'He likes his own company.'

'Spray a little perfume on my back as well, it's cooling,' Abigail said. She shivered slightly as the perfume hit the skin exposed by her low-cut dress. 'The continuity of the creek will be threatened if men like Joe don't settle down and rear families in it. I suppose women flock around him, a good-looking eligible bachelor.'

Rebecca knew Abigail was watching her again and she answered with a straight face. 'Joe doesn't seem much interested in women, Mrs Fiennes.'

'That's because he hasn't met one yet who's taken his fancy,' Abigail said archly, making Rebecca frown in puzzlement.

—

'Did you have a good time on the coast?' Abigail asked Alex while they waited for Loveday and Lilian Grubb, who was helping her to serve dinner tonight, to tell them the meal was ready.

'Yes. Has your headache gone?'

'Yes, I feel much better now. A walk in the fresh air of the creek does wonders.'

Abigail helped herself to another cocktail. Alex was drinking beer. He looked particularly handsome tonight. There was more colour in his face and his dark eyes were brighter and livelier from the coastal air and the interest he'd found in his excursion. Apart from a clean shirt, he was still in his casual outdoor clothes. He hadn't put on his dinner suit since they'd arrived. He'd refused to let anyone unpack for him and it was probably still in his suitcase.

Abigail swung her long string of jet beads with her fingers and lingered by him as he lounged across an armchair going through the letters Mr Drayton had left for him. She was wearing her most provocative evening gown, a flimsy sheath in shimmering pink chiffon with shoe-string straps, cut low at the back down to her trim waist, with a scoop neckline at the front as low as she dared. A red-sequined headband dressed her sleek short hair, which she'd pushed behind her delicate ears. She wore a slave bangle above the elbow and fluttered an ostrich-feather fan. She looked elegant and beautiful, and hoped Alex would notice her efforts.

'Stephen thoroughly enjoyed himself. He was absolutely tired out and went to bed early. And little Tamsyn enjoyed herself too, Mrs Wright is terribly grateful to you for taking her out. How about Rebecca?'

'What about her?' Alex said absentmindedly, his eyes rooted to what he was reading.

'Did she enjoy the day out?' Abigail asked sweetly, determined not to get exasperated with her uncommunicative brother-in-law tonight.

'Yes.'

'Oh good, I'm so glad. I apologised to her for being short with her this morning. She was so sweet about it. I hope she has a good evening with that awful father of hers.'

Alex did not reply and she knew he hadn't heard a word. She looked over the letter he was reading. 'Anything important?'

'Mainly a lot of boring legal stuff. There's this,' and he handed her a card in an official envelope.

'It's an invitation from the mayor and mayoress of Truro to a dinner party. How super! I'm going to luncheon with the vicar and his wife and the churchwardens tomorrow.' She looked at Alex carefully. 'I'm beginning to get a social diary. Cornwall is certainly agreeing with Stephen, I adore the creek and I do like Truro so. I'm so glad we came down here, aren't you?'

'Yes.' Alex shuffled the letters together and looked at the door. 'That's Mrs Wright coming for us.'

Abigail was careful not to chat too much during dinner. She knew Alex found it tiresome and she didn't want him going off after coffee in a huff. He sat at the desk in the sitting room hurriedly writing letters and advice to Mr Drayton while she sat quietly near the door with an empty brandy glass in her hand. When he'd sealed the letters, he got up and made to leave the room. Abigail held out the brandy glass.

'Would you pour me a teeny drop more, please?'

Alex took the glass from her and went to the drinks table. She came and stood close beside him.

'Aren't you having one?'

He looked at her squarely. 'No.'

'You're not retiring already?'

'I thought I'd have an early night. I'm up early in the morning to take one of the boats out into Falmouth Bay. After that I've got business in the town.'

'Won't you stay and talk for a little while? I haven't seen anyone all day.'

Alex didn't actually sigh but he was fidgeting to get away. 'What do you want to talk about? Anything in particular or just chit-chat?'

She had made up her mind to try to pin Alex down on his plans for Trevallion and he had given her the perfect opening. 'I'd like to know what you're planning to do about Trevallion, Alex.'

'I haven't decided. Stop pushing me for a decision, Abigail.'

He moved away but she held his arm. 'Please, Alex, I need to know. I have a son without a future. Ralph's son has a right to a secure future, hasn't he? It's what Ralph would have wanted.'

Alex looked right into her. 'You want me to settle Trevallion on Stephen? Is that it?'

'If you don't want it for yourself, yes. You wouldn't have had Trevallion at all if Miles and your other relatives hadn't died, and you have all your other property and interests to leave to your own children should you decide to marry. Please, Alex, do this for Stephen. He's your nephew and goodness knows you've paid little enough attention to him since he was born.'

Alex looked over Abigail's head. The vision of Miles standing over his bed last night and the things he had said were burning through his mind.

'Miles wants the Kennickers to have it,' he murmured.

'I beg your pardon?' She slid her hand up to his face and made him look at her.

'I'm sorry, I just can't decide yet. I'll think about Stephen and I'll do something for him, I promise, Abigail.'

It was good to get some sort of promise but Abigail didn't want to go back to Carsham Hall or to London. She had too much to live down and Stephen must never know of her exploits during the war.

'That's very sweet of you, Alex,' she said softly.

It was good being close to Alex. He might have psychological weaknesses but his rangy body was strong, he was tall and so very good-looking. He had a smell of outdoor ruggedness about him. It was different to that of manufactured aftershaves; masculine, basic. Abigail felt a longing for him.

Alex was looking at her steadily, as if he was trying to read her thoughts. Surely he could sense them? He hadn't moved away. Did he want her too? He was a man and she could give him something better tonight than terrible memories.

She slid her other hand up over his chest and put her arms round his neck. 'Alex, please...'

She had him mesmerised and sought his lips. When she found them he pulled her in close and kissed her almost brutally. This was exactly what she wanted. She realised with an almost painful intensity that she wanted him above all other men, the stand-offish, silent, brooding, Alex Fiennes. Then, afterwards, perhaps he'd be filled with remorse and a sense of duty and marry her and everything he had would be rightfully hers and Stephen's.

Alex lifted his head away and gazed at her, looking stunned.

'It's all right,' she whispered. 'Mrs Wright and Mrs Grubb have gone home. Stephen won't stir for the night and Rebecca won't be back for ages.'

He looked confused and Abigail tilted her face to kiss him again. He didn't respond and shook his head. 'No, it's wrong.'

'It's all right. I can't have any more children. Nothing like that will happen. It's just me and you here, Alex. Don't let's waste this time together.'

'No.' Alex thrust himself away, filled with shame and a little revulsion.

'Don't do this, Alex,' she pleaded. 'I will be good for you.'

He rushed from the room, up the stairs and locked himself in his room.

–

Upstairs, alone, Alex shuddered. What had that woman been trying to do to him? He didn't want any feelings stirred to life in him, particularly those. He wanted only to be dead. He'd told himself that, wished it often enough.

He couldn't sleep and an hour later lit a cigarette and looked out of the window. He saw Rebecca walking to the gatehouse with Trease. They said goodnight and he felt relieved when he heard her coming up the stairs and going into her own room. He knew he could sleep now and face another day. He didn't want to be cold stone dead like Miles and Ralph and Georgie Gilbert any more but he wanted all his other feelings, all other areas of his life, to stay dead. He didn't want anyone reaching down into them, trying to awaken them. At least there was one woman here whom he could trust.

Chapter 17

It was warm, with an early morning mist rising off the water, when Alex, Jossy Jenkins and his sons Donald and Victor set sail in Miles Trevallion's favourite boat, the *Lady Harriet*. The craft, named after Miles's fiancée, was locally built and painted white like the *Iseult*. Long and slender and purpose-built for racing, its canvas sails were beating a magnificent tattoo as they made a match for the fresh winds. The boat had meant so much to Miles. He had spoken of it the last time he had visited Carsham Hall just before the war and Alex had agreed to come down to Cornwall and sail in it the next summer. But that had never happened.

Alex could picture the beautiful lady in the portrait in Miles's study gracing the deck with her presence, layers of white silk billowing from a wide-brimmed straw hat in the wind. He could see Miles looking at her with all the love he'd borne for her. Alex was pleased he had met Harriet Bosanko. He would be calling on her great-aunt, a figure of some mystery and great interest to him, later in the day.

As on their previous trip, Jossy was only too happy to give Alex the benefit of the mine of information he seemed to have stored inside his old head. He explained that the seven cargo vessels that towered over them in the narrow deep-water channel of King Harry Reach were temporarily redundant and berthed there because it was one of the cheapest places in the country to lay up a ship. The *Lady Harriet* sailed on down Carrick Roads to the Fal estuary and out into Falmouth Bay between the twin castles of Pendennis and St Mawes which, with St Anthony's Headland, formed a natural entrance to the estuary. The castles had been built under the orders of Henry VIII to protect the harbour from the French and Spanish fleets, and St

Anthony's lighthouse, Jossy went on, warned ships of the treacherous rocks of its headland and those of nearby Zone Point. St Mawes and St Anthony were on the end of the Roseland peninsula and Alex decided on another day he would sail up the Percuil River which separated the headlands.

Out in the bay the sea was teeming with craft, fishing boats, cargo steamers, racing yachts and topsail schooners. The *Lady Harriet* rode the choppy waves undaunted and the experience held Alex spellbound. The Jenkins waved to people they knew and Alex was kept fully informed about each of the boats' occupants.

The men watched a pair of dolphins cavorting. The mammals came close to the boat for a few playful minutes then swam away. Before they were out of sight, Jossy trotted out the information that sometimes grey seals would follow the mackerel into the Fal estuary as far up as Loe Beach.

About six and half miles south-east of Falmouth, off Coverack, was the dreaded reef of the Manacles, the undoing of many a ship and its mariners. They didn't sail close but gazed at the pinnacles rising up from a depth of twenty fathoms or more. A great variety of fish could be found around the reef and its wrecks, bass and pollack, immense conger, wrasse, huss, whiting and many more.

They turned back at this point and the *Lady Harriet's* new captain and crew devoured a crib of pasties, comparing the Jenkins women's to Loveday's supreme effort. There were chicken and ham pies, yeast buns, heavy-cake and flasks of strong tea, and a stiff tot of rum produced by Alex to loud cheers.

The boat practically found its own way to the land mass of Falmouth harbour, as if it remembered the way there from its last trip many years ago. They moored up at Custom House Quay. Donald and Victor decided to look around the town but Jossy refused to budge from the boat. He'd waited so long to sail in the *Lady Harriet* again, he wasn't going to let her out of his sight.

Following Jossy's instructions, Alex walked along Arwenack Street, carried on along Grove Place, turned off into Avenue Road and round the corner at its end where it met Melvill Road. He crossed over the road and walked briskly up to the front door of Miss Susannah Bosanko's residence.

The maid asked him politely into the hall and took his card to her mistress. She was back in a minute. 'Madam says you are to step this way, sir, into the parlour.'

Alex's burning curiosity about the elderly lady he was about to meet turned to excitement. It was years since he'd been this interested in something. If her love letters were anything to go by, Susannah Bosanko had been a very passionate lady in her youth. Alex had felt like a voyeur as he read the intimate details of her affair with Roland Trevallion while he had been married to local beauty Arabella Kerseys. At one time Susannah had thought she was pregnant. There had been tears and frustration when she miscarried, and thinly disguised jubilation when Arabella had died suddenly, leaving Roland with a small son, Vyvyan. Susannah had expected to step in as second wife and stepmother. There had been a long gap in dates before the next group of letters. They contained pleas to see Roland, demands for an explanation as to why he seemed reluctant to see her. The last letters had been the most interesting; not love letters, quite the reverse, full of hate and spite. Roland had apparently taken up with another woman and Susannah Bosanko threatened revenge.

What had happened next was a mystery. Roland hadn't married anyone else and he had hanged himself soon afterwards. According to Jossy, people reckoned Roland's tragic death at just thirty-one years of age had nothing to do with the death of his wife. What then? The affair with Susannah Bosanko seemed to have been simply that to Roland, an affair. If he had fallen in love with somebody else, why hadn't he married her? Why had he killed himself like that? Alex was curious to know and hoped Susannah Bosanko would be able to enlighten him.

He was shown into a large square room and went forward to meet Miss Bosanko. She was sitting in a high-backed winged chair from where she could watch people walking along the pavement outside. Alex paid no attention to the room and did not notice that both it and Susannah Bosanko were entirely swathed in green, but he felt the same revulsion as Neville Faull had at her repugnant features. He gulped but managed to keep his face straight.

'It is very good of you to see me, Miss Bosanko,' Alex said quietly, lowering his head to meet the beady stare fixed on him.

Her head came up sharply. 'And what can I do for you, Major Alexander Fiennes?' she said quietly, her eyes piercingly bright in her skull-like face. She held out her hand and Alex, unable to tear his eyes away from hers, kissed it lightly. He instinctively knew that a gentleman did not shake this old-fashioned lady's hand.

'Owing to the sad demise of my second cousin, Captain Miles Trevallion, I've just inherited the Trevallion estate, Miss Bosanko. While sifting through my cousin's papers I came across your name and on finding that you were the great-aunt of Miles's late fiancée I thought I'd look you up. I hope you don't mind,' he concluded, trying a brilliant smile on the old lady.

It worked, much to Alex's surprise. He had never considered himself a man of charm. Up came her head again, her sharp chin jutting forward, the look in her eyes one of shining acceptance as if it was her right to receive this sort of attention from a man.

'I have few visitors nowadays and I would not turn a handsome gentleman such as yourself from my doorstep, Major Fiennes,' she said, the words seeming to melt off her lips. She leaned forward a little. 'Or may I call you Alexander?'

'Of course,' he replied gallantly. Obviously flirting was the easiest way to get to know this strange and hideous old lady. 'Or Alex if you prefer.'

'Oh no.' With a thin bony hand she waved him to the chair nearest to her. 'Alexander sounds so much more noble, to suit your strong dark looks. One hears gossip from the river and I had heard that the new heir of Trevallion had taken up residence in the gatehouse of the property. I consider it most courteous of you to call on me, and so soon, Alexander. What a pity you cannot stay in the great house. Such a charming place, not so very big by some standards but in such a lovely setting. Will you be staying in Cornwall long?'

'My original plan was to come down to wind up Captain Trevallion's affairs, perhaps to stay for the summer, but I really don't know what I shall be doing in the long term, Miss Bosanko.'

She wagged a finger at him. 'Susannah! I insist upon it. Now, Alexander, my dear, may I offer you a sherry? Or a Scotch?'

'A small Scotch would be splendid,' Alex said, speaking in the sprightly manner of his hostess. 'Please, don't ring. I shall help myself.' He sprang up and realised she was watching his movements as he walked to the drinks cabinet. 'And for you, Susannah?'

'A sherry, please.' It came out deep and husky and Alex was sure she was trying to sound sultry.

As she took the sherry from him, Alex found his eyes rooted to hers. She had him absolutely mesmerised, riveted to the spot on her Axminster carpet. A chill ran up his back but it wasn't fear. Susannah Bosanko was ugly and disfigured but utterly fascinating. There was an extraordinary aura of strength and vibrancy about her. Alex could almost feel the passion with which she had written those love letters.

Alex took his Scotch to his chair and continued to gaze at her, to Susannah's pleasure.

'It was a terrible tragedy about Miles. Such a handsome, robust young man. It nearly destroyed him when Harriet died, as it did me.' Tears glistened in Susannah's ice-clear eyes and Alex had to restrain himself from leaping up and holding her hand. 'Harriet was my niece's child, an unwanted child, and I took over the task of bringing her up. I loved her as if she was my own daughter. It was a terrible shock when she died and I felt an enormous blow when Miles died this year. I couldn't bring myself to go to his funeral, it would have been like burying my dear Harriet all over again. Miles should not have died like that!' she said angrily. 'He was not only a perfect gentleman but a real man, not like his weak pathetic father, Vyvyan, and his wretched grandfather before him!'

Alex said quietly over his whisky glass, 'I wish I was in this part of the country for reasons other than having inherited Miles's property and having to go through his personal things.'

Susannah cheered immediately, surprising him again. 'Life goes on, Alexander. No more gloomy talk, I won't have it. A young man like you, vital, full of energy, must look to the future.'

He smiled ironically. 'I would hardly describe myself as that.'

'You will,' she said shrewdly. 'Whatever happened to you during the war, you'll get over it. You'll find something to live for. Fall in love perhaps. And before you say never, if there are any young women worth their salt out there, like I was in my younger days, one of them will see to you.'

'See to me?' Alex was amused.

'You'll know what I mean when it happens. You've come down with your brother's widow and son, I understand.'

'Yes, Abigail and Stephen.'

'What are you going to do with them?'

'What do you mean? What am I going to do with them?'

'Well, you haven't married the woman. She's a war widow – I know all the gossip. You haven't married her and yet she's come down here with you, which means she's penniless, has to tag along with you because there's nothing else for her to do.' Susannah sipped her sherry, keeping her eyes riveted on Alex. 'Take my advice, Alexander, get rid of her. She'll drag you down. I know the sort of female she is. Probably wants you to marry her to set herself and her son up, and from what I've heard he's a fine piece of obnoxious spawn. Bet the woman has tried to bed you. I can't see how she could keep her hands off a splendid man like you.'

Alex hadn't blushed since his schooldays but right now he didn't know where to put himself 'You can't tell me I'm wrong, can you? She wouldn't have tried it on home ground. It's happened since you came down here. Speak up, don't be embarrassed.'

'It was only last night actually,' he admitted, astounded to find himself telling this stranger such an intimate thing. He cleared his throat and looking longingly at the Scotch bottle.

'Don't wait to be invited, help yourself,' Susannah said on a high-pitched note.

Alex knew she was thoroughly enjoying herself but wasn't so sure about himself. When he was seated with his replenished glass he took a gulp of the strong liquor. What Susannah said next made him choke on it.

'And you, my sweet, are too much of a gentleman to have given in to the whoring bitch.'

'I… I, no I didn't, but—'

'I understand that you are having repairs done to Trevallion. When you have brought it up to the mark, you will invite me there. I do not travel by boat any more but I shall come by car. It will be good to see it again.'

Alex was heartily relieved Susannah had changed the subject and said enthusiastically, 'I shall be honoured to have you there. It should be ready to receive people in another couple of weeks.'

'Excellent. Two weeks to the day then. I shall put it in my diary.'

Alex knew she was an active patron of the National Lifeboat charity but he wondered if she received many invitations. As if she had read his mind, she smiled slightly, revealing pointed teeth. 'I don't get out much nowadays and I shall look forward to it. I understand that most of the families who lived in the little creek below Trevallion in Roland's day are still there.'

'Yes, the Jenkins, the Grubbs and the Allens.'

'Allen? I don't recall any of that name.'

'Trease Allen, the chauffeur, and his daughter Rebecca.' Alex said the last name a touch more softly and Susannah noticed.

'Oh, yes? And what is this Rebecca like?'

Alex was colouring again. 'She usually works on a farm on the estate but Abigail has commandeered her as a sort of lady's maid. She's good-natured, honest.' He wanted to stop but Susannah kept silent and he had to go on. 'She's um, twenty years old.'

'And has exquisite…?'

Alex looked dumbstruck but Susannah wasn't going to let him off the hook. 'Go on, she has something exquisite about her, I'll be bound.'

He coughed. 'Very long, thick black hair and dark eyes.'

'Ah, I shall look forward to meeting Rebecca Allen.'

Alex could hardly believe what he was doing. He had called on Susannah Bosanko hoping to find out more about her than her love letters and Jossy Jenkins could tell him, but she had expertly got him to talk about himself, quite intimately too.

'Rebecca is my friend,' he said, feeling he must qualify his relationship with her.

Susannah gave a little nod. 'Mmmm. **Are** there any Carlyons in the creek?'

'Just one, the last of the family, the groom Joe Carlyon.'

'Really? I have such fond memories of the creek.'

'I shall be glad to stroll round it with you, Susannah.'

'Stroll, you say? As if I'm halfway to being infirm. I may be heading towards my ninetieth birthday but I'm quite able to walk round that creek a dozen times in one afternoon I'll have you know.'

Alex felt chastened. He looked at his wristwatch. 'Is that the time?' he said. 'I have to go, back to the quay to meet my boat.'

Susannah beckoned him to her. He obeyed. 'You will call on me again before the two weeks is up, Alexander.'

'Yes, of course.' She'd flustered him, almost terrified him, but he would come again.

'You will kiss me.'

The skin of her cheeks was cool and incredibly soft. She moved so her lips met his and despite her age and appearance he did not feel repulsed as he had with Abigail the night before.

Chapter 18

While Alex was out on the boat, Rebecca was required to help Joe exercise the horses. Joe made sure he was in the stable yard when she arrived and followed her about until she was forced to stop and speak to him. She had her mount, a smooth-coated grey pony named Claudius, saddled and Joe pulled down the foot she was about to put in the stirrup.

'Keep still,' he ordered quietly, putting his huge hands gently on her shoulders. 'I've got something I want to say and you are going to listen to me.'

Rebecca wasn't given to petulant displays and stayed put without protest. She sighed wearily. 'There's no need to say anything, Joe. As far as I'm concerned the fight you had with Dad is over and forgotten.'

'So you don't want an apology then?'

'It's not necessary.'

'Then why are you avoiding me? It doesn't make sense.' She had backed herself into a corner here. She could hardly tell him the truth. That she was hurt because he had ignored her when she'd got herself all dressed up, that she felt humiliated because that had been the reason for the fight with Trease. All she could say lamely was, 'I don't know.'

Joe laughed, kissed her forehead and pulled her close to him in a cuddle. 'Oh, Becca, you little idiot. We're too close to fall out. Come on, my dear, let's gallop the horses across the fields. Their limbs need stretching to the full and mine feel the same way this morning.'

They trotted out of the stable yard and when they reached the first field of the estate they raced the horses until their breaths were ragged. High up on Verrian Farm they came to a halt and dismounted beside an old oak in the middle of a field. Joe leaned his back against the tree and Rebecca leaned against him, as she had done from childhood. Anyone seeing them would have thought nothing of it, it was just Joe and Rebecca together. But now she was this close to him again it revived her hopes that he would at long last notice she was an available young woman.

'How's Mrs Fiennes this morning?' Joe asked, chewing on a long grass stalk. 'I saw her down in the creek yesterday, she was trying to walk off a bad headache.'

Rebecca ran a fingertip lightly over the back of his hand as she replied, 'She was grouchy again. Her headache hadn't returned but she was upset over something. She seemed reluctant to leave her room. Kept asking me if I was sure that the Major had left on the boat for Falmouth. Sounds like they'd had a quarrel or something and she didn't want to see him.'

'Aye, they don't seem to get on too well. Anyway, 'tis grand so many of us are back in our old jobs again. I'm happy with the horses and Trease is happy with the cars.' Now that the last bad feelings over the fight had been put to rest they could talk about Trease without hurt feelings. 'I hope the Major decides not to sell the estate. I'd really like to work for him. He's a good bloke, loyal to his men, if you ask me, and a decent sort of gentleman where women are concerned. Loveday's got nothing against him and if he's not too proud to take young'uns out with him in the car – well, speaks for itself. You can tell he's got the same blood as the Captain had.'

Rebecca nodded in agreement then her face darkened. 'So has Stephen but he's a horrid spoiled brat.'

'That's his mother's doing,' Joe said.

'Some folk are saying that Mrs Fiennes is flighty, but I do like her. She went out of her way to make me feel comfortable in the first awkward moments I met the family. She's kind and generous and is eager to mix with the creek folk. She's even going to Margaret's wedding on Saturday. I think she's lonely and worried underneath her gaiety, and from what I can gather her future depends on what the Major decides as much as ours does. I hope the Kennickers won't turn against her.'

'I won't,' Joe said, flexing his hands and running them down his legs. 'I like the woman.'

Rebecca snuggled her head in closer to his chest. She closed her eyes and allowed the sun to warm her face. Up here under a beautiful summer sky lying like this against Joe's solid flesh was heaven. It was no use trying to get Joe to notice her by wearing fancy clothes, perfume and make-up so she'd try a more direct approach. Taking one of his hands between hers, she held it tightly.

Joe lifted their hands and rubbed his thumb along her chin. 'I haven't felt this content in ages,' he said dreamily.

'Nor me.'

'I wonder how the Major's getting on with the *Lady Harriet*. Took my breath away to see it sliding out of the creek this morning. I almost expected to see Captain Miles at the bow.'

'As long as the Major falls in love with the river, that's all that matters.'

'Be even better if he fell in love with some local lady. He wouldn't be in a hurry to go back to Berkshire then.'

'Whatever he decides to do, I'm quite confident he won't sell the estate unless it's to someone he can trust to look after it and keep all of us on as workers.'

'He's taken to you, Becca. Whatever you're doing, just keep it up, the rest of us are relying on you.'

Rebecca turned her head and laid the side of her face on Joe's chest, fiddling with the buttons on his shirt. 'It would be wonderful if he fell in love and reared a family in the big house. It must be wonderful to fall in love.' She tilted her head and looked up at him. 'Don't you think, Joe?'

He shrugged. 'I s'pose so.'

Rebecca lifted her face to him and hoped he would kiss her. She looked at his lips then into his eyes, then back at his lips. She wanted the feel of that wide full-lipped mouth on hers. But when she glanced up to his eyes again, he wasn't looking at her at all. He was gazing over her head at the river. He pulled his hand away from hers.

'There's the *River Princess* on her way to Truro. Time we were going.'

In desperation Rebecca kissed his cheek. Joe kissed her back in the same way then used his strength to lift them both to their feet. 'Come on, maid, or you'll have Mrs Fiennes after you.'

He moved off to the horses and Rebecca looked down at the ground, crestfallen. 'I might just as well be that dandelion there.'

—

When Rebecca got back to the gatehouse, she ran up the stairs to change.

'Good morning, Miss Allen.'

She jumped in fright and nearly missed her footing. 'Mr Faull, you gave me quite a turn.'

'Where are you going in such a hurry?' he said, placing an arm on the bottom of the banister and leaning towards her. 'To change, Mr Faull.'

He eyed her casually. 'Pity, riding clothes suit you.' He smiled. It seemed to make his features melt and reform, making him even more handsome. He reminded Rebecca of one of the heroes in Stephen's adventure comics, solid, utterly strong, able to overcome all opposition. Foolish thought, she chided herself and made to continue up the stairs.

'Will you excuse me, Mr Faull. I'm running late.'

Neville put a finger on her wrist and ran it gently up and down. 'Only if you agree to come to the cinema in Truro with me one evening next week.'

After her disappointment with Joe she wasn't going to say no out of hand. 'I'll have to think about it.'

'How can you refuse? Every young lady is an admirer of Rudolph Valentino. Don't tell me you're not.'

'Charlie Chaplin, more like it,' Rebecca said pertly.

'You do have an evening off once a week, I take it?'

'I have no set hours, Mr Faull.'

'I could meet you outside your uncle's house. I know where he lives. Shall we say seven o'clock next Thursday? I'll treat you to supper at the Treleaven Restaurant afterwards.' He looked at her appealingly. 'I'll bring my Aunt Mildred along with me.'

'Rebecca! So, you're back at last. Go and change at once and brush your hair. You look like a raggle-taggle gipsy.' Abigail had appeared and looked irate.

Neville Faull had his back to her. He grinned at Rebecca and mouthed the words, 'Will you come?'

Rebecca looked defiantly at Abigail. She knew Abigail would object to her going out with Neville Faull. She looked back at Neville and gave a brief nod then turned and ran up the stairs.

'Leave her alone, Neville,' Abigail said harshly, spinning him round by his arm.

Neville smoothed the place on his expensive pinstripe suit where she had grabbed him. 'Just saying hello, Abby. What's wrong with that?'

Neville Faull's demeanour was as smooth and sleek as his voice, his suit and his hair. Abigail was tempted to slap the confidence off his impertinent face. 'I know what you're after and Rebecca's not that sort of girl. I'm ordering you to stay away from her.'

With the expression of a satisfied cat, he ran a finger along the neckline of Abigail's dress. 'You don't mind me getting close to you though, do you, Abby? Would you like to meet me somewhere? I know some very discreet places we could go.'

She was tempted. Neville was a very good lover, and his position as solicitor and on the rural council demanded discretion, so he wouldn't advertise it if they carried on with their association. But if Alex found out he would pack her and Stephen onto the first train out of Cornwall – and besides, Faull wasn't the only man around.

She stroked his chest and moved his tie. 'Better not, at least not until I'm settled down here.'

'If Alex decides to settle you down here,' Neville said cruelly, knowing how much she was relying on him.

'Until I've got him to settle my son's future then!' she spat, turning on her heel.

Neville looked up the stairs. He had been disappointed not to be able to see the Major today and try his hand at obtaining Susannah

Bosanko's generous commission, but he had achieved something else he desired. 'I wonder if Rebecca needs any help changing into her dress.'

Abigail came back to him. 'Please, Neville. Don't do anything to her.'

He grinned like the Cheshire cat. 'I wouldn't dream of hurting such a sweet young creature.'

—

After lunch Rebecca and Abigail went into the sitting room to collect the box of lingerie bought for Margaret Grubb's honeymoon. Rebecca hadn't had time to go into Truro and buy new clothes with the ten pounds Alex had given her and she was wearing a dress that Abigail had given her. Loveday had altered it for her, making it less extravagant.

Rebecca was feeling excited and rather daring after agreeing to go out with Neville Faull. 'Margaret will be thrilled with this,' she said, putting the lid on the box. They were about to go down to the creek to join the estate women in a little good luck celebration for the bride and to present her with their gifts.

'Do you really think so, Rebecca?' Abigail was worried that her gift might be seen as too risqué for a quiet country bride, even though she wasn't exactly a maiden at the age of twenty-seven. 'I'd hate to cause offence. Perhaps I should have bought her something for the kitchen like you have.'

'It'll be like a dream come true for her, to wear something like this on her wedding night.' Neville Faull certainly wouldn't expect his bride, or his conquests, to go to bed in Victorian cotton.

'I hope you're right.' Abigail picked up the box and nodded at the table. 'We'll take that bottle along with us.'

'Champagne?'

Abigail was suddenly impatient at worrying about the Kennickers' possible narrow-mindedness. 'If they don't want to drink it now they can keep it for the toast at the reception. Is Mrs Wright ready?'

'Just putting her hat on.'

The women met in Jenny Jenkins' cottage, the biggest in the creek. It was spick-and-span but Abigail had the feeling it was always like this and that the old lady wouldn't stand on ceremony even for her.

'How are you today, Mrs Jenkins?' Abigail asked, sitting down on an old-fashioned black-stained settle beside the wide fireplace.

The old lady smiled and rubbed at the back of a knee swollen with arthritis. 'I'm fine, Mrs Fiennes, but I've got this leg today, aching all over.'

'Oh dear. What does the doctor say about it?'

'Says 'tis my age and that's the last word on it,' Jenny Jenkins replied, taking a strong cup of tea from Ira. ''Tis nothing really. I'm some glad you could come to our little gathering.'

'I was thrilled to be asked,' Abigail said truthfully. It meant a lot to her to be accepted by the local women. When she could bring herself to face Alex again, she would mention it. 'Perhaps we could all gather for tea at the gatehouse one afternoon.'

All the women smiled their acceptance. Abigail felt warm inside. They did not expect to go, it wouldn't be fitting, taking tea with their mistress on her home ground, but they were honoured by the invitation. Abigail scored another point by asking to hold baby Miles George, a chore which she endured for a full five minutes.

After the second round of tea, and jam and cream scones, the presents were given to the delighted bride. Margaret Grubb was a plain big-boned woman with an ordinary face covered in freckles and coarse red hair. It would take a lot of lace and frills to transform her into a traditional beautiful bride but she was thrilled with the sheer silky negligée set Abigail had bought for her.

Abigail was amazed at the generosity of the gifts from the ordinary estate folk. Tea sets, sheets of fine linen, a canteen of cutlery, towel bales, kitchen utensils. She felt shy about the champagne but Rebecca held up the bottle and said loudly, 'Who's for a drop of this? This is also from Mrs Fiennes.'

It was accepted with gusto and out came a tray of glasses, with a bottle each of sherry, gin and brandy. Jenny winked at Abigail. 'Tedn't only the menfolk who know how to enjoy themselves.'

By late afternoon the Jenkins' cottage was filled with much female laughter and giggling. Mild innuendoes about the wedding night abounded and Abigail relaxed and thoroughly enjoyed herself. As far as she was concerned, her contribution to the hen party had been a runaway success.

When she wanted to leave, she shouted down Rebecca's ear above the noise, 'I think I'll slip out and see what Stephen's doing.'

'Loveday checked on Tamsyn a few minutes ago. She and Master Stephen are playing happily in the creek.'

'I suppose the boat will be back soon.' Abigail didn't want to leave the cottage at the same time as Alex arrived back in the creek.

'No, they'll be gone out for a spot of fishing,' Jenny said. 'My old man will keep them as long as he can.'

Abigail felt too ashamed of her actions last night to risk it. 'I think I'll slip away now, Mrs Jenkins. You stay here, Rebecca, enjoy the rest of the party.'

Abigail didn't go back to the gatehouse but made her way to the big house. She often felt drawn to it and she was in luck today to find the workmen had all left.

She had managed to procure a spare key to the front door from Alex, on the condition she didn't disturb him in the study. She sat awhile in the drawing room. She was offended to find the study door was locked. Did Alex think she was going to rifle through his silly papers! She went upstairs and looked in the nearest of the twelve bedrooms. When she'd first heard about Alex inheriting Trevallion, and considered the possibility that the house might be set aside for Stephen, she'd taken it for granted that it would need a great deal of redecorating. But many of the rooms had been superbly painted and prepared, perhaps in readiness for Harriet Bosanko, and were still in good condition.

She walked to the window and looked out over the front of the house at a glorious view of the creek and the river beyond it. She thought she heard a sound and listened for it again for a moment then moved on to the next room.

It was a double room with a huge four-poster bed. She touched the silk-shot russet-coloured coverlet and heard the sound again, like footsteps. She listened hard. It was footsteps. Abigail told herself not to be so silly, but the footsteps came again. She felt nervous. This was silly. If there was someone in the house with her it would be Percy Gummoe, or Alex come back from his river trip, but somehow she knew it wasn't either of them. The footsteps came nearer, and nearer. She stepped further into the room and hid behind the drapes hanging round the bed. Her heart stopped and she wished she had shut the bedroom door behind her.

The footsteps came to the doorway and stopped. She clamped a hand to her mouth to stop herself from making a sound. The next moment the footsteps entered the room.

Chapter 19

She clutched the bedcurtain tightly and tried not to cry out.

The curtain was snatched out of her hand and she screamed.

'Did I frighten you?'

'Joe Carlyon! You fool! I nearly died of fright.'

'What on earth for? You didn't think I was a ghost, did you?'

'Well, the house is supposed to be haunted, isn't it?' Abigail was embarrassed and she couldn't stop shaking.

Joe took her by the arm and led her to sit on the high bed. She picked at the coverlet underneath her, feeling a fool. There were framed pictures on the walls of the river and woodlands and she flicked her eyes from one to the other rather than look at Joe. She was glad to be alone with him though, to have him standing in front of her, his magnificent body towering over her, his hands resting on his wide hips. She felt rather shy, like a girl alone with a man for the first time.

'Wh–what are you doing here, Joe?'

'I saw you come in. I wanted to know if your headache had gone.'

'Yes, it has. How sweet of you to be concerned.'

He was close to her and she could smell him. It was a natural animal smell, that of a man who used his strength and muscles to earn his living. Abigail was dizzy with excitement and longing for him. Her momentary girlish panic vanished. She stood up, moved in a slinky fashion to within an inch of him, and tilted her lovely face to his dark eyes. 'Is that the only reason?'

'No.'

She clenched her fists. She knew what he was here for, why he had followed her into the house. He was no fool, he had read the signals she'd given him on the creek bank. There would be no beating about the bush but she mustn't touch him first. He wouldn't like that and she didn't want to have to beg him like she had Alex.

She raised her delicate brows and purred. 'What other reason have you for being here?'

'I wanted to see you again, alone.'

His hands came up swiftly and pulled her body against his. He kissed her savagely. Abigail gave him her mouth open and demanding, thrusting herself into him. She hoped he would be rough with her. Neville Faull liked to take his time, tease and tantalise and heighten his own and his lover's awareness. But Abigail wanted Joe this instant. If he had hesitated, she would have ripped his clothes off. He lifted her off her feet like a daisy in a meadow and dropped her onto the bed.

When their first need was spent, they undressed and took their time twice more. Finally she lay against his massive hairy chest, looking up at the brown painted plaster ceiling, the pale orange walls and gold-coloured curtains at the window.

'I like this room. I like autumn colours,' she sighed contentedly.

'I shall always have fond memories of it,' he murmured, kissing her soft hair.

He was thinking about their lovemaking. He'd been amazed at her agility and imaginativeness. Joe had never bothered much with women. There had been a short burst of fervency in his youth and the odd encounter since. He'd thought he'd known all there was to know; after all, he had been in the army where there'd been much talk of the physical side of life. But he had discovered more with Abigail in one hour than he had all his adult life. He stroked the glistening skin on her shoulder and grinned manfully to himself. She might even know something more.

She leaned up and kissed his lips. 'You were wonderful, Joe.'

He grinned proudly. 'I'm glad you thought so.'

'We must meet again but we'll have to be careful.'

Joe knew the main reason for subterfuge was because of the Major's disapproval if he found out. And it would be more than that. Alexander Fiennes obviously knew his sister-in-law for a loose woman, but he would feel they'd both betrayed him. Joe suddenly felt disloyal to Miles

Trevallion, performing an illicit act under his roof. But he couldn't simply say 'no more' to this lady. She wouldn't allow him to and he didn't want her to. He knew that when she'd had enough of him or if she ever found it inconvenient, she would finish it. Best to leave it at that and enjoy himself while it lasted.

Abigail was thinking about Joe's performance. He had great virility but he didn't seem to know very much for a man in his thirties. Her demands had taken him aback to begin with but then he'd cast off his inhibitions like autumn leaves. She lay still, enjoying the sensation of his big rough hands grazing her back and wished there was time for one more tussle.

'When I heard your footsteps I thought the rumours about there being a ghost here were true,' she said.

'I've never believed those stories myself. There's bound to be a lot of creaks and groans in an old house, sudden draughts making doors slam, mice scurrying about.'

'Many of the locals seem convinced of it. Stephen says that Tamsyn refuses to come anywhere near the house and apart from Rebecca none of the other women in the creek will come in here alone. What's the story behind the haunting, Joe? Rebecca said the ghost is believed to be of Roland Trevallion.'

'All I've heard is that he had money troubles because of the mining slump. It's all anyone's said to me, anyway. People will think differently if and when the house is lived in again. They'll be in here fast enough then if the Major offers them work.'

Joe waited for Abigail to confide in him about her hopes for the house but mention of her brother-in-law had set her thinking about Alex rather than Trevallion's eventual fate.

If she had been successful with him last night, she was certain she wouldn't have been able to let herself go as she had this afternoon. With a sudden burning urgency she wanted to know what it would have been like with Alex. With his careless clothes, lean rangy body, gaunt face and haunted eyes, she wanted him even more than this rough-cast groom whose naked flesh she lay upon. She used her imagination on what it might have been like with Alex last night and felt the heat surging through her again. Alex wasn't here but Joe Carlyon was. Oh, to hell with the time!

—

When Alex and the Jenkins moored the *Lady Harriet* in the creek, they found themselves doing so in front of a female audience. The women in Jenny's cottage had just finished washing up their teacups and glasses and were getting ready to disperse to make the evening meal when Tamsyn had rushed through the door to tell them the Major was back. Refusing to watch with the women because he hadn't been allowed to go on the boat that morning, and furious with Tamsyn for wanting to watch Alex come ashore, Stephen stamped back to the gatehouse.

Jossy and his sons grinned as wide as their mouths would stretch as they brought the craft in expertly to its usual berth. Victor jumped out and tied the rope securely to a post on the bank. Rebecca sought Alex's face and was satisfied to see him looking quietly exhilarated. The sea air and winds had put colour in his cheeks and he seemed to be holding himself straighten.

She was holding baby Miles George to give Gwen a rest and Ira Jenkins nudged her arm. 'Looks like he's enjoyed himself, the Major, doesn't he?'

Rebecca agreed and Ira moved closer to whisper in her ear, 'We've all noticed that he likes you, Becca. You just go on making him feel at home and we'll keep him here for good.'

'It's not up to me what the Major decides to do, Ira,' Rebecca replied, frowning. She was receiving too many of these sort of remarks.

She didn't want the responsibility for the estate's future to rest on her shoulders. Ira smiled out of the side of her face and nodded wisely then walked away.

Rebecca was a little dismayed that when Alex leapt ashore he came straight up to her. She felt a dozen knowing faces on her and forgot she was holding the baby.

'Is that the baby I named?' he asked cheerfully.

'What? Oh, yes,' she replied, feeling herself go red and holding Miles George at an angle so Alex could see his tiny face.

The audience came closer and watched proudly as their new master put a gentle finger on the baby's cheek. Miles George puckered up his pink features and Alex smiled at Rebecca.

'I think he likes me.'

'And why shouldn't he?' spoke up a smiling Jenny Jenkins. 'He knows a fine man when he sees one.'

Rebecca was feeling uncomfortable but Alex nearly died of embarrassment. 'I... um, yes. I hope you ladies had a good bridal party.'

'We did,' Ira Jenkins said, pushing the bashful bride forward.

'Congratulations,' Alex said to Margaret.

'Thank you, sir.' She bobbed an awkward curtsy.

'See you at the church, will we, Major?' Jenny asked, half-teasingly, half-hopefully.

Alex looked horrorstricken at Rebecca. 'I suppose Miles went to every wedding, baptism and funeral.'

'Never missed a single one,' Rebecca replied cheekily. She couldn't help being amused at his discomfort.

'I wouldn't miss it for the world,' Alex told Margaret gallantly.

'I'll have to dig a suit out from somewhere now,' Alex said accusingly as he and Rebecca walked back to the gatehouse in front of Loveday and Tamsyn.

'I'll do it for you if it's that much trouble.' Rebecca was swinging the empty champagne bottle by its long green neck. Alex watched the pendulous movements with a glum face.

'Some friend you are.'

'It's expected of you to go, and don't be so grumpy. How did you get on with Miss Bosanko? Did you actually see her?'

The inconvenience of having a wedding to attend was instantly forgotten. 'She's remarkable, Becca. I've never met anyone like her in my whole life. There are portraits of her as a young woman in her house. You couldn't have called her beautiful then, not like Harriet was, but she was very appealing. Now she is hideously ugly. But there's plenty of life in her. She's a risqué old thing and rather formidable,' he laughed. 'I couldn't tear myself away from her. I've invited her over to Trevallion in two weeks' time when the house should be ready to receive visitors.'

Overhearing parts of what was an interesting conversation, Loveday quickened her pace and closed the gap between them.

'I hope I get the chance to meet her,' Rebecca said. It would be interesting to meet the author of those love letters. She knew Loveday would be dying to know whom she and the Major were talking about; she could imagine Loveday's disgust if she read the letters.

'You will,' Alex said, his eyes twinkling. 'She said she's looking forward to meeting you.'

'Why me? She doesn't know me. Why did you talk about me? What did you tell her?'

'The truth,' Alex said, putting an arm round her shoulders and shocking Loveday who was almost on their heels. 'That you're my friend.'

Rebecca could imagine the expression on Loveday's face and heard her tell Tamsyn off for giggling. She knew that allowing Alex to keep his arm round her would fuel Ira Jenkins' observations but she couldn't push his arm away without hurting his feelings.

The roadmender had already done much to repair the road they were walking along and they admired his work. Then Rebecca said, 'It's not my place to tell you, but Mr Neville Faull was here this morning hoping to see you.'

Alex scowled. 'I'm glad I was out. Did he say what he wanted?'

'I've no idea. You'll have to ask Mrs Fiennes.'

'I can't stand that man.'

'So I can see.'

'If he had his way he'd get me to sell Trevallion off in little chunks and have the house turned into a hotel. I won't do that to Miles, I won't have tourists tramping all over his property. He would have trusted me to do things for the best.'

'That'll be a big worry off the estate's mind,' Rebecca said, hoping Loveday had heard that and could see that the Major was capable of making up his own mind about estate affairs.

She thought about Neville Faull and her agreement to go out with him. No one on the estate would approve and her father would be furious if he found out. Alex despised Faull and Mrs Fiennes seemed to have no time for him either. It would be simpler to write to the young solicitor and break their arrangement but she was feeling rebellious and it would be fun to go out on the handsome, sophisticated man's arm. She'd just have to be careful to keep his amorous attentions at bay. She'd go out with him this once and take care to keep it quiet.

–

'You're getting some friendly with the Major, aren't you?' Loveday said prudishly. They were in the kitchen preparing the evening meal.

'What do you mean?' Rebecca asked defensively. She had expected this from the moment Loveday had begun to breathe down her neck on the walk back.

'You and him all armed up, that's what I mean.'

'We're friendly because that's how he looks on me, Loveday, as a friend.' Rebecca tried to sound patient but she wanted to shake the sanctimonious look off Loveday's face.

Loveday plonked down a saucepan of carrots on the range, making water splash over the top and hiss. 'Friend indeed! He's your employer and a gentleman. You're setting your sights high, aren't you, Rebecca Allen?'

Rebecca was suddenly very angry. 'Sometimes the lot of you on this estate make me sick! Keep in with the Major, Becca. He's taken to you, Becca. We're relying on you, Becca. If I was rude to him or ignored him you wouldn't like it, but because we've actually become friends you don't like that either! I'm fed up with the lot of you putting pressure on me and I won't have you turning on me and making sarcastic remarks. Get the meal yourself, Loveday. I'm not a slave here. I don't have to stay here. I could go and live with my Uncle Bert in Truro. I could easily get a job in a shop there if I wanted to. I'm sure Mr Faull could arrange something but you wouldn't like that either, would you!' Rebecca stamped out leaving Loveday thunderstruck.

Chapter 20

Loveday apologised to Rebecca but, although the apology was readily accepted, Rebecca became quiet and withdrawn. Abigail didn't seem to notice, she didn't want Rebecca at her beck and call any more; it seemed she had developed a liking for her own company. For the past three days she had gone riding and walking about the creek alone, and she often went to the great house when Alex wasn't there. Abigail had told herself that the reason she didn't want Rebecca around her was because it would hamper her assignations with Joe; she wouldn't admit it was more to do with being jealous of the girl's closeness to Alex.

Alex asked Rebecca more than once if she was ill or if anything was worrying her but she simply replied she was fine. She was perfectly civil and attentive to him but he knew something was wrong and was disappointed she did not confide in him. He wondered if Trease was drinking again but the chauffeur always seemed sober and busy about his work.

Alex thought about Rebecca as he stood on the roadside spot at Perranporth where long ago Aristotle Trevallion had built his house. Unlike at the old mine ruins, there was no sign that a building had once stood here. Rough grasses, heather and bracken had reclaimed the area, a small plot of land which Robert Drayton had confirmed he owned. Alex liked the spot. The wild rugged atmosphere revived his spirits which had dipped with Rebecca's apparent melancholy.

You need to come here, he told the sad image of Rebecca in his mind. It might help you feel the same way as I do now. He realised that Rebecca was never really full of sparkle. He'd heard her laugh but never in the carefree way of other young women of her age. There were things about her that reminded Alex of himself. She didn't seem to look forward to the future; she was concerned about the future of Trevallion but more for the others who lived and worked on it than for herself. Thanks to her mother's selfishness and father's bitterness she hadn't enjoyed much of her life. Alex wondered what her ambitions were. Did she want to get married? She didn't seem to take any interest in young men, although he had noticed the way she looked at Joe Carlyon. Perhaps that was it. It was obvious that Joe saw her only as a friend, a sort of niece. Could it be she had been rebuffed once too often from that quarter?

Alex walked away from the road and made his way through the prickly gorse ablaze with bright yellow flowers. There was no pathway through the growth and it tore at his trousers and scratched his legs. He had to make a detour round a thicket of hawthorn slanting at a deep angle from the buffeting winds.

He came to the cliff edge and gazed out across the sea. It was the same spectacular view as from the ruins of the Wheal Fortunate mine but from here he could see all the way to St Ives Bay. He used his binoculars to watch a tiny ship drop off the pale blue horizon, then swung round to take in Shag Rock off Penhale Point which, like much of the coast along here, was a breeding ground for gulls. A smattering of gulls triumphantly fought the winds out there and used the upcurrent to hover over the top of the rock while the waves rode in and smashed against it, sending up frothy white spray several feet into the air. Alex had brought a camera with him and he used half a film here, intending to walk the short distance to the mine ruins and use the rest up there.

The sea thundered onto the golden beaches and crashed against the tall granite cliffs, invading the numerous coves that pitted the cliff face. Many a village that had grown up round the tin and copper mining and fishing communities along the coastline had succumbed to the relentless sea over the decades. Smugglers had trodden these cliffs and Alex could hear the echo of their stealth and courage as they'd defied the authorities to bring in uncustomed goods to augment their meagre living. The place had a timelessness and purpose which seemed to infuse the air and seep down to the very roots of his soul. It declared its own unique and inexhaustive energy without humility, yet imparted a deep peace.

The sun shimmered in the vastness of a brilliant blue sky and Alex felt he was the only person who existed. He felt a part of Nature, part of the cliffs formed millions of years ago, part of the strong winds and awesome living sea which soothed away his mental fog. He felt a deep loneliness creep over him. Not the brutal sort of loneliness that had dominated his mind following his loss and failure, but a strange welcome warmth that made him feel he was himself, and himself alone, a man without nightmares, without a death wish, a man capable of being strong and useful and alive.

Alex liked it here, this tiny spot of the world that was his. He liked the county; he always had. He'd always meant to come down to Cornwall and spend a summer with Miles. But all those years ago life had been busy and there seemed to be plenty of time. They didn't know then that both their worlds would be shattered. Miles's sorrow had started before the war. When Harriet Bosanko had died, Miles had wanted to be alone, then when he began to come to terms with his loss and had invited Alex to his home again, the world had been rocked with rumours of war and both men had joined the army.

It was terrible, what had happened to Miles, losing his fiancée, coming back from the war a disabled imbecile. But at least he had loved someone, had once had a future to look forward to. Alex felt his life had stopped that day when all the men in his unit had been killed. He never looked back beyond it. As Abigail had observed to Rebecca, he had always been quiet, but he couldn't remember that there had been a time when he had looked forward to inheriting the Fiennes' empire on his twenty-first birthday. That he had enjoyed a social life not unlike Miles's. He'd taken little interest in his reckless younger brother's wife and her child. Miles had been more like a brother to him; they had shared many interests, not least in sport.

Alex had forgotten the carefree days of his youth but not the deep camaraderie a respected commanding officer enjoyed with his men and it was this which made his loss all the more unbearable. The misfortunes of war had brought his life to a halt. Nothing since then had interested him or given him any hope. Not until he had found this little place on the north cliffs of Cornwall, and the friendship of Rebecca Allen.

—

Joe kept his promise to Stephen to teach him to row. He borrowed Rebecca's boat to take him and Tamsyn out on the river, showing him the rudiments of how to make powerful sweeping movements with the oars. As they neared Church Creek, he handed the oars over to Stephen. The boy quickly picked up a good rowing action but his shoulders were straining to breaking point, his face was red and his breath almost gone when he brought the boat towards the slate shore. Tamsyn, who had encouraged him all the way, was full of admiration.

'A good show all round, Captain Redbeard,' she asserted, using one of Stephen's phrases.

Joe grinned in amusement but he was impressed by the boy's efforts. 'Aye, you'll make a good rower and a good leader,' he said as he tied up the boat.

The muddy creek was typical of the river, having a small area of salt marsh at its head, but it was one of the few along this stretch where access to land could be gained by foot. When Stephen had recovered they clambered carefully over the foreshore which was well colonised by bladderwrack and eggwrack. Passing through some willow trees, they made the short distance to Old Kea church and the crumbling tower they had seen rising above the oak-wooded banks. Stephen listened to the lazy cawing of the jackdaws up on the tower.

'There's a lot of bird life on the river,' he remarked, recalling the wood pigeons that flew startled out of Trevallion's woods and the herons he'd watched patiently fishing along the river bank where he'd walked with Tamsyn the day before.

'You won't go a day without seeing or hearing something, Master Stephen,' Joe said. 'The kingfisher is my favourite.'

'I like the woodpeckers,' Tamsyn said in a serious tone.

Her face was so solemn that Stephen ruffled her hair and teased her. 'I'll buy you one for your birthday.'

He was about to chase her when Joe coughed sternly. 'Remember where you are.' He expected rebellion but Stephen merely shrugged and stuffed his hands in his pockets.

They spent ten minutes looking over the small graveyard and the pretty little mission church then Stephen and Joe took turns rowing to Turnaware Bar which was just round the bend from the King Harry Ferry. They drank lemonade on the long stony beach, Stephen so tired he was hardly able to bring his bottle up to his mouth. Joe told the children more about the war history of Falmouth which Stephen had yet to visit. The moment he heard there was a wrecked aeroplane on board a ship in the harbour, he wanted to go home to demand that his mother take him there at once.

So, later in the day, Rebecca found herself getting off the *Iseult* at Falmouth with Stephen, Tamsyn and Abigail. Abigail had readily agreed to take Stephen to Falmouth because she wanted to shop for a gift for Joe at the same time, but because Stephen refused point-blank to go without his little friend, Rebecca had been told she must come too.

The sun was blazing down, bouncing off the boats and quay, and for this outing Rebecca kept her sunhat on. Abigail managed to disembark with a dignity and grace that made sailors and pleasure-boat passengers alike give her a second appreciative look. Stephen and Tamsyn jumped off unaided and fell into excited talk about the unfortunate aeroplane they were about to see and what he would get his mother to buy as props for their latest adventure as the captain and mate of a smuggling ship. Stephen's attachment to Tamsyn and the way he enjoyed playing immature games with her annoyed Abigail; it was not what was expected of a gentleman's son, but she could not object without him throwing a tantrum and at least his preoccupation kept him from being curious about why she was suddenly spending so much time going off alone.

Abigail gave Jossy an approximate time for their arrival back at the boat and then they set off in a straggly line to view the aeroplane. It had ditched in the sea to the west of Ireland when its fuel supply had run out. The first ship on the scene had rescued the pilot and the second had picked up the aircraft and taken it to Falmouth harbour. Abigail found the time looking at the remains of the aeroplane tiresome. She agreed with her son that, 'Daddy piloted and died in an aircraft far grander than this' and urged the group into the town.

Rebecca kept a respectful few inches behind Abigail and allowed her to lead the way but when they reached Arwenack Street Abigail slowed down and walked beside her.

'Stephen wants me to buy some bits and pieces and material for play clothes for his silly games. Mrs Wright said she would make them up.' Abigail sniffed haughtily. 'And he needs a pair of new shoes. I want him well turned out for the wedding and he's scuffed every pair he owns playing in the creek. Where do you recommend we go and look for them, Rebecca?'

Rebecca resisted an impatient sigh and suggested they go to Market Street to Downing's drapery shop and some premises called the Old Curiosity Shop where just about anything could be bought. For shoes she indicated a high-class shoeshop just across the road. Abigail gave her a stiff 'thank you' and after waiting for a slow-moving horsedrawn public vehicle to plod out of the way they crossed the road. As they inspected the display of shoes in the shop window, Abigail looked crossly at the children who were whispering and giggling beside her.

'It's a pity that I had to drag you along today,' she said to Rebecca. 'But I couldn't manage both of the children on my own. I daresay you would have preferred to go with Major Fiennes on his little jaunt.'

Rebecca frowned. She had come in for several cutting remarks from Abigail recently and could only think it was because she had been overheard quarrelling with Loveday; perhaps Abigail had been angered at the way she had walked out and left Loveday to serve the meal on her own. Loveday had told Rebecca that she'd apologised to the Fiennes on her behalf, explaining her absence by claiming she'd had a sudden headache. It would seem that Abigail hadn't believed the lie.

'It's nothing to do with me where the Major goes, Mrs Fiennes,' Rebecca replied in a firm and distant voice.

Abigail looked at Rebecca with hostility. She wanted to buy a present secretly for Joe and hadn't wanted anyone else with her apart from Stephen who, given a large sum of money to treat himself with, would have taken no interest in anything she might buy.

'Well, come on, all of you,' she said. 'Let's get our shopping done and I'll treat us to tea and fancy cakes.'

Stephen was uncharacteristically cooperative and new shoes were obtained for him within ten minutes. He even carried the parcel as they moved on to the Old Curiosity Shop. Abigail and Stephen were amazed at the variety of items on sale and he picked out several for his games with Tamsyn, including a pair of old-fashioned high boots ideal for 'bootlegging', a black cloth eyepatch for Tamsyn to wear, and wooden swords. While Rebecca and Tamsyn studied a collection of foreign-dressed dolls, Abigail looked around quietly by herself Then she told Rebecca to take the children to the draper's and allow Stephen to choose anything he wanted for the play clothes, saying she wanted a longer browse in the shop.

With the others gone, Abigail went straight to a particular cigarette lighter that had caught her eye. It was small and square and a dull silver, quite an ordinary thing, something no one would be surprised at Joe Carlyon owning. Abigail knew Joe wouldn't accept a flashy gift. He would probably be embarrassed at her giving it to him but he usually gave her a few flowers when they met and she wanted to show him she cared about him too.

She joined Rebecca and the children in the draper's and paid for the material Stephen had chosen, leaving behind an assistant amused by the boy's pedantry over what he'd wanted. Outside the shop, with each person carrying a parcel, Abigail said they would head for the nearest tea shop.

'According to Joe there's a six-ton stock anchor that can be seen near Gyllyngvase,' Stephen said. 'It came from the *St Vincent* and costs threepence to view and the money goes to naval charities. Can we go and see it, Mother? Then Tamsyn and I can play on the beach. Joe said there's a splendid tea room on the beach.'

Abigail smiled at her son indulgently. 'Well, if Joe says it's splendid it must be worth a visit. What do you say, Rebecca?' She looked at Rebecca critically. 'Is it far?'

'It's rather a long way to walk, Mrs Fiennes,' Rebecca answered, not missing the slight reproach in Abigail's voice.

'Then we'll take a horse cab there.'

The tea room was spotlessly clean containing long tables laid with floral tablecloths, lace-covered trays, tall white jugs, plates set at precisely spaced intervals, big shiny metal and cloam teapots, deep glass sugar bowls, and vases of flowers. Pictures adorned the walls, patterned jugs hung in rows on big hooks and snowy white nets were at the windows. Two slim women in long white aprons were in attendance and after taking their parcels from them they showed the party of four to one of the tables. Abigail sat elegantly on a stout chair and ordered tea and scones for herself and Rebecca, and told the waitress to ask the children what they wanted. Tamsyn stood and stared at the shelves stacked with huge jars and big square biscuit tins as she tried to make up her mind what she wanted. Stephen told her to order whatever she had for him too, then went to talk to an old salt with a walrus moustache. He wanted to pick his brains about the wrecked aeroplane and the massive anchor he had seen today.

Rebecca smiled at the elderly sailor, who doffed his cap to her, then she looked out of the window at the changing huts and boats. This was preferable to looking at Mrs Fiennes and warding off more of her unkind remarks.

'What an absolutely charming little place,' Abigail said, drawing Rebecca's attention away from the view. 'Have you been here before?'

'I can remember coming here as a little girl with my mother,' Rebecca replied, her voice moody.

Abigail had been looking for another way to put Rebecca down but the unusual mention of the girl's mother and the way it had been said made her feel guilty at her churlishness. 'You must have few good memories of your mother,' she said softly.

Rebecca picked up her teacup and looked blankly over its rim. 'I have nothing but good memories of my mother. It's my father who hates her.'

'You understand why she left you?'

'I understand why she left the creek.'

Rebecca's frosty answer and the challenge in her eyes forbade further questions. Abigail realised her behaviour was unwise. She worried what Alex would say if he found out she'd been unkind to his favourite person in Kennick Creek.

Chapter 21

The bells of All Hallows Church, Kea, peeled out the joyful news of Margaret Grubb having just become Mrs Archie Magor. The wedding party gathered outside the church for the photographs, and because the new heir to Trevallion was there a photographer from a local newspaper had also made an appearance. While Abigail, in a new suit and matching hat she'd had sent down from London, made sure she was in a good position to be photographed beside Alex, he was more interested in spying out Rebecca, who was keeping a low profile at the back of the group.

When just the immediate family were required for the next photograph, he grabbed Rebecca by the arm and pulled her round to the side of the church, not caring if anyone thought this odd.

'I want to know why you're so damned miserable,' Alex said under his breath.

'We can't talk about it now,' Rebecca whispered back from under the wide brim of her hat. 'We're at a wedding.'

'I don't care where we are. You've been miserable for days and I won't let it go on any longer without an explanation. Well?'

She shrugged her shoulders. What could she tell him when she didn't really know herself? She'd been hurt by Joe's lack of interest in her but had come to accept that there could never have been a future there, that her feelings for him had just been infatuation. Her feelings now were muddled. Did she really want to stay for ever where she was? She had never thought of herself as being attractive to men, but she was soon to go out with the handsome Neville Faull, a man his class would call a cad. Rebecca wasn't naive enough to believe he was looking for anything lasting or innocent; it had been unwise to accept his invitation but part of her, a part looking for relief and a little excitement, wanted to go.

Added to her mixed-up feelings was the fact that she baulked at the other Kennickers' pressure over Alex and the fate of Trevallion. Whatever he finally decided to do about the estate would be his own affair and had nothing to do with her. It wasn't fair; why couldn't they just be glad to have an employer again and wait patiently, like she was? Loveday's self-righteousness had particularly got under her skin, and Mrs Fiennes' recent behaviour towards her was inexplicable. One minute she was barking her head off, the next she was kind and understanding. What was the matter with the woman?

Seeing he wasn't going to get a quick answer, Alex tried a different approach. 'You look lovely, Becca, if that's what you're worried about. You look as good as any other woman here, much better than Abigail and even the bride.'

Rebecca gave him a wry smile. It was a sweet thing to say. 'Thank you, Alex.'

'No, really, you do. I mean it.'

He did mean it. Without realising it, Rebecca had a flair for clothes and with the money he had given her she had bought a dusky pink georgette suit to go with the hat Abigail had bought for her. She had tied her hair at the nape of her neck with a red silk bow.

Running out of patience, Alex pulled at his stiff collar. 'Please tell me, Becca. What's the matter with you? I know something's bothering you.'

'Oh, I don't know,' Rebecca sighed. It was a struggle to find the right words. 'I've just been feeling down these past few days, that's all.'

'Is it?' he asked suspiciously. The hurt was in his voice again. 'Why haven't you come to me? We're friends. You could have told me how you were feeling.'

Rebecca felt guilty at his concern. Although she couldn't think of him as a friend in the same way he seemed to think about her, he had been good to her, never flaunting his superiority over her as Abigail sometimes did. He deserved better. She smiled into his searching eyes. 'It's nothing really, Alex. We women get a bit peculiar at times, that's all.'

He put a hand on her arm. 'You would tell me if there was anything worrying you?'

'Yes, of course,' and she smiled again to reassure him.

'Don't she look a picture today, Major Fiennes?' Jenny Jenkins said mischievously as she approached them. 'Be a bride herself soon if she would only let the young men notice her, if she smiled a bit more like that. There's many who would have her.'

Rebecca made a protesting noise but Alex suddenly paled. The feeling of security that had been with him since he'd stood on Perranporth's cliffs was slipping away. 'I... I'm sure there are, Mrs Jenkins.'

The wedding party was leaving the churchyard and the guests surged after them. Rebecca walked away with Mrs Kellow and Alex was left behind, standing alone and worried. If Rebecca married, what would he do without her? He only felt able to face the future with hope and confidence knowing that she would be near him. He'd even considered taking her back to Berkshire if that was what he decided to do.

A harsh young voice broke through his reverie. 'Come on, Uncle Alex! Mother's waiting for you in the car. All the good food will be eaten up by the time we get to the reception.'

'All right, Stephen,' he said angrily. 'I'm coming.'

Stephen looked curiously at his uncle. Alex had made more fuss about having to attend this wedding than he had himself and now the ceremony was over that old film of worried emptiness had settled back on his face.

'You weren't lagging behind to have a pee, were you?' Stephen sniggered.

'Of course not,' Alex snapped.

Poor Uncle Alex, the boy thought with contempt. You're so dead inside that you can't even cuff me round the ear for being rude.

Rebecca had gone on one of the horsedrawn carts that were taking the party to the reception in an upstairs room of the Oystercatcher pub. Trease was acting as chauffeur to the bridal couple today in the Spyker, and Alex brought up the rear in the Mercedes. As he drove along the narrow twisting lanes, Abigail looked ahead and said very little. At least that was one good thing to come out of her proposition to him the other night, Alex mused spitefully. The resulting embarrassment kept her silly mouth shut.

He stayed for only a short time in the noisy room where Jacky Jenkins played his fiddle while the guests ate from packed buffet tables, then made his way down to the main bar room. He liked it in here, a long dark room with small-paned windows, solid dark furniture, horse brasses above a huge open fireplace, a stone-flagged floor, and the friendly masculine smells of beer and tobacco. He knew that the male Kennickers who had been unable to attend the ceremony because of work commitments had come the half-mile up the river by boat. He would do that himself on most nights in the future; it would provide a welcome respite from Abigail over the dinner table and give him the opportunity to get to know the local men better.

Rebecca watched Trease from an upstairs window. She was feeling proud of him today. He was standing guard over the two cars, letting none of the excited children playing about go near them. Every few moments he gave one of the cars a polish. He had kept off the drink since the day he had hurt her and had even refused to step inside the pub to toast the bride and groom. Alex appeared from the large projecting porch below carrying two pints of beer. He gave one to Trease and they began to chat – about the cars, by their looks and gestures.

Trease had shown he was truly sorry to Rebecca for hitting her. He worked hard, kept out of arguments and tried to keep their cottage clean and tidy. He was even quite affectionate towards her on occasions and Rebecca wished she did not have to sleep in the gatehouse but could go home.

Tamsyn was running about the room and Rebecca's attention was drawn from the window by Loveday's voice imploring her daughter to sit still and not to get her dress dirty. Rebecca looked at Loveday who darted her eyes quickly away. Rebecca felt guilty at being so unforgiving. She may have accepted Loveday's apology but she had not been friendly. Loveday had taken her in when her mother had deserted her and had been her friend much longer than Alexander Fiennes. What was making her behave so irrationally?

Rebecca took a fresh cup of tea over to Loveday. 'Here, you look like you could do with this.'

'Thanks,' Loveday replied uncertainly. 'It's quite an effort trying to stop my child tearing her lovely dress.'

Rebecca smiled at Tamsyn who was about to throw a piece of cake at a cheeky-looking small boy from Archie's family. Mrs Kellow wagged a stern finger at her and Tamsyn immediately dropped the cake onto the nearest plate. Big Mrs Kellow in her flowery best dress and huge feathered hat was enough to make her sit quietly.

'Look at that,' Loveday said, amazed. 'The little tyke wouldn't do that for me.'

'Well, children often ignore what their mothers tell them, don't they, Loveday?' Rebecca smiled, sitting down beside her.

'You're right there. You look… um, brighter today.'

'I'm sorry I've been so moody.'

'I suppose I asked to have my head bitten off, but it took me by surprise, seeing the Major putting his arm around you. I didn't know what to think then but I know I took it the wrong way. I am sorry, Becca.'

Archie's younger sister, a precocious-looking creature of about thirteen who had the audacity to be wearing lipstick, came up to them. 'You're Rebecca Allen, aren't you?' She twirled about in her bridesmaid's dress, a bigger version of Tamsyn's.

'Yes,' Rebecca replied. 'And you are Madeline Magor. It's been an exciting day for you.'

'Yeah,' the girl said lazily, sitting herself down on the opposite side of the table. 'Mother was beginning to think she'd never get rid of Archie. They've got a little house in Fairmantle Street. It'll be nice having a brother in Truro, be somewhere to go when I'm waiting to catch the bus home. Wish I lived there meself. Life's dull in Feock.'

'I've always thought it was a pretty little place,' Loveday said tartly.

Madeline's pale eyes suddenly grew in size and she leaned forward and giggled. 'That Major's some good-looking, isn't he? Like something out of the moving pictures.' She added dramatically, in a tone copied from something she'd heard at the cinema, 'I thought I'd simply die when I saw him in the church when I walked up the aisle behind Margaret. I've never seen anyone so gorgeous in my life. And you're his servants. Oh, you lucky creatures!'

Loveday sipped her tea then pursed her lips. She looked over the head of the young madam to show her disapproval. Madeline didn't care. She turned to Rebecca.

'I've heard he likes you. I'd simply die if someone like him took an interest in me. What's it like being alone with him? Has he kissed you? Are you his mistress?'

Rebecca gasped. 'Don't be ridiculous! If you can't talk sensibly then I suggest you go somewhere else.'

Loveday's teacup shook in her hand. She wanted to put that hand round this outrageous young miss's face.

Madeline wasn't going to go until she'd had all her say. 'I would be his mistress if I were you.'

'If you were Rebecca you would be decent and respectable, my girl. Now go away before I tell your mother what you've said.' Loveday was boiling mad. 'I blame these modern films for these young girls' fancies,' she sniffed when the girl had gone. 'Romantic they call them. I call them filth!'

Rebecca suddenly wanted to laugh. Alex Fiennes' mistress? Well, if that's what people were likely to construe from their friendship they could go ahead and good luck to them.

'She probably doesn't know what a mistress is in that sense. Madeline's just a young girl trying to grow up.'

'Well, I hope my Tamsyn won't turn out like that. And you certainly didn't, Rebecca.'

'Don't I know it,' she replied with a feeling of regret.

–

Loveday was in Truro, taking Tamsyn's bridesmaid's dress to the steam laundry to have it professionally cleaned. Despite her watchful eye and exhortations, Tamsyn had managed to get a mixture of chocolate and motor oil on the dress. Her next stop was Louise's Drapery to pick up a dress Mrs Fiennes had ordered. Loveday was shown the finished creation and thought it too racy; but then her mistress liked to show off as much flesh as she could. Loveday thought it a scandal that the woman was buying yet more clothes, spending a good deal of the Major's money, when her wardrobe was already bursting at the seams. With the box held stoutly under her arm, she walked up the hill of Lemon Street on the last of her errands to hand in a letter from the Major to the offices of Drayton, Handley and Faull, Solicitors.

With that done, she started down the hill again. A small stone got into her shoe and she stopped by the railings outside St John's Church to eject it.

'Oh, my dear Mrs Wright,' came the voice of Mr Drayton, who was coming up the hill. 'What has happened to you? Have you twisted your ankle?'

'Mr Drayton!' she exclaimed, her face colouring as she straightened up and explained what she'd been doing.

'I'm so glad to hear you did not take a fall. I was thinking hard as I climbed the hill and did not realise it was you coming towards me until you stopped.' He picked up the dress box leaning against the railings. 'May I see you to somewhere?'

'I've just come from your office. I delivered a letter there for Major Fiennes. I said I would as I was coming into town, to save him having to post it.'

'How kind of you. I haven't seen Major Fiennes since he arrived. I'm afraid he's rather elusive. Um, where are you going now, if I may ask?'

'I've got an hour and a half before my bus home. I was thinking of having a cup of tea somewhere.'

Mr Drayton's face turned bright red. 'I… I… have some spare time. Would you care to take tea with me, Mrs Wright?'

Loveday looked down shyly at the ground. The invitation was totally unexpected. She hadn't gone anywhere with a man since Stanley's last leave. In fact Stanley had been the only man she had ever gone anywhere with. She'd met him at school and back then he'd been the only boy she'd felt comfortable with. As a youth he was cheerful but not noisy or over-enthusiastic. He didn't wolf-whistle at women or make crude remarks about them. She had accepted Stanley's courtship and his quick proposal of marriage because, in the only way that Loveday could consciously put it, there had been something about him that 'felt right'. She still missed him about the house; folk would be amazed to learn she missed him in the bedroom too. Stanley had been kind, gentle and understanding. She looked up at Mr Drayton. Did he 'feel right'? She was sure he shared the same attributes as Stanley had been blessed with. She'd always felt comfortable in his presence. Surely it wouldn't hurt to have tea with him. She said, with a little surge of enthusiasm, 'I would be delighted, Mr Drayton.'

On the way to the tea shop Loveday told herself that she had accepted his invitation because it might give her the chance to find out if the Major had said anything about his plans. She told herself that his reason for inviting her was to return her kindness in making him tea and sandwiches that day at the gatehouse. That was all there was to it.

–

Meanwhile, in Falmouth, Susannah Bosanko opened a local newspaper and a picture on the third page gave her a start. It was a report about a wedding which had taken place at the weekend, but the accompanying picture was of Alexander with a young dark-haired woman. He was holding her by the arm and looking into her eyes. The caption underneath read:

> 'Major Alexander Fiennes talking to his employee Miss
> Rebecca Allen outside the church.'

Of course the heir to Trevallion was more newsworthy than the bride and groom whose picture would be somewhere near the middle of the newspaper. Susannah cut the picture out then rang for her maid to go and buy another paper. Picking up the scissors again, she cut off the half of the picture showing Rebecca and snipped it into tiny pieces.

Chapter 22

Neville Faull picked up Rebecca from her uncle and aunt's home in St Austell Street. She was waiting outside for him, wearing the outfit she had bought for the wedding. He had dressed with restrained elegance, a red carnation in the buttonhole of his dark suit. He gave her a carnation wrapped in tiny feathery ferns.

'You look beautiful, Rebecca,' he said. She knew he had not missed a detail of how she looked and she was glad she had taken more trouble than usual with her appearance. 'Let me help you with the carnation.'

She sniffed the flower's strong scent and declined his offer, asking suspiciously, 'Where's your Aunt Mildred?'

'I thought I'd come for you first and then we could collect her together,' he smiled. He handed Rebecca a pin and when the carnation was secure under her suit collar, he offered her his arm.

'I didn't bring the car. We haven't got far to go and I thought, like Aunt Mildred, you'd prefer to walk on such a lovely warm evening.'

Rebecca was glad of this. It would have caused a lot of public interest if she'd alighted from his flashy car outside the Palace Cinema. If they walked quietly up to the queue with Neville's Aunt Mildred, people wouldn't be able to make as much of that. She thought he'd try to keep his meeting with her discreet, with him being on the rural council and she being of no consequence, but he walked proudly through the town with her as if he was showing her off.

When they got to one of the elegant Georgian terraced houses of Walsingham Place, a maid showed them inside. Mrs Mildred Cummings was laid out dramatically across a chaise longue and warning bells began to ring in Rebecca's head.

'Oh, my dears,' said Mildred Cummings in a faint voice. 'I'm so very sorry. I was out shopping this afternoon and was overcome by a dizzy spell and my head is still spinning. I won't be able to go out tonight and I was so looking forward to seeing *The Sheikh*. I'm afraid I've quite spoiled your evening. I do hope you will forgive me.'

'Well, we'd better leave you to rest, Auntie dear,' Neville said softly, going to her and kissing her hushed cheek. 'I'll escort Miss Allen back to her uncle's house.'

'I hope we will have another opportunity to meet soon, Miss Allen,' Mildred Cummings sighed softly.

'I hope you will soon feel better, Mrs Cummings,' Rebecca said.

Back outside in the wide curved street, Rebecca turned to Neville. 'I suppose you're going to say it's a shame to waste the evening and wouldn't I like to go to the cinema anyway?'

'Honestly, Rebecca,' he said, putting his hand over his heart, 'I fully intended to get rid of Aunt Mildred later in the evening but I didn't plan that dizzy spell. Poor old duck. She can't get enough of Rudolph Valentino. I've never seen her looking so poorly before. Well, what would you like to do? It's up to you.'

'You're a brazen man, Neville Faull.'

'I've never pretended to be otherwise.'

His beautiful blue eyes were sparkling, exuding playful wickedness. Rebecca smiled ironically. 'Oh, all right. It can't do any harm in broad daylight, but I'm warning you, I can look after myself.'

'Never thought for a moment you couldn't, my dear.' Inside the Palace Cinema, she knew he was looking at her more than he was the film. The couple in front of him were snuggled up but Neville didn't try to be familiar. He stood smartly to attention when the National Anthem was being played and she wondered what he had done during the war. With such a straight stance, shoulders proudly back, he must have served in one of His Majesty's armed forces.

When the last note had died away, Neville led her carefully out of the cinema, shielding her from the dispersing crowd. Outside in the gaslight from a nearby street lamp she saw his face smiling down gently at her. 'A bit of supper, Rebecca? The Treleaven Restaurant? It serves excellent fare.'

She was surprised he was asking her if she wanted to go on for supper with him. She thought it was already taken for granted. He wasn't being as pushy as she'd thought he would be, but it could be a ploy. She didn't want to go to a popular place like the Treleaven Restaurant, however, and hoped Neville would not press it.

'I'd rather go to Opie's Dining Rooms. I'd feel more comfortable.'

'Certainly, anything you say.'

'Thank you for taking me to the cinema, Neville,' Rebecca said as they strolled across the town to Kenwyn Street. She had not called him Neville before but it seemed silly to call him Mr Faull now.

'You make delightful company.' He lifted the chiffon scarf she wore round her neck and held it against the lower half of her face. 'Do you see yourself as a film actress like Miss Agnes Ayres? I must say I'd like to have you in my harem.'

She knew Neville was teasing her and answered him in the same vein. 'I don't see myself as any man's slave.'

'Nor do I. That's why I'm so attracted to you. I see you more as a Miss Mary Pickford, the cinema's sweetheart.'

Rebecca felt a flush of pleasure but she made a wry face. She mustn't drop her guard tonight or she could end up as another of this man's conquests. Looking into his beguiling eyes, she could see why so many women were rumoured to have succumbed to him. Neville Faull had more than charm. He had more than clean-cut good looks. He seemed thoughtful and good-humoured too and Rebecca found herself liking him.

'I haven't seen any pictures with Mary Pickford in.'

'You haven't been to the cinema much before then?'

'Only twice. Each time with my cousin Raymon. Die first time we saw the Keystone Cops and then a Charlie Chaplin film.'

'But wouldn't you rather see those dark intense Valentino eyes looking back at you from the screen?'

'Perhaps.'

'Well, if you like comedy films, there's an Oliver Hardy film next week.' He left the sentence hanging and they walked on to the restaurant, reaching it by ascending a short flight of stairs over a haberdashery.

It was quiet inside, with just two other couples taking supper. Red velvety curtains were drawn across the wide windows, giving the room a warm rosy glow in the gaslight. The service was quick, friendly and efficient. They sat in a secluded corner and ate a light meal of asparagus soup and grilled plaice followed by a delicious lemon souffle. Neville ordered just one bottle of white wine and didn't insist Rebecca drink more than the one glass she wanted. He paid the bill so discreetly Rebecca didn't even notice.

After retrieving her scarf from the back of her chair, she excused herself to go to the ladies' room. She studied her reflection in the mirror over the sink. She'd secured her hair back in a chignon and it had stayed tidy under her hat. She had the lipstick Abigail had given her in her handbag and considered whether to apply some. She decided not to. Her face was bright enough as it was and Neville might see the addition of cosmetics as an open invitation. One thing she was sure of, and she wanted it to happen, was that she would be kissed on the lips for the first time before this night was over.

If Joe had kissed her in the field she wouldn't be here now. Up until now Rebecca had been a serious young woman, not given to flights of fancy or romantic thoughts apart from her infatuation with Joe. But she took her time now going over her feelings. Who would she rather be kissed by? Joe or Neville? A romance with Joe might have gone on to him offering her a steady life in the creek as his wife. Neville would probably offer her nothing more than a brief affair; he would certainly be looking upmarket for a wife. But it wasn't as if she wanted to marry either of these men.

Come on, Rebecca, she told herself, picking up her handbag and squaring her shoulders. Go out and see what the night will bring.

Neville was waiting for her by the restaurant door. Out in the cool evening air, he reached inside his jacket and produced a long cigar. 'Do you mind, Rebecca?'

'Not in the least.'

He lit the cigar and tucked her arm inside his. 'Shall we go for a stroll down by the river?'

'Just for a few minutes then. I have to be in by ten-thirty or my uncle and aunt will start worrying about me.'

'I take it they know who you are with tonight?'

'Yes, of course. They were rather surprised.'

'Did they try to talk you out of it?'

'They weren't keen about it but as I was supposed to be having a chaperone, they let me go. In the end they said they trusted me to be sensible, and besides, you have a reputation to keep in your position in the city.'

Neville laughed and squeezed her round the waist. 'My God, surely they don't want me to live up to the reputation I've got as a womaniser.'

'Not that.' She laughed too. 'They meant your position on the rural council and as a solicitor. You admit it then? Being a womaniser?'

'Why shouldn't I? It's what most men would kill for. But no one can prove a thing, you know. It's all rumours, Rebecca, my dear. Could all be lies.'

She looked at him sideways. No one would believe that.

'I bet your father doesn't know you're with me though, does he?'

'No. He thinks I just fancied a night away from the estate.'

'Trease hates me. Probably thinks you're having a quiet evening in with your favourite uncle and aunt and will be tucked up in bed like a good little girl at ten o'clock with a cup of cocoa.'

Her father probably did think that but Rebecca didn't feel guilty about it.

They retraced their steps to the Palace Cinema and crossed the road to stand on the Boscawen Bridge, looking down on the quiet water where the Rivers Allen and Kenwyn merged to form the Truro River.

Neville leant on the railings. He threw the cigar butt down where it joined forces with a scrap of curled-up cardboard. He watched the odd-looking boat he had made float away then he looked at Rebecca.

'Your boss is a hard man to track down. Mr Drayton and I have been requesting a meeting with Major Fiennes for several days and he keeps putting us off. He may not have made up his mind about the estate yet but there are some decisions he must make soon.'

'All of us are waiting for him to make up his mind about Trevallion but since we've got to know him we've learned to trust him.'

'He must be causing quite a stir among the women on the estate.'

'In what way?'

'Well, he's an attractive man. The ladies of the city are straining themselves trying to think of a way to lure him out of his shell and make social contact with him. A rich man like him would make a good catch.'

'The Major's more interested in a very old lady who lives in Falmouth,' she said, to distract him from making observations about her own relationship with Alex.

'Oh really?' Neville arched his back and dropped his eyes back to the river. 'And who is that?'

Rebecca knew she shouldn't be talking about Alex's business but she thought it possible Neville might know something about Susannah Bosanko. He must have gone through the estate's papers closely over the years and might have seen something interesting. If he could ask her questions then she could do the same to him.

'Her name's Miss Bosanko. She was the aunt of Miss Harriet who was the fiancée of Captain Miles.'

Neville's face was grim. Fiennes must have come across Susannah Bosanko's name in connection with her late niece. Why was he bothering with the hideous old wretch? Nobody took a step near her if they could avoid it. If the Bosanko woman got him to agree to sell Trevallion to her, it would deny Neville the handsome commission he'd been promised. He would have to step up his attempts to talk to the Major alone.

Wondering why Neville had gone quiet, Rebecca took a step closer to him. 'Know something about her, do you?'

'No.' Neville looked up and ran the back of a finger gently up her arm. 'I've heard Fiennes rather likes you.'

'Have you now?' she said tartly, cross that he had clammed up about Miss Bosanko and that he knew about her friendship with Alex.

'Is it true?'

'We get along well, yes. Is that why you asked me out? To try to find out something about the Major?'

'Hell, no,' Neville said huskily, standing up straight. 'I've wanted to take you out for ages. I think you are so very, very beautiful, Rebecca, and I don't think you realise it one bit.'

'I haven't exactly got men falling at my feet.'

'That's because they haven't got the gumption or imagination to see past your rather gloomy exterior. Well, I have and I find you absolutely fascinating.'

A lump rose in Rebecca's throat. This was the first time she had received a lover's flattery. Said in Neville Faull's own inimitable way, it was dizzying. More dangerously, he sounded sincere. She looked up into his eyes.

He said softly, 'I'd like to kiss you, Rebecca.'

Time stood still for a moment. Then she closed her eyes as he took her into his arms. Thinking it was probably her first kiss, Neville was tender and understanding. Rebecca responded with a passion that amazed her. It felt wonderful, being in this man's arms, feeling his strong body against hers, the sensation of his warm lips pressing down and moving over hers. He was awakening new and exciting instincts in her. It was almost like being attacked by a million delicious little pains, a heady exhilaration that she had never imagined existed.

Neville took his mouth away and pulling off her hat he buried his face in her glorious hair. 'Oh, I could drink you in, Rebecca,' he moaned. 'Every tiny bit of you.'

She laid the side of her face against his chest, wanting to stay in his strong masculine warmth.

He lifted her chin and kissed her again, steadily increasing his depth and passion. Rebecca returned his embrace with equal fervour and was shocked by the sensuality of the thoughts skimming through her head. With a ladylike restraint, she pulled herself away from him.

Fighting to regain her breath she said, 'We'd better go.'

Neville seemed to devour her in one lingering look, then putting his arm around her shoulders he held her close beside him as they began the walk back to St Austell Street. The streets were quiet under the still night air, the yellow glow of light around the gaslamps making the atmosphere cosy and friendly.

'We'll have electric lighting in Truro next year,' Neville said.

'Really? That will be much more convenient.' Rebecca smiled to herself She'd expected him to carry on with his lovemaking, and she was amazed that she could chat like this, so soon after being kissed for the very first time so wonderfully.

'Much more convenient and cleaner and it's about time too. Even many small villages have electricity laid on.'

They talked in this way until they were standing outside Uncle Bert's front door.

'No lights are on,' Neville remarked.

'Shush, they must be in bed.'

He smiled and shook his head.

Rebecca was puzzled. 'What?'

He gave another of his mysterious smiles. 'Oh, my beautiful Rebecca.'

She had been trailing her hat from her fingertips. Neville took it from her and put it on the garden wall, quickly followed by her handbag. He put a hand on each side of her face and leaned forward to kiss her. Rebecca turned away. She shouldn't be doing this on her uncle's doorstep. What would the neighbours think if they saw her? And it wasn't as if she was out with just any young man.

'There's no one about,' Neville whispered, bringing his head down towards hers.

Rebecca didn't have time to protest before his lips were on hers. She allowed him to pull her in close and she put her arms round his neck. His kiss was long and ardent and conjured up those forbidden feelings in her again. It seemed it would go on all night and finally she broke free.

'We can't stay here like this,' she said breathlessly.

'Let's go inside then.'

She looked around wildly for a moment. 'My uncle and aunt—'

'Are away visiting their son Raymon who now lives in Plymouth and is recovering from having his appendix removed. There's no one in the house. It's quite empty. You've got the key, Rebecca.' Neville took her in his arms again. 'Well, my darling, are you going to invite me in?'

Chapter 23

Tamsyn and Stephen were playing down in the creek. They had spent the early part of the morning shrimping on the low spring tide and taken their plentiful catch to Ira Jenkins to be boiled for their tea. Now they were in Tamsyn's hideout, dressed in the pirate outfits Loveday had made for them. Tamsyn was wearing a black and white striped top, red leggings and a red spotted scarf around her head. Stephen was in a ruffled shirt, gold waistcoat, big shiny belt, black leggings and high boots. Tamsyn had a black moustache painted over her top lip and Stephen was wearing a long crinkly red wig and a sweeping black hat with an ostrich feather filched from his mother's wardrobe.

'Why can't I be Captain Redbeard for once?' Tamsyn demanded, folding her arms crossly and pushing out her bottom lip. 'I don't want to be first mate or a prisoner all the time.'

'I've told you a hundred times! Don't you ever listen to me, you stupid girl? You can't be the captain because I'm bigger and older than you and because you're a girl.' Stephen whacked his toy wooden sword against the wobbly old stool that served as a table.

'It's not fair. And don't do that again or I won't let you play in my hideout ever again.'

'Huh! All this is on my uncle's property so it's mine more than yours. I wish this creek had boys of my own age then I wouldn't have to play with you.'

'You said we were blood brothers. I even cut my thumb like you did to prove it.' Tamsyn held up the thumb still with a tiny scratch on it then she looked down and picked at a scab on her knee.

Making Tamsyn his 'blood brother' was something Stephen had instantly regretted. She might be a tomboy but she was still a girl.

Calling her Tam and blacking her face with creek mud didn't make her a boy. The chaps at school would think him a complete ass if they ever found out. They'd think he was an ass anyway for playing such childish games, but he had never had the opportunity to play like this before and with only a little girl as witness, and with his mother and uncle taking no notice of him, glad he was out of their way, he was enjoying it.

He smacked her hand. 'Stop doing that, Tam. You'll make it go bad and it's a beastly thing to do anyway.'

'Grumbleguts,' the little fair-haired girl murmured. Despite himself Stephen couldn't help smiling. He did it every time she called him that. Wherever did Tam pick up such a word? Her mother would have kittens if she heard her say it. He took a cigarette, lifted from his mother's gold case, out of his waistcoat pocket.

'Now, One-Eyed Pete, where did you leave your eyepatch?' he said patiently. 'You must have some idea. Think hard. Where did you have it last?'

'I didn't have it when Joe took us out on the boat last.'

'You've already said that, dead-brain.'

Tamsyn poked her tongue out at him at his use of his favourite nickname for her. When she saw the cigarette, she gasped indignantly. 'You're not lighting that thing in here! You might burn my hideout down.'

'Never mind that, I'll smoke it outside.'

'You'll get into trouble if one of the grown-ups sees you. And anyway, it's bad for you. Uncle Joe says so. He says he wishes he'd never started to smoke.'

'I've been smoking for ages and it's done me no harm,' Stephen said defensively. 'All the chaps at school do it. Don't go on about it, I'll make sure no one sees me. Now what about your eyepatch? I bought it specially for you, Tam.'

'Could be anywhere. We last played pirates up by the stables. When we were stealing Jumping Jake's smuggling booty out of his hiding place.'

'Well, let's go and take a quick look there. If we can't find it, we'll think of another game. Think yourself lucky, Tam. I've got to get myself all washed and dressed up by two o'clock. Uncle Alex has invited some decrepit old woman to the big house now it's all been done up and he's insisting I be there too. Can't think why. What have I got to say to the old bat? I'd rather go rowing with Joe again. He says I'm a natural.'

Tamsyn sympathised with him as they walked to the stables. 'Glad I'm not rich and a somebody. I'd hate to have to take tea with a strange old lady I've never met before. Do you think it's really true that she's half lizard?'

Stephen exhaled smoke from the stolen cigarette. 'I only said Uncle Alex told Mother her eyes are like a lizard's. Don't let them hear you saying it or you'll get me into trouble. Uncle Alex has visited the old crow three times and wouldn't let me go with him once. He said he wants me to meet her here. Uncle Alex can be a real pain at times.'

'But he always brings Captain Action comics and buttercream toffees and something for the model railway back with him for you. And he did take us to Perranporth that time. I'd never been to that sort of beach with golden sand before. I think the Major's a nice man. He always pats me on the head and asks how I am.'

'That's because he thinks you're a scruffy little dog.' Stephen ruffled her hair and they fought playfully as they went along.

'I wish I had an uncle like the Major. I have Uncle Joe although he's not my real uncle. I know he's taken us rowing twice but he's always busy these days, wanting to go off somewhere alone.'

Stephen gave a superior huff. 'That's probably because he's got a woman somewhere. A bint. The sort he doesn't want decent people to see him with.'

From the expression on Tamsyn's face he could see he was about to be hit with a barrage of questions he wouldn't like to answer. 'Look for your eyepatch,' he said gruffly. 'You might have dropped it along the path somewhere. I'm going to be on my best behaviour this afternoon for Uncle Alex's old bat and then I'm going to ask him to take us to Perranporth again.'

'Well, it will have to be at the weekend because I've got to go to school next week.'

'I wish I knew where I was going to school next term. Mother's talked Uncle Alex into providing me with a tutor until he's decided on the estate's future.'

Tamsyn slipped her hand into Stephen's and he let it stay there for a few moments. 'You don't want to go back to Berkshire, do you?'

Stephen looked back at the creek behind them. 'No, of course not.'

Their route took them past the big house. Percy Gummoe and the gardeners were bustling about putting finishing touches here and there for Susannah Bosanko's visit. Alex waved to the children from a window and tapped his wristwatch to indicate to Stephen that he must watch the time.

'I'll be late if I want to,' the boy muttered defiantly.

As they passed the back of the house, Loveday came running out of the kitchen. 'Where are you two off to?'

'Only to the stables, Mum,' Tamsyn said, edging away with Stephen, hoping her mother had no other plans for her.

'You come back to me for your dinner, Tamsyn, and then you're to spend the afternoon with Ira Jenkins. And Tamsyn, you must behave yourself this afternoon. The Major has a very important guest coming here and he will be very cross if anything happens to spoil it.'

'I'll be good, Mum,' Tamsyn promised.

'I'd hate to have a mother like that,' Stephen said darkly when they were out of earshot. But he went quiet for a while. In fact it would be really nice to have a mother who took a proper interest in him. All his mother seemed to want to do these days was to slip away on her own. When they'd arrived here she'd wanted Rebecca near her all the time. Now she seemed to have lost interest in her too.

–

When they reached the stable yard they separated to look for the eyepatch. Tamsyn didn't understand why it was so important to find it but pirates was Stephen's favourite game and he liked it to be authentic. Tamsyn had refused to be a one-legged pirate but she could hardly be One-Eyed Pete without her eyepatch. As soon as the game began he would put on his red beard – a piece of cardboard with long lengths of red wool glued all over it, attached to his head by a length of elastic – and give the most bloodcurdling cries.

Stephen looked around the yard and Tamsyn went into the hay barn. She remembered they had sat on a hay bale chewing buttercream toffees the day before. She saw the little black eyepatch almost at once and ran to pick it up. She was about to put it over her head and rush out to show Stephen when she froze in fear. She could hear strange noises and thought the ghost of the big house had moved into the barn. She looked all about and realised the noises were coming from the hayloft. Trance-like, she moved to the foot of the ladder. There she got a second shock. She heard a voice moan but it was clear enough for her to recognise whose it was.

'Ohh Joe.'

There it was again. Mrs Fiennes was with Uncle Joe and she recognised a grunt from him. Instinct told her that they were doing something wrong and Stephen must never know. She rushed out of the barn and collided with him.

'Ouch, be careful.'

'Sorry, Stephen. Look, I've found my eyepatch. Let's get back to the creek.'

'We might as well play in the yard now we're here.'

'NO! I want to play in the creek.' And One-Eyed Pete ran pell-mell out of the stable yard disobeying his captain's orders.

–

It was nearly two o'clock and Alex was on tenterhooks waiting for Susannah Bosanko to arrive. He peered out of the windows and looked at his wristwatch every few seconds. He paced up and down the hall, his shoes echoing on the wooden floor. There was a light step behind him and he swung round. 'Oh, Becca, it's you.'

'I couldn't find her, Alex.'

'Who?' he asked impatiently, wringing his hands.

'Mrs Fiennes, of course. You sent me to find her, remember?' Rebecca looked at him with a hint of amusement on her face. 'Anyone would think you were expecting your lady love to arrive to introduce her to your parents for the first time.'

'It isn't funny, Becca.' He thought he heard a car pull up and leapt to a window. 'Damned woman,' he said under his breath.

Rebecca stood beside him. 'Who? Miss Bosanko?'

'No, not her. Abigail! She should have been here by now. Stephen is, he's been sitting quietly in the drawing room for fifteen minutes. I thought you might have had to drag her away from her make-up and mirror to meet Susannah but I didn't expect her to disappear. You look lovely, by the way.'

'Thank you.' Rebecca could see the tension in his lean body and deep lines creased his forehead. She touched his arm and it twitched. She caught his hand and pulled down hard on it to attract his full attention. 'Calm down, Alex. You've been like a taut spring ready to snap all morning You haven't eaten a thing all day. You'll make yourself ill. Miss Bosanko is only an old lady. Why are you in such a state over her?'

He looked at her and blinked and his battered nerves seem to relax in front of her eyes. He sighed deeply and managed a small smile. 'I don't know. Sometimes I think I'm going off my head, Becca.' He took her other hand and squeezed it. 'Thank God you're here to calm me down. I don't know what I'd do without you.'

'That's better,' she said, straightening his tie. 'I'll go to the kitchen and bring the tea in when you ring.'

'No. Stay with me and greet Susannah.'

'Not me. My place is in the kitchen.'

When Rebecca's footsteps had died away, Alex asked himself why he was in such a nervous state over Susannah's impending visit. There was no doubt that she fascinated him but there was something disturbing about her too.

The moment he had kissed her cheek the second time he had called on her, three days after Margaret Grubb's wedding, she had held out a newspaper cutting to him.

'So this is your Rebecca, Alexander?'

He took the piece of paper and saw it was a photograph of himself and Rebecca at the wedding. 'Why on earth did they put this in the paper? It was the bride and groom's day. I had very little to do with it.'

'They are not newsworthy, darling. You are. She's a very beautiful young woman, Rebecca Allen.' Susannah watched Alex's face closely. 'Don't you think?'

Alex took the newspaper cutting to the window to see it more clearly. In the picture he and Rebecca were standing outside the church, where he had taken her to question her about her bad mood. He had his hand on her arm. 'Yes, she is lovely,' he said, smiling down at her face in the picture.

'You look as though you are a couple,' Susannah observed in a dry voice.

'Yes, I suppose we do. I hope you'll get the chance to meet her soon.'

He had given her back the cutting and felt alarmed when she had crumpled it in her hand and tossed it into a wastepaper bin.

On his next visit to Melvill Road, just one day ago, Susannah had chattered excitedly about her forthcoming visit to Trevallion. She had been animated, on her feet most of the time, whirling about the drawing room like a young girl and he had been surprised at her vitality.

She had wound up the gramophone and insisted that he dance with her. Alex had laughed at first and waltzed with her, expecting them to sit down afterwards. But she had put record after record on to play, making him dance with her until he was dizzy and out of breath. He had implored her to sit down, thinking that if he was worn out, she, at her age, could drop exhausted and he would be responsible for her sudden demise. But Susannah had insisted on dancing just one more tango. Her movements had been as lithe as someone years younger and she had gripped Alex so tightly he thought he'd choke. When the music finished he'd let her go but Susannah stayed close to him.

He was embarrassed. 'I... think I need a drink.'

He'd poured himself a large Scotch with shaking hands. For one awful moment he thought she was going to follow him but she had sat down and behaved with perfect decorum for the rest of his visit.

I'm afraid, Alex admitted to himself. I'm afraid she might get familiar again and if it happened in front of somebody here…

A car's horn sounded and he went outside to receive Susannah. She refused her chauffeur's hand and allowed Alex to help her alight. She was dressed as usual in green, in a short sleeveless dress which showed her raddled flesh, emerald clips flashing on its low V neck. Tucking her clutch bag under her arm, she kissed both of Alex's cheeks than his lips. He tried to escort her into the house but she held him back.

'Let me look at you, Alexander. You are very pale and look agitated. Are you not pleased to see me?'

'Of course I am. I've been looking forward to it for two weeks.' He kissed her as she had him and she seemed to be satisfied.

Alex showed her into the drawing room and after apologising for Abigail's unexplained absence introduced her to Stephen. Susannah shook Stephen's hand and stared at him. Stephen had been stared out by Rebecca and that had taken several moments. With Susannah Bosanko he gulped and dropped his eyes immediately.

'I don't suppose you wanted to meet me for a minute,' Susannah said coldly. 'Having to get all spruced up when you'd rather be out doing what little boys like you do, no doubt causing some kind of trouble for someone else. I don't like children. You've done your duty, Stephen Fiennes, so you can run along at once.'

Stephen intended to be on his best behaviour in the hope of getting another trip to Perranporth out of his uncle and he had wanted to impress this old lady with what he called his wit. But all he said meekly was, 'Yes, Miss Bosanko.'

Alex gaped as Stephen obediently walked from the room without another word.

'Close your mouth, Alexander. It's most unbecoming in a gentleman. I'm glad to be rid of the tiresome child and have no wish to meet his mother either.'

'Um… do sit down, Susannah. I'll ring for tea.'

Susannah seated herself at the side of the fireplace, her head sinking down on her chest. 'I've always liked this room. Miles had it decorated for Harriet. We were here only a week before she died.'

'I forget sometimes that this house must hold poignant memories for you.'

'Yes,' she said slowly, fixing him with her lizard eyes. 'You only have memories of Miles away from the property. You weren't here in the old days. I am glad to see that nothing has been changed.'

A few minutes later Rebecca entered the room with the tea tray. With narrowed eyes, Susannah watched her put the tray down on the table in front of her.

'Let me introduce you to Becca,' Alex said, and there was an element of pride in his face as he presented Rebecca to the old woman.

Rebecca came forward with her hand out. Susannah's head shot up and as Rebecca saw her face more clearly, she gave a shiver and grasped Alex's hand instead. 'P-pleased to meet you, Miss Bosanko.'

Susannah motioned with a gnarled hand, the veins of which were purple and prominent. 'Come here, girl. I can't see you if you hide behind Major Fiennes.'

Alex smiled encouragement at Rebecca and she obeyed. Susannah looked her up and down very slowly.

'Mmmm, a pretty dress but serviceable for a girl such as you. Sensible shoes, trim calves and shapely ankles but your stockings are not put on properly. Firm breasts, although a trifle too big to be ladylike, and well-set shoulders. Your best features are your beautiful eyes and, yes, your magnificent black hair. Alex told me you had beautiful hair.'

Rebecca almost expected this hideous old woman to order her to open her mouth so she could inspect her teeth. She found her voice from somewhere low in her chest. 'Thank you, Miss Bosanko. Shall I pour the tea or would you care to do it?'

'I shall entertain Major Fiennes, Rebecca. Return to the kitchens at once.'

Rebecca couldn't get out of the room fast enough. Whatever did Alex find so fascinating about Susannah Bosanko? She was barely human! As she reached the door, Susannah's voice halted her.

'And Rebecca, we do not wish to be disturbed.'

Rebecca turned and nodded and threw Alex an astonished look before hurrying out and closing the door.

'The child is afraid of me,' Susannah said, leaning towards the tea tray.

'Rebecca isn't afraid of anyone.' It was an automatic reply because it was how Alex had always seen Rebecca. But now he saw Susannah Bosanko as Rebecca had, what she was really like. The fascination she'd held for him evaporated and instead he felt distinctly uneasy.

He took his tea over to the french windows.

'Do you have plans to live here, Alexander?'

'None as yet.'

'That's a pity. This house should be lived in.'

'Well, it has a resident ghost.' He forced a laugh. He was finding conversation difficult.

'A ghost?' Susannah raised an eyebrow. 'And of whom is that supposed to be?'

Alex turned and faced her. This could be interesting. He hadn't been able to draw her out on her lover who had lived and died here. 'Roland Trevallion. He died violently in the cellar, as I'm sure you know.'

Susannah's face turned purple and he thought she was going to have a seizure. 'He was the most vile of men! I would prefer it if you did not mention him to me again.'

Alex felt his skin crawl. So she had not forgiven the man who had spurned her. She was probably pleased he had met a tragic and untimely end if the vindictive look on her wrinkled face was anything to go by. He put his teacup down and went to the drinks cabinet. He needed something to take the taste of decay out of his mouth. He kept his eyes rooted to the old lady's face, watching her every move and praying she would not come anywhere near him. He had a great rapport with Rebecca and now he shared something else with her. He was suddenly very much afraid of Susannah Bosanko, and of what she might be planning inside that gnarled old head.

Chapter 24

Rebecca was walking back from Verrian Farm. A car roared round a bend and she had to throw herself in the ditch.

'You mad fool!' she screamed, shaking her fist.

Neville Faull brought his vehicle to a swift halt, throwing up dust and grit. He got out of the car, laughing as he held out his hands to her.

'Sorry about that, darling. I took the bend a little too tightly.'

'It's a good job the front wheel of my bicycle is buckled and I left it on the farm for Clifford Kellow to mend or I would have been tossed sixty feet up in the air! And if I wasn't wearing my riding breeches my legs would be cut to ribbons on the brambles in this ditch. If you had met Farmer Bocock on that bend you'd have two dead horses on your conscience by now. And if—'

'Are you going to stay there all day shouting at me or are you going to let me help you out? By heavens, Rebecca, you look beautiful when you're angry.'

She took his hands and leapt out of the ditch then shook dust and bits of dead twig off her breeches. 'Beautiful when I'm angry indeed. Who do you think you are? Rudolph Valentino?'

Neville took off his cap and placed it on her head. 'No, my dear, just an ordinary man who's besotted with you. I wouldn't make much of a film star but,' he lowered his voice huskily, 'I'd love to kidnap you and take you to my desert tent.'

'Fool,' she said, playfully hitting him with his cap and putting it in his hand. 'And there's nothing ordinary about you, Neville Faull.'

'Glad you think so, my dear.' He was looking at her admiringly. 'Let me tidy your hair for you. It's—'

Rebecca pushed his hands away. 'I'll do it myself. What would people think if they saw us?'

'They'd probably think I was trying to seduce you,' and he winked saucily.

'Neville!'

They laughed, and he kissed her cheek then gestured towards his car. 'Can I give you a lift to the gatehouse? It's where I'm going. I've written to the Major requesting that he stays in to receive me but I also hoped it would give me the opportunity of seeing you again.'

'Only if you promise not to drive like a madman.'

In the car he reached over to the back seat and dropped a small box wrapped in floral patterned paper in her lap.

Rebecca picked it up and gently shook it. 'What is it?'

'Just a little gift, a box of chocolates. I was hoping I'd see you alone to give it to you.'

She lifted the tiny red silk bow on the box with a fingertip and stared down at it.

'Aren't you going to say something?'

'I've never been given anything like this before. Thank you, Neville.'

'My pleasure, Rebecca.' He leaned across and put his arm round her. Rebecca glanced along the lane. There was no one in sight and she accepted the long full kiss from him.

'How about coming into town and dining with my Aunt Mildred? She's dying to meet you properly and she thinks it will give her an opening to meet the Major,' he said, placing tiny soft kisses around her ear. 'Or would you prefer to go to the pictures again?'

Rebecca rested her head against his shoulder and said nothing. She was turning things over in her mind. Neville brought his hand under her chin and lifted her face to his.

'You do want to see me again?' He looked quite worried.

'Yes, but it'll be difficult to get away so soon. I don't want you bringing me back here. Mrs Fiennes wouldn't approve and she might tell my father. I don't want a quarrel about it. I'll have more of an idea when I can get away in a few days' time.'

'The Regatta Fortnight has begun. Are you going to the St Mawes Regatta? I hear that the Major is attending and Kennick Creek will be involved. Mr Drayton wants to go, for some obscure reason, and I was thinking of popping along myself. I don't want the old boy pulling a fast one over me with the Major.'

'Why should Mr Drayton do that?' she frowned. 'What are you up to?'

Neville tightened his mouth but the humour was still in his eyes. 'Talk about instant distrust.'

'I'd forgotten for a moment that you're a man not to be trusted.'

'Oh, I see,' he said softly, running a finger delicately along her chin. 'Does this mean I'm wasting my time?'

She looked into his eyes. They gazed steadily back at her. What could she read in those blue depths? She looked at his lips and recalled his wonderful kisses. 'I'll be at the regatta. I'll tell you then when I've next got time off. And I would like to meet your Aunt Mildred again.'

He smiled and she felt warm and lighthearted. This was just what she needed, a romance with a handsome man, and what young woman could blame her?

'Aunt Mildred's it is then. We can get to know each other better,' Neville said. He added, looking straight into her eyes, 'We could have done that last week if you'd invited me into your uncle's house.'

'It wouldn't have been wise for many reasons.'

'Why?' He kissed her forehead. 'Wouldn't I have been safe alone with you?'

Rebecca raised her eyes to the sky and shook her head at him. They kissed again then she looked at his wristwatch. 'I'd better get back or I'll have Mrs Fiennes after me.' Neville drove at speed along the narrow lanes and Rebecca's hair flowed out behind her like a length of black satin. Her face was flushed from the wind when they pulled up.

When they entered the gatehouse Abigail came running down the stairs. She had seen the car pull up and was furious to see Rebecca getting out. Their friendliness was obvious and to Abigail that amounted to nothing less than mutiny on Rebecca's part. 'So there you are at last! I gave you permission to take your bicycle to the farm to be repaired. I did not expect you to stay there all day. You may think you can do what you like where the Major is concerned but don't forget you're only an employee. Go and change this instant, Rebecca! And if you can't keep your hair tidy, I'll make you have it cut short.'

Rebecca was about to open her mouth and explode when Neville, who had been standing behind her, pushed her aside to speak up angrily on her behalf He was beaten to it however.

'*Abigail!*'

Abigail jumped out of her skin as Alex stormed out of the sitting room. 'What on earth do you think you're doing? Shouting at Rebecca as though she was a worthless menial.'

'I wouldn't speak to a dog like that,' Neville muttered loudly. He recognised spiteful jealousy when he saw it.

'I don't require your opinion on this, Faull,' Alex said coldly. 'Please go into the sitting room. I'll be with you in a moment.'

Neville glanced regretfully at Rebecca but did as he was bidden.

'You go on up to your room, Becca,' Alex said quietly. 'I want to speak to Mrs Fiennes alone.'

Rebecca obeyed with a stony face. Alex and Abigail were glaring at each other and neither noticed the box she was carrying. The instant Rebecca cleared the top step of the stairs, Abigail turned on Alex.

'Don't you dare give me a lecture, Alex Fiennes.' She made to storm off but he gripped her arm tightly.

'I won't allow you to speak to Becca like that. She's not employed here to be at your beck and call. First of all you insisted on trying to turn her into something she isn't and lately you don't seem to want her around you at all. As it is she would prefer to work on the farm. You must remember, Abigail, people are not so eager to go into service these days. They can find work in factories, shops and in offices.'

'So servants aren't so subservient these days. I know that. But that's not the real reason you're angry with me. It's because I shouted at your precious Rebecca, or *Becca* as you so endearingly call her. It's you who wants her around all the time and you don't like it when someone else wants her to attend to her duties.' Abigail pushed his hand away and added spitefully, 'You'd drop dead of fright if she left the estate, wouldn't you, Alex?'

Alex looked at Abigail with the utter contempt he felt for her. 'Probably, and that would be too bad for you, Abigail. Ralph gambled away all his money, remember, and I haven't changed my will in your or Stephen's favour since his death. I've got other relatives and you would be left out in the cold.'

Abigail gulped and went white. 'I thought you were going to make arrangements concerning Stephen. Ralph wouldn't have—'

'Ralph couldn't stand the boy any more than I can. He wouldn't have been too worried about Stephen's future. He's an evil little sod, your son, Abigail, selfish and arrogant and he'll almost certainly grow up to be as immoral as you are.'

'But Ralph did have some feelings for Stephen and I'm sure you have too, Alex,' Abigail cried. 'It's because I shouted at Rebecca that you're saying these things. Just what does Rebecca mean to you?'

'Mind your own damned business!'

Abigail began to sob. 'Please, Alex, don't let's quarrel like this. I'll apologise to Rebecca and I won't ask her to do anything for me ever again. Mrs Wright is quite happy to see to my room and clothes anyway. All I ask is that you provide something for Stephen's future. You can even cut my allowance if you like but please don't throw us out.'

Some of the heat went out of Alex's face and he sighed. 'Stop crying, Abigail. We'll carry on as usual until I've made up my mind what to do about the future. Then I'll decide something definite for you and Stephen. In the meantime I'll settle a sum of money on you both, just to be on the safe side. I'll talk to Faull about it while he's here.'

Neville had his ear to the sitting room door and heard every word. So Fiennes had a need for Rebecca, did he? He mulled this over.

'Having problems?' he asked smugly as Alex entered the room.

Alex glared at him. 'I've got half an hour to spare so let's talk business. Can I offer you a cup of tea, Faull?'

Neville shook his head slowly and put on an expression that poked fun at Alex for talking like an old maid. Then he turned on his quiet professional voice. 'No, thank you, Major. Shall we sit at the table? I have a lot of papers in my briefcase that need your signature.'

'Where's Mr Drayton today?' Alex asked stonily.

'I know you prefer to discuss your business affairs with Mr Drayton but he was called away urgently from the office earlier this morning. His mother died suddenly.'

'Oh, I'm sorry to hear that.'

Neville laid out papers and documents on the table. 'These are the deeds to all the properties Captain Miles Trevallion owned and in due course they will be transferred to your name. There's not a lot left to the once wealthy and influential name of Trevallion but, as you know, the total amount exceeds the worthy sum of seventy-five thousand pounds. If you wish to sell I could get more than that sum for you, Major Fiennes. I know of parties who would be interested in buying Trevallion House and its grounds for a most handsome amount. The rest of the estate will sell readily in separate compartments. You could make a sizeable profit on your inheritance to take back to Berkshire with you.'

Alex looked at Neville with distaste. 'Whatever I decide to do with Trevallion House, Faull, you can rest assured that I won't allow the house to be sold for the holiday trade.'

'Of course, Major Fiennes, but I have been approached by someone of local standing who would be guaranteed to carry it on in its tradition.' His words fell on deaf ears. He mentally shrugged his shoulders and pushed some papers towards Alex. 'These need signing. Perhaps you would be good enough to look them over and let us have them back in the office early next week. They are needed urgently. They entail the house transfer from Mr Drayton, myself and the other trustees to you to manage the estate yourself. The monies you want put into the estate cannot be released without your signature. Now, is there anything you would like to discuss with me before I leave?'

'Yes,' Alex rejoined in a carefully modulated tone. 'I want to add a codicil to my will.'

–

When Neville left he found Abigail waiting by his car and fully expected a roasting for taking Rebecca's side over her harsh reprimand, but she was subdued.

'I take it you are going back to Truro, Neville. Can I beg a lift?'

'Certainly, Abby. Going to raid the dress shops?'

As Neville pulled out into the lane, she said in an accusing tone, 'You gave Rebecca a lift home.'

'She was walking along the lane. I could hardly just drive by and leave her there.'

'I hope you're not trying to wheedle your way into her affections, Neville.'

Neville side-tracked that remark. 'Abigail, do you like Rebecca?'

Abigail looked ashamed. 'I know I sometimes behave unforgivably towards her but I ask you, Neville, how could anyone not like the girl? That's why I don't want her falling under the spell of a sophisticated man like you. Anybody else and I know she could take care of herself.'

'Of course Alex would make you the ideal husband,' Neville said thoughtfully. 'You're jealous that he likes Rebecca so much. He rarely leaves Trevallion and then never to mix socially, but it still doesn't leave much room for you to manoeuvre.'

'How shrewd of you, Neville, but even if Rebecca didn't exist Alex wouldn't marry me if his life depended upon it. You must have overheard him crying blue murder at me.'

'He strikes me as a strange sort of fellow, your brother-in-law, even without his war experiences.'

'Yes, he was always quiet and moody.'

Neville became thoughtful again. 'It's understandable that he should take to Rebecca. She's of a similar nature, the sort of woman that plays easy on a man's mind. Do you think there's any possibility of something going on there?'

Abigail snorted. 'In the bedroom? Absolutely not. Even if Rebecca presented herself naked to him tonight, nothing would happen.' She added bitterly, 'Alex doesn't know what to do with it.'

As they sped under a canopy of tall trees, Neville glanced at her knowingly. 'I see. Quite a waste as far as you're concerned.'

'Well, can you think of anything better in the world to do?'

He grinned as he watched the road ahead. 'Any particular place you'd like to be dropped off in Truro, Abby?'

'How about your flat?'

Neville smiled.

Chapter 25

Robert Drayton was in the kitchen of his small house halfway up Mitchell Hill in Truro when there was a knock at the front door. He thought it would be another neighbour or acquaintance come to give their condolences on his mother's death. He quickly wiped his hands, took off the apron round his waist and put on his black coat before answering the door. His face broke out in a mixture of smiles and tearful emotion when he saw who was on the other side.

'Mrs Wright. How kind of you to call. I take it you've heard...' He was more pleased to see this woman on his doorstep than anyone else on earth. Her appearance took some of the sting out of the despair and loneliness he'd been plunged into. Neighbours, friends and colleagues had been kind and sympathetic but none had the genuine personal touch about them that Mrs Wright possessed.

'Yes, Mr Drayton. I heard this morning.' Loveday shuffled her feet on the paved doorstep. 'Mr Faull called on Major Fiennes and he told him. I'm so very sorry. I felt I had to come. I hope you don't mind. I... I thought there might be something I could do.'

When Alex had conveyed the sad news to her, Loveday's first thought had been to go to Mr Drayton. Their time together in the tea shop had been most agreeable and Loveday felt they were on friendly terms. She'd immediately asked the Major if he minded if she went into Truro, and without asking any questions he said he'd drive her there himself. Loveday had run along to the creek, made arrangements with Ira Jenkins to cook lunch at the gatehouse and fetch Tamsyn from school, then, after she had changed into a black dress and stockings, the Major had driven her to Mitchell Hill.

'Pass on my condolences to Mr Drayton, Mrs Wright,' Alex had said kindly as he indicated which house was the solicitor's. 'I might as well look around the town while I'm here. I'll call back here in a couple of hours but if you want to stay longer I'll send Trease Allen for you.'

'But Major,' she had faltered. 'Supposing Mr Drayton doesn't want me to stay? Supposing he doesn't want me calling here?'

'If you feel you ought to be here, Mrs Wright, then I'm absolutely certain that Mr Drayton will be pleased to see you.'

He had been right and she passed on his condolences.

'How thoughtful of Major Fiennes. Well, as it happens I was trying to clear up a few things. Um… yes, well, perhaps you'd care to step inside, Mrs Wright, if you have the time, of course. I could make us a cup of tea.'

Loveday smiled shyly and stepped into the hall. It was dark, like the whole house; every curtain was pulled over to tell the world of the bereavement.

'Come into the sitting room, Mrs Wright. I'll just pop along to the kitchen and put the kettle on.'

After Robert had lit the gaslamps in the semi-darkness, Loveday was left alone in the sitting room. She walked to the piano, a highly polished upright, and took a photograph off the top. An elderly lady with a kind face and a white bun on top of her head smiled back at her.

Robert returned and Loveday said softly, 'Your mother?'

'Yes.' He smiled gently, gazing down at his mother's face. 'It was taken only last year, just after Christmas. She'd hardly had a pain in her life up until a few weeks ago. It… it was very sudden… Mother didn't suffer. She, um, she… had a pain in her chest about three o'clock this morning. I telephoned for the doctor at once. He was here in five minutes and telephoned for the ambulance to take Mother to the infirmary. She…' A solitary tear crept down Robert's face. 'She died at four twenty-four. It was very peaceful. I, um, ah, that's the kettle. Please excuse me, Mrs Wright, I shall be back in a minute.'

Loveday looked around the room. There were vases of flowers on every table and shelf, and on the piano. Photographs were prominently displayed on the walls and mantelpiece. Mr and Mrs Drayton with a fat baby, presumably Robert. Mr and Mrs Drayton with Robert as a small boy dressed as if they were attending a wedding. Robert with his school class. Robert in gown and mortarboard receiving his degree at university. Mrs Drayton and Robert, now a man of about twenty, at another wedding. Robert in officer's uniform with his Duke of Cornwall's Light Infantry unit. Robert and Mrs Drayton in party hats and raised glasses at a Christmas party not many years ago.

Mrs Drayton's knitting basket sat at the foot of what was obviously her favourite chair. On the long needles on top of the basket was the nearly completed back of a jumper in brown wool, a garment she had no doubt been making for Robert. A shawl was put tidily on the back of the chair, in case the old lady felt chilly in the evenings. A cushion was plumped up against the arm, embroidered with the figure of a lady in crinoline in a flower garden.

The chair on the other side of the fireplace was Robert's. His cushion had a symmetrical design in blues and greys. His spectacle case was sitting on a neat pile of books and papers on the floor nearby, work brought home from the office last night. Loveday felt a lump rise in her throat as she pictured mother and son sitting in companionable silence as they got on with their respective tasks. They probably listened to the wireless set standing on its own shelf as they worked. There was new linoleum on the floor, patterned in a green and yellow design with a tiny red rose dotted here and there on the corners, a mixture of feminine and masculine design. Mother and son had lived in harmony.

Loveday left the sitting room and walked quietly along the passageway to the kitchen. Robert was at the draining board wiping up spills from the teapot.

'A little accident,' he said, blushing with embarrassment. 'I'm afraid I'm being rather clumsy today.'

'Let me,' Loveday said soothingly. 'It's why I'm here.'

She took off her coat and Robert gratefully relinquished the responsibility of making the tea. Searching in the cupboards she found a biscuit barrel and put pieces of shortbread on a plate on the table. Robert was standing about, his arms folded, smiling uncertainly.

'Why don't we drink our tea in here?' Loveday said. 'Then we won't make crumbs in the sitting room.'

'Thank you, Mrs Wright. It's so good to have someone here with me.'

Loveday poured the tea as they sat at the small table. She smoothed down the tablecloth absentmindedly. It was perfectly tidy but she wanted Mr Drayton to feel he was being cared for.

'How did you get here, Mrs Wright? I hope you didn't have to wait hours for a bus, and of course in the first place you would have had a long walk to the main road.'

'Major Fiennes ran me over in his car. He's very kindly coming back for me later.'

'That was very thoughtful of him. You must thank him on my behalf but I will be happy to run you back myself... if, if the Major were to find it inconvenient.'

Robert dunked his biscuit and bit off the wet soggy bit without realising at first that he'd done it. Then he said quickly, 'I'm so sorry, Mrs Wright. Mother didn't mind me doing it, you see. She was never a bossy woman.'

'It's a very great loss for you, Mr Drayton. I can remember all the things you told me about your mother when we had tea together in town. I do understand how you're feeling.'

'Of course you do, you lost your husband in the war. I feel so numb. I can't believe Mother's gone. She was seventy-six years old. She lived for thirty years after my father died. I know some parents are selfish when they lose their spouse and rule the lives of any children still living at home, but Mother was never like that. She used to encourage me to go out and would have been delighted if I had got married and left home. She was a wonderful woman.'

'It's the right thing to do,' Loveday said gently, 'to talk about her.' She couldn't help wondering why Mr Drayton had never got married.

'And to keep yourself busy, as one of the neighbours told me. I want to clean and polish the sitting room. Mother will be coming back home later in the day. She'll lie in her coffin in the sitting room until her funeral.'

'And when's that, Mr Drayton?'

'Well, the undertaker will be calling on me later in the day to make the arrangements but I suppose in three or four days' time. Mother will be buried on top of Father in Kenwyn churchyard, that's where we've always worshipped. I think I'll order lots of flowers. Mother would have liked that.'

'I'm sure she would. Mr Drayton, will you allow me to see to the sitting room for you?'

'There's not a lot that needs to be done in there but, Mrs Wright, I wonder if you would be kind enough to...'

'Yes? I'll do anything I can. Do go on.'

'Would you, um, tidy up Mother's room for me, please? And... and... look in her wardrobe and find her wedding dress? It was her wish to be buried in it. She was as slim as the day she was married. I just couldn't...'

'Of course, Mr Drayton. Leave it to me.'

'You're so kind.' Robert's eyes filled with tears. 'Everyone's been so kind, friends and neighbours. We haven't got a lot of relatives, you see. Not in Cornwall. I've sent telegrams to those who live in London and Kent. I expect they'll come down for the funeral. My partners in the practice were here earlier today. Mr Handley and Mr Faull. Strangely it was Mr Faull who was the most comforting. He knew just what to do and what to say. He suggested he and Mr Handley halve the work I was supposed to do today and they took it away. I intended to go with Mr Faull to Trevallion this morning.' He coloured as he went on, lowering his voice, 'I was hoping to see you and have a cup of your tea, Mrs Wright. But here you are doing it anyway. Strange, how things work out...'

Loveday got up from the table to allow Mr Drayton to compose himself. She felt a sudden warmth rush over her as she thought about what he'd said, that he'd hoped to see her. She busied herself looking for duster and wax polish. 'Do use Mother's apron,' Robert said.

'Thank you. There's two tins of polish and lots of dusters. We'll make short work of the sitting room and your mother's bedroom, then I'll sweep down the stairs and the hall and passageway. Then when we've finished, I'll make a light lunch. You must eat something, Mr Drayton.'

'Oh, indeed,' agreed Robert at once. He wanted Loveday to stay as long as possible. 'Mother's bedroom is the first one on the right-hand side. There's clean linen in the cupboard next to the one you found the polish in.'

There was little for Loveday to do in Mrs Drayton's bedroom. Everything was clean and tidy. The double bed which the old lady had slept in since her wedding night was as she had left it last night. The covers were pulled back where Robert and the ambulance man had helped her out. Loveday stripped the bed and replaced the crisp white sheets. She put a doll dressed in a faded crinoline dress, a treasured toy from Mrs Drayton's childhood, on the pillow. Next she opened the wardrobe and moved the garments along on their hangers looking for her wedding dress. It wasn't hanging up but Loveday found it in a box on the wardrobe floor. She took out a simply styled Victorian creation, gone an off-white now, the sleeves and high neckline covered with fine lace. She shook out the folds of the dress and laid it out reverently on Mrs Drayton's bed. She stood back and surveyed the dress, tears pricking her eyes for the end of the life of a lady she had never known.

She slipped downstairs and went into the sitting room. Robert had finished his work and was staring down at the pullover his mother would never finish for him. Loveday had a small vase in her hand.

'I thought I might take a few of the flowers from this room for your mother's bedside table, if that's all right with you.'

'Yes, yes, that would be lovely, Mrs Wright.'

Loveday swept the stairs and passageway then found Robert at the kitchen sink staring down aimlessly at a few potatoes he'd put in it. 'I can't seem to apply myself to anything this morning,' he said apologetically.

'Well, that's understandable. You sit down, Mr Drayton. There's no need for you to do anything while I'm here.'

The telephone rang in the hall and Robert excused himself and went to answer the call. Loveday busied herself peeling the potatoes then peeped out through the curtains to see what Mr Drayton's back garden was like. The garden had a high wall on one side and three immaculately trimmed privet hedges on the other three. Robert had vegetables growing in neat regimented lines on one side of an ash path; flowers and shrubs grew on the other side.

'Would you like to go outside and take a closer look?' Robert said behind her. 'I know I could do with a breath of fresh air. I could cut a cabbage to go with our lunch. You will stay with me and eat?'

Loveday smiled warmly in answer. She took off the apron and stepped outside with him. There was a shed, a small greenhouse and an outdoor water closet, all in good condition.

'You keep a splendid garden, Mr Drayton,' Loveday said, genuinely impressed. 'I'm afraid I spend so much time at the gatehouse these days that my own little garden has been neglected.'

'What a shame. I find gardening so relaxing. I can't take the credit for all this myself Mother used to spend hours out here. It was nothing for her to dig over the ground and put in the bean sticks.' Robert took a penknife out of his pocket and cut a round-headed cabbage. 'There,' he said proudly. 'You'll taste none better, Mrs Wright, I promise you.'

'I can quite believe that, Mr Drayton.'

'There's some lamb chops covered up in the cold room. We could grill them and have boiled potatoes, my own potatoes of course, and I think there's a little rice pudding left over from yesterday we could warm up in the oven. Will that suit you, Mrs Wright?'

'A feast fit for a king, Mr Drayton,' she replied.

'You must allow me to pick you some flowers to take home.' He had a sudden thought. 'Oh, I mustn't keep you. I quite forgot your little girl. You'll have to get back for her.'

'Oh, Tamsyn will be all right. Ira Jenkins is looking after her and has taken over my duties for the day.'

'I'm so glad. I saw your little girl when I called at the estate in the hope of finding Major Fiennes at home.' Robert searched his mind for something complimentary to say about Tamsyn. He knew all mothers were proud of their children and, in Mrs Wright's case, very protective. 'She has, um, an intelligent little face.'

Loveday smiled proudly then made a wry face. 'I bet she was untidy with a dirty face. Tamsyn is a tomboy but then she has a whole creek practically to herself to run about in. She can be cheeky. I hope she wasn't cheeky to you, Mr Drayton.'

'No, actually she said hello and after that she stared at me. Children have their own special way of staring at you, I've found. Usually it makes me feel uncomfortable but Tamsyn was only being curious. Master Stephen Fiennes was with her but I'm sorry to say he was rude to me.'

'He can be a horrid child,' Loveday said. 'Most of it's attention-seeking, I think.'

'Yes, I'm sure you're right.'

'I'd better put the vegetables on if we are to have lunch,' Loveday said.

After they had eaten, Loveday washed the dishes and Robert dried them. When they were all back in their places and the tea towel was spread out to dry, he turned to Loveday. 'I can't tell you how much I've appreciated you coming here today, Mrs Wright.'

'I'm glad I've been able to help.'

The doorbell rang. 'That will be the undertaker,' Robert said nervously.

'I'll bring some tea into the sitting room.'

'When you do, please stay, Mrs Wright. It would be helpful to have a lady's contribution to the arrangements.'

'Well, if that's what you want I shall be honoured, Mr Drayton.'

It wasn't the undertaker at the door. It was Alex, calling to see if Loveday was ready to go home. He shook Robert's hand and went through the routine of offering his condolences and help. He saw he had thrown the solicitor into a nervous dither.

'Shall I send Trease Allen for you at about five o'clock, Mrs Wright?' he said. 'Then you will have time to prepare something for Mr Drayton's dinner.'

Mr Drayton looked at Loveday with an expression that pleaded with her to stay.

'If it's of no inconvenience to you, Major, that would be greatly appreciated,' she replied.

'Such an understanding man,' Robert said, when Alex had gone. 'I do hope he decides to keep Trevallion. You could work under no better an employer after Captain Miles.'

Loveday agreed wholeheartedly then suggested they return to the kitchen for another cup of tea and wait for the undertaker. They sat at the table, talking about the changes for the better that Major Fiennes had brought to the Trevallion estate, the weather and their respective gardens. Then suddenly Robert's face broke and tears of loss and sorrow ran from his eyes.

'It's just hit me, Mrs Wright. My dear mother will never share another meal with me, tend the garden and sit across the room with me in the evenings. I'll be glad when they bring her home. To be here for a little longer. I wish she had died at home.' Robert searched for a handkerchief and dried his eyes. 'Do forgive me, Mrs Wright.'

'There's nothing to be ashamed of in showing your grief, Mr Drayton.' Loveday reached across the kitchen table and put her hand in his and he held it very tightly.

Chapter 26

The St Mawes Regatta was the third to last to be held during the River Fal's traditional Regatta Fortnight. Excitement bubbled in the picturesque town; its streets, alleyways, the sea frontage and harbour were gaily decorated with streamers and flags, evergreens adorned every windowsill and door mantel. Another good day's holiday and sport was anticipated and the younger folk looked forward to the fun of the music and dancing and the amusements St Mawes was famous for – climbing a greasy pole to win a leg o'mutton, ducking for apples and, finally and best of all, a dazzling fireworks display.

Everybody agreed it was a fine day for it. Competitors and sight-seers crammed the quay, the sea wall and rocky beach below, while others filled a great many boats on the water. Three majestic top-sail schooners swayed in the wind, decked out with hundreds of colourful flags.

The town's brass band sat proudly on a raised platform playing a hardy selection of marches, waltzes, hymns and country music. Chairs and benches had been put out and some people sat on blankets with their picnics. Refreshment and cheap-jack stalls had been set up and a fortune-teller had brought her gipsy caravan along the network of pretty but narrow and winding roads of the Roseland. Most people had come straight from their creeks and villages by boat.

The Kennickers had arrived by boat, either their own or one of Trevallion's. Rebecca had sailed in the *Lady Harriet* with Trease, Alex, Percy Gummoe and some of the Jenkins. She was amused to see her father, Alex and Jossy were whispering to each other. If she looked at them or moved close to them they instantly became silent. After the long years of absence, the *Lady Harriet* was being entered in a scratch race for those with boats over twenty-eight feet in length. The three men were probably planning tactics for the race. When Rebecca caught their collective eyes, she looked at them scornfully. She wouldn't have divulged their secrets.

A dark-blue thirty-five-foot fishing boat swept up beside them. It was the *Emmeline*, skippered by Miles Trevallion's long-time rival Pat Vincent, a St Mawes fisherman.

''Tes 'an'some t'see she out again, Jossy,' Pat called across the boats, nodding his bulky head at the *Lady Harriet's* name freshly painted black on gleaming white.

'We're back to give 'ee a run for your money,' Jossy beamed proudly. 'Let me introduce you to Major Fiennes, her new owner.'

'You won't do much against we, Major,' Pat Vincent boasted good-humouredly to Alex. 'Your crew 'ave been too many years out of practice, but like I said, 'tes nice to 'ave a Trevallion boat back in the races again.'

Alex smiled, studied his rival's mainsail, and repeated a term he'd heard Jossy use often as they'd practised for the races, 'It's good to meet my cousin's old rival, Pat, but you've got sails fit only for cruising there.'

Pat Vincent slapped his knee in delight. 'Did 'ee 'ear that, boys?' he asked his crew, entirely made up of his family. ''Tes just like the old days when we belonged to exchange a bit o' banter with the cap'n.'

'We don't seriously stand much chance of being placed today, do we, Jossy?' Alex asked, after the crew had helped Rebecca and the other women off onto dry land.

'The races are held in the spirit rather than the letter of the law, Major,' Jossy replied. 'My boys should do well with their oysterdredger but like I promised Pat, we'll do our best.'

Rebecca would have preferred to watch the regatta from one of the boats but she'd stepped ashore in the hope of seeing Neville about the town. She caught sight of Mr Drayton, who was looking about for Loveday, who in turn was chasing after Tamsyn in the hopeless task of trying to keep her clean and tidy. Tamsyn had given her mother the slip and was wandering about the town, spending her few pennies of pocket money on sweets with some St Mawes children she knew, a hurt look on her face because Stephen didn't want her today; he preferred to stay close to Joe who'd helped row over the Trevallion gig. Mrs Fiennes had arrived on the *Iseult* and had decided to sightsee from the motor launch.

The races began with a handicap class, boats of twenty-two feet and upwards, racing against the clock on handicaps decided annually. Rebecca watched with the same degree of enthusiasm as she did every year, but kept her eye alert for Neville. Cheers from the sightseers for their favourite boats echoed across the water. People on land jumped up and down to encourage their heroes and a huge blast of sound went up as a Falmouth quay punt edged its bow over the winning line first.

'Going to be some close races this year,' Trease said at her side as he clapped the winning crew.

'Looks like it,' Rebecca agreed. 'How come you're ashore, Dad? I thought you'd be getting ready for your class and you're in the gig racing.' She hoped Neville would stay out of sight if he turned up now.

'Got plenty of time yet. Jossy broke his flask of tea. The rest of us have brought beer or coffee but he won't touch either, says he can't get his brain tuned into the winds and currents if he hasn't had a mug of strong tea.'

'There's a refreshment stall behind us,' Rebecca pointed out.

''Tis run by women and there's only women round it. Be a dear and get a mug for me.'

Rebecca raised her eyebrows playfully. 'That's hardly the spirit of a brave crewman about to pit his wits against the famous Pat Vincent and his precious *Emmeline*.'

Trease wasn't listening. He was staring down at the boats clustered on the water.

'What are you looking at?' She peered in the direction he was staring, her hand over her eyes.

'Look at 'em. Showing themselves up in public now!'

'Who?'

'Carlyon and that Fiennes bint. They're all over each other again.'

Rebecca looked down at the *Iseult*. She could make out Abigail Fiennes in her straw cloche hat with perky feather. She was leaning over the boat and talking to Joe who was standing up in the gig. 'They're only talking to each other, Dad. What do you mean "again"?'

Trease snorted. 'You must be the only one on the estate who doesn't know. She and Carlyon have been carrying on for weeks.'

'Joe and Mrs Fiennes?' Rebecca gasped. 'I don't believe it.'

—

Loveday finally located her daughter on the waterfront. 'Tamsyn! Just look at your hands and face, and the ribbons of your dress are trailing on the ground. And look at your shoes. How did you manage to get into this state in such a short time?'

She grabbed her daughter, wetted her handkerchief on Tamsyn's tongue and attempted to wipe a dirty mark off her chin. 'Keep still, Tamsyn, and stop making that face or you won't have an ice cream later on.'

When her face passed inspection, Tamsyn was turned round so Loveday could tie a big bow at the back of her dress. 'Will you please keep still?'

'Mr Drayton's coming this way,' Tamsyn said, moving away as Loveday's hold on her slackened. 'I think he wants to talk to you, Mum. Can I go back and play with the other children now? I promise I won't get dirty.' Tamsyn looked at her mother for an answer and watched her face turn a soft pink as Mr Drayton approached them.

Mr Drayton smiled as he held out his hand. 'Mrs Wright. How nice to see you again, and your little girl. Tamsyn, isn't it?' He turned to Tamsyn with his face abeam and held out his hand to her too.

Tamsyn shook hands as her mother had taught her to do. 'That's right, Mr Drayton. Have you come to watch the races?'

'Yes, I have, Tamsyn. I'm happy to say I have very little business to attend to this afternoon. Now, can I get you a cup of tea, Mrs Wright? And would you like a glass of lemonade, Tamsyn? Perhaps an ice cream?'

'Oh, yes please,' Tamsyn blurted out before Loveday could make a reply.

Tamsyn was thrilled; having a drink of lemonade bought by Mr Robert Drayton who did business with the Major would put her one up on Stephen. She led the way to the nearest refreshment stall. A short time later she left her mother drinking tea with Mr Drayton while she clutched a big ice cream.

'That was very generous of you, Mr Drayton,' Loveday said, sitting on a chair vacated by a surge forward to watch the next race. They were in full view of some of the Kennicker women, who included Mrs Kellow.

'Tamsyn is a delightful child, Mrs Wright. It's easy to see she's had a good upbringing.'

Loveday flushed with pleasure. 'I'm sure I do my best, Mr Drayton. How are things with you after your mother's funeral?'

'Well, I miss Mother terribly of course but I'm sure I'm coping better than I thought I would because of the support you gave me on the day she died. It was very thoughtful of you to attend her funeral.'

Loveday ran her teaspoon round her saucer. 'Funny really, after making her bed and putting flowers in her room I felt I knew her.'

'My mother would have liked you, Mrs Wright. It's a shame you never met.'

Loveday looked down at her lap. 'If… if there's anything more I can do for you, Mr Drayton…'

'Actually, Mrs Wright,' Mr Drayton swallowed hard, 'Mother always said that when her time came she would like her clothes to go to charity. If you were, um, to get the time, I was wondering…'

'Yes?' Loveday prompted, still looking down.

'If… if I were to give you a key to the house, would you, could you, I mean, would you be so kind as to gather all Mother's clothes together and pack them in a box? I think such an undertaking needs a woman's touch. Then I'll arrange for the Salvation Army to call for them. I think they are the best people to put them to good use. And please, don't be offended, but if there is anything you would like, do… do take it.' Mr Drayton looked nervously about and when he glanced at Loveday she was smiling at him. He smiled back.

Unknown to them, there was a collective 'Ahhh' from the women watching.

'I will let you know when I next have a day off, Mr Drayton, and I would be happy to do that for you.'

'Oh, splendid.' Then Mr Drayton added boldly, 'If I may, by way of thanks, I'd like to help you with your garden. May I suggest we watch the regatta together, Mrs Wright?'

'I shall be delighted, Mr Drayton.'

As Loveday left on Robert's arm, Rebecca came up to the stall and bid them good morning.

'What about that then?' Mrs Kellow said to Rebecca, nodding after the couple.

'What about what, Mrs Kellow?' Rebecca frowned, hoping she wasn't going to hear any more gossip. She hadn't got over the shock of Joe's affair with Mrs Fiennes yet; Trease had been adamant it was true.

'Can I have a strong mug of tea, please?' she asked one of the serving women at the stall.

'They that just passed you!' Mrs Kellow raised her voice at Rebecca's back and she dutifully turned round. 'Loveday Wright and that Mr Drayton solicitor bloke. If you'd been here five minutes ago you would have had the surprise of your life, maid. Some friendly they were, weren't they, Myrtle?' Myrtle nodded enthusiastically and Mrs Kellow prattled on. 'I reckon something could be going on there. I heard she went to his mother's funeral.'

'Mrs Kellow,' Rebecca said airily, 'are you seriously telling me that Loveday is having a romance? *Loveday?*'

'Yes, I am, maid. And it's about time you were romantically attached too.' Mrs Kellow couldn't resist giving a little dig but she wasn't prepared for Rebecca's reaction.

'What makes you think I'm not, Mrs Kellow?' Rebecca plonked a few pennies on the table for Jossy's tea and flounced away, leaving Mrs Kellow gaping.

Rebecca rushed the tea to Trease who took it to Jossy. She watched the bustle on the water and wondered if Neville would turn up. It was unlikely that he would have come by boat. A familiar waft of cigar smoke reached her nose and she smiled.

'Are you enjoying the races, Miss Allen?'

'Yes, thank you, Mr Faull.' He was behind her but she did not turn round.

Neville dropped his voice. 'I want to see you alone.'

'I think I'll take a walk along to the castle.'

'I'll follow you in a few moments.'

Rebecca walked on a little way past the castle to a quiet spot where there were few spectators watching the water sports, making sure there was no one about she knew. From here she looked across Falmouth Bay to Pendennis Castle. A keen wind chilled her bare arms but this was warded off a few moments later by Neville.

Before she could speak he kissed her fully on the lips so passionately it took her breath away.

'Neville!' she gasped, struggling out of his grasp and looking around hastily to see if anyone was watching them. 'What a way to greet a girl.'

'Well, I've missed you, sweetheart.' He smiled confidently. 'There's too many people about here, let's walk on.'

They took a path that led away from the town of St Mawes in the direction of St Just until they found a deserted spot. Neville took off his blazer, put it down on a grassy slope and they sat down side by side. He put his arm round her and she rested her head on his chest.

'Lovely scenery here but not as lovely as you are, Rebecca,' Neville said and sought another kiss. Rebecca obliged him. He caressed her hair. 'You like being with me, don't you?'

'Mmmm,' she murmured into his shirt. She did like the feel of his arms about her, the strength of his body as she leaned against it, the fresh smell of him. She liked to be kissed by him. She planted a small kiss on the back of his hand and he lifted her hair from her neck and kissed her there, making her shiver with pleasure.

'When is your next full evening off? Aunt Mildred has suggested dinner next Thursday or Friday evening.'

'I can make it on Thursday. I'll write to Uncle Bert to ask him if I can sleep over.'

'Back, is he? And your aunt?'

'Yes, Neville.'

'That's a pity.'

Rebecca ran a fingertip over the back of his hand where she had kissed it. She knew it wasn't sensible to tease this man but Neville made her feel young and light-hearted. She looked up at him and asked softly, 'Why is it a pity?'

He smiled and raised an eyebrow. 'Because Uncle Bert will want you in by ten-thirty and I would like to keep you out much later. Will you tell him where you are going?'

'He knew the last time,' Rebecca said defensively.

'All the way from Plymouth? You didn't tell him, Rebecca. You knew he'd tell your father and there would be trouble. I think you're going to suggest that we meet somewhere rather than have me collect you from your uncle's house.'

'At the front of the cathedral,' Rebecca admitted. 'I was planning to tell Uncle Bert that I'll get a taxi to a friend's house for a musical evening.'

'Well, I can promise you the music.'

They gazed at each other in silence for several moments, Neville stroking her hair and shoulders. Then he kissed her longingly and Rebecca responded in the same way. Afterwards he held her tightly, murmuring into her neck and running his lips along her neck and behind her ears.

'We'll have to go back to the others in a minute before I'm missed,' she sighed.

'In a little while,' Neville said huskily and kissed her again.

—

Alex took off his hat, raised himself on the deck of the *Lady Harriet* and looked about for Rebecca. The boat's class had been called and he wanted to wave to her for good luck.

Jossy tapped on his arm. 'We're off to the starting line, Major.'

'Oh, right then,' he replied, disappointed at not being able to find Rebecca. 'Let's do our best for Kennick Creek.'

Six boats lined up with the *Lady Harriet*, two quay punts, three oysterdredgers and the *Emmeline*, all with different shaped hulls. The wind was light and Jossy had tied a few lengths of wool to the shrouds to see which direction the wind was coming from. He told his crew they would have to keep the sails flatter so as not to disturb the wind over the leeward sail area. Most of the crews numbered seven men, the usual for a scratch race. Two men worked the jib, two on the staysail, one on the mainsheet, one working the backstays and the last man on the helm.

Alex's crew included Victor, Donald and Royston Jenkins, fresh from victory in their oysterdredger, Joe, Trease and Percy Gummoe. They were all tense as they waited for the starter flag to drop and Alex could hardly contain his excitement. When the flag was dropped he surged forward slightly before the *Lady Harriet* did and nearly toppled over. Jossy, behind him at the helm, grabbed his shoulder and Alex looked at the old Kennicker in apology but Jossy's eyes seemed to be riveted on sails, spars, water and the winning line all at the same time.

The *Lady Harriet* cut through the water, the other six craft with her, none stalling. It was a magnificent sight to see the mass of canvas, fifty feet high and spanning forty-five across boom and spinnaker pole on each boat, surge forward as one.

They had not gone far when one of the quay punts, whose captain had not checked the wind as Jossy had, dropped back and Alex was pleased that at least his boat would not be last. He felt a strong surge of competitiveness but allowed Jossy to shout the orders. It had been years since he had done any serious sailing and the boats he was used to were nothing like these strong Cornish vessels. His few weeks of experience could not match Jossy's years. The old man knew the *Lady Harriet*'s every creak and flurry and instinctively ordered the sails to be trimmed when needed.

As the pace increased the Trevallion boat took third place to the *Emmeline* and an oysterdredger. The rival boats were about half a length ahead on either side of the *Lady Harriet*. Pat Vincent turned round from the helm of the *Emmeline* and shouted to Alex, 'You've got no chance, Major!'

The *Lady Harriet* was gaining steadily on the oysterdredger and Alex began to hold his breath. When his boat overtook it, he yelled in delight.

'Keep her steady, boys, and we'll catch that bugger up front,' Jossy shouted above the fluttering sails. 'We're coming after you, Pat!'

Pat Vincent turned his great head and waved in defiance. He was a highly skilled helmsman, able to get his fishing boat out of any dangerous situation on the high seas. He would not be easily beaten.

The *Emmeline* was keeping a steady speed of nine knots and the *Lady Harriet* did her best to catch her. With the finishing line coming up fast, Alex broke out in a sweat. 'What can we do to catch her, Jossy?'

'Not a lot more, Major,' Jossy said resignedly. 'Our girl's doing her best and Captain Miles would be proud of her.'

Alex was disappointed but only for a moment. They had done well to come runner-up against a captain who spent more hours sailing in one season than the average yachtsman did in several years. At a slight turn of his head he saw the remaining five boats had dropped further back and he felt proud of the *Lady Harriet* and her crew. He was aware of the cheers of the crowds as the *Emmeline* creamed over the finishing line and knew there would be congratulations too for the return of Trevallion's grand old lady. He couldn't wait to see Rebecca's face.

She was nowhere about when they sailed in close to the sea wall to receive a rapturous reception from the party of Kennickers gathered there. Tamsyn was also absent and Alex assumed Rebecca had gone looking for the errant little girl. When she appeared half an hour later with Tamsyn, no one was any the wiser.

The gig races were starting and Alex got into Trevallion's racing gig and took up oars with Joe, Trease, Percy Gummoe, Frank and Leslie Kellow, Donald and Victor Jenkins, and Jossy as cox. Alex saw the wind buffet a girl's long black hair but he had no time to wave to Rebecca because Jossy had called 'Off' and they were on their way to the starting line. The Kennickers had no problems with this race, and thanks mainly to Joe's massive shoulders they saw off the opposition by two full lengths.

On shore Alex proudly accepted the cup and turned at once to shake the crew of both Trevallion boats who had gathered behind him. 'This is all thanks to you. This is a proud day for the estate.'

'Thank you, sir. You pulled a surprise or two on us,' Joe answered for them all. 'With a bit of practice, perhaps next year we'll do it again.'

'Who knows, Joe? Are you coming to the pub after the fireworks with the rest of us? I'm buying everyone a round of drinks.'

Joe glanced towards Abigail, who had come ashore. 'Probably not, sir. I want to spend a bit of time with the horses tonight. I haven't seen much of them today.'

'Anyone would think they were your children, Joe,' Alex grinned.

Stephen went up to Joe and proudly shook his hand. 'I shall row like you one day, Joe.' Joe ruffled his hair.

Alex turned to Abigail. 'Have you enjoyed yourself?'

'Oh, yes,' she said enthusiastically. 'It was absolutely thrilling. It would be good to be here again next year, Alex,' she added hopefully. But the response she got was curt.

'Where's Rebecca? She seems to have disappeared again.'

'I don't know. I haven't seen her for a while.' When Alex frowned she said, 'Slipped away for a cup of tea, I expect. Ah, here she comes now.'

Alex watched Rebecca walking towards the group of Kennickers. She couldn't look Joe in the eye after what her father had told her and went straight up to Trease and congratulated him. Then she turned to Alex.

He was so excited he kissed her on both cheeks, which provoked a cheer from the others. 'Would you like to hold the cup?' he asked.

She took it from him and held it up high. 'Keep it there,' Alex said, running to Mrs Kellow and taking the camera he had asked her to look after. He took several photographs as the cup was passed from hand to hand. For the first time in years he felt happy and clear-minded.

When he got the cup back, he read the name of the donor. His heart gave a little start. 'Kindly donated by Miss Susannah Bosanko,' it stated. He pointed it out to Rebecca. She looked at him wide-eyed and as if on cue the old lady stood before them.

'Well done, Alexander, you and your crews put up a splendid show. I'm so pleased that you won the trophy.'

'I expect you've donated many,' Alex said, not wanting to be singled out on any terms by this strange ugly creature dressed in green.

'Oddly enough, just the one you're holding.' Susannah turned her reptile eyes on Rebecca. 'I might have known you wouldn't be far away from your master,' she hissed.

Rebecca made to move away but Alex caught her arm. 'I hope you've enjoyed the regatta, Susannah. I've promised Becca some refreshment. If you'll excuse us.' He hauled Rebecca away with him before Susannah Bosanko could make a protest and suggest she join them.

'Alex, you're hurting me!' Rebecca struggled.

He apologised and loosened his grip but kept up the same pace, eager to be away from the old woman.

'You were very rude to Miss Bosanko,' she said accusingly after he pushed the trophy into her hands and ordered two cups of tea at a stall.

'And two of those huge saffron buns.' He smiled at the serving woman, relieved at his escape. 'I wish I'd never got to know her,' he said to Rebecca. 'There's something unnerving about her.'

'Well, I agree with you on that. Something evil about her, if you ask me. You needn't worry about her bothering you again today. I saw her march off through the town with her chauffeur. She won't be pleased at the long drive back. She's too afraid to cross the river on the King Harry ferry. Jossy told me she's terrified of water, for some reason.'

'As long as it keeps her away from me, that's all I care about. Eat your saffron bun, Becca, my dear. I'm starving; it's this wonderful sea air.' They sat on the sea wall sipping their tea. Alex looked contentedly at the water, teeming with craft of every size and colour. 'It's been a wonderful day. Nothing could have happened here to spoil it.'

Chapter 27

The customers of the Oystercatcher were in a celebratory mood at the end of the evening, with all the talk centred on the regatta. Most members of the Trevallion estate had sailed on from the regatta to the pub. The men crowded round the bar, the women round two tables.

The drinks flowed, and Donald Jenkins, who was in charge of the Trevallion crew beer kitty, did not have to squeeze through the crowds asking the men for regular top-ups, thanks to Alex's generosity. Joe offered his hand to Trease and complimented him on his rowing that afternoon, and Rebecca was pleased to see they had found something of the old friendship they'd had before the war.

Abigail had not wanted to go on to the pub and had surprised everyone by offering to mind Tamsyn for the evening so she could play with Stephen at the gatehouse. It had taken a lot of cajoling to get Loveday to agree to come to the pub and she sat next to Rebecca, feeling uncomfortable and complaining about the din the men were making.

Jacky Jenkins started up on his fiddle and the singing began. The Cornishmen filled the air with rowing songs and boisterous sea shanties.

The landlord came over to the women's tables with a tray of drinks. 'On the Major, ladies,' he said cheerfully. A sudden loud cheer went up from the bar as another song was finished and Loveday spilled her tonic water.

'Look at them,' she said crossly. 'Grown men behaving like irresponsible schoolboys. The Major shouldn't be encouraging them.'

'Don't hurt to let your hair down now and then, Loveday.' Jenny Jenkins laughed and raised her port and lemon to Alex, who nodded back with a king-sized grin. Jenny took a sip and stroked Rebecca's hair. 'Becca's enjoying herself but then she's got her hair down nearly all the time.'

The women cackled and Loveday made an angry sound and turned away from them. An old man sitting at the next table caught her eye and winked at her and she turned back in a huff 'I know I shouldn't have come. It doesn't set a good example to Tamsyn.'

Rebecca glanced around to make sure none of the other women were listening then whispered into her ear, 'I suppose Mr Drayton's company is more to your liking, eh, Loveday?'

She expected Loveday to blush furiously and tell her off sternly. Instead her face took on a soft glow. She lost her prim demeanour and looked like someone of Rebecca's own age. 'Mr Drayton is a friend of mine, Rebecca,' she said in a mellow voice. 'There is nothing more to it than that.'

Rebecca listened to the next song for a while then plucked up the courage to ask, 'Has he asked to see you again?'

Loveday looked shyly round the bar, then hid behind her glass. 'Actually he's going to help me with my garden.'

'Oh, that's nice.' It had sounded a bit lame but Rebecca knew Loveday would be frightened to continue her association with Mr Drayton if others made too much of it.

'What are you two whispering about?' Mrs Kellow, her stout body squeezing Ira Jenkins up the corner of a bench, asked loudly. 'Don't tell me you've got yourself a young man at last, Becca? I haven't forgot what you said at the tea stall.'

'Are you all right, Mrs Jenkins?' Loveday asked Jenny, ignoring Mrs Kellow.

Jenny was massaging the side of her neck. 'I'm fine, m'dear, I've just had this neck all day. Everything gets a bit stiff when you get to my age.'

This caused an outbreak of female tittering which Loveday did not join.

The main party of Kennickers left just before closing time. Joe was eager to leave. Alex and Trease were among those who decided to stay on for a private party with the landlord.

Rebecca tapped Alex on the arm as she filed out with the women. 'Father's well on the way to getting merry. I'm relying on you to bring him home in one piece.'

Alex raised his whisky glass. 'Your wish is my command, my lady.' He smiled a little drunkenly. 'Trust me.'

'Get along with you all!' Trease shouted at Alex's side. 'Blasted women spoiling a man's fun.'

'You can't trust any man with anything when he's drinking,' Loveday muttered on her way out of the door.

Sitting next to Rebecca in the *Iseult* taking them home, Loveday asked quietly, 'Have you got a young man, Rebecca?'

Rebecca looked through the still night air. A pale round moon lit a magical path for the boat to follow. There was hardly a breeze to stir the screen of trees on the shoreline and the only sound was the engine puttering and the water lapping. The boat was making good speed, passing dark nooks and crannies on shore. A bird called out, a long mellow drifting sound. It was a dreamy, peaceful end to the day and the memory of being with Neville was fresh in Rebecca's mind. Should she tell Loveday about him? She thought not. But it wouldn't hurt to admit there was someone special in her life.

'There is someone.'

'Oh, I'm so pleased for you. Who is he?'

'I'm not prepared to divulge his name,' Rebecca said mysteriously.

'But you can tell me what he's like. Is he kind and handsome?'

'Very.'

'Is he a professional man?'

'Yes.'

'Do I know him?'

'Yes. He's closer to you than you'd think.'

Loveday gasped at what she thought was the truth dawning on her. 'The Major. It's the Major, isn't it? You're very close to him. He's obviously very fond of you. Has he been making romantic talk to you? Be careful, Rebecca. Men of his class tend to make sport of women of ours.'

Rebecca laughed and the sound rippled over the water. 'I never thought you would be this fanciful, Loveday. I can tell you honestly that it's not the Major, he's simply a friend to me – like Mr Drayton is to you,' she added mischievously.

'Is that the truth?'

'I swear it.'

'Who is it then?'

'I'm not telling.'

Loveday chewed over what she'd been told. If Rebecca was seeing a 'professional man' then it wasn't any of the young men of the estate or surrounding area. She hoped Rebecca had not set her sights too high and would end up getting hurt, but it was good to see her bright and happy as a young woman of her age should be. But then, what did age have to do with it? She had felt old and finished, resigned to life as a war widow when Stanley had been killed. But she was only nine years older than Rebecca. Why shouldn't there be someone for everyone? Of course Mr Drayton wasn't good-looking or anything, but what did that matter?

She leant on Rebecca's shoulder to whisper, 'It is romantic though, isn't it?'

When they were all safely on shore Joe offered to walk Loveday to the gatehouse to fetch Tamsyn. 'I'm the only one with a lantern and I don't want you spraining your ankle in the dark,' he said. 'Are you coming, Becca?'

'I think I'll go home and wait till Dad gets back. I won't sleep until I know he's got back safely.'

Loveday knew she wouldn't find a sleepy little girl whom Joe would have to carry back down to the creek. Tamsyn was full of beans anytime of the night or day and although Loveday didn't like her missing her usual bedtime, a regatta day was special.

—

When she was sure that Stephen was sleeping, and knowing her brother-in-law would not be back yet, Abigail slipped outside and stole along to Joe's cottage. Joe would have seen the Wrights safely home by now and would be waiting for her.

They sat side by side on his small lumpy sofa, with only the moon as light.

'Stephen enjoyed the regatta,' Abigail said. 'I don't have to worry about him not wanting to stay and live here.'

'The Major's made his decision then?' Joe asked, putting his arm round her.

Abigail leant contentedly on his huge chest. 'Seems like it. He hasn't said anything but he's showing so much interest in the estate, especially some little nook he's discovered on the other coast, and after the way he enjoyed himself today, well, it speaks for itself After you'd won that rowing race, Alex looked almost human.'

'Almost human? What a strange thing to say.'

'He's a strange man,' Abigail said defensively, with a hint of spite. She hadn't got over the shame of having her advances to him rejected or the hurt at the cruel things he'd said after she'd told Rebecca off. 'Anyway, never mind him. I'm glad you and Stephen are getting along so well, he was very proud of you today.'

Joe said thoughtfully, 'He's not a bad boy when you get to know him. He got an earwigging from Tamsyn for leaving her to her own devices, but on the way home they were chatting nineteen to the dozen. Stephen's got her eating out of his hand.'

Abigail gave a small laugh. 'I think that works both ways. She made him apologise and that's something Stephen hates.'

Joe kissed the top of her head. 'Do you want to go upstairs?'

She settled her head more comfortably. 'No, I'm quite happy just to stay like this.'

–

Rebecca was dozing in the kitchen of Allen Cottage when she was awakened by a knocking at the door. She opened it to find the landlord of the Oystercatcher and his son there.

'Evening, m'dear. We've got someone belonging to you,' Basil Hartley informed her cheerfully.

'Don't tell me,' she sighed resignedly. 'One very drunken father.'

Basil Hartley moved aside and his son, Tom, carried Trease into the kitchen. Trease was fast asleep and snoring, beer all over his moustache. 'Shall I carry un upstairs for 'ee, Rebecca?' Tom grinned.

'You know the way, Tom. The bedroom to the left.'

Basil disappeared outside and dragged Alex, who wasn't quite in the land of nod, in through the door. 'Where does this one belong? The gatehouse or has he moved into the big house?'

Alex lifted his head and tried to speak. 'Oh look, ish my lillal Becca. Shesh my right-hand man, you know, B-b-Basil. Ishn't she pretty?'

'There's no point in taking him up to the gatehouse and disturbing Mrs Fiennes,' Rebecca said drily. 'And I'm sure you want to get back home, Basil. Will you carry him up to my room? I'll sleep on the settee.'

–

Alex woke up and stared round the strange room he was lying in. The rose-patterned curtains were drawn across but he could see the sun was up and it was a hot bright day. He tried to clear his brain and make out where he was. It was obviously a woman's room. Pink walls, pink candlewick bedspread, a frilled pillowcase, a few feminine things on the tiny dressing table. On a pink-painted wooden chair, the only other piece of furniture in the room, was a hand-knitted woman's cardigan and a doll which had seen better days.

'Where the hell am I?' he murmured to himself. He hoped he hadn't gone home with a strange woman from the pub and… He didn't want the estate to think badly of him. 'Probably wouldn't have been up to it anyway,' he comforted himself. Then he frowned. What if the woman lied? What if she blackmailed him? What if she was married and had a huge angry husband? This is what you get for getting legless, he reprimanded himself. Bloody idiot.

Alex pushed back the bedcovers and saw he was only in his underpants. He heard someone coming up the stairs and pulled the bedcovers swiftly up to his neck. He broke out in a cold sweat as the person turned the door handle.

'Becca!' he sighed with relief.

'Who did you think it was?' she asked sternly. 'By the look on your face I would guess somebody's husband.'

'Don't be silly. I know precisely where I am.'

'Liar,' she said, throwing back the curtains.

Alex cried out as the sunlight hit his eyes. 'Close them again, for goodness sake!'

'Just realised we've got a thumping headache, have we?' She looked down on him with a superior expression on her face.

'Why are women so heartless when a man's had a few too many? What's wrong with it? It damn well infuriates me. It isn't as if I do this every day of the week.'

'As long as it doesn't encourage my father to.'

'Well, there is that, but I don't think Trease will go back to drinking like he used to before I came here.'

'Oh? Think yourself a good influence on him, do you?'

Alex looked ashamed. 'You have a horrible way of putting me in my place at times, Rebecca Allen. What I meant was that Trease is happy now he's back working entirely on the cars. It's given him a new lease of life.'

'Well, I'm grateful for that.'

'I suppose he's just woken up with a splitting headache too?'

'No,' she said briskly, tossing Alex's clothes on the bed and making him wince. 'He was up and out at work hours ago. He went to the gatehouse first to tell Mrs Fiennes she needn't worry about you. There didn't seem any sense in hauling you all the way up there last night. Get dressed. Breakfast is in ten minutes.'

'My clothes are damp and crumpled,' Alex said, holding his shirt away from his body in disgust when he came into the kitchen.

'That's because you fell into the creek while Basil Hartley was trying to get you out of his boat. By the way, he'll be expecting someone to pick up your boat later today – and your gratitude.'

'I know, I know,' Alex said irritably, sitting at the table because his legs were still a bit wobbly. 'I suppose that's why Trease undressed me.'

Rebecca put a pot of tea on the table. 'Dad wasn't fit to even undress himself last night.'

'Who did then?'

Rebecca said nothing, pursing her lips as she poured the tea.

'Not you? It wasn't you?'

'It was. How do you like your eggs?'

A bright colour crept all the way up Alex's neck and face and disappeared under his untidy dark hair.

'Well, I could hardly leave you in wet clothes, could I? And don't you look pretty when you blush?'

'Damn and blast it, Becca, you've got a mouth like a shrew! I think you're damned well enjoying this.'

Rebecca smiled at him very sweetly. 'You didn't say how you like your eggs.'

'I don't want anything to eat,' he said tartly, spooning sugar into his tea.

As Rebecca made toast for him, he came up behind her and put his hands on her shoulders. 'I'm sorry about you having to undress me, Becca. That was out of order on my part.'

She looked at him over her shoulder. 'Don't take it to heart, Alex. I'm used to it.' He was bedraggled and needed a shave. He was looking very serious and it made him seem young and vulnerable. It was no wonder Loveday had thought that he was the handsome young man she was seeing.

'I don't want you to have to do the things you've been used to like that, Becca. That's not the sort of life you deserve.'

–

'That was a good time the Major had with you men last night in the pub,' Ira Jenkins said to her mother- and father-in-law as she shared a mid-morning cup of tea with them outside their home. They were sitting with their backs to the kitchen wall, on a bench Jossy had made in his younger days.

'Yes.' Jenny laughed brightly, putting her cup down on an old washtub that served as a table. She rubbed at her stiff fingers. 'He got a bit too merry. Basil and young Tom had to leave him to sleep it off at Trease and Rebecca's cottage so Mrs Fiennes wouldn't be disturbed. That dear maid, she's a good little soul. She took it all in good part.'

'The regatta was a great success,' Jossy said, screwing up his wrinkled old face in huge satisfaction. 'The Major thoroughly enjoyed himself. Reckon we'll be hearing good news from un soon about keeping on the estate. Can't see any reason why he wouldn't want to keep it on, even if it was only for the summers, t'come down for the regattas. He's a natural river man.'

Ira nodded. 'And Mrs Fiennes loves the creek. She told Joe and Joe told Loveday and Loveday told me. Master Stephen positively revels in it. He was a bit nasty to little Tamsyn to begin with but they're good pals now.' She chuckled. 'They'm always off somewhere up to mischief, and he being a big boy too. He takes good care of her, mind. I've hardly had to look after her while Loveday's working lately.'

Jossy lit his pipe. 'And if the Major keeps Trevallion, 'tis all down to Becca, we mustn't forget that. Somehow she's managed to bring the Major out of his shell, and I bet he's been brooding over something to do with the war, I've seen the look he used to have on his face before.' Jossy tapped his big nose. 'You mark my words, m'dears, all we got to do is just sit back and wait for good news. The big house won't be empty much longer.'

Chapter 28

From the moment that Alex had triumphed at the regatta, he felt more confident in himself, enough to come to a decision about the Trevallion estate. He was going to keep it. He hadn't made up his mind exactly what he was going to do with it but he wanted to make sure the Kennickers, in particular Rebecca, would have no fears for their future. He felt good, he was beginning to feel in charge of himself at last, like he had been before the war when decision-making had come easy, when he had faced the world with ease, taking it for granted he'd sow his wild oats, then one day get married and raise a family at Carsham Hall.

As he rode Polonius through the fields early one morning, he realised that he'd hardly thought of Carsham Hall since coming down to Cornwall. It hadn't meant much to him when he'd come back from the war; it meant nothing to him now.

Where do I belong? he thought, as he slowed the horse to a trot and looked down on the river. Here? Miles's face sprang into his mind, the angry, taunting vision of it he'd seen in his nightmare when Rebecca had comforted him. He felt uneasy. He shook the memory from his mind and let his thoughts travel to Perranporth, to the old mine ruins and the site of Aristotle Trevallion's house. Miles didn't haunt him there. A heron soaring up from the river below captured his attention and brought him back to the present. His dream of Miles may have disturbed him, but there was no doubt that he had found some peace here on Miles's property.

Throughout the week since the regatta Alex had visited many of the farms, he had sailed the Trevallion boats and continued to spend money on the big house and grounds. He knew the estate workers had relaxed too, he was sure that most of them took it for granted he was going to keep the estate. He was on his way to Verrian Farm now.

'Good morning, Frank, Howard,' Alex said gaily as he trotted into the farmyard. Howard, the young farmhand who had taken over Rebecca's job, was standing beside his boss holding on to a sheep. 'I'm glad I caught you. I thought you might be out working on the harvesting. I'd like to give you a hand.'

'I'm waiting for the vet,' Frank explained. 'I brought the ewe into the yard to show the boy here her bad foot. Be glad to have your help in the fields, Major. 'Tis good of 'ee to offer.'

'What's the matter with her?' Alex asked curiously, stroking the ewe's shorn back. She was a small animal who yielded a small amount of wool, as was typical of most Cornish sheep.

'Bit of foot rot, I believe,' Frank replied. 'I don't want to lose her, she's a good breeder, is Pandora.' He affectionately touched the ewe's ear and she seemed to respond to him.

'The estate men did us proud at the regatta,' Alex said, grinning at Howard over the fuss the farmer was making of his sheep.

'Aye, and the Jenkins boys did well the following week racing their boat up to Fowey. That can be a tricky journey if 'tis bad weather, specially round Dodman Point. They did well in the harbour races too. Wish I'd seen them.'

'So do I,' Alex agreed. He thought the talk about the regatta would go on but what Frank said next nearly sent him reeling across the yard.

'I was surprised to learn that young Rebecca is seeing that estate trustee bloke.'

Alex thought he couldn't have heard right. 'What are you talking about, Frank?'

'Mr Faull. Rebecca's been seeing Neville Faull.'

'But she can't be!' Alex gasped. 'Becca wouldn't go out with Faull if he was the last... Are you serious about this, Frank?'

Frank wished he'd kept his mouth shut. 'They've been seen, sir. At the cinema in Truro, canoodling in the lane and walking together through St Mawes last week.'

Alex's face turned purple with rage. Forgetting why he'd come here, he left Frank and Howard standing with the ewe and ran to

Polonius. His mind was in a fever. He knew Rebecca had nurtured hopes over Joe but apart from that he'd thought she wasn't interested in men. He had seen men casting admiring glances at her but he had never seen her reciprocate. Now to be told she had a man in her life, and of all people Neville Faull! He rode out of the farmyard at breakneck speed, Polonius's hooves showering dust over the astonished farmer and his young hand.

–

Rebecca was in her room at the gatehouse thinking about the evening she had spent with Neville at his Aunt Mildred's house, unaware that a storm was about to break. She was hanging up the dress she had worn, freshly laundered and ironed, in the small wardrobe, remembering Neville's compliments on how she had looked.

Neville's Aunt Mildred was a charming woman and had quickly swept away Rebecca's misgivings about dining in her house. There had just been the three of them and after dinner they had gone into the large cosy sitting room to drink coffee. Neville relaxed with a cigar and brandy. They had played cards until ten o'clock. Then Aunt Mildred 'remembered' there was a letter she 'simply must write' and left Rebecca and Neville alone.

Neville had put the cards back into their box and smiled at Rebecca from across the table. 'Good old Aunt Mildred, she knows when to make a strategic withdrawal. Well, my dear, what shall we do now?'

'You can tell me about the paintings in this room, Neville. I'm fascinated by them.'

Neville looked over his shoulder at a portrait of a young man in early Victorian clothes and long side whiskers. 'So that's who you've been glancing at all night. My grandpater, Edward Arthur Penlewey Faull. And I thought you were making eyes at me. That's not very flattering, Rebecca.'

Rebecca laughed at him and got up to take a closer look at the portrait. 'He was a very good-looking man, your grandfather. He had longer hair and more of it about the face but you look just like him, Neville.'

'That's better,' Neville said, stroking his neat moustache.

He came to where she stood with her head slightly tilted. Moving her hair away from her shoulder he kissed the soft skin he had uncovered, then he did the same on the other side. Rebecca closed her eyes and leant against him.

'Have you got any more family apart from your Aunt Mildred?' Not having had much of a family life herself, looking at Neville's grandfather's portrait had aroused Rebecca's curiosity in his.

'Not many. Like you, I'm an only child. My parents died when I was a youth. My cousins, Aunt Mildred's children, are married and scattered around the country. Pity really, I'd like to have more family around me, specially at Christmas and times like that, nieces and nephews to spoil.'

Looking again at the portrait, she said, 'So you feel you've missed out on something?'

'Yes, I do.' Neville didn't have to think about it. 'And I take it you do too.'

'Yes,' Rebecca replied. 'But at least Dad's trying harder these days. He was thrilled to have rowed in a winning gig at the regatta.'

'That's good.' Neville moved back to more immediate things. 'I like your dress, Rebecca,' he said, touching the straps on her shoulders. 'What colour do you call this?'

'It's cobalt blue.'

'It suits your beautiful hair.' Neville put his arms round her and placed his hands over hers which were clasped in front of her. 'You're very beautiful, Rebecca,' he whispered in her ear. 'Do you really want me to tell you about the paintings? I can do that another time.'

'No,' she replied, turning round to him.

Rebecca had told her Uncle Bert she was meeting an old school friend and he had given her permission to stay out until eleven o'clock. The evening rushed by all too quickly and soon she was putting her coat on against the chilly night air and saying goodbye to Mildred Cummings at the door. Neville walked her home and they kissed goodnight in the shelter of a doorway several yards from Uncle Bert's front door. Neville watched from a distance until she was safely inside the garden gate then waved to her. It had been a wonderful evening and she would be going out with him again sometime next week.

Rebecca was daydreaming and took no notice of the sudden shouting from downstairs. Then she shook herself back to the present and put the dress in the wardrobe, listening to the voices. It was Alex and he was ordering an argumentative Stephen, who was the only other person in the gatehouse, to go outside to play. Rebecca was about to go downstairs to find out what the trouble was when Alex came bounding up, marched across the landing and pushed her from the doorway back into the room. His face was as black as thunder.

'What's the mat—'

'Is it true that you've been seeing Neville Faull?' Alex shouted at her.

Rebecca was stunned at his fury and said blankly, 'What?' Alex leant towards her, clenching his fists. 'Are you? Answer me! I demand an answer from you this minute.'

'I don't have to give you an answer at all!' Rebecca shouted back defiantly. 'It's none of your business.'

'It damned well is. The man's a cad. He's a bastard.'

'He is not,' Rebecca replied coolly. She was not going to allow herself to get into a rage like Alex and became perfectly calm. She moved to her dressing table, putting her back to him. 'It is none of your business, Alex, now please leave my room.'

Alex charged up to her. He was about to speak when he noticed what was on the dressing table. 'What's this? Chocolates! Expensive perfume! Did he give you these? What is he to you? Just because he's got a Military Cross—'

'So Neville won a medal in the war, did he?' Rebecca said evenly. She was determined not to get ruffled. Alex clutched her shoulders tightly and swung her round to him 'Neville! Why is he Neville to you? I demand to know why!'

Trying not to blink under the barrage, Rebecca said, 'Why are you Alex to me? You're not to anyone else.' She struggled to free herself. 'Now let me go, you're hurting me.'

But Alex shook her violently. 'Are you going out with Faull?'

'Yes!'

'Are you mad, going out with him? The man who keeps encouraging me to sell Trevallion out from under the Kennickers' feet for a blasted hotel just because he'd make a hefty commission on the sale! What's the attraction, Rebecca? Is he a good lover? Is that it?'

Despite the pain he was inflicting on her, Rebecca clamped her mouth tight and refused to answer.

A look of intense pain passed over Alex's face then he pulled Rebecca towards him. 'Well, if it's lovemaking that you want...'

He forced his mouth down on hers and Rebecca fought against him with all her might. He had not shaved that morning and his one day's growth of beard scratched her face. She tore her lips away and tried to scream at him to stop. Alex raised a hand to the back of her neck and used brute force to kiss her again. She could hardly breathe. She reached out with a hand to try to secure something on the dressing table to beat him off with but only succeeded in scattering things on the floor. The perfume bottle Neville had given to her broke and its strong scent filled the air.

Rebecca struggled against Alex's desperate strength. She thought she was going to black out when she felt his hand close over her breast and with a rage that gave her renewed strength she kicked and flailed at him with her fists and wrenched herself away. She was shaking and out of breath but delivered a slap across Alex's face so hard it made his head rock and sent him reeling across the room.

It brought him to his senses. 'Oh, Becca, forgive me?' he wailed. 'I don't know what came over me. I was so afraid...'

Tears of disgust and anger were falling down her face. Gulping in air, she said hoarsely, 'I have been out with Neville Faull twice and seen him at other times too, but not once did he force a kiss on me and he knew how to keep his hands to himself.'

'Becca...' There was pleading in Alex's eyes and his body was shaking. 'Please, Becca. I couldn't bear it if you didn't forgive me. I need you...'

His face was ashen and pathetic and the morbid, frightened mask that she had seen there when she'd first met him had returned. She couldn't bear to look at him and sat down on the bed with her face in her hands.

'You Fiennes have been nothing but trouble to me since you came to Trevallion. And I mean all of you. You're selfish and detestable. Do what you like with Trevallion, Major Fiennes. I don't care what happens to it any more. I'm going home tonight and somehow I'll have to hide from my father the true reason why. He'd probably want to kill you for what you did and I don't want him getting into any trouble on my account, but tomorrow I'm leaving—'

'No, Becca!' Tears of anguish rolled down Alex's face. 'Oh, please, don't say that. I need you. You make me feel safe. Without you I'll die. I beg you—'

'Rebecca? Are you all right?' It was Stephen calling timidly outside the bedroom door.

Alex ran out of the room and turned on his nephew. 'You rotten little bastard! No one but you would be capable of interrupting when two people are quarrelling over a sensitive matter. You're an evil little swine. You're no Fiennes, boy! You're not my brother's son! You were spawned by one of your mother's many lovers. Now get out of my way or I'll damn well knock you out of it.'

Stephen made a strangled sound and ducked aside as his uncle pushed past him. He thumped down the stairs and slammed the front door as he left the building. The boy came into Rebecca's room and stared at her in a state of shock.

Rebecca was standing numbly, her hand held in horror to her face.

'Did you hear?' Stephen murmured painfully. 'Do you think it's true?'

She shivered. 'What he said about you not being Ralph Fiennes' son? I think your uncle was just lashing out at you.'

Stephen looked as though a mighty truth had just dawned on him. 'It must be why he hates me. He's always hated me.'

Rebecca wanted to be left alone so she could pack the few belongings she kept here and take them home to Allen Cottage, but she could not turn away the shocked boy, who had been brave enough to come to her aid, without giving him some word of comfort.

'People say terrible things when they're in a foul temper, Stephen. I shouldn't take any notice of him.'

'That's easier said than done.' He looked close to tears and abruptly turned his concern to her. 'Are you all right? Did he hurt you?'

'I'll be all right, Stephen, and I'd be grateful if you didn't talk about what you heard.'

'Are you joking? Admit my barmy uncle is no more than a disgusting rapist? If that got around I wouldn't be able to hold my head up anywhere.'

'Let me make one thing very clear, Stephen,' Rebecca said firmly, rising from the bed and facing the boy squarely. 'Your uncle is not a rapist. If I thought for a moment that he was then I wouldn't hesitate to tell my father. He just panicked, that's all.'

'Then you're not going to leave here?'

'Oh yes, I am. Tomorrow I'm going to go to live with my uncle and aunt in Truro. If you don't mind leaving now, Stephen, I would like to be alone to pack my things. I'll leave a note for your mother to say where I'm going. I won't come back here. If Mrs Fiennes wants a full explanation, she must either ask the Major or come down to Allen Cottage.'

Stephen nodded. 'I'll go downstairs and make you a cup of tea. You can drink it before you go. I must be growing up because for the first time in my life I feel that I could do with one. I don't know how long we're to stay here. Some people seem to think it's for good but my uncle hasn't made any arrangements for me to attend a local school. But no matter how long I have left here, I shall miss you, Rebecca. And I'll tell you one thing. Whether it's true or not, I'll never forgive Uncle Alex for what he said.'

Chapter 29

Joe and Trease were sitting at the kitchen table in Allen Cottage playing cards. A sudden battering on the door brought them swiftly to their feet.

'What now?' Trease growled. 'If that's any of the Fiennes come down here to demand that Becca goes back for the night I'll have something to say.'

Over the cards the men had been discussing Rebecca's explanation as to why she had suddenly come home. She'd said the Major had spoken to her harshly and she'd had enough of being treated like a skivvy and wanted to live in Truro. Trease had spent hours trying to get her to change her mind. He'd begged her to stay and keep house for him as she had until a few weeks ago but she had packed a suitcase.

'Well, it would hardly be Mrs Fiennes tripping down here this time of the night.' Joe frowned. 'Something must be wrong with one of the Kennickers. 'Tis a wet windy night. P'raps one of the boats has broken free from its moorings.'

'They wouldn't bang on the door. They'd walk straight in. 'Tis rarely locked,' Trease said testily as he went to open the door.

The moment it was ajar, Abigail and Stephen, soaked through in summer coats, tumbled through the door together.

Joe went to Abigail at once.

'Where's Rebecca?' Abigail said urgently, pushing past him to plead with Trease. 'It's imperative that she comes to the gatehouse straightaway.'

'You can't order my maid about like that,' Trease retorted sternly. 'She was treated badly by the Major today and is threatening to go to

Truro to live. You're driving her away from her home between you. She's in bed and I won't disturb her.'

'But you don't understand,' Abigail said, wringing her wet hands. 'The Major's gone mad and Rebecca is the only one who can calm him down. We thought at first he was just having another of his nightmares but he's shouting and screaming out all the time and it sounds like he's throwing things around his room. We tried to open the door but it's locked and we're afraid. Rebecca must come or he'll hurt himself. He might do anything in this mood.'

'Well, I don't know,' Trease began.

'Don't forget what some men suffered in the trenches, Trease,' Joe said. 'Could have been me or you.'

'I'll go, Dad,' Rebecca said. She was in the doorway that led to the stairs, standing in her dressing gown.

'After the way he upset you?' Trease asked.

'Oh please come at once, Rebecca,' Abigail pleaded with her. 'If he does something silly,' she added to Trease, 'who knows who will look after the estate.'

Rebecca threw a coat over her dressing gown, and with Joe and Trease to break down the Major's door if necessary, she ran all the way to the gatehouse with Abigail and Stephen. Inside they could hear moans of anguish and banging coming from Alex's room.

'Stay down here with Master Stephen,' Joe ordered Abigail. 'You'll find it warm in the kitchen from the range. Dry yourselves off.' He turned to Rebecca. 'Me and Trease will go upstairs first. You keep back until we've got the door open.'

Trease knocked on the Major's bedroom door, hoping the sound would penetrate through the wailings and bangings coming from within. 'Major! Major Fiennes! Can you hear me? Open the door, sir. We just want to make sure you're all right.'

The terrible sounds went on. Joe said grimly, 'It's no good. We'll have to break away the lock.'

Rebecca leant back against a wall. Her heart was pounding, her mouth dry. What was Alex doing in there? What did all those noises mean? What was he doing to himself? There was an unearthly howl and Rebecca clutched her wet coat about herself. 'Hurry! For goodness sake, hurry!'

On the count of three, Trease and Joe rammed their shoulders against the bedroom door. It took three more blows before the wood round the lock gave way and the door burst open.

'Bloody hell!' Joe gasped.

'It's like the trenches all over again,' Trease breathed in horror.

Rebecca ran up behind them but Joe held her back. 'Don't go in, Becca. This is no place for you.'

She could hear Alex muttering and a scream ripped from his throat. 'I must go to him!' She struggled and Joe let her go. She rushed through the door and came to a standstill. 'Oh, my God. Alex, what have you done?'

The furniture had been turned over as if Alex was making a defensive position. There was blood along the walls where he had repeatedly slammed his fists and head against them. He was lying flat on his stomach behind the overturned wardrobe. He was wearing only his underpants and there was blood on them too. He was muttering to himself and Rebecca could just make out what he was saying.

'We'll get them this time, boys. Be over the top and back again without a scratch on us. I'll go first. If they get anyone it will be me first.'

He scrabbled about on his hands and knees to a pillow which was stained with blood. 'Who's that?' His voice was forlorn and trembling. 'You can make it? Don't give up. I'll call for a stretcher. Oh no, it's Jimmy Clark!' His voice rose with each succeeding word. He picked up the pillow and hugged it to his chest. 'He's only a boy. He can't die now. What shall I say to his mother? Aargh! Jimmy! Jimmy!' He rocked the pillow and howled again.

Rebecca climbed over the broken furniture, ignoring Trease and Joe's warnings, and ran to Alex. In one hefty pull she tore the pillow from his desperate grip and knelt in front of him. As he screamed in terror, she threw her arms round him and pulled him to her.

'It's me, Alex. It's Becca. I'm here now and I'm going to take care of you and you don't have to be afraid any more. It's Becca.'

Trease was over the furniture a split second after Rebecca, ready to pull her away from the Major if he threatened to turn his violence on her. But something in her voice penetrated through the horror in Alex's brain and he went quiet and limp like a rag doll. Trease watched in fascinated disbelief as his daughter held his employer's bruised and bleeding head against her breast and stroked his hair, talking soothingly to him.

'We'll have to get the doctor to him, Trease,' Joe said at his side. 'What a mess he's in. Wonder he didn't bash his head in.'

'I'll go for the doctor in one of the cars,' Trease said, wanting to weep at the pathetic scene before him. 'Will you stay here and make sure he doesn't hurt Becca?'

'Aye.' Joe put a hand on Trease's shoulder. 'Be as quick as you can.'

Joe moved broken furniture aside to make a clear passage from the door to Rebecca and the injured Major. Rebecca went on with her comforting words, rocking Alex as he had the pillow he'd thought was one of his dead men.

A hand on Joe's arm made him jump. It was Abigail. He put his arm round her as she gazed in horror at the room. She said quietly, 'Mrs Wright is downstairs. She heard us shouting outside Rebecca's cottage and came up here to help. Will you come down to Stephen, Joe? He could do with a man to comfort him right now. He was terrified by all the noise Alex was making. It was like nothing on earth.'

'I know. It made my blood run cold. I can't leave Becca though.'

Abigail looked at her brother-in-law, quiet and unresponsive in Rebecca's arms. She thought back to the night Rebecca had comforted him in another nightmare. 'She won't come to any harm, Joe, I promise you. No matter how much out of his mind Alex is, he would never harm Rebecca. Anyway, I think it would be better to leave them alone and we won't be far away.'

Joe wasn't sure but reluctantly conceded and went downstairs with her. Stephen was sitting at the kitchen table, sobbing wretchedly over his arms. Loveday was stroking his head. For the first time in years, Abigail gathered her son into her arms. She was shocked at his distress and he clung to her.

'It's going to be all right, darling. Joe's here now. And Rebecca's with Uncle Alex. She'll make sure Uncle Alex doesn't hurt himself any more.'

'I don't care about him!' Stephen cried brutally. 'I hate him. I hope he dies! I hope he kills himself!'

Abigail looked at Joe. Thinking that she had no right to hear what was coming next, Loveday excused herself and left the room.

Abigail lifted Stephen's chin, which had sunk down on her chest. 'Why, darling? Why do you say a thing like that?'

It was Joe's eyes the boy sought. 'He told me I'm not a Fiennes. He called me a bastard. He said I was evil.'

'God in heaven,' Joe murmured, stooping to hold Stephen's hands in his. They both looked at Abigail.

Abigail couldn't meet their eyes. She said, 'What your Uncle Alex said is true, but you are a Fiennes, Stephen, because your father took you as his and that's all that matters. If he hadn't gambled away his money, it would have come to you when he died.'

She glanced anxiously at Joe to see what he thought of her, and she was ashamed to see that he didn't even look surprised.

Stephen was quiet for a while, then without looking at his mother, he asked quietly, 'Then who is my father?'

Abigail's face was ashen. How could she tell her distraught son that she didn't know? What lie could convince him? Then Joe spoke.

'I don't think your mother should have to explain any more in front of me,' he said softly. 'But Mr Fiennes obviously cared deeply for your mother and that is what is important.'

Stephen leant away from his mother and rested his head on Joe's shoulder. He whispered, 'Whoever he is, I hope he's like you, Joe.'

–

Rebecca had been aware of Abigail coming into the room and leaving with Joe and she was glad. When Alex came back to his senses, he would be embarrassed to have Joe watching him. She went on rocking him. 'It's all right, Alex, it's Becca. I won't leave you. You're safe now.'

Suddenly he gripped her round the waist. 'Becca… is that you?' His voice was husky, barely above a whisper.

'Yes, Alex. It's Becca. Everything's going to be all right now.'

'Becca…' He breathed her name over and over again. 'I was so afraid I'd lost you.' He wept and his tears mingled with his blood and the rainwater on her coat.

She took a handkerchief out of her coat pocket and gently wiped some of the blood from his head. 'You've hurt yourself, Alex, but don't worry. My father has gone to get the doctor.'

He became panicky and held her tighter. 'You won't go?'

'No, I promise you, Alex. I'll stay with you all the time. Do you think you can get up? You'll be more comfortable in my room.'

'No, I can't move. I feel so weak.' He pressed his head closer to her breast and she held him tightly.

'I could call for Joe. He'll carry you through.'

'Not yet, Becca. I'll make it with you helping me in a few minutes.'

Becca doubted if Alex would be able to stand up but she knew he needed to retain a little pride. She wiped away fresh blood dripping from his head.

'Alex,' she said, as softly as she could. 'What happened to bring you to this? Did you have another nightmare?'

'M–Miles,' he whimpered. 'He was here again… his eyes blazing… telling me he hated me. He's not happy with me because I haven't made a firm decision yet. But… but I do have a plan forming in my mind, Becca.' Alex's voice began to rise again and his eyes were glazed. 'But Miles wouldn't listen… he said I was worthless… that he was furious I'd inherited Trevallion.'

Alex ran out of breath and became quiet for a few moments then, without prompting from Rebecca, he started talking again. 'He said I had to fight the war again… that if I didn't… if I didn't bring my men back alive…' His voice turned to a squeak. 'That he'd kill you, Becca.'

She smoothed his hair. 'You must remember that it was only a terrible dream, Alex. Captain Miles would never have hurt you, me or anyone else. He was a good man and would have been delighted with what you've been doing with Trevallion. You mustn't lose sight of that. And, Alex, it wasn't your fault that the men under your command died and you survived. I know you and I'm sure you'd have done all you could to ensure their safety. What's happening is that you're getting all your guilty feelings mixed up. You've become happy here and you probably feel you have no right to be. But you have. You're a good man, Alex.'

Alex pulled his face away from her body. Blood was on his face and dark shadows circled his eyes, making them look too big for his gaunt face.

'Do you really think that, even after what I did to you this morning, Becca?'

'Yes, I do.'

'But it was unforgivable, and you threatened to leave. You've cleared everything out of your room.'

Rebecca pictured her suitcase packed ready to leave first thing in the morning. 'It was only a threat. I got into a temper myself, that's all,' she said quickly, then wiped at the blood on his face in fear he would see the truth and panic again. He had broken out in a feverish sweat during his ordeal and was now shivering with cold. 'Alex, you're going to get a chill if we stay like this and you really ought to put on some more clothes. Let me call for Joe and we'll get you into my bed and clean you up. You'll feel much better for when the doctor comes.'

'I can manage with you, Becca. Please don't call for anyone. I'd hate anyone to see me like this.' It struck Rebecca then that Alex didn't realise that Trease, Joe and Abigail had seen him in this state. He probably had no idea how he had been shouting and howling, of the fear and distress he had caused. If she could get him into the bed she had slept in, Joe could clear up the room.

It was a struggle getting him to his feet. Alex used the upturned wardrobe to lever himself up and he had to cling to Rebecca to keep his balance. His sight became blurred and he breathed deeply, waiting for his eyes to clear. One of his bloodied hands dug into the bruises he had made on her shoulder that morning and she flinched, trying hard not to cry out in pain. A bit at a time she helped him to the door and out of the room. They stumbled across the landing and she had to hold all his weight with one arm while she opened her bedroom door. They fell through the doorway and hit the floor. Alex groaned and lay panting. Rebecca disentangled herself from his clinging arms and got to her feet.

'We only have to get you on the bed now,' she said.

'Becca? You all right?' Joe called up the stairs. 'I heard you moving about.'

'I'll be back in a minute,' she told Alex and went to the top of the stairs to speak to Joe.

'I've managed to get the Major into my room. Can you come and tidy up his room, Joe? And ask Loveday to bring up a bowl of hot water, towels and a flannel and leave it outside the door?'

Joe signalled he understood and disappeared. Becca dashed back to Alex and found him sitting on the bed, his eyes tightly closed, his fists clutching the covers.

'Becca...'

'I'm here, Alex.' She went to him. 'You'll feel better if you lie down.'

'No, I'll be all right in a minute.' He hoped he would be. He was dizzy, felt thick and stupid and he was frightened he would stay like this for ever.

'I'm just going out of the room for a minute but I promise I'll be right back.'

She sped to Alex's room. He had pulled out all the drawers from the chest and his clothes were scattered everywhere. She tossed clothes aside, searching for his pyjama bottoms.

'What are you looking for?' Joe asked behind her.

'These,' she replied, holding them up. She picked up a pullover and made to leave the room.

Joe held her arm. 'I'd better put them on for him,' he said sternly.

'Oh, Joe,' she sighed impatiently. 'It's hardly the time to be thinking about modesty.'

'Well, I don't think your father would like it, Becca.'

'Then don't tell him!' Rebecca snapped.

266

She went back to Alex and waited for Loveday to leave the things she had asked for outside the door and go downstairs again. Loveday's primness would provoke a much harder argument about the impropriety of a young unmarried woman dressing the Major.

Rebecca put the hot water on the marble-topped washstand and wrung out the flannel. Alex was watching her out of huge frightened eyes, like a child afraid of being left alone, and she felt a lump rise in her throat.

Hoping her voice would sound normal, she said gently, 'I'll wash your face first.'

'I can do it,' he said, his voice full of pain.

'You're shaking too much, Alex.' She wrapped a big bath towel round his shoulders. 'This will help to keep you warm.'

As she gently wiped blood and sweat from his forehead, large tears fell from his eyes at his humiliation. He didn't have a shred of pride left to cling to.

'Oh, Becca, I'm so sorry about this.'

'There's nothing to be sorry about, Alex,' she said, cleaning carefully round his eyes. 'All we need to do is get you prepared for the doctor and you'll feel much better.'

'Have… have I done much damage?'

'It looks worse than it actually is but you'll have two black eyes in the morning.'

He raised a hand to his head. 'I've got a terrible headache.'

'That's hardly surprising.' Rebecca smiled to cheer him.

'Promise me one thing, Becca. Don't let the doctor send me to hospital. I hated it in the field hospital. I couldn't bear it.'

'I'm sure the doctor will be happy for you to stay here but if he thinks it's best, the infirmary in Truro has some very nice private beds, so I'm told.'

She was washing one of his hands and he snatched it away and gripped her arm tightly. 'Promise me!'

Rebecca gently prised his fingers away. 'Listen, Alex, no one can make you do anything you don't want to. You're in charge of your own life.'

'Am I?' he said harshly. 'What kind of man must I be to end up like this?'

'A man who's suffered greatly. No one blames you for having nightmares, Alex.'

'What kind of man speaks to a child the way I did to Stephen this morning?'

Dropping the flannel, Rebecca lifted his face between her hands and made him look at her. 'Stop feeling sorry for yourself. You've done something wrong and you can change things by making up your mind to put it right. Speak to Stephen, tell him you're sorry, do all you can to make it up to him.'

Alex stared back into her eyes and a little measure of determination filtered into his face. 'Becca, I've done something that will settle Stephen's future and not only his. I've decided I will never sell Trevallion. I made up my mind the day of the regatta. I should have told you before but I was planning to throw a party at the big house and break the news then.' Alex sighed and his shoulders drooped. 'I haven't got the heart for a party now but at least the people on the estate can look forward to a secure future. You can tell them that. I'll tell Stephen and Abigail myself.'

'Everyone will be pleased to hear it,' Rebecca said, stroking his damp hair.

'You are staying?'

'I told you I was, Alex. Now, no more worrying.'

He yielded to her like a child again. When she had done as much as she dared to clean and dry him for the doctor's examination, she picked up his pyjama trousers. 'Now, let's get you into these.'

Alex blushed. 'I'll do it.'

Rebecca twisted her mouth. 'You can't touch these with those hands, you'll get blood on them.'

'Oh God,' Alex moaned.

'Just pretend I'm a nurse. Or would you prefer I get Joe?'

'No! I mean, I know it's indelicate but I'd rather you did it, if… if… if you don't mind too much.'

'Well, I have worked on a farm. I daresay I won't see anything too shocking,' she said, tongue in cheek. 'Stand up, please.'

The blood drained from Alex's face as he clung to the bed, he felt giddy and nauseous as Rebecca eased off his blood-stained underpants and put his pyjama trousers on. She pulled back the bedcovers and eased him into bed, sitting him up against the pillows. Then she put the pullover round his shoulders to keep him warm.

'You didn't blush once,' Alex grumbled, resting his stinging hands gingerly on the covers. 'You reminded me of one of the VAD nurses in France. She was ruthless about anything of a delicate nature. She never took enough care to pull the screens round if you were on a bedpan.'

Rebecca put her fingers to her face. 'I think you will pass inspection for the doctor, Major Fiennes. Are you comfortable or would you like me to fetch a bedpan?'

Alex's face changed from shock to a relieved smile when she laughed. 'It's good to see you aren't angry with me any more. You're not, are you? And you are staying?'

A great weariness overcame Rebecca and she slumped down on a chair. Apart from the traumas of the day, it was tiring to have to keep reassuring him. 'I've told you before, Alex, I am staying. You can accept my word on it.'

A short time later there was a knock on the bedroom door and the doctor entered accompanied by the district nurse. Alex scowled at Maisie Uren.

'Good evening, Rebecca.' Dr John Pearn, a young man who wore bright unconventional clothes and had the habit of consulting his pocket watch every few minutes, smiled cheerfully at her. 'I hear you've been having a spot of trouble.' He turned to Alex after looking at his watch. 'Major Fiennes, I presume? I hear you're still fighting the war. Nurse Uren, will you take Rebecca downstairs, please, and see she drinks a cup of hot sweet tea. She looks rather shocked.'

Rebecca felt so weak that Maisie Uren had to help her to her feet.

'You'll come back, Becca?' Alex said in a panicky voice.

'Now, now, Major Fiennes, we mustn't be selfish,' Nurse Uren said stoutly. She and the doctor had been told by Trease how Rebecca had managed to quell Alex's ravings. 'If Rebecca doesn't get out of this wet coat and have some refreshment, we'll have two patients on our hands.'

As if the nurse hadn't spoken, Alex cried, 'Becca?'

'I'll be back when the doctor's finished with you, Alex,' she promised, and the district nurse and doctor raised their eyebrows.

'I won't go to hospital,' Rebecca heard Alex declare loudly after Maisie Uren had closed the door.

The kitchen was warm from the fire Loveday had built up in the range and Nurse Uren shooed Joe, Trease and a tear-stained Stephen out of the room. She helped Rebecca out of her coat and frowned. 'Got out of bed, were you, dear? Well, your dressing gown is splashed and muddy. This will never do.'

'I'll go and fetch something of mine,' Abigail said. 'How's the Major?'

'He's quiet but we'll know more when Dr Pearn's finished with him. The doctor and I had just attended a difficult birth when we happened to meet Mr Allen in a Trevallion motorcar.'

Abigail brought back her most substantial dressing gown but it still received a tut-tut from Maisie Uren. 'Have you got a warm woollen cardigan to go round the child, Mrs Fiennes?'

'Oh, I'm sorry,' Abigail said, weary-eyed with delayed shock and worry. She was worried about Stephen, worried about what Alex had in store for them if he hated her son so much he'd told him the truth of his parentage. Then there was Joe. Would he end their association now? If he chose to gossip about her she had nowhere to go, and even if she did, no money to go there.

She looked at Rebecca with new respect. Goodness knows what Alex might have done to himself if Rebecca hadn't been willing to face him, and she'd shown not the slightest fear.

'Are you all right, Rebecca?'

Rebecca looked up from the cup of tea she was sipping. 'Yes, thank you, Mrs Fiennes.'

'What would we do without you?' Abigail said, then left to fetch a cardigan.

'Yes, that's what I would like to know,' Loveday muttered tightly, coming back into the kitchen.

Rebecca returned to Alex when Dr Pearn and Maisie Uren had left. He had bandages round both hands and his head. 'A few stitches and lots of bruises the doctor said,' she commented, sitting on a chair by the bed.

'I've got to have that woman calling here to nurse me for the next week,' he said darkly. 'She'll probably get her own back on me for not showing her my hand a few weeks ago.'

'Going to sulk about it, are we?' Rebecca said, in an impersonation of Maisie Uren's voice.

'No,' he replied sulkily. 'But I suppose it wouldn't be fair to expect you to nurse me. She wanted me to go into hospital for observation.' His voice changed to a serious tone. 'Dr Pearn talked to me for a long time. He said I'm still suffering from shell-shock. That I've got a morbid obsession with the death of my men, that in spite of Miles's terrible injuries, I've been envying him, the very fact that he was left in such an awful condition and that some of his men came home.'

'He's right, Alex. None of it's your fault. You must accept that or you'll never find any peace.'

Alex looked away for a moment. 'The doctor said I should talk about my feelings.'

'And will you?'

He reached out with a bandaged hand. 'I might, if I find the right person, but I'm not going to burden you, Becca.' His voice became softer. 'How are you feeling?'

'I'm all right now, but you did frighten me, Alex.'

'I'm sorry about that, but I'll make it up to you the moment I'm allowed out of this bed, though I can't see why I have to stay in it. We'll move into Trevallion and you can choose any bedroom you want, even the master bedroom if that pleases you.' He looked at her critically, at the flimsy dressing gown and fluffy cardigan. 'Abigail's clothes don't suit you. I'm going to buy you the biggest wardrobe of clothes a woman's ever had.'

'That's not necessary,' she protested, looking weary again.

'You aren't going, are you, Becca? I mean right this minute?'

'When Dr Pearn reassured us that you probably won't… get ill again tonight, Dad, Joe and Loveday went home. I told Mrs Fiennes I'd sit up with you.'

'You'll get cold,' Alex said softly. 'You can come in here with me. I promise there won't be a repeat of what happened this morning – I'm not capable of doing anything anyway.'

She didn't have the strength to argue. So, not only was she to sleep in the gatehouse tonight, once again she had to climb into bed with Alex Fiennes to comfort him.

Rebecca took off Abigail's cardigan and dressing gown, turned off the oil lamp and in just her simple cotton nightdress climbed into the bed beside him. Alex turned on his side and put his arm over her.

Thoughts of the distressing events of the day jumbled about in her mind but one kept coming to the fore. There was something she wanted to know. 'Alex?'

'Yes, my love?' he murmured, nuzzling closer to her.

'Is it true? What you said this morning about Stephen not being your brother's son? He was very upset.'

Alex sighed heavily. 'I shouldn't have said that. I never intended he'd find out. I'll have to tell him I only said it in temper. I owe it to Ralph to look after the child he owned as his son. Ralph was impotent, he wasn't capable of being a complete husband. He fell in love with Abigail and was delighted when she accepted his proposal of marriage. He didn't expect her to stay celibate and he wouldn't have minded too much if she'd kept to one lover but she took several. When she got pregnant, he talked her into having the baby because he loved children and it would make him feel more of a man in front of his male friends. I don't dislike Stephen because he's not Ralph's. It's because he's such a horrid young swine.'

'Stephen can be horrible, Alex, but he's not as bad as you think. I feel sorry for him. You don't understand children and I expect you've never tried to.'

'No, I suppose you're right. I'll see him in the morning and tell him I'm sorry.'

'I don't think it's going to be that easy, Alex. You see, Stephen asked Mrs Fiennes if what you'd said was true and she admitted it was.

Loveday overheard them talking. She wouldn't have told me but she fears there could be more trouble.'

'I'll do what I can to put things right between me and the boy first thing in the morning,' Alex said irritably. His head was aching cruelly and he didn't want to face the hurt he'd caused Stephen through the long night ahead. 'I'm only really interested in putting things right with you, Becca.'

Her nightdress had slipped off her shoulder leaving her breast half exposed. Alex put his head there, the universal place to find comfort. He clung to her tightly. 'Promise that you'll never leave me, Becca?'

Rebecca thought of the plans she had made for the morning and the man she had intended to turn to for help in getting her a new job and a fresh start in life. Then she thought of the consequences for the man in her arms if she did just that.

Tears pricked her eyes as she whispered, 'I promise, Alex.'

Chapter 30

Susannah Bosanko was writing a letter:

> *My dearest Alexander,*
>
> *Why haven't you come to see me? I haven't seen you since the day of the St Mawes Regatta and that was two weeks ago. To my regret we had so little time to talk then. It's such a bind that Trevallion House is not connected to the telephone.*
>
> *I shall wait three days for a reply to this letter or I will call at Trevallion and root you out.*
>
> *Yours ever affectionately.*

She signed the letter with a scratchy version of the S.B. that had appeared on Roland Trevallion's love letters then rang for her maid.

'Hilda, post this letter without delay and purchase a box of Fraser's Superior Mints on your way back.'

'Yes, ma'am.' Hilda curtsied and dutifully took the letter. She hurried to the servants' hall to collect her coat then slipped into the kitchen to alert the rest of the staff. When Miss Bosanko asked for Fraser's Superior Mints it meant she was in a particularly foul mood and heaven help anyone who crossed her.

–

Neville Faull was at his office desk opening his mail. He always did this in a deliberately unhurried way, tossing aside the serious-looking letters, especially those marked urgent, and opening up any interesting personal ones first. He had made two haphazard piles when he came across one written in a firm open hand.

'Definitely from a female,' he drawled, sniffing the envelope for perfume.

'What was that, Mr Faull?' Miss Penmere, his secretary, asked from across the room where she was lifting files out of a cabinet.

'Nothing of importance, Miss Penmere,' Neville replied, a full grin on his face. Taking a silver paperknife, he slit the top of the envelope open carefully, lingering over the task as he made guesses at the identity of the writer. He took out a single sheet of white paper and read its contents swiftly with his brows raised and mouth half open. Then he pushed the letter into his pocket and sprang up from his desk.

'Miss Penmere, ask Mr Drayton to take over my appointments for this morning.'

'But Mr Faull—'

'I have to go out,' he shouted on his way through the door.

—

The Fiennes were officially moving into Trevallion today. Not so Rebecca. Despite Alex's pleas she had resolutely refused to live in at the big house and was back home in Allen Cottage. There would be female staff living at Trevallion and she was no longer needed as a chaperone. If she had to stay in the creek to prevent Alex from killing or crippling himself she would at least keep some independence. She now found herself in the position of Major Alexander Fiennes' personal assistant, whatever that meant. Trease was doubly proud of her and the other Kennickers had congratulated her, thanking her for what they believed she had done towards making the Major decide to keep Trevallion and live there.

She cleared up the mess Trease had made getting his breakfast then carried the bag containing the few belongings she had used in the gatehouse upstairs to her room. She put the bag down on her narrow little bed, where not long ago Alex had slept after his drinking session with Trease. It was a relief to be home and to be able to sleep in her own bed again.

She put her hairbrush and comb on the dressing table, and shook out her dressing gown and hung it on its old hook. She had brought none of the things that Abigail had given her but next out of the bag came a dress she had bought with the money from Alex. She put it on a clothes hanger and hung it behind the curtain of a small alcove that served as a wardrobe. The dress suited her perfectly and she had received many compliments while wearing it. The same was true of the one she had on her back now, which along with other items was also bought with Alex's money. Rebecca liked her new clothes but they made her feel he owned a part of her.

In her new role as personal assistant she would have little to do as Alex did not need any such thing. He just needed to see her every day to stop him going berserk again. Dr Pearn warned he might be very near the edge for several months to come.

During the last week she had thought over her decision to pack and leave after Alex's panic-stricken assault on her and realised that, while she hated being restricted, she would always love Kennick Creek and was happy to live here for the foreseeable future. But this turn of events meant she would not be able to see Neville for ages and he would probably soon find someone else to dally with. She knew nothing would have come of her relationship with him but she had wanted it to last as long as possible. Tired from the tensions of the last few days, Rebecca threw a pair of shoes dolefully at the floor. Neville must have read her letter by now.

She'd told Alex she wanted to give Allen Cottage a thorough cleaning and catch up on her father's washing and wasn't expected up at Trevallion until the afternoon. Changing into her old clothes, and enjoying the familiar feel of them, she made a start on Trease's room, lamenting the state he'd got it into since her few weeks at the gatehouse but happy to be doing it. She checked his cupboard and drawers and was pleased to find no hidden bottles of liquor.

As she put the final rub to his washstand, she heard someone coming up the stairs. 'I'm in your room, Dad. I've given it a spring clean and it certainly needed it. I can't understand how you managed to get it into such a mess,' she said, backing out of the room and holding the door open. 'There, what do you think?'

'I think you've done a wonderful job, my dear,' a man said from behind her, his arms winding round her waist.

She twisted round. 'Neville! What are you doing here? How did you know where to find me?'

'I've just received your letter, Rebecca. I drove to the gatehouse at once and the roadmender told me where I could find you. What's all this about the Major having a brainstorm and you not being able to see me? What on earth's been going on here?'

'A brainstorm was the only way I could think of to describe what happens to the Major sometimes.'

'Sometimes? You mean it's happened before? Has he seen a doctor?'

'Yes and the district nurse is keeping an eye on him. It's to do with his war memories, all his men getting killed. He feels guilty about being the only one left alive. When he gets upset he has terrible nightmares and relives his experiences.'

'I see,' Neville sighed thoughtfully. 'That can be pretty terrible.'

Rebecca knew Alex and Neville despised one another but she wasn't surprised that Neville didn't sneer at Alex's attacks. 'You men who fought in the war, you're all sympathetic to each other, aren't you? The Major was understanding about my father's drinking when he first arrived here.'

'I've seen men shoot themselves because they couldn't bear to go on any longer. I've heard of another who slaughtered his entire family in one moment of madness. No man came back unchanged, that's certain.'

'Including you, Neville? You were very young. The Major told me you won a medal.'

'Did he now?' Neville looked away, somewhat embarrassed, then as if in retaliation he said, 'I bet he didn't tell you he won the Military Cross for bravery in trying to rescue one of his men single-handed while under heavy fire.'

'No, he didn't,' Rebecca said humbly. She pushed Neville's arms away. 'We can't stay up here. If my father came in he'd go mad.'

'Let's go downstairs then. He couldn't accuse me of trying to seduce you down there. I came here to see you and I'm not going just yet.'

'Would you like a cup of tea?' Rebecca asked, leading the way into the kitchen.

'Why does everyone think a cup of tea is the answer to every problem in the world! I'm sorry, Rebecca, but I don't understand what Major Fiennes' state of mind has got to do with you holing yourself up here on the property.'

'I'm the only one who can get him to calm down. He seems to rely on me, says he feels safer when I'm around. Dr Pearn says it's very important that he doesn't have another attack in the near future or he could do something so terrible he'd end up in a mental institution. I can't take the chance of that happening, Neville. You haven't seen him. It's terrifying.'

'I'm sure it is, but you can't go on like this forever.' Neville's handsome face creased with concern. 'Rebecca, I don't like this. What if Fiennes hurts you? You could be taking a big risk.'

She shook her head firmly. 'There's no chance of that. The Major would never hurt me. You don't think my father would let me near him if there was any risk of that, do you?'

'Well, maybe so,' Neville returned doubtfully. 'But surely he'd be all right if you came into Truro once a week. You could make it during the daytime. I'd bring you back, you wouldn't have to be away for long.' He tried to hold her again but she moved away.

'This is so difficult. I can't take the risk of seeing you, Neville.'

Against her protests, Neville pulled her close. 'Is he having funny turns because you're seeing me? Is that it?'

'Only the last one. I will see you again if you want me to but not until he's stronger, when his mind is clearer. When he's settled in at Trevallion—'

'Settled in? So he's decided to stay on then?' Neville had resigned himself to the fact that if Alex Fiennes decided to sell the estate then it wouldn't be to someone he had recommended. He was philosophic about the lost commission and saw no reason to bother informing the vile old lady in Falmouth that he had failed. According to Rebecca the Major had been in touch with Susannah Bosanko direct anyway. But he was uneasy at the thought that he might have competition over Rebecca.

'Yes, he has, but I don't know his long-term plans,' Rebecca replied. 'When he's stronger I'll tell him gently that I'm seeing you again.'

'How long will that take?' Neville asked impatiently.

'I don't know. A few weeks, months—'

'Months! I couldn't stand the wait. I care for you, Rebecca. I wouldn't be here now missing a very important meeting if I didn't. I've never done anything like this before. You've got your own boat, we could meet somewhere on the river. You suggest a place and I'll be there.'

'No, not yet. If you'd seen him the other night...'

'Very well,' Neville said angrily. 'But that doesn't mean I can't come here. Fiennes has asked the office to look into some possible business ventures for him, boatbuilding, china clay, tin, etcetera. I'll have an excuse to be on the estate and if I happen to see you I'll damn well speak to you and that's that!'

'Don't make things difficult, Neville,' she begged. 'If anything happens to the Major it will affect Trevallion and if he has just a small bad experience I'll be tied here even longer.'

He caressed her hair then held her face tightly between his hands. 'Don't worry, darling, I know how to be professional. Just don't ask me to stay away from you for good.' He kissed her long and hard and Rebecca nestled in against him.

'Are you happy I came?' he murmured.

'Yes, very happy.'

When Neville left Allen Cottage, he drove on to Trevallion. If the Major found out he'd been here and not called on him he'd know he'd been to see Rebecca and might go barmy again.

'What do you want?' Alex snapped at him as Emily Jewell, the fourteen-year-old daughter of an estate farm labourer, nervously showed him into the study. 'Thank you, Emily.' Alex smiled at the girl. 'If you're not sure what to do next, ask Mrs Wright.'

'Yes, sir.' Emily bobbed at the knee and ran out of the room.

Neville closed the door, which Emily had forgotten to do. 'So you've moved in here, Major Fiennes? Mr Drayton will be pleased. He'll be able to carry on with the little gardening interest he's taken on here.'

Alex returned Neville's sarcasm. 'What about you, Faull? It's spoiled your hopes for a little commission from selling this place for a hotel. What are you doing here now?'

'I called at the gatehouse with some information you asked for about local investments. I think you'll find the boatbuilding the most interesting to you.' Neville had a folder under his arm. It had been lying on the seat of his car and was quite empty. He was gambling that Alex was in no mood for talking business; from the bruises and cuts still visible on his face, he looked in no fit state for anything much. 'Perhaps the moment is not opportune,' he said in the voice he reserved for wealthy elderly ladies in bereavement. 'You are obviously not well.'

Alex stared at him stonily and Neville retreated to the door.

'I'll call again next week, Major. I do hope you feel better soon.'

–

'The Major's sulking in Captain Miles's study,' Ivy Gummoe, wife of Percy the caretaker, paused in her dusting to inform Rebecca as she stepped inside the big house.

'Has someone upset him?' Rebecca asked, sighing. She'd have stern words with Neville if he'd caused any trouble.

'No, I don't think so. That Mr Faull was here this morning but he left almost at once. He made young Emily come over all strange, she thought he was so handsome. Percy and I have been given a lovely room, Rebecca. It will be much better than living in that cold draughty cottage we had. I don't think I could have faced another winter there. Want to have a look-see later on?' Ivy's small urchin face was alight with joy and Rebecca was pleased for her.

'I'd love to, after dinner tonight, eh?'

'S'pose you must be feeling some pleased with yourself,' Ivy remarked, dusting the long hall table with gusto. 'You're somebody important now. Don't know why you didn't want to move in here, could have had the best room in the house so I've heard. Still, I suppose home's home and that's all there is to it.'

'The Major is my employer, Ivy, just like he is yours,' Rebecca stressed.

'Oh, don't look like that.'

'Like what?' Rebecca asked, getting impatient with Ivy's chatter.

'All mournful looking. Where's that nice smile we've been seeing of late? You were beaming on regatta day.'

'I'll see you later, Ivy.'

Rebecca went into the study. One look at Alex's face brought on the compassion she felt for him. It was easy to feel vexed with him when she was apart from him but it was different when they were face to face. He was lounging at his desk, his chair turned away so he could stretch his legs. His shoulders were hunched over, his head held stiff, his eyes staring at nothing.

She went up close to him. 'Are you all right, Alex?'

'Mmmm, I suppose so,' he said wearily. He lifted his head and searched her face and Rebecca was certain that he wanted to ask her if she had seen Neville Faull.

'Did you eat your lunch?'

'You sound like that bloody nurse,' he said tersely.

'If you're going to speak to me like that I'll go to the kitchen and chat to Loveday,' she threatened but kept a calm voice.

For the first two days after his nightmare she had taken the full brunt of his moods, which had changed more quickly than unsettled weather. It had taken great patience and strength of will to cope with him. Nurse Uren, who was unshakeable no matter how badly he behaved, advised Rebecca not to pander to his every whim and not to be afraid to give him a good ticking off when she felt he needed it.

Alex had learned to sidestep her. He got up and wandered round the room. 'I wonder how Stephen is getting on with his first day at Truro Cathedral School. Miles was schooled there. I'm going to get Stephen his own pony. Did I tell you?'

'Yes, several times.'

Alex had tried as many ploys to get Stephen to talk to him as he had in trying to get Rebecca to live at Trevallion. While Rebecca's promise not to leave the creek gave him a measure of peace, Stephen had been unrelenting in his unforgiveness; he was only sorry to be going to boarding school during the week because he'd miss the creek, riding and rowing with Joe and, most of all, Tamsyn. He was disgusted with his mother. When Abigail had been told by Alex of his decision to stay, she seemed to forget his cruel behaviour and had talked only of the exciting future they would have.

Alex had not missed the slight note of impatience in Rebecca's reply. 'At least Abigail's in her element,' he said, thinking of all the measurements she had taken and all the design charts she had consulted during the last week. 'I've given her a generous budget for decorating and new furnishings. She has a wonderful sense of colour and design so I'm confident she won't ruin the place. Miles would have hated that.'

Rebecca looked at a large space on the wooden floor which she was sure hadn't been there before. 'Have you been moving the furniture around?'

'Yes. I'm having a desk put in here for you.'

'What on earth for?' she asked sharply. 'I can't type or anything and I don't want to learn.'

He moved close and gazed at her. 'You don't want to be here at all, do you, Becca?'

She threw her hands out hopelessly and watched his dark face for signs of trauma. 'It isn't that... I just want...'

'Your freedom? I know how hard this must be on you, but if you can just bear with me for a little longer, allow me to get my bearings in this house, as it were. Will you do that for me, Becca? We can forget the desk. You don't have to do anything but be around for a while.'

Rebecca felt a weight being lifted off her shoulders. It would still be unwise to see Neville for the time being but she felt less of a prisoner now. She should have known really. Alex Fiennes wasn't the kind of man to be unfair.

She smiled at him. 'I'm happy to stay around you, Alex.' He looked relieved and rubbed his hands together. 'Well, we'd better get on with some work. Plenty to do. What I would like from you is help to get things running smoothly here. If you wouldn't mind taking notes, I'll get someone to do any typing that's needed. Perhaps I could get someone to come here two or three times a week.'

'That would be ideal,' Rebecca said, pulling up a chair on the other side of his desk.

He looked through a notebook he had been keeping since he'd arrived at Trevallion and called out the things that had to be seen to in order of priority. Three dangerously-uprooted trees needed to be felled in the woods. Rubbish dumped near Kennick Creek by some unsocial individuals had to be removed before there was an accident on the river. The reintroduction of pheasant breeding needed to be looked into. Certain items were required on the farms, mainly help with financing equipment which the farmers couldn't afford themselves, including new parts for the engine of Frank Kellow's creaking old tractor.

'Do you think I've hired enough staff for the house, Becca?'

'You'd better ask Mrs Fiennes that. Of course the more people you can employ, the better it is for the locals.'

'I'll put an advertisement in the local press for an under-gardener and a stable boy. Abigail wants me to have a tennis court built. What do you think?'

'It would be nice, I should think,' Rebecca said, tilting her face to the side. 'I'm quite good at tennis. I used to play against my cousin Raymon on the new public courts at Boscawen Park.'

'Perhaps I'll give you a game one day,' Alex said, throwing down his fountain pen and rubbing his eyes.

'Are you getting tired?' she asked, her mind only half on him. She'd noticed Susannah Bosanko's love letters to Roland Trevallion on the desk. 'I see you've still got those letters from that ugly old woman. It wouldn't do for Stephen to read them.'

'You're right as usual,' Alex said, grinning as he rooted them out from the other papers on the desk. 'Have you read any of them, Becca?'

'No, not in detail, but I know what sort of thing they contain. Actually Tamsyn came across them when we were trying to clean up the house for your arrival.'

Alex gave a loud laugh. 'Thank goodness Loveday didn't read them. She would have refused to make tea for the old dear when she called here.'

'"Old dear"? Witch more like. We ought to have the place exorcised.' Rebecca went over to the chest and bent down in front of it.

Alex joined her. 'Frightened of Susannah, are you? What are you looking for?'

'It's just occurred to me. If someone wrote such strong letters to you, very intimate ones at first then hateful vengeful ones, you wouldn't just push them in under a chest to conceal them. There must be a hiding place under here. Perhaps it broke and the letters fell out. And yes, I am frightened of the old lady. She gives me the creeps.'

Alex tried putting his hand under the chest but the space was too narrow. 'I'll lift the chest up on its side. You take a look and see if there's anything there.'

'Mind your hands then.'

'It's not heavy,' he said, lifting the bottom of the chest. 'Can you see anything?'

Rebecca lay flat on the floor and looked up under the chest. 'There's a thin piece of wood broken free. I'll just give it a pull.'

The piece of wood came away in her fingers and something fell out from behind it. She picked it up and Alex lowered the chest.

'It's more old paper, rolled up like a document,' Rebecca said and gave it to him.

Alex frowned.

'What is it?' she asked.

Alex tilted the paper to show her and whistled through his teeth. 'It's a last will and testament.'

Chapter 31

The following day Alex was poring over the newly discovered will when Rebecca came into the study and told him he had a visitor.

'Oh, I hope it's not Susannah Bosanko! I had a letter from her this morning. I couldn't bear to see her now, Becca. Tell her to go away. Tell her I'm out. Tell her I'm dead, anything, but just get rid of her.'

Rebecca wrinkled her nose at him then smiled. 'It isn't Miss Bosanko but it is a lady and she said you probably wouldn't be pleased to see her.'

The lady in question came into the room behind Rebecca and Alex sprang up as if his chair was on fire. 'Well, Major Fiennes,' she said in a stern voice. 'I've heard that you've been getting yourself into a fine pickle.'

The will fluttered from Alex's fingers to the floor. 'Sister Eddington!' he gasped.

Rebecca studied his face. It was white with disbelief and he looked like a child who had been discovered doing something naughty.

'You may well look guilty, Major Fiennes. I understand you've been giving everybody here the runaround.' After each sentence, Sister Eddington closed her colourless lips and tightened them at one side. Her unwavering gaze followed Alex's movements as he sank weakly into his chair. She sat down on the opposite side of the desk without waiting to be invited.

Alex looked at Rebecca as if he was pleading for help. She did her best to keep a straight face.

'Emily will be here with the tea shortly, Miss Eddington,' she said in an efficient voice and tried to look busy beside the old chest.

Miss Eddington gazed stonily across the desk. 'What's the matter, Major? Aren't you pleased to see me? It's been a long time, about eight years now. It's not Sister Eddington any more. I left the nursing corps soon after the war ended and studied to become a pharmacist. I work for a chemist in a quiet little town in Essex. I have my own little house and car and am considered to be something of an oddity, especially as I've never married, but we women must forge ahead and take our place in the commercial life of the country. What do you say, Miss Allen?'

'Yes, indeed, Miss Eddington,' Rebecca agreed, shuffling papers.

'Have you nothing to say, Major? Are you just going to sit there with a face as blank as a sheet of notepaper?'

Alex hastily cleared his throat and collected his wits. 'What are you doing here, Sister Eddington?'

'Miss Eddington. I don't call that a greeting after I've gone out of my way to look you up. I have a cousin who lives in Polperro. I've come down to Cornwall for a week's holiday. Had the surprise of my life to read in an old local newspaper that you had inherited some property down here. I couldn't bring myself to go back to Essex without seeing the worst patient I ever had during my entire war service once again.'

'Your worst, Miss Eddington?' Rebecca said, her curiosity getting the better of her. Why did this tall, neat, middle-aged lady with severely bobbed hair strike Alex dumb with horror?

Miss Eddington pointed a finger across the desk and Alex looked as though he was trying to disappear into his chair. 'I nursed men in France for four years, all ages, all ranks, in all conditions, but he was by far the most difficult. He was brought into the field hospital with a terrible head wound and when he came to after a couple of days he demanded to be allowed out of bed and dressed so he could go straight back to the fighting. He could hardly raise his head, let alone stand, but he fussed and moaned and cursed every waking moment of every day until he was released to go back on active duty, and even then he wasn't really fit. He drove my nurses to distraction, except for a pretty American nursing aide who took a shine to him, but that's another story. Never was I more glad to see the back of a patient.'

Rebecca came closer to Alex. 'I can well believe that. He treated Nurse Uren as if she was an interfering old busybody instead of a woman just trying to do her job.' She picked up the will from the floor and Alex swiped it out of her hand.

'I won't be talked about like this!' he snarled.

'I was told you had a little accident, a fall of some sort out on the river.' Miss Eddington fixed Alex with a hard question in her clear blue eyes.

He looked at Rebecca with raised eyebrows. She said, 'Miss Eddington and I had a little chat before I showed her in here and I told her about your boating accident, Major.'

'Boating accident?' Miss Eddington tightened her lips. 'I bet he was drunk.'

'He wasn't… this time,' Rebecca replied.

Alex slammed a hand on his desk. Cushioned by just a light bandage it hurt badly but he didn't show it. A nerve twitched in his cheek. 'If you two women persist—'

There was a knock on the door and Rebecca opened it for Emily to enter. When Emily had gone, she poured out a cup of tea and handed it to the ex-nurse. 'I hope that's how you like it, Miss Eddington.'

'It looks just right. Call me Trixie.'

'Trixie!' Alex scoffed from across the desk.

Trixie Eddington ignored him. 'Did you help nurse him, Miss Allen?'

Before Rebecca could answer, Alex said stiffly, 'Becca is my personal assistant.'

'Then I pity you greatly,' Trixie said, sipping her tea. 'There can't be many men more troublesome in the whole of Christendom than the dashing Major Alexander Rupert Ignatius Fiennes.'

'Ignatius?' Rebecca couldn't help giggling.

'That's his full name. I saw it on his army papers. Do you know, he was so upset at not getting a visible scar. He wanted to be hideously disfigured. Didn't like it one bit that his splendid face was untouched. But he had a terrible gash on the top of his head.'

Trixie got up and went round the desk. Alex had no time to escape his chair before she grabbed a handful of his hair and pulled it aside.

'Come and look at this, Rebecca. Among these fresh cuts he's got the most awful scar here.' Rebecca came and looked and made a suitable noise of exclamation. 'It's a good job his hair's so thick or the scar would be easily seen.'

Alex had had enough. He got up abruptly, pushed the two women aside and stormed for the door. 'I have never been treated so appallingly in all my life. If I'd been captured and tortured by the Hun I'm sure they would have shown me more respect!'

'Told you he was easy to send up, didn't I?' Trixie grinned at Rebecca. 'Come and sit down, Major Fiennes, and drink your tea. I had to get my own back on you somehow for all the past strife you gave me.'

Alex looked at Rebecca's gently smiling face then at Trixie. 'You mean you planned this between you?'

'We did,' Trixie replied. 'It was my idea, but I do apologise if seeing me again has brought back too many unpleasant memories. I know how you suffered, losing your men, the frustration of being relegated to a desk job and having to fight the end of the war from there. I've seen a lot of ex-soldiers in the last few years. I've seen the many different effects of what is called shell-shock. Forgive me, Major, but I don't believe the tale of a boating accident. I've more than a shrewd idea how you recently hurt yourself.'

Rebecca was worried for a moment that a sudden rush of painful memories would send Alex into a frenzy. Several emotions seemed to vie for a hold across his face, then he grinned, and she sighed with relief.

'I suppose it was good of you to look me up, Sister Eddington. Who knows, perhaps a talk over old times will do me some good.' His grin broadened. 'But if I'd known back then that you were called Trixie it would have put a very different complexion on the whole war for me.'

—

Stephen was home for the weekend and Alex went to his room. He knocked on the door and put his head round it. 'May I come in, Stephen?'

'I can't stop you,' Stephen replied frostily, placing homework on a small desk and tossing his school bag into a corner. 'This is your house.'

Alex moved into the room, tidy now but which would be reduced to a shambles by Monday morning. He stood with his hands in his pockets. 'I have tried to say I'm sorry to you, Stephen. It would help if you could at least meet me halfway.'

'Why? Because it would make you feel better?'

Alex shrugged. 'I suppose so. It would make Becca and Tamsyn feel better too and you care about how they feel, don't you?'

'Listen, Uncle Alex,' Stephen said, looking down at his school books. 'I know how much you hate me and having to put up with me and Mother and paying for everything we need. I can't do anything about that now but I intend to do my best at my studies and get into a well-paid profession so I can relieve you of the responsibility. One day I shall pay you back every penny.'

'I don't hate you, Stephen, and I don't care about the money.' Alex shuffled his feet awkwardly. 'I've been so preoccupied with myself and my problems I've never really thought about you. If I hadn't neglected you we would have been closer and not in this position now.'

Stephen raised his chin. He looked at Alex coldly but there was a new maturity in his face. 'I don't see it that way. You knew right from the start that I wasn't your brother's son. You haven't neglected me because you owe me nothing. In fact I should be grateful to you for supporting me and Mother all these years, when you owed us nothing. You're not my uncle and I shouldn't really call you that. I wouldn't like to have to call you Major. Perhaps I could call you Alex.' As he spoke Stephen's face coloured. He'd thought over his situation carefully and these were his considered conclusions. It was hard to hate a man who although he'd shunned him all his life had not relegated him to a life of poverty.

. Alex took his hands out of his pockets. He clenched his fists then put a hand uncertainly on the boy's shoulder. 'As far as I'm concerned you are Ralph's son and I had no right to say those terrible things to you, no right to call you those vile names. You are not responsible for your parentage. You were never meant to know, Stephen, and it wasn't my place to tell you. I am very sorry. I've been cruel to you but I want to stay your uncle. Can't we start again? Can't we at least try?'

A huge tear slid down Stephen's face. 'Do you know who my real father was?'

Alex shook his head. 'No, I'm sorry. It was something I never asked about.'

'Mother said he was a fighter pilot like your brother. She said he was handsome and brave and I would have been proud of him.'

If that was what Abigail had told him, Alex would not disillusion the boy. 'I'm sure he was a very good man, Stephen.'

They were both embarrassed and Alex moved away and picked up one of the school books. 'How are you getting on at school?'

Dashing a hand across his face, Stephen spoke quickly. 'Oh, just fine. All my masters are pleased with me. The headmaster sent for me today. He'd just received my old school records and, well, they weren't very good or anything, but he was impressed to see I'd made a marked improvement in all my subjects in just two weeks. He says I'll have a good future if I carry on in the same way.'

'Good for you,' Alex said, leafing through a geography exercise book. 'I was considered a bit of a swot at school. If you need any help…'

Stephen couldn't quite grasp his uncle being this kind and interested in him. 'Perhaps… thanks, Uncle Alex.'

Tamsyn ran into the room and Stephen grinned happily at her.

'Are you coming out to play, Stephen? Motley's jumping about outside. He's dying to go for a long walk.'

Stephen glanced at his uncle. 'Well, I've got some homework to do, Tam.'

Alex put the exercise book down. 'Go on, Stephen, you need fresh air in your lungs after a week at school. I'll help you with your homework later.' He made for the door, ruffling Tamsyn's fine hair as he passed her. Outside the room he smiled to himself, thinking how pleased Rebecca would be that he and Stephen were on good terms at last.

His smile widened when he heard Tamsyn say excitedly, 'You'll be able to ask your uncle about a trip to Perranporth now, Stephen.'

–

'You don't think we were too hard on the Major, do you?' Trixie Eddington asked Rebecca. They were out on the river in Rebecca's rowing boat.

Rebecca stopped rowing and frowned anxiously. 'No, do you? I know he was angry with us but he soon came round. He wouldn't have asked you to stay for dinner and agreed to talk to you afterwards if he was really upset.' She pulled on the oars to continue their trip downriver. Trixie had expressed the wish to see something of the river, and feeling the need to stretch herself after being stifled by Alex's possessiveness for so long, Rebecca had jumped at the chance and suggested a trip to the King Harry Ferry.

Rebecca's thoughts were never far from Alex these days and she added, 'Alex needs something, or someone, to help lift him out of his moods, to help him put the past behind him for good. That could be you, Trixie. You knew him when he was injured. You nursed him. You're a figure of authority to him. Perhaps you could help him to get things into some sort of…' She searched for the right word.

'Perspective?' Trixie asked, trailing her hand in the ripples of water the oars were making. 'It's not as easy as it sounds, Rebecca, but you seem to have made significant inroads into breaking the awful pattern he's obviously been controlled by since he lost his unit. Shell-shock is a terrible thing. We medics saw it in many forms. Some men suffered, and still do, from the sheer physical shock of an explosion or their wounds. Others were ground down by the relentless daily noise and carnage, which finally shattered their nerves. Men like Alex are sometimes the most difficult to help. They suffer mainly from guilt. He wasn't too badly hurt and all his men were killed. If he'd lost a leg or been disfigured or something, if even just one of his men had survived with him, then he would have coped a lot better.'

'Poor Alex. It's hard to understand how much he must have suffered.' Rebecca stopped rowing again. 'And my father. He became bitter and turned to drink. He was injured and he lost good friends. He couldn't bear to think of the way Captain Trevallion ended up.'

'The chap Alex inherited the estate from?'

'Yes, they were cousins. The Captain lost his legs and his mind. He lived, well, if you can call it living, in a nursing home, having all his needs attended to until he died this year.'

'It would have been hard for your father, Rebecca. He not only depended on the Captain for employment but he probably looked up to him and respected him. I imagine your father felt safe while the Captain was in charge, but when he was injured he would have felt at a loss.'

Tears stung Rebecca's eyes. 'Things might not have been so bad if my mother hadn't run out on us while he was away fighting. Coming home to the creek and finding she wasn't here must have been the final straw.'

'It's hard not to see them as no more than the men they've become, Rebecca. It's all they see themselves as most of the time.' Trixie bent forward and took Rebecca's hand. 'Come on, my dear. You've got nothing to blame yourself for. Where would the Major and your father be without you, eh? Or is that half your trouble?'

Drying her tears, Rebecca smiled. 'I don't really mind but the responsibility weighs me down at times.'

'Of course it does. They've both asked a lot of you. But perhaps I'll be able to help a little with Alex before I go.' Trixie looked along the river. 'Is that the ferry up ahead? You live in a beautiful part of Cornwall. Why don't we forget Alex and your father for a little while and just enjoy ourselves?'

–

The dining-room table was laid in Trevallion House that evening and sitting round it were Rebecca, Alex, Trixie, and, because he wanted to show his nephew he had meant what he'd said earlier, Alex had invited Stephen, who had been taking his meals with Tamsyn. Abigail was in Truro at a social engagement.

The talk was rather stilted to begin with but they were soon chatting comfortably, mainly to Stephen about his school, which made the boy feel wanted, as Alex had hoped. Stephen was delighted when Alex suggested the ladies leave them while they remained at the table. Stephen wasn't allowed to have any port but he did manage to secure a small glass of wine.

When Stephen retired to look over his homework, Alex joined Rebecca and Trixie in the drawing room. They were talking about the Trevallion estate in general and Rebecca rose to leave when he entered; it was time Trixie and he were left alone for their talk. He was nervous and he squeezed Rebecca's arm as she walked past him.

'I don't know what I'd do without Rebecca,' Alex said, shuffling his feet about in embarrassment. 'I don't tie her down,' he hastily defended himself.

'Sit down next to me, Alex,' Trixie said softly. 'Try to relax. I'm not strict Sister Eddington now. I've looked up a number of my old patients since the war ended. I know what you all went through. It might be a comfort to learn that you're not alone in how you feel.'

Alex sat down beside her. There was no need to tell her about the events that had led up to the death of his men and his stay in the field hospital. There was no need to tell her about the hell he had lived through since. She knew. She understood. She cared. His throat became choked with tears.

He put a shaking hand to his brow. 'I... I've wanted to kill myself so many times.'

Trixie placed a hand firmly on his shoulder. 'I expect you have.'

'The nightmares... I can't stop them, they keep coming back.'

'They will, Alex, until you acknowledge what happened. Your men are dead but it wasn't your fault. You were fighting a war. It wasn't you who gave the order to take your men over the top. That came from higher up. You were only doing your duty. Your men wouldn't have wanted you to be maimed or killed, would they?'

'Rebecca said something like that.'

'And you've got to believe it.' Trixie stressed her words. 'You've got to realise that you won't ever forget the horrors you went through, but you have to think about the future too. Believe that there is one. Reach out for it, try to grasp it. Believe that you can do it. When you are faced with a bad memory, acknowledge that it's there, then replace it with a pleasant thought. Do something positive. Get out on the river. Or get involved with the running of the estate. You had men who relied on you in the past, Alex. They're gone. Now you've got people relying on you for their present and future.'

'I know.' Alex let his hand fall from his head and he clasped it tightly in his other one. Trixie prised them apart and held them in hers. For a moment he grasped her hands as if he was afraid he was going to fall from a great height. Then his grip loosened and his body sagged, as if the years of stress, fear and failure were slipping out of him. Trixie stood up and gathered him against her. Alex wound his arms round her and sobbed gently.

'Things will get better if you try,' she whispered, her voice hoarse with tears of her own. 'You'll see.'

–

The trip to Perranporth took place the following afternoon. It was a very noisy outing. Tamsyn was thrilled that Motley was allowed to go this time and he barked all the way there with his head sticking round the side of the car. He knocked off Rebecca's straw sunhat and instead of putting it back on she allowed the wind to whip her hair in a long black stream. When Alex started to sing, they all joined in.

They settled the picnic basket and rug on the same spot as on their last visit then walked a mile along the clifftop in the direction of Perranporth beach.

'Can we go beaching later, Major?' Tamsyn asked, tugging on his hand as Motley rushed past him on the narrow path.

After struggling to keep his balance, Alex said they could. When their legs had been stretched and Motley was satisfied that he had sniffed out all the strange and wonderful scents, they returned to the picnic spot. Stephen and Tamsyn drank some lemonade and went off to play, eating an apple.

'You know the safety rules, Stephen,' Alex reminded his nephew. 'I'm trusting you to look after Tamsyn.'

Rebecca watched the boy's broad back as he strolled off with the little girl and the scruffy dog. 'Stephen looks so much more settled now you've made friends. There's a more responsible attitude about him.'

'I feel much better now that we've got things sorted,' Alex said, breaking off bits of rough heather and twirling them in the palm of his hand. 'I think you're right, Becca. Stephen does seem more grown up. I hope he doesn't encourage Tamsyn to do anything silly though. It would break Loveday's heart if she lost Tamsyn. I always feel a bit unsettled looking after other people's children.' He was silent for a while then he looked at Rebecca with a twinkle brightening his dark eyes. 'Mr Drayton has called at the big house twice this week. Loveday has the best-kept garden on the estate and I've had so much advice on business lately I can't keep up with it.'

'Aren't you the lucky one,' Rebecca said, passing him a flask cup of tea.

'I was rather thinking Mr Drayton was. Loveday always just manages to be in the vicinity of his motorcar when he leaves. I don't know why he doesn't just ask her out properly and be done with it.'

'Some things can't be rushed, Alex. Loveday would run a mile if things happened too quickly, and Mr Drayton's not a brash man.'

Alex looked as if he was about to say something but changed his mind. Rebecca was sure he'd wanted to compare Mr Drayton to Neville Faull. They had talked about many things in the ten days she had worked at Trevallion House but, even though Neville had called there again, not once had he been mentioned. Rebecca had managed to snatch a few moments alone with him and he'd told her to look out for him at the end of the following week. She wondered how Alex would take it if she told him she wanted to see Neville again. Alex had changed remarkably since moving into Trevallion. Dr Pearn had been pleasantly surprised and put it down to the fact he felt settled at last. He looked stronger and stood straighter and there had been no nightmares. Rebecca knew Trixie Eddington's visit had had something to do with his newfound peace.

'I think it's terribly romantic,' Rebecca said. 'But I don't know what Tamsyn would think if Mr Drayton became her stepfather.'

'I don't think she'd mind too much. I've noticed that she seems to like him. It's a pity we can't think of something to help bring her mother and Mr Drayton closer together.'

Rebecca had a sudden thought. 'What would happen if Mrs Fiennes wanted to get married again? How would it affect things at Trevallion? Stephen may not take kindly to a stepfather.'

'It wouldn't matter to me if she wanted to move a husband into Trevallion, as long as he was a good man. I don't intend living there for good. It still belongs to Miles. The study is Miles's, the boats are his. The Kennickers respect me but they will always think of everything as belonging to Miles.'

'I see.' Unaccountably Rebecca felt disappointed. She had baulked against feeling trapped and had privately blamed Alex. But now she didn't want him to go away. She was used to being with him. She realised she felt a little hurt. 'You mean you're going back to Berkshire?'

'I haven't made up my mind yet, but not necessarily. I've had another idea.'

Alex paused to allow Rebecca to ask him what this other thought was, although he was sure she wouldn't. She thought of him more as her employer than a friend of whom she had the right to ask personal questions. After she had dug out the hidden will from under the chest in the study she had left the room to fetch them some coffee and had not asked him a thing about it.

He was right; she asked about something else. 'Does Mrs Fiennes know that you have other plans?'

'It's none of her business. All that woman should concern herself with is getting herself decently married,' Alex said harshly.

'Why say it like that?'

'No one is unaware of Abigail's goings-on with Joe Carlyon. They're like a couple of blasted rabbits. Up in the stable loft, in the fields when they've been out riding. She even sneaks into his cottage in the dead of night. They probably used Trevallion when it was lying empty.'

'That's not a nice way to talk, Alex.'

'I don't approve of such loose sexual encounters. Abigail left Berkshire in fear of Stephen finding out about her reputation. He knows now, thanks to me, that he isn't Ralph's son. How's the boy going to feel if he knows she's with the groom at every opportunity?'

'I understand your point. Sometimes I feel sorry for Stephen.'

'Well, at least I've made things up to him a little.' Alex looked at Rebecca closely. 'You had an infatuation with Carlyon once, didn't you?'

Rebecca smiled at the memory and blushed a little. 'It seems a long time ago now. How did you know about that?'

'I noticed the way you used to look at him.' Alex threw the dregs of his tea away and lit a cigarette. 'It must be nice for a man to be looked at in that way by you.'

Rebecca was flattered by his last remark. She studied his profile, his hair, dark and grown long over his collar, his strong brow, proud nose and square jaw, finishing at his wide firm mouth. She realised how attractive he was. Actually he was more. He was gorgeous. He turned and gazed at her. Reaching out he pushed back a thick tress of hair from her face.

'Are you thinking that if I don't have my hair cut it will soon be as long as yours?'

Unable to tear her eyes away from his, she murmured, 'Something like that. Next time you go down into the creek you could ask Jossy Jenkins to cut it for you. He's always done it for the creek men.'

'I've rather fallen in with the slower-paced Cornish way of life. I think it's time I made a trip into Truro. I'll get myself smartened up at a barber's there.'

'Why not Falmouth?'

'Because I've been to Falmouth often but only once to Truro since I stepped off the train.'

'Could it be because Miss Bosanko doesn't live in Truro?' she teased.

Alex turned away to draw on his cigarette and blow smoke up into the air. 'That's another factor, I admit. I replied to her letter and put her off but I'll have to see her soon. You can come with me.'

'Do I have to?'

He put his face close to hers. 'Yes. I feel uncomfortable being with her alone. If she were a lot younger you might have had to look out for my chastity.'

Rebecca's face took on a look of disbelieving shock. 'She doesn't feel like that about you, does she?'

'Does that surprise you, Becca? That a woman could find me attractive?'

'No, of course not. You're a very attractive man, Alex,' she blurted out and immediately felt embarrassed. She looked away. Only a moment ago she had been ogling him.

'But not to all women?' he went on.

'I didn't mean that. What about that American nursing aide Trixie Eddington mentioned?'

'Val Hendrikson. Boy, was she full of grit!' Alex smiled. 'Our VADs were rather jealous of the Americans, and not surprisingly so. They had much more freedom, less petty rules and were even allowed to go to parties. Val brought me back a half-bottle of whisky once. I promised I'd only take a few sips a day but I drank the lot to get drunk and annoy Sister Eddington. It worked like a dream.'

Rebecca felt her stomach tighten. She told herself she couldn't possibly be jealous of this American woman in Alex's past, but she had to admit she didn't like the thought that another woman had been close enough to him to give him comfort.

'Do you keep in touch with this Val Hendrikson?'

'No.'

'Have you never thought of looking her up like Trixie did you?'

'It's passed through my mind.'

Rebecca picked up the flask cup he had used and screwed it back on the flask. 'Trixie's visit did you good, didn't it?' she said stiffly. Damn it, she was even jealous of the ex-sister now!

'We talked for hours after dinner. I think she's helped me come to terms with my morbid obsession.'

Rebecca said nothing more and he got up and walked towards the edge of the cliff where he tossed away his cigarette end. Rebecca felt disappointed again, that he had moved away from her. She watched him as he gazed at the sea's horizon then turned and scanned each direction of the clifftop. He came back to her quickly.

'I can't see the children or the dog. Where on earth could they have got to?'

Chapter 32

Rebecca stood beside Alex and scanned the cliff. She pointed to the mine ruins. 'There's Stephen and Motley but I can't see Tamsyn.'

They exchanged a fearful look and ran to Stephen and the dog.

'Where's Tamsyn?' Alex demanded, clutching the boy's arms.

Stephen pointed to a small black opening gaping from an overgrown grassy bank. 'She wanted to look in that hole. I told her not to.'

'What?' Rebecca screamed, running to the opening and shouting Tamsyn's name.

'You were supposed to be looking after her,' Alex shouted furiously before following on Rebecca's heels.

'Wait, Uncle Alex—'

'Stay put,' Alex shouted back over his shoulder. He was more concerned about Rebecca now and called her to stop. If she went in after Tamsyn with nothing to light her way then both of them could end up lost or hurt.

'Come back, Becca! We can't do anything without the right equipment.'

Rebecca heard him shouting and Stephen's voice crying after him in the background but she could think only of Tamsyn. Loveday had entrusted her precious daughter into her care. She would never forgive her if anything happened to Tamsyn and Rebecca would never forgive herself. She should have been watching the children, not making eyes at her employer. If Tamsyn was lost she must be terrified in the dark. Perhaps she was hurt, had fallen thousands of feet and was... Fear clutched Rebecca's heart.

She eased herself through the small black opening. The inside was low and narrow and she edged her feet along uneven stony ground. Her own body was shutting out the fight and with each awkward step it was getting darker until the light was gone altogether. She took several steps into pitch blackness, calling Tamsyn's name. The tunnel widened and soon she found she could not touch the walls. She began to feel vulnerable.

She called to Tamsyn and stayed still in the hope of hearing a reply. But there was nothing. She took another step forward and something overhead whacked her on the temple and she was sent sprawling to the ground. She shook her head to clear it and that's when she realised she was in total darkness and absolute silence and she had no way of knowing which was the way out. Panic overwhelmed her and she screamed from the depths of her soul.

'Becca, it's all right! Just stay where you are.'

'Tamsyn!' she screamed.

'It's Alex, Becca. Just stay put. I'm coming for you.'

Alex's voice broke through the terrifying fog of her mind and she quietened to a whimper. 'Hurry, Alex. I'm so frightened.'

It was only seconds later but it seemed like hours before his hands reached out for her. She clutched at him and he pulled her into his arms. She threw her face against his chest and sobbed. 'I was so scared. What must poor little Tamsyn be feeling?'

'We can't do anything for Tamsyn like this, Becca. My cigarette lighter will light the way out of here and then we'll go for help. It needs experienced miners to go further in and find Tamsyn. I'll run to Cligga.'

'Loveday will never forgive me for this,' Rebecca wailed, clutching his shirt.

'First things first, my love. I'm going to take you outside. It's not very far. Just keep calm and mind your head.'

Alex kept one hand on Rebecca's head to guide it under the tunnel roof and with the other he flicked on his cigarette lighter to light their way out. A minute or two later they emerged in the bright sunlight and she was taking in deep gasps of fresh air. Rebecca wiped dirt from her face and gasped as she was met with another shock.

'Tamsyn! We thought you were lost down the mine.'

'It was only a game, Becca. I hid away from you,' Tamsyn said shamefacedly and looking as though she was about to burst into tears.

Alex put his arm round Rebecca, who was still shaking. 'Stephen,' he said sternly. 'Explain.'

'I'm sorry, Uncle Alex. It was only a joke. I did call after you but you wouldn't listen. We didn't mean you to go inside there.' The boy was looking at a trickle of blood on Rebecca's head and seemed to be near to tears himself. 'I'm sorry you were hurt, Rebecca.'

'I have never heard anything so... so damned irresponsible! I'll have your hide for this, Stephen. This time you've gone too far. Back to the car. We're going home at once.'

'Yes, Uncle,' Stephen muttered, lowering tear-filled eyes to the ground.

Rebecca eased herself away from Alex. 'You take Tamsyn back to the picnic spot and give her some lemonade, Alex. I want to talk to Stephen alone.'

'What?'

'Do as I say, please, Alex. I'll explain later.'

Her voice brooked no argument and Alex complied. He held out his hand to Tamsyn and they walked away together, a striking contrast, the small fair girl and the tall dark man. Sensing he had to behave, Motley went along quietly with them.

Rebecca and Stephen were left outside the mine opening. The ground was sunken here and Alex and Tamsyn were soon out of sight.

'I didn't mean you any harm,' Stephen said, his voice thick with tears.

Rebecca handed him her handkerchief. 'I know, Stephen. That's why I told your uncle to leave us. Let's sit down, my legs are still a bit shaky.'

He flopped down, drying his eyes on the hanky and she sat close beside him.

'I'd never do anything to hurt Tamsyn. Never,' he stressed. 'I'm very fond of her, you know, and I'm not ashamed to admit it.'

'I know that. Now I'm out of there I can see it was only a bit of youthful fun and if your uncle and I hadn't panicked but had stopped and listened we would have heard what you were shouting at us.'

'You're a good sort, Rebecca... for a girl. I wish my uncle liked me as you do. Just as we were beginning to get along with each other I have to go and spoil it. He probably won't buy me a pony now.'

Rebecca took his hand. 'He will, don't worry, and I'll talk him round to carrying on with our day out. I want to go beaching myself and I'm not going home until we do.'

Stephen laughed through his tearfulness. 'I wish my mother was more like you, Rebecca. It's no wonder Uncle Alex likes you round him all the time. You would have been quite safe in the mine if you'd only known you couldn't go far in. I've seen the old map and it's only part of an adit, used for ventilation, and it's been blocked up for years.'

'Now you tell me.' Rebecca lifted her eyes to the heavens and gave a small laugh.

'I wouldn't do anything to risk hurting Tamsyn,' Stephen stressed again. 'If she had really been in danger I would have been screaming and shouting for help. I'd be distraught if anything terrible happened to her.'

He couldn't check his tears any longer and Rebecca put her arms round him and he cried on her shoulder. Rebecca kissed the top of his head, and when he was sure there was no evidence on his face to show he had been crying they rejoined the others.

–

'If you're going to keep on sulking with me then I'm going straight home,' Rebecca said crossly as Alex lifted the picnic basket out of the motorcar in front of Trevallion House.

Percy Gummoe came forward and took the picnic basket from him.

'I don't expect my orders to be disobeyed,' Alex retorted. 'Stephen should have been punished. You had no right to say he could spend the evening setting up the model railway in one of the spare bedrooms. You're not the boy's mother and you're supposed to be my assistant, not my boss!'

Percy moved off grinning and Rebecca raised her eyebrows and smiled at Alex sardonically. 'Has anyone ever told you how handsome you look when you're angry?'

'Rebecca Allen! I've a good mind to put you in...' He scratched his head while he thought about it.

'In what?' she teased him, enjoying herself and laughing. Alex had not stopped grumbling since she and Stephen had returned to the picnic spot and she had sent the children off to play.

'What on earth do you think you're doing?' he'd demanded as she'd unpacked the basket he'd been piling things into.

'As far as I'm concerned, the incident is over,' she replied, sitting down on the blanket and biting into a sandwich.

He had snatched the sandwich out of her hand and thrown it away. 'It's not as far as I'm concerned. Stephen's prank nearly went horribly wrong. You were frightened half to death and could have been badly hurt. I said we're going home and we're going!' He threw the basket lid open to start repacking. Rebecca tore it out of his hands.

'This is Stephen's day out, not yours.'

'What's that got to do with anything? His behaviour—'

'Was that of a boy having fun. There was no malice intended in what he did. Don't be so hard on him, Alex.'

Alex slumped down beside her. 'You... you... I don't know what to say about you. Here I was worrying about tying you down because I need you and you're the one calling the wretched tune!'

'Do you want a chicken sandwich?'

'No, I bloody don't!'

'There's no need to swear.'

'Becca!'

'There's ham as well.'

Alex snatched the proffered sandwich from her, bit off a huge chunk and nearly choked on it. Rebecca sat quietly, eating demurely.

'And they say it's a man's world,' he complained to the cliff, sky and the breakers of the Atlantic Ocean rolling towards Perranporth's beach. 'Well, I had good men under my command and all of them had their faults. But,' and he looked straight at Rebecca, 'not one of them was as cunning and as conniving and downright insubordinate as a certain woman I know.'

'I bet they all moaned when they couldn't get their own way, just like you do,' she said sweetly. 'Tea? I think there's coffee in the other flask.'

Alex leant on his elbow and pushed his cheek out with his tongue. With narrowed eyes he said, 'I know what I would have done to you if you were under my command. Coffee, please.'

'I'm sure you were a fair officer and I just want you to be fair to Stephen,' she returned, pouring his coffee. 'He doesn't seem to have had much of a life and now at long last he's got the chance to get really settled. He's got a new home and he's got Tamsyn. Given a bit of attention and encouragement he could be turned into a fine young man.

'Hasn't it occurred to you, Alex, that he could have asked one of the boys from his school to Trevallion for the weekend and taken him on this trip? He's told me he's made friends. But instead he wanted Tamsyn to come. It shows he has loyalty. You would have bent over backwards to do anything for your men, wouldn't you, so why not Stephen? You're always so quick to punish him. Can't you try to understand him a little bit more? Try to build up a good relationship with him?'

His face tight and dark, Alex sat up and lit a cigarette. 'I've said it once before but you've got a tongue like a shrew, Becca Allen.'

'But do you understand what I'm trying to say?'

'Yes, yes, all right! I'll take the boy into Perranporth and buy him the biggest damned kite I can find and then I'll take him up the dunes and teach him how to fly it. A one-to-one relationship. Is that all right with you? God save me from a woman who's always right!'

Rebecca stole a glance at his outraged face and thought it wise to stay quiet. She rubbed at the dirt on her dress.

'Where's your handkerchief?' Alex said suddenly.

'Stephen's got it.'

Alex took a napkin from the basket. 'This will do. You've got some blood on your head.'

He leaned over and gently wiped at the trickle of blood on her temple.

'Ouch.'

'You've got a bad bruise. You were lucky I suppose, could have been worse.'

'I was so glad you got to me quickly,' she said seriously, her eyes on his chin as he cleaned up her head. 'I can imagine something of what you've been going through with your nightmares.'

He looked into her eyes. 'Perhaps you realise now how comforting it is to have someone you trust put their arms round you and help you through the ordeal.'

'Yes. It's good to have a friend close by in those circumstances.'

'Some people are good to have close by all the time and not just because they're a friend.' Alex said no more and got up to call the children.

They went into Perranporth to buy a kite and then to the beach. As Rebecca and Tamsyn built sandcastles by the stream running across the beach, the kite-flying up in the dunes went well and both Stephen and Alex were smiling when they scrambled back down. Stephen excitedly promised to take Tamsyn up into one of the fields after church the next day and show her how to fly the kite.

The journey home had been quieter. Alex was still smarting at having his orders so blatantly disobeyed but he wasn't a man who bore grudges.

'You're going to put me in what, Alex?' she teased him as they stood in front of Trevallion House.

With a glint in his dark eyes, he replied, 'In your place I think, Miss Bossyboots.'

Rebecca squealed and ran round the car. Alex caught her by the shoulders and swung her round and as they laughed together and she playfully struggled, a voice boomed out at them.

'Just what the heck do you think you're doing with my daughter, Major?'

Rebecca turned and found herself facing her furious father. Before either of them could explain, another voice assailed them from the main doorway of the house.

'Yes, Alexander. What are you doing with that girl? It's not the way for an officer and a gentleman to act. Mauling a servant girl in front of her father.'

'Susannah!' Alex gasped, dropping his arms from Rebecca. He felt embarrassed in front of Trease but disturbed to see Susannah and angry at the way she had spoken to him.

'Dad, we were only having a bit of fun,' Rebecca said, red-faced.

'I didn't know my daughter's new position meant you could fool around with her any time you liked, Major,' Trease said angrily, striding forward and taking up a threatening stance.

'It was only a little harmless horseplay, Trease,' Alex said. 'We… we had a good day out. We were in good spirits, that's all.'

'Is it?' Trease asked. 'Are you sure about that, Major? I've been thinking about you wanting my maid round you all the time. 'Tisn't healthy in my reckoning and 'tis time it was stopped. I've been thinking too about the time she come home from the gatehouse all upset and packed her bags to leave. 'Twas through you, wasn't it? You tried to have your way with Rebecca and that's why she came scurrying home. Now you're trying a different approach. Your sort's all the same. That sister-in-law of yours can't keep her hands out of Joe Carlyon's trousers.'

'Dad!'

'You dare to speak—'

Alex broke off as Trease grabbed Rebecca by the arm and pulled her towards him. 'Tell me it's not true, girl. Go on, tell me he hasn't tried to get you into bed!'

'He hasn't!' Rebecca shouted back. She didn't count the time Alex had been out of his mind with panic. 'Major Fiennes is an honourable man and he has never made advances towards me.'

'Then explain why you are in such an untidy state, girl,' Susannah Bosanko's shrill voice cut through the air. 'Look at your dress and face. What have you been doing?'

Rebecca wrenched herself free from Trease and marched up to the old woman. 'If you must know, I was trapped down a mine adit and the Major rescued me. Nothing untoward has happened between us.

It's only yours and my father's dirty minds! What business is it of yours anyway?'

Susannah raised her hand to strike Rebecca across the face.

'Don't you dare, Susannah!' Alex shouted, the rage in his voice terrifying.

'My dear boy,' Susannah purred, the expression on her hideous face changing from wrath to simpering softness with a speed that made Rebecca blink. 'I was only going to slap the girl because I was afraid she was getting hysterical. Now I suggest we all calm down. Everything has been suitably explained, wouldn't you agree, man?' she called to Trease.

All eyes were on Trease, who was looking angry and uncertain. He didn't like the way the old baggage had addressed him. 'I'd be obliged, Major, if you didn't make so free with my daughter in future.'

'Fair enough, Trease,' Alex said coldly. 'And I'd be obliged if you kept your mouth shut about the lady of this house. I won't tolerate that kind of filthy talk from you again.'

Trease gave a curt nod but he went up to Alex and said in a hard voice, 'You're a brave man, Major Fiennes, when you've got my daughter holding your hand.' He got into the Spyker and drove it round to the garage.

Alex turned to Rebecca and said quietly, 'I'm sorry about this, Becca. You may please yourself what you do for the rest of the day.'

'Thank you, Alex,' Rebecca said, glaring at Susannah. 'I think that first I'll go home and change.'

'Have you tried to seduce the girl?' Susannah asked as she watched Rebecca's long-legged strides towards the creek.

'Of course not,' Alex snapped. 'Shall we go inside?'

'Why "of course not", dear? Have you no feelings in that department? Rebecca is a beautiful healthy woman. Don't you want to lie with her?'

'Inside, Susannah,' Alex said through clenched teeth. He took Susannah's arm and tried to propel her into the house but she resisted him.

'Your chauffeur was right about your sister-in-law, Alexander darling. There is no lady residing in this house. The silly bitch has been trying to entertain me while I've been waiting for your return and I could see she was itching to get away. Your groom, isn't it? I don't understand why you tolerate it.'

'They're in love,' Alex said savagely, making a stand for Abigail's reputation for the first time in his life. 'And you know all about affairs, don't you, Susannah?'

Susannah's eyes seem to glitter with a strange malevolent energy. Alex felt sick to his stomach and began to tremble.

The old lady smiled through her lizard eyes. 'Are you quite well, Alexander?'

'I'm a little tired, Susannah. I shall go to my room and bathe and change my clothes. I'm afraid you will have to do with Abigail's company for a while longer.'

—

'Alexander is back and has gone upstairs to freshen up,' Susannah informed Abigail as she returned to the drawing room. She stood next to the fireplace and glared at Abigail as she lit a cigarette.

'I was wondering where you were, Miss Bosanko,' Abigail replied uncomfortably, gazing at the red tip of her cigarette. She'd just spent a most trying hour playing hostess to the harridan who had arrived at Trevallion unexpectedly and insisted she would wait for Alex's return. Susannah had plied her with personal questions about Alex and had criticised everything Abigail had done to the house. 'You found the bathroom all right, I hope? I was about to come and look for you.'

'Smoking is a beastly habit in a lady,' Susannah hissed.

'Oh, I… I… do beg your pardon,' Abigail stammered, hastily stubbing out the offending article.

'What does that creek girl mean to Alexander?' Susannah asked sharply.

'You mean Rebecca? He's just made her his personal assistant. Why do you ask?'

'Because I wish to know. Is Alexander bedding her?'

Abigail had endured enough and shot to her feet. 'What my brother-in-law does in his private life is his business, Miss Bosanko.

If you are going to be insulting I shall ask you to leave. This is my home and I will not tolerate it. You have been ungracious to me from the moment you arrived.'

Susannah crossed the room with frightening speed and grasped Abigail by the wrist. 'Are they lovers? Tell me!'

'No, they are not! Why do you want to know, you evil old bitch? Get out of here at once!'

'I'm going now but let me tell you this. A creek girl tried to cross me once before and lived to regret it. No one will keep me out of this house for good, least of all you, a so-called lady who'd be happy to service a tomcat. Trevallion is mine by rights. It should have been mine years ago and I mean to have it!'

Susannah rang for her car to be brought round. The moment she was gone, Abigail dashed up the stairs and into Alex's room. He was coming out of his adjoining bathroom with just a towel round his waist.

'Abigail!'

'You've got to stop that evil old woman coming here,' she cried, close to tears.

Alex led her to a chair. 'Sit there and tell me what happened.' He threw on a dressing gown while Abigail took several deep breaths. 'Is she still in the house, Abigail?'

'No, she's gone. Alex, that woman said Trevallion should be hers. What does she mean?' Abigail held out her wrist. 'Look what she did to me. She was demanding to know if you and Rebecca were sleeping together. She went berserk. She said a creek girl had crossed her before and she'd made her sorry. Alex, you've got to do something. She threatened both me and Rebecca and God knows what she'd like to do to you. What if she tried to hurt Stephen? She terrified me. I can't get that evil look in her eyes out of my mind.'

Alex went to a window and saw Susannah's car disappearing through the towering trees. 'Don't worry, Abigail, I'll make sure she doesn't come here again. I wish I'd never looked that old woman up. It's a pity Roland Trevallion didn't burn his love letters.'

'Love letters?' Abigail joined him at the window. 'What are you talking about?'

310

Alex told her about the love letters written by Susannah Bosanko and their hiding place. 'There was also a will in the hiding place, Abigail.'

'A will? This is all very mysterious. It doesn't mean anything, surely. You are the rightful heir to Trevallion, aren't you?'

'Legally, yes, but perhaps… Abigail, I'm going to ask you a delicate question and I want you to tell me the truth. What exactly does Joe Carlyon mean to you?'

Chapter 33

That evening Rebecca went to the kitchen to talk to Loveday. She found her in the washroom where she was adding water to a bowl of cold strained tea.

'Hello, Becca. I'm just putting this black silk dress of Mrs Fiennes' in to soak. She spilt coffee on it this afternoon when that dreadful Miss Bosanko was here.'

'I've just been talking to the Major about her,' Rebecca said, an expression of distaste on her face. 'He told me he's going to write to her and tell her she mustn't come here again. Apparently she was very rude to Mrs Fiennes and she ruined the end of our lovely day out with the children.'

'I'll thank the Lord for that,' Loveday replied with feeling, pushing the soft material gently into the cold tea. 'Emily told me she and Ivy heard raised voices coming from the drawing room. If you ask me, that old woman is evil. I'm glad Tamsyn's never come across her.'

When the silk dress was fully immersed, Loveday dried her hands and looked deeply into Rebecca's face. 'There was another visitor here today.'

'Oh?' Rebecca replied hopefully. Neville had called twice recently and each time she had not been at the house and had missed him. 'Who was that?'

'As if you didn't know, my girl. Here,' Loveday dug into her apron pocket. 'He asked me to give you this.'

Rebecca took the sealed envelope. It was Trevallion stationery and her name was written on it. She recognised Neville's writing from documents in the study. Her face brightened up and Loveday made a smug sound.

'I had a suspicion you were seeing him. All those extra calls on the Major were just excuses to see you then.'

Rebecca studied Loveday's face. 'I take it you don't approve.'

'I can understand how a man like him would turn a young girl's head but I thought you were more sensible, Becca. I don't trust him one iota. Just you be wary of him, my girl. You could end up being very sorry.'

Loveday didn't mention that Neville Faull had seemed almost distraught that he had missed Rebecca for a third time. He had begged Loveday to let him into the study so he could write a quick letter to her. It seemed he was actually fond of Rebecca, but Loveday had taken it upon herself not to encourage her.

'I'll leave you to read it in peace and check on the vegetables for dinner,' she said.

Tamsyn skipped into the kitchen looking for her mother to ask if she could stay on at Trevallion for the evening. She and Stephen had already eaten and were busy in one of the spare bedrooms laying out the model railway. He wanted her to stay long enough to help him complete a new complicated piece of tracking.

Emily and Ivy were laying the dining table and the kitchen was empty. A saucepan of cauliflower was boiling over on the big black range. Tamsyn called out, 'Mum!' There was no answer and she went over to the range and twisted her small face as she decided what she ought to do. Her mother had warned her many times not to go near an oven while something was cooking on the top, but Tamsyn felt she was grown up enough to lift the lid off the bubbling saucepan to stop its contents boiling over. She lifted up the lid but burnt her fingers and crying out in pain she snatched her hand back. Her elbow caught the handle and tipped the saucepan over. Boiling hot water and cauliflower tipped over her, scalding a path all the way down one side, and she screamed in agony.

'Tamsyn!' Loveday cried as she came through the doorway. 'Tamsyn! Oh, my God, my baby!'

Rebecca had slit Neville's letter open but at Tamsyn's first scream she dropped it. She rushed into the kitchen and found Loveday trying to pick Tamsyn up in her arms and Tamsyn fighting her off, rolling around on the floor, screaming and screaming.

'She's been scalded!' Loveday shrieked at the top of her voice. 'What shall we do? Help me, Becca!'

Rebecca ran back to the washroom and grabbed a bucket of cold water. Shoving Loveday out of the way so forcefully she ended up on her bottom, Rebecca snatched a big jug off the table and began to pour the cold water over Tamsyn's squirming body.

Alex ran into the kitchen. 'What's happened?'

Rebecca was in tears like Loveday. 'Take hold of her, Alex. I've got to get as much of this cold water as possible over her. I daren't throw the bucketful over her, it might send her into shock.'

Alex held Tamsyn as best he could against her struggling and screaming. Emily and Ivy ran in at the same time. They went to Loveday and held her tightly. She moaned and wailed, hot tears skimming down her face and dripping off her chin.

'Let Becca and the Major see to her for now,' Ivy said wisely. 'Tamsyn will need you later.'

When the last jugful of water had been poured over the desperate little girl Alex said grimly, 'We must get her to the infirmary immediately.'

'I've already sent Gummoe for Trease to bring a motorcar round,' Abigail said. She was standing in the doorway, clearly shaken, and clinging to her, his face white with shock, was Stephen.

'Thanks, Abigail,' Alex said. 'Can you fetch a sheet and a blanket?'

Abigail nodded and tried to take Stephen with her but he refused to budge and she went off quickly by herself. Rebecca watched as Stephen edged closer to his friend.

Tamsyn's screams had turned to whimpers. Loveday had stopped struggling to get away from Emily and Ivy and was staring down numbly at her daughter. The skin visible on Tamsyn's right side was an angry red.

'Don't come any closer, Stephen,' Rebecca said softly when he was a foot away.

Tears suddenly spurted from his eyes and he let them fall unchecked. 'T-Tam… sh-she'll be all right?'

'We'll get her to the infirmary, Stephen,' Alex said gently. 'She'll be well cared for there.'

'Mum,' Tamsyn whimpered.

Loveday started, as if she had come back to life. 'I'm here, my handsome,' she sobbed. 'Just lie still against the Major, he's going to look after you.'

'Come and hold her hand, Loveday,' Alex said soothingly. He held up Tamsyn's left hand, which was unhurt.

Loveday did as he bid her, kissing Tamsyn's hand and murmuring reassurances to her.

Abigail returned and passed the bedclothes to Rebecca.

Percy Gummoe rushed into the kitchen a moment later. 'Car's ready, sir.'

'Right, we'll get going then. Tamsyn's gone quiet and I think she'll stay like that. We'll wrap her carefully first in the sheet and then in the blanket and she can lie across her mother and Becca's laps. She's in shock and must be kept warm. I'll drive them myself.'

'I want to go, Uncle Alex,' Stephen implored with a fresh outpouring of tears. 'Please let me go. Mother, say I can go. Tamsyn will need me. I'm her blood brother. She's my chum. I must go too.'

'Trease can take one of the other cars,' Alex said, glancing at Abigail.

'We'll all go,' Abigail said quickly. 'We're all one big family now.'

The cars sped through the narrow lanes and on to the main road to Truro in the darkening cool night air. When they reached the infirmary Alex took Tamsyn off the women's laps and carried her into the gaunt dark-stoned building. Medical staff quickly took her from him. As he gave a nurse some details, Rebecca came up behind him, her arm around Loveday.

'Take a seat, Mrs Wright,' the nurse said kindly. 'Someone will come and tell you what's happening as soon as we know exactly what Tamsyn's condition is.'

A long wait began.

'It's all my fault,' Loveday sobbed into her cardigan sleeve. 'I should never have left the kitchen with food cooking on top of the oven. Oh, my poor baby.'

Rebecca held her close and fought to hold back her own tears. Alex crouched in front of them and held both their hands. Moments later they were joined by Abigail, Stephen, Trease and Joe. Joe had heard the commotion from the stables where he had been doing his evening round and had jumped in the motorcar with the others.

'How is she?' he asked Rebecca.

'We don't know anything yet,' she replied, her voice choked.

'Sir?' Joe inquired of Alex.

Alex rose to his feet and Abigail pulled up a chair where he had been and held Loveday's hand. Stephen sat down beside Rebecca and put his head on her shoulder. He stared at the opposite wall and every few moments Rebecca rubbed his hand in comfort. The three men walked away to where the women and boy couldn't hear them talking.

'It's not good,' Alex said huskily, his voice full of pain for the suffering little girl. 'She's been scalded all down one side of her body.'

'Oh no,' Trease wailed softly, rocking on his feet. 'The poor little maid. She's Stanley's little girl. How could this have happened? She won't… die, will she?'

Alex ran a hand through his hair. 'I… I shouldn't think so… Oh, God,' he murmured under his breath, 'not this little girl too.'

Twenty minutes ticked by agonisingly slowly. The group stayed close together, in an overbearing atmosphere of disinfectant, chloroform, ether and their own fears.

Loveday stopped sobbing and stared at the ceiling, lowering her eyes only when someone walked up or down the corridor or came out of a doorway, desperately hoping it was someone come to tell her of Tamsyn's condition or to say she could go to her. The others tried unsuccessfully to think of something to say to comfort her. But the men had seen too many burnt men on the battlefields, dead or horribly scarred, and Rebecca, Abigail and Stephen had seen Tamsyn thrashing about in agony.

More time passed. Stephen wanted to ask how long the doctors would be but he knew this was not the moment to make a fuss and he bravely kept quiet, planning all the things he would do for Tamsyn when she was better. He'd ask Mrs Wright if she could stay at the big

house when she was well enough to leave hospital and he'd lay out the
model railway so she could watch the trains rocking along the tracks.
He'd read all his Bonzo dog comics to her; Tamsyn adored Bonzo dog.
He'd get her all the sweets and lemonade she wanted. He'd ask Uncle
Alex to buy her a pony of her own. Tamsyn would love to have her
own pony and in the meantime of course he'd look after Motley for
her. He thought hard about what he'd do for her and tried to get the
picture of her suffering on the kitchen floor out of his mind.

A senior nurse came to speak to Loveday and the group crowded
solemnly round her. 'At this point, Mrs Wright, the doctor wants you
to know that he's confident that Tamsyn's life is not in danger.'

'Thank God, thank God,' Loveday moaned. 'But how badly hurt
is she, nurse? Can I go to her now?'

'You can go to her in a little while. I can't say much more at this
point but it's not as bad as we first thought. You did the right thing by
dousing the child in cold water right from the start. It took away the
heat and stopped the burning or things would have been much worse.
I have to get back now. The doctor will come and talk to you as soon
as he can.'

'Thank you, Becca,' Loveday said, mopping up her tears. 'If it hadn't
been for you…' She looked up at Alex's grave face. 'And thank you,
sir. You were such a help. You've been so kind. And you too, Mrs
Fiennes.'

'We're all in this together, Loveday,' Alex said firmly and Abigail
nodded in agreement and squeezed her hand. 'We'll stay for as long as
it's necessary,' she said.

Another nurse appeared and offered Loveday a cup of tea which
she declined. People drifted up and down the corridor, moving in
and out of the doors, medical staff, ancillary staff, visitors and patients.
The daylight had gone and gaslights were lit. Another hour had passed
when a door at the end of the corridor was opened and Loveday sprang
to her feet.

'Mr Drayton!' She ran to him. 'Oh, Mr Drayton, thank you for
coming.'

Robert Drayton took Loveday's outstretched hands in his. 'I had to
come the moment I heard, Mrs Wright. How is Tamsyn?'

As Loveday told Robert what she knew, Trease remarked to Joe, 'I wonder how he found out.'

Rebecca was wondering that too. She thought about Neville's unread letter and thought it likely he'd written to say he intended coming to Trevallion tonight and on finding out about the accident had driven straight to Mr Drayton. Her assumption was proved right when Neville came through the same door a few moments later.

'I'm sorry to hear about your daughter, Mrs Wright,' he said, pausing where Loveday and Robert were talking quietly. When Loveday had thanked him for his concern, he moved past the couple and went straight to Rebecca.

'Darling, are you all right? The servants told me what had happened and I thought Mrs Wright would like to have Mr Drayton with her.'

Rebecca glanced at Alex. His face was tight, his dark eyes blazing.

'You did the right thing, Neville,' she said awkwardly.

Neville took Rebecca's hand and informed Alex curtly, 'I didn't call at Trevallion to see you.'

'Becca may see whom she wishes,' Alex said acidly, then he turned his back on them.

Rebecca pulled her hand out from Neville's. It wasn't proper what with Alex's mood and with her father glaring at them.

A middle-aged doctor, wearing uncomfortable-looking formal clothes covered by a spotlessly white starched coat approached Loveday. He exuded an air of confidence and superiority.

'We're preparing to take your daughter up to the ward, Mrs Wright. You may thank the person responsible for being so quick off the mark with the cold water that her scalding is in the main only superficial. I'm reasonably confident there should be very little scarring. We're more concerned with the shock she's received but we don't foresee any complications from that. We've given her a painkiller and she's very drowsy. She'll soon sleep for hours. A nurse will come in a few moments and take you to her.'

'Thank you, doctor,' Loveday said, sniffing back more tears. 'She'll make a good recovery? Is that what you're saying?'

'She's going to endure a rough time in the next few days but ultimately I'm confident all will be well.'

Loveday suddenly keeled backwards. Many hands shot out to catch her but Robert Drayton caught her and supported her strongly. He sat her down gently and when he was sure she wasn't going to faint he looked the doctor directly in the eye.

'I shall go to the ward with Mrs Wright,' he said with quiet but absolute authority. 'I am her fiancé and Tamsyn will shortly be my stepdaughter. They are my family and they need me.'

Loveday's head shot up to look at Robert. Rebecca expected an outraged denial from her but when the look of shock vanished from her face it was replaced by acceptance, pride, admiration and inner happiness.

While the gathering gazed in astonishment at Robert, the doctor nodded and said, 'Of course.'

'I want to go too,' Stephen interjected, pulling himself up from his forlorn state to his fullest height. 'I'm Tamsyn's brother and she needs me.'

'I don't think you are her brother,' the doctor said, smiling sympathetically, 'but I'm sure you're a special friend. The important thing for Tamsyn now is that she gets plenty of rest to ensure a quick recovery. I'm sure as a special friend you will understand that she can't have everyone round her bedside tonight. Perhaps in a day or two. I'm sure Mrs Wright will tell her how concerned you are when she's fully awake tomorrow.'

Stephen nodded and his chin fell on his chest. Alex took him by the shoulders and turned him round. Stephen's temporary assertiveness crumpled and he cried bitterly in Alex's arms.

'I'll see that Mrs Wright gets home when she wants to leave, Major Fiennes,' Robert said firmly. Then he took Loveday by the arm and they followed a young nurse who had appeared to take them to the ward.

Abigail suddenly burst into tears too. Rebecca went to comfort her but Joe was there first and no one took offence as he put his arm round her shoulders and led her away.

'I'll drive you home, Rebecca,' Neville said, holding out his arm to her then looking at Alex in challenge.

Absentmindedly smoothing his hands over the crying boy's back, Alex looked into Rebecca's face and waited for her reaction. Rebecca knew she couldn't allow Neville to drive her home even though she wanted his strong arms round her at that moment. Before she could think of a suitable reply, Trease butted in.

'Rebecca's coming home with me,' he snapped and stalked off.

Alex's expression did not change and a moment later he led Stephen away.

'They don't own you, Rebecca,' Neville said angrily. 'Come with me now and make a stand. I talked to Mrs Wright this morning. She told me that the Major is already much stronger, but even if he does have one of his mad turns it's not your responsibility to nurse him through every one.'

'I'd better go with my father, Neville,' Rebecca sighed, rubbing at her forehead.

'You do want to be with me?' He held her face and tried to kiss her, even though they now had an audience of smiling young nurses who were going off duty.

'Yes, of course I do,' she said rapidly, pushing his hands away and moving her face from the region of his lips. 'I must go now, Neville. Don't try to stop me.'

'When will I see you?' he demanded, holding her tightly. 'You can struggle all you like but I'm not letting you go until you promise to see me tomorrow, Rebecca. Surely you're not expected to work on a Sunday. If you don't promise me then I'll come over to Trevallion first thing in the morning, you can count on that.'

'No, don't do that,' she said in a panicky voice. 'I'll meet you in Victoria Gardens tomorrow morning, about eleven o'clock, after I've come here first to see how Tamsyn is. Now let me go, Neville. If my father comes back and sees us like this there'll be even more trouble.'

'I don't care,' Neville said vehemently. 'I told you in my letter how I feel about you and I won't let anyone stand in my way.'

'Rebecca!' Trease shouted from the door. He only used her full name when he was furious with her. Neville let her go but not before he had kissed her swiftly on the lips.

'I'll see you tomorrow like you promised or I'll be out to Trevallion within the hour.'

'Don't be late tomorrow,' one of the nurses called out cheekily to Rebecca.

Rebecca thought she would scream with rage. What sort of mood would Alex be in now? She walked wearily to join her father, knowing she was in for a barrage of angry questions from him about Neville Faull.

Alex went into the kitchen to gaze down at the scene of the accident. Tamsyn's screams were still echoing inside his head. Ivy and Emily had cleaned up the mess and kept the dinner warm but no one had eaten a thing and Abigail had sent them and Stephen to bed. She had said she was going to retire herself but Alex knew she had slipped out to see Joe and he envied her for having someone to turn to.

On the kitchen table lay Rebecca's letter from Neville. Alex read her name and recognised Neville's handwriting. He picked the letter up and turned round as he heard footsteps behind him.

'You've come for this?' he asked Rebecca in a soft quiet voice, holding the letter out to her.

She took it from him without a word. She waited for him to speak and hoped it wouldn't be anything similar to the furious tirade pitted with foul words and vile accusations about her character that she had received from Trease.

She was so tired. Tamsyn's pain and Loveday and Stephen's grief hung heavily over her and she was afraid the terrible event would send Alex into his world of nightmares. Neville turning up at the infirmary was the final straw. But she had seen Alex as a strong and able man today. He had been there to rescue and comfort her when she'd been terrified of being trapped in the profound blackness of the abandoned mine. He had taken charge of Tamsyn's accident. He had comforted Stephen. Was he likely to have a nightmare? She looked into his face. Not if he was as quiet and self-assured inside as he seemed outwardly. He looked steadily back at her.

Rebecca suddenly wished she had left Trevallion before Alex had inherited it, and yet she knew she wouldn't have wanted to miss knowing him. He was a noble man, kind and caring, quite unconscious of class barriers. He was not always easy to read and understand but he was honest and likeable. Oh, but he was more than likeable, much, much more. To add to the complexities of her feelings, Rebecca was now aware that she was torn between him and Neville. She sighed and her body seemed to cave in; she was amazed to find herself still on her feet. She glanced down at the letter in her hand then back at Alex.

What if you are torn between these two particular men? she asked herself. At the end of the day you can't have either of them, at least not for good.

Alex looked sad but had nothing to say to her. He simply nodded, and said in the same quiet voice, 'Goodnight, Becca,' then he left her standing there alone.

–

'Bloody hell and blast fires! Damned girl. Did she think I brought her up to go out with that ruddy swine?'

'I won't tell you again, Trease,' Basil Hartley said sharply to his drunken customer across the bar. 'Stop that bad language or I'll ban you from coming here for the next six months. It's nearly closing time. Victor is about to go home, why don't you go with him in his boat?'

'I'll row me bloody self home,' Trease said stubbornly, shrugging off Victor Jenkins' hand from his shoulder.

'You're in no fit state, Trease,' Victor said sternly. 'Come on, I'm going back to the creek.'

'Then go back! I don't need a nursemaid. I've rowed home many a time in a worse state than this.'

'But you aren't usually so upset,' Basil said, glancing at Victor. The two men exchanged a look of mutual determination to carry Trease out of the inn and into Victor's rowing boat.

'Oh no, you don't!' shouted Trease, slamming his hand on the bar. 'I know what you're up to. Just leave me alone.'

The last two customers in the bar got up, tut-tutting and shaking their heads, and left the inn.

'That's right, bugger off the pair of you,' Trease bawled after them. 'I don't like drinking with your sort anyway.'

'Trease!' Basil pointed a warning finger. 'Either you go peacefully now or you're barred for the next six months.'

Tears suddenly welled up in Trease's bleary eyes. 'Poor little maid. She's Stanley's little maid, his little baby and he never ever saw her. And now her mother's got someone else. "Her fiancé," he said as bold as brass, a bighead solicitor, marrying Stanley's wife.'

'Stanley's widow,' Victor gently corrected him, not fully understanding what Trease was rambling about.

'Bah! All women are the bloody same. Look at my precious daughter, my Rebecca. Now the Major's made her his assistant she's got ideas above herself, going out with that blasted Neville Faull. Neville Faull! We all know what he's after! Just like her mother, just like Nancy Ann.'

Basil and Victor knew Trease was upset over Tamsyn's accident but they didn't know what to make of his babblings about Rebecca and Loveday.

'He's in no fit state to row home,' Basil whispered to Victor. 'When he's had too much to drink in one of these moods he feels the whole world's against him.'

Victor nodded but when the two men looked at Trease he was standing bolt upright smoothing one hand over his hair and wiping beer froth off his moustache with the other.

'I'm sorry,' he said feebly. 'I'm just upset over the little maid. I'll be all right. There's no need to worry about me, I'll just take a walk and breathe in a little fresh air and I'll row myself home.'

'You're welcome to stay here for the night,' Basil offered.

'I'd rather go home, thank you all the same,' Trease said firmly.

He seemed calm and reasonable and Basil and Victor reluctantly allowed him to have his own way.

Trease stayed out of sight on the river bank while Victor rowed away and all the pub's lights went out. He had made a supreme effort to appear sober in the pub but now he was stumbling and lurching about. The angry things he had said out loud were going round in a turmoil in his mind and every so often he swore profusely and stamped his boots.

When all was dark and quiet, he lurched towards his rowing boat. He untied the mooring rope and without bothering to pull the boat in close to shore he jumped into three feet of cold water and cursed as he hauled his body clumsily on board. The boat rocked wildly as he tried to find the seat and sit down.

'Bloody Nancy Ann! Bitch!' The rowing boat had once been called Nancy Ann but Trease had painted it out years ago and had never renamed it. He blamed the boat now for all his problems.

Grabbing the oars he managed to push out into the flow of the river and head for home. With a dark band of cloud obliterating the moon and a thick mist rising off the water, his one good eye had trouble seeing where he was going. He thrashed at the water with the oars and sent the boat on a haphazard passage. Once he rowed into the bank, which painfully jarred his neck.

'Hell to it! Hell to everything! I wish I was dead!'

Tears of frustration seared his puffy cheeks and he threw one of the oars away. He beat on the seat with his fists and howled in rage. He kicked out with his feet, trying to make a huge hole in first the side then the bottom of the boat, but it was too well crafted and he achieved nothing more than a lot of noise which reverberated across the lonely waters.

He'd gasped in so much oxygen lambasting the world and everyone in it he began to hyperventilate and had to force himself to calm down. When his breathing was under control he sat and stared vacantly into the mist-laden night air. He shivered and put his hands on his arms to rub them and realised he had left his coat in the pub. It was only a little thing, forgetting his coat, but it fed his belief that the whole world was against him and sent him into a fury again. Clutching the sides of the boat he rocked and rocked, making water splash over him. The boat moved away from the bank and drifted off in the current. The other oar fell out of the rowlock and floated away.

'That's right!' Trease ranted after it, spittle drooling down his chin. 'Desert me too! Everybody deserts me. Nancy Ann left me. Joe didn't want my friendship when we got back from the war. Loveday's got herself a fancy solicitor. Rebecca too. My daughter! Letting me down, turning out like her rotten mother.'

Although he tried to block them out, Tamsyn's burns filled his head and he gave a great cry of anguish. 'Oh God! Stanley's little maid. Poor little Tamsyn. Nothing ever goes right! What's the bloody use? Even Captain Miles left the estate.'

He brought to mind all the things and people who had hurt him, his drunkenness distorting everything. He saw Neville Faull taking Rebecca's hand in the infirmary and he imagined them in bed together. And then it wasn't Rebecca's face he saw in ecstasy in the throes of lovemaking with the handsome young solicitor but Nancy Ann's.

He beat at his face with his fists, howling like a tormented animal. He wanted physical pain equal to that of his emotional agony. 'No! No! No! I can't bear it.'

The boat was in deep water, drifting slowly with the flow of the river. Trease suddenly stood up and the boat rocked precariously. His head was spinning and his balance unsteady. He lurched forward and toppled out of the boat. As he hit the water he instinctively twisted his body and rolled over onto his back. He floated with ease. The water was soothing and he felt that somehow it had arms and was holding him close and comforting him. The mist was like a covering of soft blankets and Trease relaxed and let the current take him. He felt safe and warm and sleepy. He closed his eyes with a peaceful smile. He'd go to sleep now. And he knew nothing would ever hurt or worry him again.

Chapter 34

As Rebecca walked from the infirmary to Victoria Gardens she thought about Neville's letter. She had read the few hurriedly written sentences many times and knew each word by heart.

> *My darling Rebecca,*
> *I have to go to London for a week on Monday and I'll go quite mad if I don't see you before then. I've missed you terribly. I shall be back on the property at 8 o'clock tonight. Meet me by the gatehouse or I'll come looking for you.*
> *With my love,*
>
> *Neville.*

Last night Neville had said his letter would tell her how he felt about her. His words were impatient, ardent, passionate, but Rebecca wasn't sure they declared he loved her. She'd never thought she had a future with Neville but what he'd written did not depict him as the cad that Alex had called him. She hadn't seen him alone for several days and, despite her torn feelings over Alex, she knew she had missed him.

She hadn't told Neville exactly where she would meet him in the gardens and thought she'd look for him by the bandstand. That was the usual meeting place for lovers. She followed the course of the Leats, a wide steady stream that ran past the gardens and on through the town. She saw Neville waiting for her at the main gates that led into the gardens. He walked rapidly to meet her and immediately took her into his arms.

'I was afraid you weren't coming.'

'It's only ten past eleven,' she said, looking up into his anxious face. 'I've been talking to Loveday at the infirmary.'

'How is her daughter?'

'She's frightened, still in shock, and in a lot of pain. The doctors are quite pleased because her skin hasn't blistered. Hopefully Tamsyn will be over the worst in about a week's time. I wasn't allowed to see her.' Tears glistened in her eyes and Neville hugged her close.

'Was Robert Drayton there?'

'Yes, apparently he's been with Loveday most of the time. He got a woman neighbour to stay in his house overnight so Loveday wouldn't have to go all the way home and come back in again. I brought her some things. The vicar's with her now. I wish there was something more I could do.'

Neville put a peck on each of her cheeks. 'You've done all you can, darling. You look all in. I suppose you didn't sleep last night. Come to Aunt Mildred's for a cup of tea. We can walk around the gardens another day.'

'Is your Aunt Mildred at home?'

'No, she's away in London and her staff have gone with her. The house is empty but I have a key.'

'Well, that's honest of you,' Rebecca said. 'But you've given me no choice but to refuse.'

'If I was intending to seduce you, Rebecca, I'd ask you to come to my flat. I promise it'll be strictly tea and sympathy and a chance for you to put your feet up. Aunt Mildred will have left something good in the larder. I'll make us a tasty meal. Now what do you say?'

'Well… I must admit I am tired and would welcome a chance to unwind a little. Just for a while then.'

He put her arm through his and they strolled like an attached couple along River Street where Neville greeted some people he knew and proudly introduced Rebecca to them. In Victoria Place he put five florins in a Salvation Army woman's collecting box and chatted gaily to her before steering Rebecca into Walsingham Place. He took the front-door key to his aunt's house out of his coat pocket and let them in.

'You'll find the curtains open and everything as it usually is. Aunt Mildred can't bear to think of the house not looking lived in. She employs a man to come and check on it twice a day. I put a note through his door informing him I might be here today.'

'You were so sure that I'd come?' Rebecca said, taking off her hat and gloves.

'I wanted us to go somewhere where we could talk alone. I haven't seen you alone for ages.' He suddenly looked unsure of himself 'If you'd rather we went out, darling, I'd be happy to leave. I don't want you to feel uncomfortable.' Rebecca smiled at him. He held out his arms and she went to him. She wound her arms round his waist and put her head against his chest. 'I want to stay here and I need you to hold me, Neville.'

Neville let her keep her head there for a few moments then he lifted her face and kissed her long and gently.

He realised they would not be able to make tea with his aunt's range not being lit and they went into the drawing room for a glass of sherry. They sat on a plush sofa covered with a watered-silk Chinese design. Rebecca kicked off her shoes and curled her legs up on the soft material. Neville took off his coat and put his arm about her and she rested her head on his neck.

'What did you make of that fiancé bit that Robert came out with last night?' Neville asked. 'I've never seen him in such a determined mood before.'

'I should think after this he'll ask Loveday to marry him and make it official.'

'Do you think she'll accept him? She's always struck me as rather a staid woman.'

'There's one thing I know about Loveday and that is she doesn't do anything she doesn't consider proper. If there wasn't something between her and Mr Drayton she wouldn't consider it proper to have him with her at the infirmary and she wouldn't have considered it proper to stay overnight at his house, even with a chaperone. As soon as Tamsyn is better I'm sure there will be an announcement.'

Neville gave a short kindly laugh. 'I never thought old Robert would get married. Did you ever meet his mother? She was a sweet old dear. I loved eating at her table, it was sheer pleasure.'

'You're not a bit like I used to think you were,' Rebecca said.

'Oh, and what was that?'

'Cunning, conniving, probably intolerant of elderly people and quiet people like Mr Drayton.'

Neville gulped down the rest of his sherry. 'Well, that's charming,' he said with a sigh. 'You've hurt my feelings now.'

She looked up at him and his eyes were twinkling. He bent his head and kissed her lips and she responded with the same gentle pressure.

'I deserved that,' he said, smiling in a way that made his blue eyes light up. 'Did you get a rough time from your father last night? I know he has a poor opinion of me.'

'He demanded to know what's been going on between us. When I told him I'd gone out with you he accused me of being a camp follower.'

Neville's face darkened with anger. 'If he wasn't your father I'd punch his face. I might have a reputation but he should know you better. And what about the bleak-faced Major? Did he rant and rave at you too?'

'No,' Rebecca replied. A picture of Alex's quiet, sad expression had been on her mind since he had left her alone in the kitchen last night. 'He didn't say anything at all.'

'Did he have one of his turns?'

'No. He was very quiet in church this morning. We all went to the early service to say prayers for Tamsyn.'

'Did he drive you into Truro today?'

'Yes, with Mrs Fiennes and Stephen. My father spent the night out drinking and I didn't go in to him in case he was still in a bad mood with me. The Major said to let him sleep it off.'

'So the Major knows you're seeing me?'

'I think he's probably guessed.'

'Then you can come and go as you please from now on?'

'I suppose I can, as long as I do my work.'

'Why on earth do you stay there, Rebecca? You're a beautiful, intelligent, vital woman. You're wasted in a little backwater place like that.'

'You can hardly call Trevallion that, Neville.'

'The creek I meant.'

'I love the creek. It's my home, but anyway I feel I must stay there for now… at least until Tamsyn's better.' Even as she said it she knew there was something more but she was tired and didn't want to think about it.

Neville stroked her hair and it rippled away from her face. He caressed her cheek and ran a tender finger down her throat. His eyes took on a soft smokiness as he looked at every tiny part of her face. He pressed his lips to her eyes then ran them round the contour of her chin and onto her mouth, kissing each corner before gently coaxing her lips apart.

Rebecca found pure enjoyment in his touch and his warmth, and melted into his hard masculine body. She needed someone to hold her now. To make her forget Tamsyn's screams, Loveday's distress, and the anger and fear she'd felt at Susannah Bosanko's evil eyes burning into her yesterday, and Alex's sad and noble face last night. Neville was just the right person to be with now. He was the only one who seemed to see her as a woman in her own right. He demanded nothing from her and put no responsibility for the fulfilment of his own hopes and dreams on her.

She let go of all her tension and felt Neville's lips becoming gently probing, a little more insistent, a little more persuasive. He put his lips to her temple and ran them down over her skin until his breath was flowing over the soft flesh in the hollow at the base of her neck. He found her mouth again in an explorative and dominant way. Rebecca shivered delightfully. He was flooding her body with fiery sensations. He was unleashing desires in her that made her forget everything. She felt eager and demanding and reached up and tugged on his hair as she hungrily responded to him. He let his head fall forward and his body followed until Rebecca was almost lying on the sofa and his top half was over her. Neville groaned in pleasure then ran a hand over her waist and down a little lower. Suddenly he raised his head and she could see his face was flushed. She touched her own cheek and found it was on fire.

'You shouldn't kiss me like that, Rebecca,' he said panting.

'Sorry.'

He laughed. 'Sorry? Only you could say something like that, darling Rebecca.'

He pulled her up and poured out more sherry. They sipped it slowly and put their empty glasses down on the table.

Neville lifted the decanter. 'More?'

'No, thank you. My head will start spinning.' It was spinning already, quite alarmingly, from their passion.

'Do you mind if I light a cigar?'

'No, please do.'

Neville took a cigar and lighter out of his coat pocket. He unwrapped the cigar and then tossed it on the table. Rebecca arched her eyebrows in question.

'I don't really want it.'

He reached for her and kissed her again.

'Rebecca...'

'Mmmm...'

He whispered huskily in her ear, 'I didn't bring you here in the hope of going any further, I swear to you, but will you come upstairs with me?'

'I... I don't know.'

She knew what he was asking her, but did she want to go upstairs and make love with him? He'd stirred up intense feelings inside her and they made her feel wanted, cherished and alive, and very much a grown woman. He'd asked nothing from her before but her company, he hoped for nothing more now than the physical act of love. He wanted her in that way and it hadn't been out of naivety or innocence she had aroused his need. She was sure loving with Neville would be tender and exciting, and he would be giving to her as well as receiving. Would the experience be fulfilling? Would it be enough?

She ran through her feelings for Neville and knew there was something holding her back. The moral question, she supposed, and the unlikelihood of there being anything permanent with him.

He held her loosely in his arms for a few moments. Then when he sought her lips again she found the passion in her response to him had not lessened. He got up and pulled her to him. He kissed her again, making his body sway intimately against hers and running his hands in slow sensual movements over her spine. She did not want him to remove his lips or his hands, nor did she want the feelings he was making sing and soar inside her die away.

He looked into her eyes and they darkened and grew immense, reflecting the passion he'd brought her to. They gave him permission. 'Come on,' he gulped huskily.

He led her up the stairs and into one of the back bedrooms of his aunt's house. 'I use this room when I sleep over for the night,' he told her.

Rebecca stood still and watched him as he undid the buttons of his shirt and pulled it out of his trousers, his movements flowing and liquid, unselfconscious, telling of his experience in doing this. His bare skin was flawless and beautiful. He was beautiful. When he moved, well-formed muscles stood out from the smooth flesh of his chest and broad shoulders.

Rebecca glanced at the bed and Neville smiled at her. He had a beautiful smile, it made his eyes shine like the bluest sky. She didn't know why but she couldn't move. She stood mesmerised as he came towards her and lifted her hair and kissed it.

'Don't be shy,' he whispered. He said it kindly. He had always been kind to her. No doubt he would be kind and gentle when he took her virginity.

He smiled again. The first time she had gone out with him she hadn't trusted his smile. Now she knew she could, but still she couldn't move. Neville was kissing her lips, very gently, softly, tenderly. Soon he would be kissing her in full passion and touching her in her most sacred places but she was rooted to the spot, absolutely immobile. It was like being in a dream.

His fingers lifted the simple lace collar of her blouse then slid lightly down to the first tiny mother-of-pearl button at her throat. He undid it, then the rest, patiently, not hurrying, then he ran his hands down to her wrists and undid the buttons there. He slipped the blouse off her shoulders and after admiring the hot glistening skin he'd exposed he kissed it tenderly. He let the blouse slide to the floor and pulled her to him. He gave a little moan of ecstasy and once more searched for her lips.

A few moments ago Rebecca had revelled in her basic womanly feelings but now she felt numb. Her body just would not work, not even her lips which had been so eagerly responding to his downstairs. And now she knew why. At the moment she'd entered the bedroom she'd seen a scrap of paper on the dressing table with Neville's hand-writing on it. It was only a little note, about something unimportant no doubt, but it reminded her of Alex passing Neville's letter to her the night before. She was staring at Neville but now it was Alex's dark eyes she saw, big and sad, with a deliberate film drawn carefully over them.

Neville drew back a little. 'Darling?'

She gulped and said in a small voice, 'I'm sorry, Neville, but I don't want to go through with this. I shouldn't have let it get this far. Forgive me, please, but I simply don't want to.'

Neville took his hands from her waist and stepped back. He walked round her and she felt her blouse being put over her shoulders.

'It's all right, Rebecca. I'll go downstairs and wait for you.'

There was pain in Neville's voice but gentleness and kindness too. She put her arms through the blouse sleeves and her fingers trembled as she fastened the tiny buttons. She tried not to think about what had nearly happened. She was confused over her feelings for Neville and Alex and consciously put them to the back of her mind where she would keep them until much later, until she could slip out onto the river alone and think.

'I'm sorry, Neville,' she said when she was back in the sitting room. She felt humble before him but not embarrassed.

He had put on his coat, combed his hair, lit the cigar and was drinking whisky. There were bright red blotches on his cheeks.

'I don't mind at all, darling,' he said tenderly. 'I don't want you to do anything that you're not ready for. I've just remembered that Aunt Mildred keeps a small Primus to boil a kettle when the kitchen's not working. I'll make you a cup of tea and then if you like I'll just hold you for the rest of the afternoon, unless you want me to take you home. It's your decision, Rebecca.'

She couldn't go back and face Alex so soon after thoughts of him had stopped her from giving herself to Neville. She didn't want to see her father recovering in a foul mood from a hangover and be subjected to more vile accusations from him. She couldn't bear to talk to anyone else at this moment.

Neville could have become very angry over her sudden refusal but his tender words and kind actions showed he was a man she could stay with alone and trust.

'I'd like to stay and have you hold me, Neville,' she smiled at him.

–

Ivy was surprised to see Rebecca in the servants' quarters of Trevallion House that evening. Rebecca explained that she wanted to know how Stephen was bearing up.

'He's been a little champion,' Ivy said, putting on her hat for Evensong. Ivy sounded offhand and Rebecca could see she was agitated. She was going to ask her if there was anything wrong but Ivy kept tucking her hair in needlessly under the hat and wouldn't meet her eyes. Rebecca thought Ivy must have guessed she'd been with Neville and didn't approve. Rebecca wasn't about to justify her friendships and made her way to Allen Cottage, hoping her father wouldn't be in a bad mood.

She was surprised to find Alex there and her heart sank. He got up from the kitchen table, his face grave. So he had something to say about her and Neville after all.

'Becca, I've been waiting for you. Did Faull bring you home?'

'Yes,' Rebecca said defensively. 'I hope you're not here looking for a quarrel over it, Alex. What I do in my own time and off the estate is my own business.'

'Yes, it is. I'm not here to quarrel with you, Becca.'

He moved towards her but Rebecca, not believing there wasn't going to be some slur on Neville's character and objections to her seeing him, turned away.

'I'm busy, Alex. I have Dad's supper to get.' She took a plate out of the cupboard. Alex took it from her and put it on the table. There was something deep and painful in his eyes and she began to feel uneasy.

'Sit down, Becca,' he said gently. 'I'm afraid I have some very bad news for you.'

'It can't be Tamsyn,' she said, backing away. Whatever Alex had to say she didn't want to hear it. 'Neville and I asked at the hospital before we left Truro and they told us she was sleeping quite peacefully.'

Alex put his hands firmly on her arms and eased her down onto the nearest chair. 'It's about your father, my dear.'

'Dad? Has he got into trouble? Has he gone too far this time and you're here to tell me you've dismissed him? I suppose I can't blame you. Dad can be terribly rude when he's got a hangover.'

Her heart froze. There was nothing in Alex's face that told her she was anywhere near the truth.

He lowered himself down and held her hands in his. 'Trease went drinking last night as you said, Becca, but he didn't come home. He got drunk and Basil Hartley tried his best to stop him from rowing home alone in the dark but Trease wouldn't listen. While we were at the infirmary this morning Tom Hartley went out with some friends to go fishing and they came across Trease's boat, floating down the river without oars and quite abandoned. They brought the boat round to the creek and when no one could find Trease, Jossy and the men went out to search the river for him.'

'But Dad's all right…?' Rebecca said, searching Alex's face. 'I didn't check on him this morning because I was afraid he'd still be in a bad mood with me and if we quarrelled it would set him off drinking again. I didn't notice that the boat wasn't there, what with rushing to the infirmary, but that's not unusual. If Dad's too drunk to row home he sleeps it off somewhere on the river bank. He must have forgotten to tie the boat up, that's all. He'll be there waiting for someone to find him and bring him home. Jossy will find him.'

Alex had not taken his eyes from her face. His expression was grim. 'Becca, my dear, Jossy found Trease's body about two hours ago. He was floating face down and was drifting out to sea. There was nothing anyone could do. He had drowned.'

Rebecca's face went white, her body rigid. 'Dad's dead?'

He nodded. 'I'm very sorry, Becca.'

She pulled her hands away and stood up. Alex rose with her and stayed close. She was surprised at how calm she felt, how in control she was.

'Why didn't someone tell me Dad was missing?'

'I knew nothing about it until I got back about lunchtime. Jenny Jenkins told me not to go looking for Trease myself but to leave it to the men who know the river better than I do. I didn't come for you in Truro because I was hoping he'd be found alive and there would have been no need to worry you. I'll send a message to your uncle and aunt if you like.'

'Thank you. Tell them not to come here and that I'll see them tomorrow. Where is Dad now?'

'Jossy brought your father back here and we informed the police and coroner and I formally identified him. I waited for you here, feeling that you would rather be told of his death at home. Jossy has taken your father's body on to Truro on the *Lady Harriet*. If you want to go to the mortuary now I'll take you, although there's nothing you need to do until the morning.'

'I don't want to go there now,' she said numbly. 'If Loveday sees us it'll upset her.'

'Would you like to come up to Trevallion for the night?'

Rebecca felt a numbness creeping over her but she could think clearly and reason things out. 'No, thank you, I'd rather stay here.'

'Then would you like me to get Abigail or Jenny to keep you company? Or someone else?'

Rebecca knew who Alex meant. Neville would still be on his way back to Truro. He would come straight back and cancel his seat on the early morning train to London. He would be kind and reassuring. He would be a great help because he would know all the legal things she would have to do. He was strong and capable and would take care of her. But strangely she didn't want him here.

She shook her head. 'No, I'll be all right.'

Alex looked uncertain. 'I'll leave you alone then, if that's what you want, Becca, but come up to Trevallion if you need anything.'

She said nothing. Just stared blankly at the hands clasping hers. She would be all right. She was calm. Her father was dead and she didn't need anyone to help her grieve.

After several long moments, Alex murmured how sorry he was again and left.

She was alone but she could cope. She looked around the room. The moment her eyes fell on a photograph of Trease in his army uniform, a smiling, proud young man with two good eyes, she crumbled inside and ran to the door, throwing it open.

Alex was standing on the other side. He hadn't gone. He hadn't been convinced she could cope alone. He was her friend and he knew her well.

'I'm here for you, Becca,' he said softly.

'Stay with me, please, Alex. I need you to be here.'

Alex gathered her into his arms and took her inside.

Chapter 35

Trease was buried close to the grave of Miles Trevallion, who had been laid to rest just a few months before. The whole estate and Kennick Creek turned out to pay their last respects. The Union Jack was draped across his coffin and Joe played the Last Post on his bugle at the graveside.

Alex supported Rebecca as he had done over the last four days since Trease's death. He led her away from the graveside on his arm and they drove off with Abigail and Stephen back to Trevallion where the funeral tea was to be held. He stood close at her side in the hallway of the big house as she thanked the mourners for coming before they filed into the dining room for refreshment.

Robert Drayton was there with Loveday. 'Please accept my condolences, Miss Allen. It was tragic. Your father wasn't of a great age like my late mother when she passed away.'

'He was forty-two, Mr Drayton.' Rebecca forced a light smile. 'At least he didn't suffer like Captain Miles.'

'Mr Faull will be back from London at the end of the week. I'm sure he will be shocked at what has happened and will be here to offer his sympathy.' He knew nothing of Rebecca's relationship with Neville and Alex's negative attitude towards it.

'If you don't mind, Becca,' Loveday said hastily, 'we'll leave now for the infirmary.'

'Yes, of course,' Rebecca said. Loveday kissed her cheek. 'Give Tamsyn my love and tell her I'm looking forward to seeing her home the day after tomorrow. I'll tell her about Dad then.'

Joe was next in line and he gave Rebecca a hearty hug. 'I'm heartbroken for you, Becca. With Trease gone there's not many of us left from Captain Miles's command now.'

The people who crowded into Trevallion to comfort Rebecca were also interested in seeing the inside of the big house. Abigail played the perfect hostess. When the last mourner had been shown out of the huge oak doors, she tried to insist that Rebecca go and lie down and rest.

Rebecca shook her head. 'I'd rather keep busy, Mrs Fiennes.'

Alex and Abigail had been kind and understanding since Trease's death and had given her a room in the house to use. She thought she'd prefer to stay in Allen Cottage but after lying in Alex's arms on the lumpy settee on the night after Trease's death she couldn't bear to stay there alone. The Kennickers took their close friendship for granted now but Alex could hardly stay there every night.

'Perhaps you'd like to spend an hour or so in the study,' Alex suggested.

'Yes, I'd like to catch up on some work, find out how things are going on the estate.'

'The parts for Frank Kellow's tractor engine will be delivered early next week,' Alex said as he shut the door of the study against the rest of the world.

'He'll be glad of that,' Rebecca said, leafing through the day's post, which Alex had not opened. 'Frank's tractor is an old bone-shaker. I know, I've driven it many times.'

'Have you?' Alex raised his eyebrows. 'You're very modern.'

Rebecca made a wry face. 'Women have been driving vehicles for years. I reckon I could drive any of the Trevallion cars. Oh, don't look so horrified, Alex. I'm not going to ask you if I can drive the Mercedes.' Then her face fell.

'What's the matter, my love,' he said softly, putting his hands comfortingly on her shoulders. 'Why have you gone quiet? You can drive any of the cars whenever you like.'

'I've just realised something. With Dad gone you'll be needing a new chauffeur. It'll be strange seeing someone else working with the cars.' She hadn't cried much before today but now tears burned her lashes and she leaned her forehead against him. 'The new man will need a home. I'd better move out of Allen Cottage.'

'Becca.' He lifted her chin. 'You can stay in the cottage for the rest of your life if you want to. I will have to employ a new chauffeur to ferry Abigail and Stephen about but if he needs a home I'll make other arrangements.'

'I… I might as well move out. Too many sad memories. My mother left us there…'

Alex rested his chin on her head. 'You aren't planning on leaving here, are you?'

'I… I don't know.'

He spoke next as if he could hardly get the words out past his throat. 'Whatever you do, Becca, don't do it in haste. You may live to regret it.'

She knew that he was afraid she'd do something rash when Neville Faull got back from London. She didn't want to think about that now. She moved away and wiped her eyes dry and returned to the letters.

'You have a letter from Susannah Bosanko.'

'Oh no, doesn't that damned woman ever give up? I thought I'd heard the last of her as she didn't immediately respond to my letter telling her to stay away.'

Alex read the letter quickly with a look of distaste on his face.

'What does she say?'

He handed her the letter. 'Read it for yourself.'

Rebecca read it out loud. '"Alexander, dearest. I was most distressed to receive your letter. I do apologise for my behaviour. Please forgive an old woman's moods. I have few visitors and I was so disappointed to have to wait for your return that day I called at Trevallion. Bring Mrs Fiennes and Rebecca here to me and I will apologise to them personally. What more can I say? Relent and forgive me, I beg you. Yours affectionately, S.B." If there's any affection in that old woman's body I've yet to see it,' Rebecca said sourly, dropping the letter on the desk. 'I can't see Mrs Fiennes agreeing to go to her house and I hope you don't expect me to.'

340

'Of course not. I'll ignore her for a little while and hope that works. If not I'll go by myself and explain to her again that our association is over. It's a pity that Susannah is as horrid as her last letters to Roland Trevallion suggested. I should have left well alone.'

They talked for twenty minutes about estate business that Rebecca had become involved in as Alex's personal assistant then he noticed how tired she was looking.

'Right, that's enough work for one day. I'm going to get you a good stiff drink.'

'Just a sherry,' she said, stifling a yawn. 'I'm not going to lie down though. A walk round the creek in the fresh air will do me more good.'

They went to the drawing room and realised the house was quiet.

'Not even the ghost is stirring,' Alex commented, passing her the sherry.

'Do you ever find this place creepy, Alex?'

'No, but then I've had a rather morbid outlook on life for many years. I suppose I've sought out gloomy atmospheres.'

Her next question was delivered carefully. 'Do you still get nightmares?'

He stroked his chin thoughtfully. 'Just bad dreams you could call them now. It's strange, but with you and the others needing me these last few days I feel I've grown stronger, more sure of myself. Left my own problems behind. I feel able to cope with life again after all these years since the war. You needed me in the old mine workings, then Tamsyn to get her to hospital. Stephen needed someone to lean on. Then you again, my love, when Trease died. But, even so, I mainly owe this new strength to your friendship and support, Becca. I'll always be grateful to you. Meeting you has been the best thing that's happened in my life.'

Rebecca sipped her sherry and recalled the time, only a few days ago, when she had drunk sherry in the company of another man, one she had nearly let make love to her. She had felt a strong attraction for Neville, not because she had needed him over Tamsyn's accident, but physically, for the man himself. She had needed Alex since her father had died. And she felt a strong physical attraction for him too. He was a very handsome man, different to Neville, his face still clinging to the gauntness that was part of him, his body tall and straight and wide-shouldered but his frame spare of flesh because he hadn't eaten properly in years.

Looking into his eyes, she breathed, 'That was a nice thing to say, Alex.'

'It's the truth, Becca.'

He finished his Scotch and put the glass down. He came close to her and she followed suit with the sherry glass. She hoped he would take her into his arms. He'd done so many times to comfort her in the last few days but this time she would feel differently about it. She wanted him to kiss her. He had forced a kiss on her out of panic in her bedroom in the gatehouse but she wanted to know what it would be like when he was gentle or passionate. She felt half-ashamed of her eagerness because she had never given him any cause to believe she looked on him in any way other than as employer and friend.

'I've promised Stephen I'll drive him into Truro,' he said. 'He wants to buy Tamsyn a present before I take him back to school. Would you like to come with me or stay here? Abigail said she would stay around in case you needed her.'

Rebecca swallowed back her disappointment and scolded herself for thinking like a fool. Alex hadn't been in his right mind when he'd forced that kiss on her and, no matter how he complimented her and valued her friendship, he was, after all, a gentleman and her employer.

She tried to sound impersonal as she replied, 'I think I'll change and take that walk round the creek and perhaps have a chat to Mrs Fiennes later.'

'You've been through an awful time lately, Becca. I was wondering if you'd like a day out tomorrow. We could take the *Iseult* and sail on the river, stop somewhere and have a picnic. A whole day of fresh air and relaxation would do you the world of good.'

He was being kind to her again and she was grateful. 'That would be lovely, Alex.'

'It'll be just the two of us. I'm not bothered about what people might think about us being alone together all day. Are you?'

'No. I suppose most people find nothing unusual about it now.'

'Good. First thing tomorrow it is then.'

—

Jossy Jenkins raised an eyebrow when Alex told him the *Iseult*, which he'd been asked to get ready for the trip, was for just himself and Rebecca.

'Jossy looks disappointed,' Rebecca remarked as they pulled out of the creek. 'He hates to see one of the big boats going out without him on board.'

'Too bad,' Alex grinned as he headed the boat downriver. 'This is your special day, Becca, and I'm only concerned about you.'

They chugged past the King Harry Ferry, down the full length of Carrick Roads, rounded St Mawes and headed up the Percuil River which divided a part of the Roseland peninsula. The oysterdredgers which worked the river here were rewarded with fine oysters. Percuil itself was a fairly busy little port and, apart from its small fishing industry, the vessels calling at it handled timber, coal, roadstone, manure, grain and farm produce.

The *Iseult* and her crew of two glided past a great variety of vessels about their business, including the rowing-boat ferry that provided a link with St Mawes and the steam ferry that ran to Falmouth. Running alongside on shore were fish cellars, storerooms for manure and roadstone, a lime-kiln works and, of most interest to Alex, a boatbuilding yard.

Rebecca enjoyed the bustle of the river, but she was content when Alex steered the motor boat into the peace and quiet of a tiny unnamed creek. He slowed the engine and Rebecca leant over the side and let her hand drift in the cool green water. She spoke to a family of ducks. They took no notice of her and tipped their tails skywards to search for food beneath the surface. The creek became narrower as they progressed, the trees on its banks beginning to meet. Alex skilfully avoided overhanging branches until they came to the tiny inlet's natural end. He jumped out and tied the hawser to a strong tree. He helped Rebecca to alight and lifted off the picnic hamper.

They didn't speak. There was no need to. The day was still young and there was time to dawdle and explore and unwind. The water would leave the creek's banks with the tide and they would be stranded for a few hours until it returned. They strolled along, twisting in and out of the trees, stopping at their leisure to gaze at the water, the wildlife and wild flowers. When they came to a grassy spot, sheltered and surrounded by an overhang of trees, Alex put the picnic hamper down and they walked on, squeezing through the trees where they grew at their thickest until they came out on the other side and were looking up at a meadow. A few sheep were grazing nonchalantly and Alex broke the silence to ask Rebecca if she wanted to climb to the top of the meadow.

'Let's not disturb the sheep,' she replied. 'They look in the same mood as us today, wanting only to be left alone.' They returned to the picnic hamper and laid out the blanket. After they'd eaten and shared most of the contents of a bottle of white wine they relaxed and chatted. Alex rested his back against a tree and Rebecca leaned against his arm like she used to do with Joe. It was a time to be quiet, one day taken out of their lives and snatched from the future where there were going to be many changes. Rebecca couldn't help wondering how those changes would affect her life.

'You told me once that you weren't going to stay at Trevallion,' she said thoughtfully. 'Have you decided what you're going to do, Alex?'

His eyes were closed and he opened them to look at the little bit of muddy water left in the basin. 'Well, I'm definitely going to stay in Cornwall. I shall sell my business and property in Berkshire and put my money into this county. I'll start a boatbuilding yard on the river like Miles had planned to do. I'm going to have a new house built on the same spot as Aristotle Trevallion's at Perranporth. I love that part of the coast. Its ruggedness soothes my soul.'

'That sounds wonderful.' Rebecca was relieved that he wasn't going far away, but she had a feeling the answers to her probings would eventually make her heart sink. 'And the estate and Trevallion House?'

'I know what I'm going to do about them. I was about to announce my decision to Abigail, but when Tamsyn was hurt and then with

Trease's death, I decided to wait a while longer. Rest assured that those who live and work on the estate have safe jobs and homes just as Miles wanted.'

Rebecca tilted her head back to look up at him. 'You really believe that Captain Miles appeared to you, don't you, Alex?'

'I know it was nightmares and with my mind being in such a bad state everything was warped and ugly, but somehow I can't help feeling that Miles was trying to tell me something.'

'What sort of something?'

'Something to do with the will we found under the chest in the study.'

She turned completely round to him. 'I'd forgotten all about it.'

'You could have read it and known what was in it but you would insist on it being none of your business. You can be a stubborn woman, Becca.'

'Never mind that now. Whose was it?'

'It was written by Roland Trevallion, not long after his American wife Arabella died. Apparently Roland was trying to finish his affair with Susannah Bosanko because he had fallen in love with a girl from the creek, Rowena Carlyon. Joe's great-aunt.'

Rebecca was astounded. 'Rowena Carlyon? She drowned in the creek. Joe never mentions it but everybody knows about it. So Roland lost his wife and then Rowena soon afterwards? There was a mining slump then and everyone blamed his suicide on that but it looks more likely he died of a broken heart.'

'It's a possibility but that's not all. Roland also left some writings. Rowena was pregnant and Roland was going to arrange for a special licence so they could marry. He wanted his second child to be legitimate like Vyvyan, Miles's father. Roland wrote that he didn't care much for Vyvyan, he thought him weak and spoiled, and in his secret will he left half of everything he still owned to Rowena and their baby. I think Miles must have found the will and felt that since his grandfather had been involved with a girl from the creek, the estate should be kept on for the workers. He'd made provisions to keep it going in the event of his death or incapacitation, and when I questioned Mr

Drayton it transpired that Miles had named Joe in particular as one person who was to be kept in employment at Trevallion for as long as he desired it. Becca, I believe that Joe has a real stake in Trevallion.'

'What are you going to do about it?'

'Well, I have Abigail and Stephen to consider too. I'll be putting a proposition to Abigail and Joe shortly.'

'I see, presumably because of their association. It sounds like you have the future all mapped out.'

Alex looked wistful. 'Not everything will be as I'd like it, but at least I know in what direction I'm heading.'

Rebecca became quiet. He had said nothing about keeping her on as his personal assistant when he moved to Perranporth, but then she had told him yesterday that she didn't know what she wanted to do with her future. Starting a new life for herself seemed the most obvious answer now. The estate was safe, she had helped make that happen by supporting Alexander Fiennes in his time of need. Kennick Creek had always been her home but Trease was dead now and Loveday and Tamsyn would be moving out as soon as the little girl was well enough to attend her mother as bridesmaid when she married Robert. It would be best to go and live with Uncle Bert in Truro and get a job there. Neville would help and he probably still wanted to see her – at least for a while.

Her mouth had gone dry and she sat up straight to drink from the bottle of wine. Alex slid down and laid himself out on the blanket, clasping his hands on his firm stomach. He had gone quiet too. Both of them were facing an uncertain, and perhaps lonely future.

She studied Alex's face. His eyes were shut, his expression slightly melancholy but, unlike most people when they weren't happy, he looked more handsome. He had become tanned by his outdoor life and it gave a healthy tint to his dark looks. His mouth was clamped in a tight line. It was nearly always like that; he'd smiled little over the years but it held a great attraction. Rebecca mentally traced the outline of his full lips, wondering what they would feel like under her fingertips.

'It's peaceful here,' she said.

'Mmmm.'

She felt he was aloof from her and lay down beside him. She put her face against his shoulder. He didn't move or speak, but then this wasn't an unusual occurrence, them lying down beside each other. Rebecca put her hand on top of his. He smiled lightly and that was all. Neville would have rolled over and started kissing her. Rebecca suddenly didn't like this 'just good friends' relationship she had with Alex. She had a burning desire to get closer to him. She had wanted Alex to kiss her yesterday, then thought herself a fool, but now she wanted to kiss him. It struck her then that she had never kissed Neville unless it was to respond to. As far as she understood, a woman didn't usually kiss a man first or he would think she was 'fast'. At this moment Rebecca didn't care about that.

She leaned on one arm and picking a long piece of grass ran it over Alex's brow and round his cheeks. He didn't move so she tickled it under his chin and down his neck. Alex grinned and without opening his eyes took the grass from her and tossed it away. He clasped his hands together again.

Rebecca felt like the sirens in the moving pictures but was determined not to give up. She pulled Alex's hands apart and laid her head on his chest. He put his arms round her, but nothing more. He didn't even stroke her hair as he usually did when they were this close. She lay still for a while listening to his heart beating. He smelled good, he always did, and she breathed him in, so much more aware of his strength and masculinity than before.

Getting impatient, she raised herself and looked down on his lips. He opened his eyes and she smiled into them, then he closed his eyes again and seemed to be settling down to doze. Rebecca ran out of patience. She pressed her lips firmly to his.

Alex's eyes sprang open. She was aware of his surprise as she kissed him. 'Why did you do that?' he asked huskily when she lifted her face away.

'Because I wanted to.'

She kissed him again, harder and longer to show she meant it. Kissing Neville had been good, it had stirred her to her first full passion. But kissing Alex was pure bliss. She felt more than mature and full of feminine longing. She was totally sure she wanted him, all of him. She didn't have to wonder if making love with Alex would be fulfilling. Her whole being longed for him and if he wanted her too, no matter what he felt for her afterwards, she wanted her first time to be with him.

Alex was stunned at her kissing him like this. He responded immediately; kissing Rebecca like a lover was something he'd wished for a long time, long before his assault on her. Despite his battle trauma and gloomy personality he'd wondered what she'd be like to kiss as far back as the journey in the trap from Truro railway station. She had seemed so natural, a quiet, beautiful young woman, lacking pretensions in her shabby clothes. He'd never been the sort of man to bother his female staff and he'd known from the start Rebecca wouldn't have countenanced anything like that anyway. He'd hoped his nightmarish existence wouldn't follow him to Cornwall, but with the appearance of Miles in his dreams it had been even worse. It had been such a comfort to secure Rebecca's friendship. After she'd forgiven him for the lunatic assault and he'd got her to promise to stay at Trevallion, he'd thought that at best she only felt a maternal tenderness for him. When Neville Faull had turned up at the infirmary and made no secret of the fact that they were still meeting, he'd found it hard but he'd accepted it and resolved to pick up the pieces if Faull used and cruelly dropped her. He was sure they'd arranged to meet when Faull returned from London, so why was she kissing him like this now?

'Are you sure about this, Becca?' he breathed, holding her face gently away from him. He had to be sure her kisses meant what they seemed to, what he'd give anything in the world to happen. He didn't want her to make a terrible mistake. 'Isn't there someone else to consider?'

She replied with the truth and said it boldly. 'I've never been sure of anything more, Alex. There is no one else I want like this, only you.'

He pulled her down to him and kissed her in the way they both wanted. Fully, possessively, passionately. He drew his hands through her hair, kneading and caressing it, making it feel like an act of intimate lovemaking in itself. She could feel his life force flowing through him, the energy, the vitality, the spirit which had been missing in him for so long.

They forgot all about their life's tragedies, their uncertain futures, the river and Trevallion. They lay down together and very soon were totally lost in each other.

Chapter 36

That evening Joe Carlyon went to the big house as requested by the Major and was disconcerted to be shown into the drawing room. If he'd known it wasn't going to be a short conference on the running of the stables in the study he would have tidied himself up and put on his suit. Abigail was there and a look of shock and guilt passed between them. What did the Major want? Was he going to rebuke them over their relationship? They were both immediately on the defensive.

'What's this all about, Alex?' Abigail asked abrasively from the chair where she was preparing to light a cigarette.

'Come in and sit down, Joe,' Alex said in an amiable tone by the drinks cabinet. 'What would you like to drink?'

Joe shuffled his feet but stood his ground. 'Drink, Major?'

'Yes, drink. Scotch, brandy, sherry? I have some beer.'

'Um, nothing for me, sir. I… I don't understand.'

'You will shortly, Joe. There is one other person to come and then I'll tell you why I've asked you here.'

'And who's that?' Abigail demanded, rising from her chair dramatically. 'I don't know what you think you're playing at, Alex—' She was stopped by a fourth person entering the room. 'Rebecca…'

Rebecca smiled and crossed the room to Alex, who put his arm round her. They gazed lovingly at each other for a moment and Abigail said sarcastically, 'Well, we don't have to ask if you two enjoyed your day out together. Does this mean we are to expect an announcement?'

'That's right, Abigail,' Alex replied proudly with a contented look on his face. 'This afternoon I asked Becca to marry me and she accepted.'

Various expressions crossed Abigail's face as she took in this news but Joe lost his nervousness and went to the couple to shake their hands.

'Congratulations, Major, Becca. I couldn't be more pleased. I'll not hide the fact that the whole estate has been hoping there might be something between you both and that it would come to this. It's a pity that Trease isn't here. He would have been as proud as punch.'

'Thank you, Joe,' Rebecca said, accepting a kiss on the cheek from him and thinking sadly of her father.

'I'm sorry to break in on your felicitations,' Abigail said harshly, waving her cigarette about in its holder. 'But where does this leave me and Stephen? And why have you brought Joe here tonight? You could have waited until tomorrow to tell him your good news.'

Rebecca looked at Abigail with sympathy. She felt she shouldn't really be here but Alex had insisted she had the right as his future wife.

'To begin with, Abigail, Becca and I don't intend to live here so you need not worry that she will be usurping your position as mistress of Trevallion. But on that position I will be laying down a condition. We are going to marry as soon as possible and until the house we're planning to have built at Perranporth is ready, we'll live in the gatehouse. We want our privacy and in that way you will have full rein here. I'm going to sell all my assets outside Cornwall and start various business ventures locally in which Becca will play a major part.'

Joe kept quiet, not understanding why he was here and being told of the Major's plans before the rest of the estate workers.

Abigail was looking at Alex with suspicion. 'This is all very touching but what is the condition you are talking about? Where does all this leave my son? Is he to have Trevallion one day or not?'

'Yes, he will, Abigail,' Alex answered evenly. 'On one condition, that you and Joe marry and provide the boy with some sort of family life.'

'Alex!' Rebecca gasped. 'You can't make a condition like that.'

'I can and I will,' Alex said coolly.

'But, sir,' Joe's face had gone a sickly colour, 'Mrs Fiennes would never want to marry me.'

'Why not, Joe? She's happy to lie in your bed or anywhere else you choose to carry out your affair – and before you raise your hands in protest, I will have you both know that your relationship is public knowledge.'

'This is outrageous!' Abigail shouted across the room. 'I won't be told what to do like this. How dare you make such a condition, Alexander Fiennes. If you have any feelings for Stephen, why can't you just turn Trevallion over to him when he comes of age and leave it at that?'

Rebecca was about to speak but Alex put a finger to his lips. She kept quiet but shook her head. When Alex had said on the river bank that he was going to put a proposition to Abigail and Joe, this was the last thing she had expected.

'I've decided on this course to protect the Trevallion estate as Miles Trevallion would have wished and to protect Stephen. I want there to be no more gossip about the two of you and if you get married people will think you have fallen in love and are doing the decent thing. Stephen will have a home, a mother and a stepfather he gets along with quite well.'

'But if we do as you want what will the other young gentlemen say at the boy having a stepfather who is only a groom?' Joe asked. He was looking at Alex as if he thought he'd gone mad.

Alex's eyes were on Abigail when he answered and she seemed to shrink in size. 'Abigail has already forfeited her place as a socialite by her past behaviour. Stephen loves the creek and I think he'll be reasonably happy with the arrangement. He won't have a groom as a stepfather, Joe, because I intend to make you general manager of the estate. I'm confident that you will learn quickly how to manage things and I trust you completely as I'm sure Captain Miles did. Also, in this way it'll make sure that Abigail doesn't marry some unsuitable lounge lizard who might suck Stephen's inheritance dry. Stephen will be able to take charge of Trevallion when he's twenty-five and until then I shall keep some control, along with Robert Drayton, as extra protection. You will have thirteen years between you to turn Stephen into a responsible young man and a worthy heir to Trevallion.'

Abigail looked thunderstruck and Rebecca fought back the desire to go and comfort her. At that moment, because she was Alex's fiancée, the gesture wouldn't have been appreciated.

Alex looked at the pinched faces of the lovers. 'You can take it or leave it. If you decide to leave it then you, Abigail, will be no more than a lodger here, with no inheritance to come to Stephen except the large sum of money already written into my will. And you, Joe, will remain as groom. I shall install a general manager to run the estate.'

'You are a hard man, Major Fiennes,' Joe said coldly.

'I prefer to think of it as practical, Joe,' Alex returned, unshaken.

'You are despicable!' Abigail suddenly screamed, throwing her unlit cigarette across the room and making Rebecca jump. Abigail ran to Joe and took hold of his arm. 'You've made me sound like a harlot but I'll have you know that Joe and I do care for each other. If we decide to marry, it will be because we want to.'

'Aye,' said Joe, puffing out his chest and holding Abigail protectively.

'I'm glad to hear it,' Alex said softly.

Abigail turned with as much dignity as she could muster and swept out of the room on Joe's arm. The door was closed loudly.

'You were a bit hard on them,' Rebecca said.

Alex was thoroughly unrepentant. 'I had to be, darling. They deserved it the way they were carrying on. Abigail was risking her reputation down here without a thought of what it could mean to Stephen or the Kennickers. Jossy himself asked me recently to put a stop to their goings-on. This seems to be the best way for everyone concerned. Joe will make an excellent head of the estate and as he seems able to satisfy Abigail's appetites, she's less likely to wander elsewhere.'

'Alex! Really.'

He smiled and went over to her, and kissed her lips. 'You've lived a rather sheltered life, my love. Straight talking is not so shocking in society.'

'I must be thankful for a quiet upbringing then,' she said, cuddling into him.

'Nothing could spoil you, darling Becca. I do love you.'

'Do you think they'll get married, Alex?'

'Joe will probably be the one to have reservations, but what choice does Abigail have if she wants to be lady of this house? She'll talk Joe round if need be. I think she was telling the truth when she said they care for each other. I asked her a while ago what she felt for him, because I wouldn't want to force her into a marriage she would hate. That wouldn't help Stephen. She told me to mind my own business though she did seem concerned for Joe. She was afraid I would throw him off the estate. But I'll tell you one thing, Becca Allen,' – he grinned with a wicked glint in his dark eyes, a sign of his newfound confidence since she'd given him her love – 'I'll get you to the altar before Abigail does Joe and maybe even before Robert Drayton does Loveday Wright.'

–

Rebecca was in Allen Cottage packing up her belongings to take to the gatehouse. She glanced out of her bedroom window and saw Neville coming up the path. She ran down the stairs to meet him. She was expecting him to come today, a week after his trip to London.

'Hello, Neville.'

'I've just read your letter, darling. I came as quickly as I could. You should have got Robert Drayton to get in touch with me in London. I would have come back straightaway. I'm so sorry about your father's death. How are you bearing up?'

'I'm all right, Neville,' she said, turning her face so his kiss landed on her cheek. 'Come inside.'

She led him into the kitchen where he tried to hold her but she nipped smartly aside. 'Would you like a cup of tea?'

'Only if you've got one made,' he replied, frowning. 'You seem different, Rebecca. Is there something wrong?'

'I've got some news for you, Neville,' she said, pouring him a cup of tea which he ignored.

'Yes?'

She squared her shoulders but couldn't help going a little pink. 'I'll come straight to the point. The Major and I are getting married.'

'What the hell – I don't believe it!' His mouth fell open and he couldn't speak for a minute. When he found his voice again it was full of hurt. 'He certainly stepped in smartishly the moment I turned my back. Good God, Rebecca, what are you doing? You can't marry half a man. You can't spend the rest of your life wiping the nose of a damned lunatic.'

'It's not like that,' Rebecca returned emphatically. She'd known this was going to be difficult. 'Alex is so much stronger and more capable these days. A lot has happened since you've been away and he's coped wonderfully. He's put the war in the past. He's got everything in perspective. Alex has made plans for the future and I'm happy to be a part of them.'

'I thought I meant something to you, Rebecca.'

'You did, Neville. But with Alex it's different.'

Neville caught her by the arms and held her fast. 'In which way different? What's different about him?' He searched her face for answers then groaned. 'My God, he's made love to you, hasn't he?'

Rebecca looked back steadily. 'We made love together.' Neville let her go. He ran his hands through his fair hair and sighed heavily to check the urge to cry. He had thought of Rebecca every minute of the week he'd spent in London. She had affected him in a way no other woman had before. He had come to adore her. He had desired her and very nearly won her completely, but when she had changed her mind about making love with him, rather than making him angry or feel rejected or become even more determined that one day he would have her, it had made him think deeply about her. She was as honest and forthright as she was beautiful. She sought neither status nor position. There was something pure about her. As the week had worn on and the longing to see her again and just hold her in his arms had grown, he had even begun to consider whether he could take her as his wife. A marriage simply to benefit his career and place in society was no longer very appealing.

And now he was too late. Alexander Fiennes had something in his character that he did not, and whatever it was, it had made Rebecca succumb to him. All he could do now was to bow out as gracefully as he could.

'Well, that's that then,' he said, his voice thick with emotion. 'I can't compete with that. You must think a lot of him to have given yourself to him. Now it's up to me leave you to your future life, but it's damned hard, Rebecca, damned hard.'

'I'm sorry, Neville, but it wouldn't have worked out for us.'

He looked at her for some time. 'Oh, I don't know, Rebecca. You've straightened out a moody shell-shocked industrialist and you came a long way to reforming a caddish solicitor.'

Neville met up with Alex on the way back to his car. It seemed Rebecca was right about Alexander Fiennes; he had changed. He looked calm and confident and there was more than a touch of arrogance in the way he looked at him. He kept his hands in his pockets and seemed disinclined to speak, as if Neville's presence on Trevallion was of no concern to him.

Neville was feeling bitter. It would take only the slightest provocation and he'd raise his fists and beat this superior looking dark-haired major into the Trevallion dirt.

'I congratulate you, Fiennes. I received a letter from Rebecca saying she wanted to see me. Mr Drayton told me her father had drowned in the river. I thought she was in need of my comfort. You pulled yourself together in the nick of time because very soon Rebecca would have been mine.'

'Sent you packing, did she?' Alex asked drily.

'Yes, she did. You've got yourselves a wonderful woman there. Rebecca is a matchless creature, and you don't deserve her. You bloody upcountry people come down here and take all our best things.'

'I know exactly what Rebecca is like. No matter where her husband comes from, you wouldn't have been good for her, Faull.'

'Well, I certainly don't think you are, Fiennes,' Neville bellowed. 'I believe you've manipulated her into agreeing to marry you!'

'You can believe what you like. I love Rebecca and you may depend on it I'll look after her with my life.'

-

Tamsyn was tucked up on pillows on the settee in Loveday's tiny sitting room, her small face peeping over a blanket. Stephen was there. His headmaster had given him permission to spend the first week of her release from the infirmary at home. Loveday came into the room and started to fuss with the blanket.

'Now just you mind you don't let Motley in here, Master Stephen,' she said in a no-nonsense voice. 'A big dog jumping all over her will hurt her and she could get an infection from him. I'm just popping up to the big house to make sure Ivy's got the lunch under control. I'm trusting you to look after Tamsyn until I get back.' Loveday wasn't working at Trevallion full time now and Alex had advertised for a replacement cook.

'You can depend on me, Mrs Wright,' Stephen said stoutly.

'I'll be back in a little while, my handsome,' she told Tamsyn. 'Just you stay put. If you want anything, I'm sure Master Stephen will get it for you.'

''Bye, Mum.' Tamsyn gave a small wave with her good arm.

'You're lucky to have a mother who loves you so much,' Stephen said. 'Mine is more preoccupied than usual. If I as much as ask her a simple question she says, "Go down to the cottage and see Tamsyn, darling. I've got a lot on my mind."'

'Wonder what it is, what she's got on her mind,' Tamsyn said, putting the large curly-haired doll Stephen had bought for her outside the blanket and refastening its cardigan buttons.

'Something to do with Uncle Alex marrying Rebecca, I expect.'

'Isn't it romantic?' Tamsyn said dreamily, copying Ira Jenkins who had been talking to Loveday about it the day before. 'I'm going to be two bridesmaids.'

'Tush! And you mean you're going to be a bridesmaid twice.'

'What's it matter how I say it if it means the same thing?' Tamsyn returned petulantly.

'You'll understand when you start the new school Mr Drayton is going to put you in. When you're living in Truro I'll be able to see you sometimes in the week. Your mother's said that she will ask permission for me to have tea with you.'

'Aren't you afraid the other boys will laugh at you, having tea with a girl?'

'I don't give a damn about them! I'll thrash anyone if they poke fun at me over you. Just think though, Tamsyn, with your mother getting married again, you might have some little brothers or sisters.'

'How can that happen?' Tamsyn scoffed. 'My father's dead and Mum will need him to make more babies. Jenny Jenkins told me that ages ago when I asked her why I had no brothers and sisters.'

Stephen made an impatient face. He wasn't going to explain the facts of life to her. 'Dress your doll in something different. The women in the creek have knitted you so many clothes, you don't have to keep the same ones on.'

'This outfit is my favourite,' Tamsyn protested but peeled off the doll's pink knitted clothes anyway.

Stephen got up and looked out of the window.

'Are there any Revenue men out there, Captain Redbeard? Any dragons or creatures from the deep?'

'There's certainly an old dragon out there,' Stephen replied, leaning over the windowsill. 'It's that ugly old Miss Bosanko. I wonder what she's doing in the creek.'

'She's not coming here, is she?' Tamsyn asked nervously, holding her doll tightly.

'No, she's going towards Allen Cottage.' Stephen took up arms in the form of Tamsyn's play sword and swept it about the room. 'But I'm ready for the old witch if she threatens us!'

Chapter 37

'We've had a week to think over Alex's proposition, Joe. Have you made a decision yet?'

While her son was standing guard over Tamsyn, Abigail had gone quite openly to Joe's cottage. If the Kennickers were gossiping about them, what did it matter if she was seen entering his cottage while he was there alone? She was dressed in a more low-key fashion than usual, wearing a longer skirt and the fluffy cardigan she'd lent Rebecca on the night of Alex's worst nightmare.

'I've thought of nothing else, Abigail,' he said glumly from the other side of the kitchen. 'I can't get over the Major coming up with something like that and I didn't like the way he spoke about you. I've hardly been able to look him in the face with any respect since then.'

Abigail looked philosophic. 'There's no need to be gallant, Joe. Alex was right. He's been very patient with me and, although you haven't mentioned it, you know that Stephen is not his brother's son.'

Joe glanced down. 'It's none of my business.'

'If it's only a carnal relationship you want with me then it isn't. But if you've been considering what Alex wants us to do, that's different. You have the right to know all about me.' She picked at the bottom buttonhole of her cardigan, feeling unaccustomedly shy. 'You must have realised I've had several lovers. I wasn't unfaithful to Ralph as such. He was incapable of making love and when he asked me to marry him he didn't expect me to stay celibate. Ralph was delighted when I became pregnant. It made him feel more of a man. He had a son to present to the world and he asked Alex to accept Stephen as a true Fiennes. It hasn't been easy for Alex. Stephen has always been a difficult child and after Ralph was killed we found out that

359

he'd gambled all his money away. I had no family and it made me and Stephen totally dependent on Alex's financial support.'

Joe felt protective towards Abigail and it wasn't a new feeling. 'You haven't had things easy over the years.'

Abigail shrugged. She had taken a long hard look at herself and had come to many uncomfortable conclusions. 'You could look at it that way but I'm grateful to Alex. He's been very generous to us. Stephen has gone to the best schools and I've had everything I've needed. Alex was harsh with us, me in particular, but all that matters is the future. I want Trevallion for my son. I might not be the most attentive mother in the world but I do love Stephen and I want something solid for his future. If you and I don't do as Alex wants then Stephen and I are going to be left in an impossible position.'

Joe was solemn. He would be left in an impossible position too. If he didn't marry Abigail he couldn't bring himself to stay on at Trevallion and work under a new general manager, any more than he could remain working there with Abigail in the house and the other Kennickers' silent disapproval of his moral lapse. He was in a dilemma. He wanted to stay single but he wanted to keep on his association with Abigail; he liked the idea of being general manager of Trevallion and felt somehow that Captain Miles would have approved of it. But he also wanted Abigail to consider all her options.

'Have you thought that you might meet someone else, someone rich and with a position who could offer you marriage?'

Abigail had thought of it and had immediately discounted it. 'No one can guarantee that and it wouldn't necessarily mean that Stephen would get an inheritance. You've seen Stephen, Joe,' she went on earnestly. 'You know how much he loves the creek. Alex said we have thirteen years to turn him into a worthy heir to Trevallion. I think if his future's settled he will become just that.'

It was Joe's turn to feel awkward and shy. 'Do you want us to get married then?'

Abigail lit a cigarette and ran a fingernail round the arm of the chair she was sitting in. Not looking up, she blew out a long puff of smoke and asked softly, 'Would that be so terrible?'

'Not at all,' Joe replied at once and he went to her. 'But Abigail, just think what it would mean, my dear. I'm not worthy of you. You'd want to entertain at Trevallion. I'd make you a laughing stock with my lack of manners, dressed up in clothes which wouldn't suit me. I wouldn't want that kind of life either. I'd hate it and we'd probably end up hating each other. It could be hell, particularly for you.'

She took hold of his big rough hand. 'Of course things wouldn't be perfect, Joe, but we could make some compromises. And you'd be making the biggest one of all. I've told you I can't have any more children. Apart from Stephen, it would be a childless marriage.'

'I can't say I've ever really wanted children of my own and Stephen will be enough for anyone to cope with.' Joe gripped her hand and added in all seriousness, 'Do you think we could make a go of it, Abigail?'

'I'd like to prove to Alex that I can live a decent life. I'd try so hard, Joe, I promise. You could spend most of your time running the estate and if you like I could learn about it too and help you. That way we'll know exactly what needs to be done when Stephen takes over. I could restrict my socialising for the most part to entertaining the Ladies' Guild to afternoon tea. We could have dinner parties but with people you feel comfortable with, like Alex and Rebecca, Mrs Wright and Mr Drayton. You'd feel quite comfortable with other people from the creek, wouldn't you?'

Joe caressed the top of her head and smiled warmly. 'I've often wished I could give you Trevallion. By marrying you I can. You make it sound like it could be quite cosy. But the biggest obstacle could be Stephen himself. What will he think about us getting married? I can't imagine him taking it meekly.'

'I've thought a lot about Stephen. He's nearly thirteen years old, he's becoming a young man. I think the best approach would be to tell him the truth. That if we don't marry his future will be uncertain. That a general manager brought in from outside might run things on the estate in a way none of us would like. That he and I would still have to go cap in hand to Alex for everything we need. I think Stephen would come round to our way of thinking. Please say yes, Joe.' Tears formed along Abigail's lower eyelids and she stubbed her cigarette out with shaking hands. 'I don't think I could bear spending the rest of my life as a lodger here.'

Joe took Abigail in his arms and kissed away her tears. 'Don't you go worrying, my dear. I care very deeply for you and I respect you. In a little while I'll go find the Major and tell him that we're getting married and then we'll tell Stephen together. We'll make a good team together, Abigail. We'll show 'em.'

'Joe,' Abigail said after a few tender moments, 'I've been thinking about Alex and Rebecca. I can understand why Alex wants to marry her and keep her close by him for ever. I'm sure he's fallen in love with her but why do you think she's agreed to marry him?'

'Presumably because she's fallen in love with him. Don't you think she has?'

'I don't know, but up to the day Trease drowned, Rebecca was seeing Neville Faull. He was besotted with her and I'm sure she was fond of him. When Alex first announced their engagement I thought she'd agreed because she wanted to be mistress of Trevallion, but that's not the case since they're going to live at Perranporth.'

'Rebecca's not a social climber,' Joe said. 'Perhaps she's marrying the Major because she feels sorry for him, but if that's the truth of it, it won't be much of a future for her.'

'If she backs out it will break Alex's heart,' Abigail commented thoughtfully.

–

Rebecca was pulling her boat towards the bank of the creek when she felt someone was watching her. Thinking it was Motley, she called his name. When no big dog came bounding up to her, she stopped to listen. She let the rope go and stiffened to attention. Someone was approaching her and she turned round hurriedly.

'Good afternoon, Rebecca. Are you going for a row in your boat?'

'What are you doing here, Miss Bosanko? I thought Alex had made it quite clear that you're not welcome here.' Rebecca folded her arms but couldn't help taking a couple of steps backwards.

'I don't consider that to be any of your business, miss!' Susannah hissed. She was in an ugly mood. Her reptile eyes gleamed in her cadaverous skull. She held her head as high as possible off her chest, revealing folds of curded flesh. She was dressed in her usual colour, a shade of green which blended with the creek foliage. Rebecca had only seen her once before and had felt repulsed at the old woman's gargoyle features but now she seemed to be rotting before her eyes.

'Alex and I are getting married. That makes it my business,' Rebecca snapped back. She was in no mood to be spoken to like an insignificant piece of rubbish.

The gruesome head was flung back and the yellowing neck folds quivered. 'Yes, I heard about that. It's utterly ridiculous! A gentleman shouldn't even dream of marrying a servant girl.'

Rebecca was totally out of patience and raised her voice. 'It's got nothing to do with you. Get back to Falmouth and keep out of our lives.'

'Think you're in love with him, do you? Think he's in love with you? Has he told you? Have you told him? The men in that big house up there have a fondness for working-class girls who live in this Godforsaken little creek. They use ladies like me then get an infatuation over some silly girl and plan to marry her. It's pathetic.'

'You have never meant anything to Alex in that way,' Rebecca said scornfully. The old woman must have taken leave of her senses. 'You're old and hideous and mad to even think it. And just what do you mean by girls? Are you referring to Rowena Carlyon? Are you still jealous because Roland Trevallion wanted to marry her and not you? I've seen some of the letters you wrote to him. The last ones were vicious.'

Susannah's decaying features twisted up in hatred. 'I was going to be mistress of this estate! After Arabella died I expected Roland to make me his bride but he said he'd fallen in love and wanted to marry that young Carlyon bitch. He'd got her pregnant. He wanted another son. But things didn't work out the way he wanted. I saw to that. I made them both pay!' She moved closer to Rebecca. More than anything Rebecca wanted to get away from the foul woman, but she stood her ground. She belonged here. Susannah Bosanko did not and never had.

But it was chilling to have the hag's eyes boring into her, to hear the hatred and threats in what she said.

Susannah smirked arrogantly. 'I killed them both.' Rebecca shuddered then froze on the spot. She didn't doubt that Susannah Bosanko had spoken the truth. She looked quite capable of something so horrendous.

'I thought that would take the pep out of your stride, my girl. Got nothing to say to that? Well, let me tell you how I did it. I drowned the Carlyon girl in the creek. Come to think of it, roughly in the spot we are now. I asked the stupid girl to come for a walk with me. We sat on the bank. The tide was in and I pushed her head under the water and held it there until she stopped struggling. It was so easy. Over in a few minutes. The end of her useless life and her bastard child. Then I dragged her body further along the bank and threw it in.' Susannah laughed triumphantly but there was a note of insanity in it. 'Of course with her being pregnant there was never any doubt that she drowned herself over her shame.'

'You're evil,' Rebecca breathed in disgust. She was frightened now and her eyes widened as she fought to keep her mind clear. It was vital to keep her wits about her to fend off this ageing madwoman. She edged away. She would quicken her pace and tear up to Trevallion and get Alex to inform the police, but Susannah opened her mouth to say more and Rebecca felt compelled to stay and listen to what else she had to reveal.

'Do you want to know how Roland really died?' she taunted. 'It was so simple. After I'd killed the girl I gave him the chance of marrying me and making me mistress of all this. I was wealthy and I would have built up the Trevallion fortune to its past glory. But all he could do was lament over that wretched girl and her child. He said he wouldn't marry me at any cost, not after the things I'd written to him. He should have been more forgiving, Rebecca. He should have seen my last letters as a jealous woman's rage. But he didn't! So I murdered him too.'

Susannah seemed to be far away, back in the past and glorying in its memories. 'I pulled out my little hand gun. Such a ladylike thing with a jade-inlaid handle. I made Roland go down to the cellar. I made him put a rope over a beam and then round his neck. I made him stand on a wine barrel. He didn't plead with me. I wasn't sure if he didn't care much for his life or thought I was bluffing. He did look a bit surprised though when I kicked the barrel out from under him. He didn't struggle much as he dangled there. If he had he would have died all the quicker, tightening the rope round his neck, but to be sure of it I pulled his legs and stayed until he was quite purple, as dead as a doornail. You should have seen him, Rebecca. He didn't look very pretty. It was a shame really because he had been such an attractive man with a wonderful proud turn of the head. And now it was lolling to the side and his tongue was sticking out and dribble was—'

'Shut up!' Rebecca screamed.

In one swift movement Susannah was standing right in front of her.

'I don't believe a word you've said,' Rebecca said desperately. 'Now, if you'll excuse me I have work to do.' She walked briskly away, intending to run to Alex. She made only two steps.

'Rebecca!'

She whirled round.

Susannah Bosanko was pointing a gun at her; it had a jade-inlaid handle. She trained it on the centre of Rebecca's forehead. 'I'm an excellent shot. I used to enter ladies' firearms competitions in my younger days.'

Beads of fear sprang out on Rebecca's face. Although Susannah Bosanko was very old, she had a steady hand. 'Are… are you going to shoot me?'

'I'll leave you to guess about that,' Susannah gloated maliciously. 'But I'll tell you one thing, you'll never get Trevallion.'

'I don't want Trevallion, I just want Alex. Please—'

'I don't want to hear any more from you,' Susannah broke in violently. 'Turn round!'

On legs that would hardly move, Rebecca obeyed and held her breath. She could feel Susannah Bosanko's vile breath on her hair. The gun was pushed into the back of her neck and she closed her eyes and bit her lip, waiting for the hot blast of pain that would take away her life.

Susannah lifted her head up and smiled to herself. Then she pulled back her hand and brought the gun down savagely on Rebecca's head. As Rebecca staggered, Susannah hit her twice more and laid her out on the creek bank.

–

Alex was in his study. He was finishing off the plans for the house he was having built for himself and Rebecca. Satisfied with his progress, he put the drawings back in their folders. Tomorrow he had an appointment with an architect in Truro, and he would take Rebecca with him to buy an engagement ring. Everything was progressing well and his future was settled. The wedding arrangements were made and he had a secret honeymoon planned for Rebecca on the Continent.

It had been here in this study that he'd first realised he loved her. When she'd looked forlorn and trapped that day he'd officially moved into the house and he knew he couldn't keep her against her will if it meant she'd be unhappy.

Alex pushed the folder aside and saw an unopened letter staring accusingly at him. It was from Susannah Bosanko and had been sitting there for two days. The writing was erratic and he knew it would contain hate-filled words and vile accusations. He sighed and made up his mind to read it. If it contained what he feared, he would have to call on her at her home and put a stop to it once and for all. Tearing the envelope open he had no time to read the first word. There was a knock on the study door and when he called 'Come in', Joe entered.

Alex leaned back in his chair, the letter between his fingers. Joe stood in front of the desk and gazed down at him with a proud, determined look on his face and Alex knew why he was here.

'You have good news for me then, Joe?'

'I think it's the way you will look at it, Major,' Joe said stiffly and formally.

'Sit down,' Alex said hospitably, his eyes drifting towards the letter while he waited for Joe to sit.

'I'd rather stand,' Joe said brusquely. 'Abigail and I have just been talking and we've come to a joint decision about what you put to us last week.'

As Joe began his explanation, Alex couldn't stop his eyes flicking over Susannah's letter and picking out half sentences: '… I won't be picked up and tossed aside… make sure you never marry Rebecca… will make her pay…'

'Oh good God!' Alex sprang to his feet and Joe, mistaking his intentions, rounded the desk and grabbed his shoulder.

'You could at least have the decency to listen to me!' he shouted. 'You say the most horrible bloody things to Abigail that a lady doesn't deserve and when I tell you're we're going to do what you want, you jump up in indignation. I'd like to punch your damned face, Major bloody Alexander Fiennes!'

Alex thrust him away. 'I wasn't getting at you, Joe. It's this!' He pushed the letter under Joe's face. 'I have to find Rebecca. She could be in terrible danger!'

Chapter 38

Rebecca couldn't breathe. She felt she was choking. Her face and shoulders were wet and she couldn't see properly. For a moment she thought she was dreaming, having a terrible nightmare like Alex used to. She opened her mouth to call his name but it filled with salty water; she swallowed some of it and gagged. She tried to lift her head but something was holding her down, forcing her head into the cold water. In the next second she understood. Susannah Bosanko was trying to drown her just as she had drowned Rowena Carlyon.

Terror coursed through Rebecca and with it came a surge of strength and determination. She wasn't going to let the evil crone rob her of her life and future with Alex. She struggled, thrashing the water with her arms, then tried to reach up behind and grab the old woman. There was a thud and a sharp pain in the small of her back and she realised that Susannah had thrust her knee there and was pushing down on her with all her weight.

Rebecca flailed out, fighting for her life with the ferocity of a wild animal. Her lungs were bursting. Her brain felt as though it was about to explode and everything turned black. She couldn't escape; her strength began to seep away and she knew she was going to die.

'Get away from her, Susannah!' Alex yelled at the top of his voice as he raced furiously towards them.

Susannah cackled and thrust Rebecca's head down even deeper under the water. Rebecca had gone limp, her arms hung in the water with her long black hair.

Alex hurled Susannah away from Rebecca with all his might and grabbed a shoulder and a handful of floating black hair, yanking Rebecca's face out of the water.

'Becca! Becca, my love.' He forgot about Susannah Bosanko as in anguish he pulled Rebecca round to him and pushed strands of hair away from her face. Her face was white and purple smudges flecked her closed eyes and lips. He shook her in desperation. 'Becca, darling, wake up.'

Joe Carlyon stepped round Susannah Bosanko where she had landed in a heap on the creek bank and joined him.

'Turn her onto her front on the bank and knead her back to get the water out of her lungs,' he advised urgently.

'No, it's better to breathe into her mouth,' Alex said, tilting Rebecca's head back over his arm. 'I learned this from a medic in the trenches.'

'No one's going to do anything to try to save that girl! Get away from her, both of you!'

The two men looked up and saw that Susannah had got to her feet and was pointing a small gun at them. Her other hand was hanging at a grotesque angle, broken badly in the fall. Alex scowled and ignored her, putting his mouth over Rebecca's and breathing deeply into her body.

'I mean it, Alexander. Put the girl down and move away from her this instant or I will put a bullet through your head.' Susannah's voice was a thunderous hiss, bitter and insane yet fully controlled.

'Get away from us!' Alex screamed at her.

Susannah pulled back the safety catch and levelled the gun at Alex's forehead. 'I meant what I said, Alexander.'

Joe took two menacing paces towards her. 'If you shoot I'll throw you in the creek. You can't kill both of us.'

'What do I care if I die?' Susannah laughed with a hint of hysteria. 'I'm an old woman. I've lived my life.'

'Then let Rebecca and me have ours together, Susannah,' Alex begged. 'What will you achieve by killing us? Why does it matter to you what we do?'

'I couldn't have Roland Trevallion and his beautiful house so I drowned the girl he loved,' Susannah rasped. She looked coldly at Joe's shocked face. 'That's right, man. Rowena Carlyon. A relative of yours, I understand. I drowned her in the creek just as I did Rebecca.'

'No!' Alex howled like a wounded animal. 'Why hurt Rebecca?'

'Because you had my beautiful house. I should have lived there all these years, and I would have done when my great-niece married Miles Trevallion but fate robbed me of my glory a second time. When you came here and called on me, you gave me another chance but then like Roland you fell in love with a creek girl and wanted to marry her instead. I won't allow it, Alexander. I need you. I won't stand aside and let you rob me of my destiny again.'

'How could there be anything between us, Susannah? We're separated by too many years.'

Susannah lifted her skirt, the gun still in her hand, and swung it back and forth as though she was showing off her figure. In a sing-song voice, she said, 'I'm young and beautiful. Everybody says so. Don't you think so, Alexander?'

'She's gone raving mad,' Joe gasped, nudging Alex's arm.

Alex saw the opportunity too. Gently he laid Rebecca on the ground and ran at the old woman, intending to bring her down in a rugby-style tackle. She cried out as he rushed towards her and as he grasped her body the gun went off.

Blood spurted down Alex's neck but he didn't feel any pain. He brought Susannah down with a terrific thump. She shrieked and spat and fought like a savage, clawing at his face with the energy of someone three-quarters her age. She managed to wriggle out from under him, kicking him in the chest and then in his face. She was hatred and fury incarnate. She got herself to her knees and when Alex righted himself she punched him in the face with her good hand.

Alex swept back his hand and slapped her hard. Her wig fell off, revealing a tiny wrinkled head sparsely covered with short wisps of white hair. Susannah bellowed and scrabbled about the creek bank for her gun. Alex saw it first and reached out and picked it up. He fought the raving old woman off and getting to his feet hurled the gun several feet away.

He and Susannah were face to face. Both of them were dishevelled and streaked with blood. He was desperate to get back to Rebecca. She read his thoughts.

'It's too late, Alexander.' Her voice rose, shrill and hysterical. The arteries in her temples stood out against her sagging flesh, her lizard eyes were like sharded glass. It was hard to imagine anything more evil and hideous. 'I've already told you. The bitch is dead.'

'You should be dead!' Alex hurled at her.

She laughed her horrible laugh again. 'How about you and me dying together, Alexander, darling? After I drowned that other girl I developed a terror of the water but now I don't feel the least bit afraid.'

Susannah thrust out her good hand and grasped a handful of his shirt. They were very near the edge of the bank and Susannah ran backwards, toppling off the edge and taking Alex with her. She didn't let him go in the water and struggled to push his face under her body and hold him down. She succeeded for a few moments, putting her own face in the creek and gulping in mouthfuls of water.

Holding his breath, Alex straightened out his legs, then brought up both his feet and kicked Susannah's sunken chest with all his might. She lost her hold on him and shot out of the water like some grotesque flying fish. She hit the water again with a mighty splash several feet away from him in the basin of the creek where the water was deepest.

Alex swam for the bank, scrambled out and ran back to Rebecca without a backward glance to witness the fate of the evil old woman.

Joe was bending over Rebecca, his mouth over hers, breathing into her as he'd seen Alex do. 'Is she breathing? Is she all right?' Alex gasped.

Joe stopped his resuscitation and Rebecca's chest rose and fell unaided. She seemed to be breathing on her own. Alex put his ear to her chest and through his panic forced himself to concentrate. Yes, thank God, he could hear a strong heartbeat. But how much had the near drowning affected her otherwise? He lifted her up in his arms. 'Becca.' He gave a gentle shake. 'Becca!'

'Careful with her sir,' Joe cautioned. Like Alex he was worried about the possibility of brain damage. He had been with Stanley Wright when he'd drowned at Passchendaele and he had seen other men pulled out of the mud in various stages of drowning. Some had fully recovered, others, starved too long of oxygen, had been permanently mentally disabled.

'We have to get her to the infirmary, Joe,' Alex said grimly. 'Fetch a blanket and tell Abigail what's happened.'

'You need medical attention yourself, sir.' Joe nodded at his bleeding neck. 'Shall I carry Rebecca to the motorcar?'

'No, I can manage.' Alex stood with Rebecca in his arms. 'If anything happens to her, Joe...'

He turned to the creek and a momentary look of hatred crossed his face. There was not a ripple on the surface but the green material of a dress could be seen floating just under it. 'We'd better tell the police that there's been a drowning in the creek.'

—

'Becca,' Alex whispered softly. 'What are you doing down here? You should be resting.'

Rebecca was sitting alone on the fallen tree on the creek shore. She smiled up at him. 'I've told you before, Alex, I feel fine now. I'm just sitting here trying to make sense of all that has happened.'

It was only two hours since Alex had brought her back to Trevallion House from the infirmary. She had not wanted to stay cooped up in the house whose fate had affected her so deeply, and she had slipped out the first moment she could. When she'd gained consciousness after nearly being drowned two days ago, she'd longed to be alone to think things over and there was no better place for that than the creek.

Alex sat down close beside her. 'It might be best to talk about it, darling.' He couldn't bear her being so quiet with him and he was worried she was bottling things up. 'You haven't mentioned Susannah Bosanko, but you don't have to be concerned about her any more, Becca. She can't hurt anyone ever again, we're safe from her now.'

Rebecca gazed at the creek bank and shivered. She hadn't seen Susannah Bosanko plunge into the water and drown but she could picture it. 'She was so evil, Alex. She killed Rowena Carlyon here, she told me all about it.'

'I know, darling,' he said grimly. 'She told me and Joe too.' She'd been preoccupied with thoughts about Alex while she'd lain recovering and had shied away from thinking about her own ordeal but now she couldn't hold back the terrible memories. 'She… she also killed Roland Trevallion.'

Alex breathed out heavily. 'Did she tell you that too?'

Rebecca shuddered. 'She made him go down to the cellar at gunpoint, the same gun she used to shoot you. She made him put a rope over a beam and stand on a barrel then she kicked it away. She told me every detail, Alex. She was enjoying reliving it, she enjoyed killing Roland Trevallion.'

'The woman was insane but she can't hurt us any more, darling,' Alex repeated softly. 'Her body's been found and disposed of. Even if Roland Trevallion's ghost haunts the house, she won't haunt the creek.'

'Are you sure her body was found, Alex?' Rebecca looked around the creek as if she was afraid Susannah Bosanko would jump out from behind a bush and threaten her again.

'I'm absolutely positive, Becca,' he replied. Placing a gentle hand underneath her chin he made her look up at him. 'I promise you. The police pulled her out of the creek and I identified her myself. She looked more vile than ever but it was definitely her. The same green dress, the same sunken head, the same staring eyes.'

'Don't, Alex.'

'Sorry, darling, but I want you to be certain she's dead. I don't want her haunting you in the same way that losing my men haunted me. Is this why you've been so quiet with me? Because you've been terrified Susannah might still be alive and could still harm you?'

'No, I've been thinking about everything that's happened since you came to Trevallion. So much has happened between us in such a short time that I needed to be by myself to take it all in.'

Alex looked down at the creek bed. 'Are you saying things happened too quickly between us that day out on the river, when you agreed to marry me?'

Rebecca took his hand and he squeezed hers tightly but kept his eyes down. 'Yes, I think it did happen too quickly, Alex. I knew I wanted you more than any other man, but Dad had just died and you were looking for something or someone to rebuild your life with.'

'But I knew before then that I loved you, Becca,' he burst in, his face going white.

Rebecca knew she was hurting him, but she needed to say what she had come to realise, and carried on, speaking calmly. 'But I didn't love you, Alex. I was attracted to you and I liked being with you. I didn't know how I really felt about you. I think I agreed to marry you because it seemed the right thing to do after we'd made love.'

Pain shot across Alex's face. 'Are you saying you don't want to marry me now?'

She looked deeply into his dark eyes. 'No, Alex. What I'm telling you is that I didn't realise that I loved you until I thought Susannah was going to kill me and deny us our life together. Then when I came round and the doctor at the infirmary told me that you'd been shot, for a moment I thought you were dead and I wished she had succeeded in drowning me.' She smiled shyly and Alex was bewitched by her. 'I knew then that I loved you so much, darling Alex, that I couldn't bear to think of living without you.'

Alex's face changed from fear and pain to utter relief and joy. 'I knew you must have had strong feelings for me to give yourself to me, but I thought perhaps you'd agreed to marry me because you felt sorry for me or out of some sense of duty to the Trevallion estate. After what I've gone through for the last eight years I would have been content with that. All I wanted was to have you always by my side.'

'I love the creek but I'm glad we won't be living in the big house. All that I care about is that wherever you are, I will be there too.'

Alex squeezed her happily. 'You know how much I love you, don't you, Becca?'

She kissed his cheek tenderly. 'Yes, I do. You've changed so much, Alex, and I've watched every step. I know you so well and I know we'll have a wonderful future together.' They kissed in a way that told of the love they would always share, a love much stronger, deeper and longer lasting than a stretch of never-changing river. High above them the sun glinted on the tall windows of Trevallion House and the grand old building seemed to smile its blessing down on them.